'I realised that you were the perfect match for my requirements,' Bastian fielded with characteristic cool. 'However, if you don't want to do it return the fee and we'll say no more about it.'

Bastian strolled forward, his lean, darkly handsome features infuriatingly calm and assured. He was disturbingly graceful in motion, with not a visible ounce of tension in his big powerful frame as he stepped unexpectedly into her space.

'What on earth do you think you're doing?' Emmie gasped, overpowered by his proximity and totally disconcerted by his behaviour.

'Maybe I want to see what I was paying for,' Bastian said succinctly, indifferent to whether or not he caused offence. After all, wasn't he hiring her to do a job?

'You haven't bought me...you *can't* buy what isn't for sale!' Emmie flung back at him in fierce rejection.

'Yet I've still managed to buy your time for the whole of one weekend.' Bastian savoured the fact, dark eyes glittering golden as hot sunlight below level black brows.

A BRIDE FOR A BILLIONAIRE

The men who have everything finally meet their match!

The Marshall sisters have carved their own way in the world for as long as they can remember. So if some arrogant billionaire thinks he can sweep in and whisk them off their stilettos he's got another think coming!

It will take more than a private jet and a wallet full of cash to win over these feisty, determined women. Luckily these men enjoy a challenge, and they have more than their bank accounts going for them!

Read Kat Marshall's story in
A RICH MAN'S WHIM
May 2013

Read Sapphire Marshall's story in
THE SHEIKH'S PRIZE
June 2013

This month read
Emerald Marshall's story in
THE BILLIONAIRE'S TROPHY

THE BILLIONAIRE'S TROPHY

BY
LYNNE GRAHAM

MILLS & BOON

First published in Great Britain 2013
by Mills & Boon, an imprint of Harlequin (UK) Limited.
Harlequin (UK) Limited, Eton House, 18-24 Paradise Road,
Richmond, Surrey TW9 1SR

© Lynne Graham 2013

ISBN: 978 0 263 90030 9

Printed and bound in Spain
by Blackprint CPI, Barcelona

Lynne Graham was born in Northern Ireland and has been a keen Mills & Boon® reader since her teens. She is very happily married, with an understanding husband who has learned to cook since she started to write! Her five children keep her on her toes. She has a very large dog, which knocks everything over, a very small terrier, which barks a lot, and two cats. When time allows, Lynne is a keen gardener.

Recent titles by the same author:

THE SHEIKH'S PRIZE *(A Bride for a Billionaire)*
A RICH MAN'S WHIM *(A Bride for a Billionaire)*
A RING TO SECURE HIS HEIR
UNLOCKING HER INNOCENCE

Did you know these are also available as eBooks?
Visit www.millsandboon.co.uk

CHAPTER ONE

Sebastiano Christou, known as Bastian to his many friends and acquaintances, studied the huge emerald ring in his hand with seething frustration blazing in his dark golden eyes, his lean darkly handsome features settling into forbidding lines of hauteur. He was holding the Christou betrothal ring, which had, until very recently, adorned the hand of his intended wife, Lilah Siannas.

Ironically, Lilah had not voiced a single word of reproach concerning the terms of the pre-nup agreement presented to her lawyer. Instead, while leaving the pre-nup unsigned, Lilah had become irritatingly unavailable and distant but her burning resentment had ultimately triumphed, culminating in her public statement that the engagement was over and the wedding cancelled. And ever since then Lilah had been noisily painting the town red in the company of a good-looking toyboy millionaire.

Bastian was well aware that Lilah was throwing down a gauntlet she expected him to pick up. He was supposed to be jealous: yet he was not. He was supposed to feel foolish: but he did not. He was supposed to want her so much that he would forget about the pre-nup: only he did not. No, Lilah was playing a losing game for Bastian would never marry a woman without first securing his wealth with a pre-nup agreement. That was a lesson learned well at his grandfather's knee.

His father had married four times and his three incredibly expensive divorces had decimated the Christou family fortune. Bastian's grandfather had taught his grandson that love was unnecessary in a successful marriage and that shared goals and principles were more important. Bastian had never been in love but he had often been in lust. Lilah, a tiny exquisite brunette, had excited his need to chase and possess but he had never kidded himself that he loved her. Indeed before he proposed, he had evaluated Lilah's worth much as though she were an investment. He had recognised the advantage of their similar backgrounds; he had admired her unemotional outlook, excellent education and her skills as a society hostess. But, as he now grimly reminded himself, he had seriously underestimated the strength and pulling power of his fiancée's avarice.

Bastian thrust the ring back in its case and put it in the safe, angry at the months he had wasted on Lilah, a woman demonstrably unfit to be his wife. He was thirty years old, more than ready to marry and have a family, bored with casual affairs. He had not realised that finding a wife would be such a challenge and he was already wondering how the hell he was supposed to avoid a scene at his sister, Nessa's wedding in two weeks' time because Lilah was one of Nessa's bridesmaids. Lilah would be outraged when Bastian didn't, at least, *try* to win her back. She would relish being the focus of all eyes at the wedding and would delight even more in a confrontation, but Bastian did not want his baby sister to be embarrassed or upset on her special day. The only way of avoiding that danger would be for him to arrive with another woman on his arm, for Lilah was too proud to overlook such a statement.

But at this late stage where on earth would he find another woman to act as his partner throughout a weekend of family festivities? A woman who wouldn't try to trap him into a relationship and who wouldn't read more than he meant into his invitation? A woman nonetheless capable of pretending to be intimately involved with him, for nothing less would keep Lilah at a distance. Did such a perfect woman exist?

'Bastian…?' He spun round as one of his directors strode in with a laptop beneath his arm. 'I've got something amusing to show you—are you in the mood?'

Bastian was not in the mood but Guy Babington was a good friend and he forced a smile to his hard mouth. 'Always,' he encouraged.

Guy opened the laptop on the desk and spun it round to display the screen to Bastian. 'There…recognise her?'

Bastian studied the photo of a stunning blonde with

bright blue eyes in a party dress. She was laughing into the camera. 'No...should I?'

'Take another look,' Guy urged. 'Believe it or not, she works for you.'

'No way...I would've noticed her,' Bastian instantly declared because she was such a beauty. 'What's her picture doing on the Internet? Are you on Facebook?'

Amused, Guy shook his head. 'I'm on a website advertising a business called Exclusive Companions. It's an escort agency for professionals, *very* exclusive,' he said, rolling his eyes suggestively.

Bastian frowned, his sensual mouth curling a little with distaste. 'Do you use escorts?'

'I wouldn't mind using this blonde,' Guy confided, ducking the question with a lascivious look.

Bastian elevated an ebony brow. 'You said she worked for me—'

'She does—as an intern on a three-month placement on this floor. Emmie...she does research for your PA.'

Astonishment gripped Bastian as he turned his attention back to the screen. '*That's* Emmie?' he queried in disbelief, mentally flicking up an image of the young woman as she looked at work: hair tied back, specs anchored on her nose, dowdy clothes. Still frowning, Bastian zeroed his attention in on the dark mole on the centre of the blonde's cheek as he recalled that the intern had the same beauty mark in the identical place. '*Diavelos*...that *is* her! She's actually moonlighting as an escort?'

'Evidently...but what I'd really like to know is why

she dresses to look like the ugly duckling when she comes into work here,' Guy confided.

'Her name is Emerald according to the site...'

Sebastiano flipped open his own computer and hit several buttons to access the list of his staff. Yes, it wasn't Emmie short for Emily or Emma as most people would assume; her true name was indeed Emerald. So, weird and unbelievable as it seemed to him, it *was* the same woman.

'Doesn't she clean up amazingly well?' Guy chuckled lecherously.

Bastian would not have described the intern as an ugly duckling although he had to admit that on the few occasions she had been around him she had thoroughly irritated him.

'Sugar is bad for your teeth,' she had told him when she handed him his coffee, strong and sweet the way he liked it.

'Manners maketh man,' she had quipped when he strode through a door ahead of her and they almost collided in the doorway.

But he had noticed that, even clad in the ubiquitous black tights, she had incredibly long legs, the sort a man thought about wrapping round his waist. An escort, he ruminated thoughtfully, a woman whose company was available for hire. If she cleaned up as well as she did in that photo, she would make a very presentable piece of arm candy and, after all, it would be in her own best interests to meet his expectations. Possibly she wasn't fully aware of the terms of her temporary employment, one condition of which specified that she must do nothing to bring the company into disrepute. And working a lucrative sideline as an escort for rich men definitely didn't fit the bill of acceptability. He had never used an escort service before, nor would he have considered doing so in normal circumstances, but for this particular occasion he liked the idea of a woman he could *hire* to accompany him to his sister's wedding. He would not have to ask anyone for a favour, nor would he have to pretend an interest in a woman that he didn't feel anything for and there would be no room for misunderstandings in such an arrangement: he would pay Exclusive Companions and she would deliver the act he told her to deliver. In fact the more he thought about it, the more he liked that idea; she would be as much under his control as a robot.

Emmie swallowed back a yawn with difficulty while Bastian Christou's PA, Marie, gave her exhaustive details on the company she wanted her to research. Her hand unwittingly rubbed at her aching leg, which always bothered her when she was on her feet too much. Her right leg had been badly injured in a car crash when she was twelve and for years afterwards Emmie had been disabled, initially forced to use a wheelchair and only later recovering sufficiently to get around on crutches. Indeed, without experimental surgery she would never have walked unaided again and so grateful was she still for that surgery that she always shrugged off the occasional ache as unworthy of note or fuss.

Unfortunately, her tiredness made concentration a virtual impossibility and, not for the first time, Emmie marvelled that she had ever believed that an unpaid internship would be the perfect solution to her unemployment crisis. After months working a temporary dead-end job in the local library, Emmie had been willing to try anything to get her career out of the doldrums. She had jumped, however, from the frying pan straight into the fire. Although she had several friends working for no money to gain some experience for their all-important CVs they were all, without exception, still in receipt of parental financial support.

Emmie was rather less fortunate in that field. Although she had an excellent business degree the economic downturn meant there were few graduate jobs and the few that there were went to applicants with the skills and practical know-how that were only attainable from actual employment. After countless unsuccessful applications, Emmie had known that she needed work experience to improve her chances and she had initially been ecstatic when she got through a tough assessment centre and first won the internship at Christou Holdings, one of the most aggressive and successful software companies in London.

Never having lived in the city as an independent adult, she had not initially appreciated what a challenge it would be simply to make ends meet. And then, her estranged mother, Odette, had got in touch out of the blue and had offered Emmie her spare room and Emmie had snatched gratefully at the opportunity for cheap lodgings without which she could not have hoped to accept the job. It had not once occurred to her that Odette might have an ulterior motive in inviting her to stay. Naively, Emmie had simply been eager for the opportunity to get to know the mother she had last seen when she was twelve years old. From that age Emmie and her two siblings had been raised by her eldest sister, Kat, in the Lake District and, although she had recognised Kat's dismay when she learned of the London scheme and Emmie's plan to live with their mother, Kat had not interfered and had merely warned her sibling that Odette could be 'difficult'. Well, the word *difficult* didn't begin to cover the problems she was having, Emmie reflected heavily, hoping that she wasn't in for yet another long-running row when she got home later.

Her first unsettling discovery after moving in with Odette had been the disturbing revelation that her mother made her very comfortable living through an Internet-based escort agency. The even bigger shock that followed had been Odette's firm conviction that Emmie should join her list of escorts and earn her keep that way. When Emmie had refused and had instead taken on waitressing work five nights a week, Odette had been furious and, even though Emmie was handing over every penny of her meagre earnings to her mother, Odette was still angry and dissatisfied with her daughter.

Perhaps the most upsetting experience of all for Emmie had been the dawning awareness that her mother didn't love her, cherished no fond wish to get to know her better and certainly didn't regret having left her to her sister's care at twelve years old. That learning curve had been steep and painful and had made Emmie appreciate that she had gone to live with her mother in the hope of reviving a relationship that had only ever existed in her own imagination. Sadly, Odette was not the maternal type. Her children were simply the by-products of relationships that had gone wrong and it honestly seemed as though Odette had never managed to form an attachment to any of her daughters.

'Ah, Marie…' a familiar dark accented drawl pronounced from the doorway. 'The meeting is about to start. Emmie can take the minutes for us.'

Emmie spun round, faint colour blooming in her cheeks as she focused on Bastian Christou's tall powerful frame. The Greek entrepreneur was a popular choice for profiles in leading business publications and she had read all about him long before she came to work for him. He took a brilliant photograph but was even more eye-catching in the flesh, where his height and breadth and the gleaming luxuriance of the ruthlessly cropped black hair that framed his lean, darkly handsome features were disturbingly noticeable even in a crowd. Of course he was taller than most men, something Emmie tended to notice because she was five feet nine inches tall but he topped her by a comfortable six inches. In truth he had the charisma and looks that no woman could ignore, added to a sun-kissed complexion the shade of dulled gold and the perfectly formed features of a fallen angel. His mother, she had read, had been a famous Italian film star and he looked exactly like her, right down to the burnished dark eyes that were currently engaged in roaming over her as though she were edible and he were starving. Startled by that analogy and the intensity of his continuing appraisal, Emmie tensed and jerked her chin up while throwing him a look of frowning enquiry, for he had never looked at her in that way before. Perhaps his reaction was an illustration of the strange mood that Marie had warned her that her boss was in, doubtless fallout from the broken engagement that nobody had yet dared to mention in his presence, she reasoned uncertainly.

'Of course,' Marie responded equably. A slender, efficient brunette in her early forties, she rose from her seat to follow her boss back out of the office.

Bastian surveyed his quarry, Emmie, and wondered what her first smile would look like. He was accustomed to women smiling at him, not at all accustomed to one scowling and challenging him with her head tilted at a scornfully unimpressed angle. Yet there was something familiar about her, some quality that nagged at him, making him feel that he must have seen her or met her before somewhere. That niggling awareness irritated him, for he was well aware that she did not move in his social circles but indeed hailed from some hayseed background in the north. Unless, of course, he thought abruptly, he had previously come across her when she was acting as an escort to someone he knew... Now that was a genuine possibility, he acknowledged with distaste, wondering what on earth she was doing getting involved in such a seedy way of life at her age. Or was he being naïve? Beautiful women could reap rich rewards and an enviable lifestyle from such pursuits. Indeed if she was to meet the right rich man and marry him, she could set herself up for life.

Bastian had learned at a young age that most such women *used* their beauty like a commodity, expecting it to work for them and win them special treatment. His own mother had belonged to that group. Why should Emmie Marshall be any different? He watched her take notes during the meeting, noting the faint dark shadows circling her eyes and the translucent quality of her skin. He did not think he had ever seen skin that perfect on anyone other than a child. She propped her chin on an upturned hand, head at a slant that defined her slender neck and delicate jawline. A fine strand of corn-gold hair had escaped from her ponytail to trail across her cheekbone. He marvelled that he hadn't noticed the quality of her looks sooner. But then the loose shirts and trailing mid-length skirts she wore with the specs provided an off-putting disguise and the attention had to linger to note that soft, full pink mouth with its delicious pout and very slight hint of an overbite, and appreciate that the eyes behind the unattractive spectacles were a truly dazzling bright blue. In some astonishment, Bastian registered that he was developing a hard-on while he imagined those pillowy lips pouting just for his benefit. And for how many others had she performed that arousing trick as part of her escort duties? he asked himself grimly, squashing his arousal at source, for while he never bedded innocents he had an innate aversion to sex being traded for a price. And he already knew what *her* price was, didn't he?

'Emerald's rarely available. She's very much in demand,' the voice at the other end of the phone had informed him smoothly when he phoned the escort agency. 'I can offer you Jasmine *or*—'

'It *has* to be Emerald,' he had countered. 'She's the only one I want. I'll make it very well worth her while to choose me as a client.'

And then Bastian had negotiated, a skill at which he excelled, and he had learned once again—had he ever doubted it?—that for the right price he could have anything he wanted, including the rarely available and already fully booked Emerald currently falling asleep across the table from him. He had bought her services for the weekend and he had paid an enormous price for the privilege. It amused him that she evidently had not the slightest idea of the fact and yet he marvelled that any woman could so irresponsibly sell her time and attention to strangers, who might abuse her trust. Her curling lashes were down on her cheekbones, her slim shoulders drooping as she sank lower into her seat. He stretched out a long leg below the table, found her feet and nudged them sharply with the toe of one shoe. She jolted awake again, her wide startled blue eyes flying straight to him in dismay, her full lips parting, cheeks reddening with embarrassment. He wondered who she had entertained the night before and whether sex had figured. Nine out of ten men would expect sex for what he had paid for her services. He wondered how she would feel about that and how *he* felt about that…no, *never*, no way was he going there, he thought in disgust.

Emmie collided slap-bang-crash with smouldering dark golden eyes that reminded her of a tiger's eyes and that fast her ability to breathe vanished while a humming warmth prickled and then pulsed between her legs. Shock rippled through her in reaction to that sexual response, for it had been a long time since she had felt like that. Emmie was wary and seldom reacted to attractive men, having found them invariably vain and self-serving. She was very picky, *so* picky she had yet to choose a first lover, although she had come very close to losing her virginity at university when she fell in love. Of course that relationship had gone pear-shaped the instant Toby looked at her and said, 'I can't believe I'm going to bed with a girl the living image of Sapphire…'

Wham, that astonishing admission had hit Emmie right where it hurt, crushing her confidence *and* her faith in the love he had pledged. Being the sister of a world-famous supermodel and, even worse, her identical twin had often made Emmie feel as though she had no identity or individuality of her own. Time after time men had made her feel like an imperfect copy or stand-in for her flawless sister and the resemblance between the two women was so strong that, to sidestep that humiliating association being made, Emmie generally played down her best assets and avoided her twin's company. Now she wondered what it was about Bastian Christou that got to her. Lashes cloaking her gaze, she studied him, her heart beating very fast. Why had he looked at her like that? All right, his engagement was over and he was supposedly a free agent again, but what was he playing at? Men didn't, as a rule, see beyond the plain, unflattering clothing she wore. And his former fiancée was as different from Emmie in appearance as to be almost another species, being tiny, dark and glittery rather like a manic fairy, Emmie recalled from her one fleeting glimpse of the imperious little Greek socialite. Lifting her chin, Emmie gazed steadily back at him.

Reluctant amusement rippled through Bastian's powerful frame. She had nerve and he liked that; he liked that very much.

'In my office—five minutes,' he told her coolly, thrusting back his chair and rising to his full intimidating height.

'He must want to check the minutes. I hope you kept pace,' Marie commented. 'At one point there, I was afraid you might be falling asleep.'

Emmie winced. 'It was a possibility…' *Until your boss kicked me awake.* The awareness that Bastian Christou had noticed that she was dropping off made her want to cringe and she wondered if that was what he wanted to speak to her about. After all he had never bothered to speak to her before except in passing and he channelled any instructions through Marie.

'Is there no way you can chuck in the waitressing?' Marie enquired in an undertone.

'Sadly not, but I do have only another few weeks to go here,' Emmie pointed out, relieved she had chosen to be honest with the older woman about the fact that she was working two jobs to survive.

'I hope the long hours you're working to do this pay off,' Marie retorted wryly.

And from the tone of that remark, Emmie gathered that Marie saw little prospect of her being offered a full-time position with the company. In truth Emmie hadn't really expected the internship to lead to a permanent job but naturally she had hoped to be proven wrong in that assessment. She knew that it was much more likely that another unpaid intern would be offered the position she had vacated. Why should employers take on extra staff and pay them when they could get young eager workers for nothing?

Emmie walked into Bastian's office for the first time and glanced around, taking in the cool contemporary furnishings and artworks, the almost palpable opulence of a décor where no expense had been spared. But then Bastian Christou had no need to count the cost of anything. A genius in the field of software development and an exceptional businessman, he had single-handedly built an international company out of the best-selling program he had developed before he even left university and had become an enormously wealthy man while still very young.

'Close the door,' he told her, his deep voice setting up a vibration along her spine. He was a very masculine man and it had nothing to do with his physical size. Raw masculinity was etched in his hard bone structure, shrewd eyes and the authority and assurance with which he spoke. Although he was always perfectly groomed there was nothing metrosexual about him. One had only to see Bastian Christou with his sleeves rolled up on his strong forearms, his tie torn off and collar unbuttoned to show a slice of bronzed flesh to know that he was *all* male in a way so few men still dared to be.

Emmie pressed the door shut and turned back, a shiver of disconcerting awareness filtering through her tall, slender length as she met his keen, intelligent eyes. Beautiful eyes, she thought absently, as arrestingly bright as starlight in that strong face. Her body betrayed her instantly as if, having found the chink in her armour with this one man, it had forced that tiny loophole into a dangerous crack, for her breasts stirred and swelled heavily within her bra so that it felt tight and uncomfortable. Her colour fluctuated as her nipples stung into straining peaks and suddenly she was as tongue-tied as an awkward adolescent.

'Miss Marshall,' Bastian drawled, tracking her every change of expression. 'Or may I call you Emmie?'

'Emmie's fine,' she muttered at the height of a drawn-in breath.

'Or do you prefer Emerald?'

Taken aback by that rare use of her baptismal name, Emmie hovered uncertainly. 'I don't use that name…'

'You…*don't*?' A winged ebony brow climbed as though she had surprised him and when he bent his head over the laptop on the desk, it was a relief for her to have a moment to catch her breath again while watching the light from the window behind her gleam over the glossy sheen of his luxuriant black hair.

Catching herself on that thought, she didn't know what was wrong with her and only wished she could kick her brain back into gear. Yes, he was a good-looking guy but that didn't impress her, it being her experience that handsome men were usually very aware that they were handsome and invariably offended if a woman didn't react with admiration. Not that Bastian Christou struck her as belonging to that category, she acknowledged grudgingly. She was of such minuscule importance on his scale that she was sure he couldn't care less how she reacted to him. No, it was her own self and her pride that were affronted by her breathless, nervous state in his presence. A grown woman didn't lose her ability to reason around an attractive man, at least not if she expected to be taken seriously as an employee in an executive office that was still very much a man's world.

'No, I don't use that name…never have,' Emmie proclaimed with a strained smile, recalling that he could only have got that name from her job application because she only employed it when officialdom required it. Perhaps it had lingered on his mind because it was unusual.

Bastian Christou looked up with a slight smile and inexplicably that smile of his suddenly chilled Emmie to her bone marrow. 'But that's not quite true, is it?'

Frozen there in front of his desk, Emmie blinked rapidly, unnerved by the ESP promptings that were warning her of a threat when there was no possible threat that she could see. 'Sorry?' she questioned uncertainly, having lost the thread of the conversation.

'It's untrue that you don't use the name Emerald,' Bastian declared, swivelling his laptop round for her to view what was on the screen.

Emmie's soft mouth fell wide when she saw the picture he was referring to, shock and disbelief vibrating through her from head to toe because she could not imagine how a personal photograph of hers could have ended up on the Internet for anyone to see. It had been taken at her graduation party on one of the very rare occasions when she dressed up and threw caution to the wind and the photo was still in her digital camera...or at least she had *thought* it was. 'What's this? Where did you find that photo?' she gasped strickenly.

'On the website belonging to the Exclusive Companions escort agency,' Bastian confided, noting that she had turned as white as a sheet at his admission and experiencing an entirely unexpected pang of conscience because she contrived to appear genuinely shattered by his discovery. Of course, he reasoned, that merely proved that she had the useful skill of being a good actress in a challenging situation.

'Exclusive C-Companions?' Emmie stammered, for it was her mother's business and she knew that her photograph could not have been uploaded to that website without her mother's involvement. She was absolutely appalled and stared fixedly at that colourful image with a sinking heart. How on earth could Odette do that to her? Her mother knew she wanted no involvement with her business. 'How did you find this?'

'*Not* because I was visiting the website,' Bastian asserted with dry emphasis. 'Someone else who works here drew it to my attention.'

Nausea curled in her sensitive tummy. Who else knew? How many people? Inwardly she cringed in embarrassment. Who else was now convinced that she worked as an escort outside office hours? My goodness, was everyone she worked with talking about this behind her back? Humiliation clawed at her and she cursed the day she had moved in with her mother. What on earth was her picture doing on the website when she didn't work as an escort? But who on earth would *ever* believe that now?

'It is you, isn't it?' Bastian Christou pressed.

In silence, Emmie gritted her teeth and nodded agreement, unable to see how she could lie on that score. 'But it's not what you think—'

'Allow me to know what to think,' Bastian Christou murmured, smooth as glass.

'It's none of your business!' Emmie told him, her mortification yielding to a sudden rush of resentment.

'I'm afraid it is my business,' Bastian countered levelly. 'Your employment contract with this company states that you're not allowed to do anything which might bring the company into disrepute and I'm afraid that advertising yourself on the Internet as an escort would fall within that category.'

Emmie lost colour. She could not believe that a foolish action of her mother's might have put her job at risk, but she could also understand that it was an association that any employer might consider distasteful and suspect. 'I'll deal with it,' she said flatly, her full lips compressing with determination.

'*How* will you deal with it?' Bastian asked, glittering dark eyes pinned to her with growing curiosity, his attention lingering on that soft full mouth. He wanted to rip off the spectacles and tug her hair out of that ugly ponytail and see her beauty as nature had intended it to be seen: that mane of golden hair, clear, flawless skin and glorious eyes. When most women went to great lengths to look the best they could, why the hell did she hide her beauty as though it were something to be ashamed of? And then unveil that beauty to be an escort? Had she been afraid from the start that someone in the office might recognise that photo and realise she was leading a double life? It was the only explanation he could see that made sense of such a disguise.

'I'll have the photo taken down from the website. It

shouldn't be there,' she declared defensively. 'I don't actually work as an escort—'

'But clearly you have a connection to the agency,' Bastian pointed out, amused by her vehemence, her eagerness to persuade him that he had somehow misunderstood. She had little hope of getting far with that objective when he had so recently booked and paid for her services, he conceded grimly.

Emmie squirmed, determined not to admit the degrading truth that her connection to the escort agency was through her mother. 'I promise you that I'll deal with it and that photo will be taken down as soon as I can get it organised.'

'If you're tied into an employment contract with the agency it won't be that simple a matter,' Bastian warned her and he pushed a business card across the desk towards her. 'Feel free to contact this lawyer if you need advice or assistance on that score.'

'There *is* no contract. I told you…I don't work as an escort,' Emmie repeated doggedly, her colour high because she knew he didn't believe her and she didn't really blame him for that when her photo was on the website for all to see. She was mortified by the entire conversation but surprised that he was offering her a legal contact who could help her cut ties that didn't actually exist. Fortunately, the only tie Emmie had to Exclusive Companions was her blood tie to her manipulative mother.

'Tell me, why isn't the HR department dealing with this?' she queried.

'I felt the issue needed to be dealt with immediately and without spreading the news round the office.'

Exerting self-control, Emmie clenched her teeth together. 'Thanks. I appreciate that,' she felt forced to say with very real gratitude.

'Take the rest of the day off to handle this business,' Bastian advised, further surprising her with his consideration. 'I'll clear it with Marie.'

Thoroughly disconcerted by that generous suggestion, Emmie stiffened, but she was very grateful for the chance to go straight home and confront her mother about what she had done as it was scarcely something she could ignore.

'A stitch in time saves nine,' Emmie muttered shakily, taut with rage and embarrassment and frustration that she could not clear her own name but, on another level, very grateful to have discovered that her face was on that website, so that she could demand it be removed forthwith.

Bastian elevated a satiric brow. 'Another one of your funny little homilies?'

'I was talking to myself,' Emmie breathed curtly, flushing slightly because she had picked up the habit of uttering proverbs when she was a child and tended to blurt them out mindlessly when she was nervous or apprehensive.

So far, so good, Bastian reflected cynically when she had left his office, having reacted exactly as he had expected her to and engaged in a frantic cover-up. Even so, she would get that photo down from the site

and cut her ties to the agency, which would perfectly
suit his requirements. He had no desire for anyone to
discover that he was keeping company with an escort
and once she was removed from the site there would
be less risk of that happening.

CHAPTER TWO

ODETTE WAS USING her laptop in her elegant lounge when Emmie entered the apartment. Her mother was a tall woman in her fifties with the same classic blonde looks that had raised Saffy, Emmie's twin sister, to super-model status and universal acclaim.

'My word, you're home early…did the old office sweatshop burn down?' the older woman commented flippantly.

Emmie's face was already flushed by the speed with which she had walked from the bus but now her slender hands clenched as anger rose inside her. 'You put my photo on your website without my permission,' she accused.

Impervious to her daughter's tension, Odette lifted and dropped a slim shoulder, her unconcern patent. 'Photos of very beautiful girls improve business. Lots of my clients have phoned asking specially for you and I simply say you're already booked—but if you weren't so stubborn, you *could* be making a fortune.'

'You must have taken that photo from my camera.'

Emmie was disconcerted by her mother's lack of re-action to her accusation.

Odette's blue eyes, so like her daughter's, were cold as a winter sky. 'Yes. I can't see why that should be a problem—'

'You...*can't*? But you know that I don't want any involvement in your business—'

'Although you're quite happy to live off my earnings from running an escort agency!' Odette sliced back with stinging effect.

Emmie reddened. 'That's not true. I'm not living off you. I give you everything I earn from waitressing—'

Odette lifted a scornful brow. 'Which amounts to peanuts!' she exclaimed. 'If I rented out that room, I could be making three times as much for it. Instead I decided to be generous and help you out with your career. Is this all the thanks I get for it?'

Emmie hovered uncomfortably. 'You know I'm grateful, but I still want that photo taken down from the site. I'm not an escort and I don't want people think-ing that I am—'

Odette settled resentful blue eyes on her. 'My girls aren't prostitutes. I've told you that before. They are companions, *professional* companions, guaranteed to be presentable and pleasant. Sex isn't included in the package.'

'As far as you know,' Emmie added jerkily. 'You don't know how your escorts behave if a man asks for something more and is willing to pay for it—'

Odette rose gracefully upright. 'No, I don't,' she

conceded. 'I'm not their keeper or their mother,' she said. 'I'm only the manager who takes the bookings and runs credit and character checks on the clients. Why are you so prudish and suspicious of my business, Emmie? The girls on my books are educated middle-class young women, who want to make a decent income. Some of them are paying their way through college...'

'I'm not condemning their choices, I'm only saying that it's not a choice I would make,' Emmie declared, lifting her head high and wondering why she was feeling so guilty and ungrateful. 'Will you take down that photo right now, please?'

'You're making such a fuss about nothing,' Odette complained. 'You wouldn't think twice about posting that photo on one of those social networking sites you use—'

'That's different. You must take that photo down and remove any mention of me from the site,' Emmie reiterated. 'Whether you accept it or not, being associated with an escort site is damaging to my reputation, and have you even thought about what it could do to Saffy's reputation? The embarrassment this could cause her?'

'What the heck has Saffy got to do with this?' her mother demanded tartly.

'My face is *her* face, or have you forgotten that we're identical twins?' Emmie retorted impatiently, wishing the older woman would stop trying to play dumb when she was as wily as a box of ferrets. 'Saffy would go spare about this if she found out—'

Odette was unmoved. 'And why should that bother you? She's already made a fortune out of her face and body. She's got a lot more wit than you have but, let's face it, according to what Topsy has told me, you and your twin are not exactly close.'

Emmie stiffened at that reference to her youngest sister, who had taken to occasionally visiting their mother and had no doubt innocently let slip personal details that Odette would happily use against her daughters if it suited her to do so. 'Saffy and I may not be close but I wouldn't do anything to harm her or her career,' she proffered tautly. 'And I certainly wouldn't want to embarrass her the way I was embarrassed when someone showed me my photo on your website today. I'm really upset about this—please tell me you'll take the photo down now...'

Odette expelled her breath on an irritable hiss, her annoyance palpable. 'I will—if it really means that much to you—'

'It does. Thank you,' Emmie pronounced stiltedly, realising in frustration that she had said nothing that she intended to say and that once again Odette had contrived to talk her down and act as the victim rather than the perpetrator. Her mother had not even apologised for stealing that photo and using it on her website, she reflected in frustration as she walked towards her bedroom to get changed for her shift at the café where she worked weeknights. But then, another voice reminded her grimly, she could not really afford to have a no-holds-barred row with her mother while Odette was allowing her to occupy her spare room. Accepting favours always came with a price.

'Unfortunately, it's no longer quite as simple as that,' Odette remarked softly.

Emmie spun round in confusion. 'What are you talking about?'

'I've already taken a booking for you—'

Emmie was stunned into momentary silence. 'How can you have taken a booking for me when I don't work as an escort for you?' she asked drily.

'The client offered me so much money, I agreed,' her mother admitted without shame or embarrassment. 'I need the money and, let's be frank, so do you.'

'Well, you're just going to have to give the money right back again!' Emmie shot back at her mother in angry disbelief. 'I'm not for hire!'

'He's a businessman. He sent a contract over by courier and I signed it on your behalf—'

'But that can't be legally binding when I don't work for you!' Emmie protested.

'How are you going to prove that you don't work for me when your profile is on the website?' Odette enquired dulcetly.

At that suggestion of outright blackmail, Emmie went rigid. 'It's nothing to do with me. Return his money—'

Odette pushed her laptop aside and stood up. 'It's not that simple. I had outstanding bills and I've paid them. There's still a healthy cut of that money set aside for you—'

'I don't want it!' Emmie flung back at her furiously. 'I'm not going to be forced into acting as an escort so that you can make money out of me… It's not going to happen!'

'But I have no way of paying the money back,' her mother declared.

'That's not my problem,' Emmie stated curtly. 'Although I had no idea you had financial problems—'

'It's a tough world out there and an escort is a luxury. This guy's young, rich and handsome, so you can't complain on that score,' Odette told her with derision.

'I don't care…I'm not doing it, not for you, not for anyone!'

'Let me tell you just how much he was willing to pay to take you abroad for a weekend,' Odette urged thinly and she mentioned a figure of thousands of pounds that shocked Emmie rigid, for there was a much greater sum of money involved than she could ever have imagined.

'Odette…' Emmie said shakily. 'It doesn't matter what he paid you or what you signed. You can't sell me or my time like a product. I'm not for sale, and after the number of arguments we've had on this subject, I can't believe that you went ahead and accepted a booking for me knowing how I felt about the idea.'

The older woman settled icy blue eyes on her defiant daughter. 'You owe me, Emmie, and I intend to collect.'

'How do I owe you?' Emmie prompted painfully. 'You never bothered with me from the age of twelve. You never visited or wrote or phoned or even paid towards my upkeep—'

'I had a hard time surviving. And you were all quite happy living with your sister, Kat,' Odette argued tautly. 'But when it *really* mattered, I was still there for you—'

Emmie's facial muscles were locked tight with self-discipline. 'And when was that?'

'When you needed surgery for your damaged leg. When you were desperate to walk again, I came through for you,' her mother declared impressively.

Emmie was knocked sideways by that announcement. 'You're saying that *you* paid for the surgery I had on my leg?' She gasped in shock.

'Where did you think Kat got the money from?' her mother enquired drily.

Emmie was too distraught at what she had been told to continue reasoning with her unrepentant parent. She changed for her shift at the café and went to work in a daze. Was it true that Odette had paid for her surgery? It was a supreme irony that as a teenager it had not even occurred to Emmie to wonder where her oldest sister, Kat, had got the cash to pay for Emmie's private surgery abroad. Even though Emmie was now in her twenties it had never occurred to her to ask, an oversight that now struck her as unforgivably obtuse and selfish. Emmie knew how much that surgery had meant to her at the time, how desperately she had craved the normality and the independence of no longer needing assistance in almost everything she did. She was dumbfounded by the assurance that her mother had paid to make her deepest wish come true.

While she served meals and drinks that evening, her mind was lost on another plane. Her sister, Saffy, had never overcome her guilt that she had not been injured in that same crash and she had been fiercely protective of her injured twin in the aftermath. Saffy had never understood that the continual presence of her physical perfection and glowing health had only made Emmie all the more aware of what she had lost. Emmie's teen-aged experience of infirmity had been wretched and she had often been depressed. People had continually looked away from the awkward gait caused by her disability, embarrassed by her, embarrassed for her, pitying, avoiding her as if her brain might be as damaged as her body. At the same time Saffy, blonde, beautiful, sporty and gregarious, had been the most popular girl in school. Emmie hadn't resented her twin and she hadn't been jealous either, but that was when she had learned to hate the wounding comparisons that people made between the two girls, one so perfect, the other so physically flawed. Those feelings had been compounded from early childhood by Odette's resentful attitude to having had twins when she had only wanted one child. Even worse, Emmie had proved to be a heavy responsibility, underweight when born and often ill afterwards, a sickly child continually requiring extra care and attention. Emmie was always painfully aware that in those days Odette had found caring for her too heavy a responsibility.

Her mother was in bed when Emmie got home and although it was a relief not to have to face the older woman again Emmie was still in turmoil. Odette might once have been a neglectful parent but that costly surgery had transformed Emmie's life, not least giving her her freedom and independence back. If her mother had paid for that operation, Emmie *did* owe her a debt. But surely that didn't mean she was honour bound to perform escort duties for some stranger? Hadn't Odette said 'a weekend *abroad*'? My goodness, could such an arrangement be any more bizarre or dangerous? A *whole* weekend out of the country? He could be a white slaver and she might never be heard of again.

'I'd like to see that contract,' Emmie told her mother staunchly over breakfast, determined not to let her emotions take control of her again. She needed a solution and another argument would be counter-productive.

A couple of minutes later, Odette passed her a slim document. Emmie glanced down it and leafed to the last page to see the signature and what she saw there astonished her. *Sebastiano Christou!* How was that possible? How could Emmie's boss be the man who had booked her as an escort? The same boss who had informed her that her supposed second career as an escort ran contrary to company policy? Emmie was so enraged by the sight of that particular name that she was vaguely surprised steam didn't pump from her ears. She stuffed the contract into her bag. 'I'll handle this,' she told the older woman tautly.

Evidently having expected more of a reaction from

her, her mother said, 'Aren't you surprised by the identity of the client?'

'Should I be?'

'You do work for the guy—'

'Oh, so you're aware of that?' Emmie fielded thinly.

'Of course I am. It puts a whole new spin on office romance,' Odette remarked mockingly.

'Believe me,' Emmie declared as she stood up, 'there's nothing romantic about this situation.'

Rage was powering Emmie like adrenalin by the time she reached the office. Bastian Christou was a complete hypocrite. Unbelievably, the same guy who had paid a ridiculous sum for her services as an escort had dared to warn her that her working in such a role threatened to bring *his* company into disrepute. But at least now she knew why he had been looking at her so oddly, doubtless imagining that if she worked as an escort she was a much more sexually exciting and adventurous personality than she appeared on the surface. Well, we'll just see about that, Emmie reflected, furiously gritting her teeth together.

'Mr Christou and I discussed a private matter yesterday and I need to see him as soon as possible to update him on…er, a recent development,' Emmie informed Marie.

Her eyes carefully veiled, Bastian's PA passed no comment and swept up her phone.

'Go on ahead,' she urged then, before adding, 'Be careful, Emmie—'

'Careful?' Emmie queried, glancing back over her shoulder.

'Before Lilah, Bastian had a bad track record with women,' his PA murmured warningly.

Her face flaming at the type of development that the other woman so obviously suspected, Emmie knocked on the office door and entered. Bastian surveyed her from his stance by the window, his arrogant dark head set at a questioning angle, his brilliant eyes narrowed. Emmie dug the contract from her bag and slapped it down on the desk top in explanation.

'So, you know,' Bastian remarked evenly, not one whit perturbed by her aggressive body language.

'And now it's time for you to know that it's not on, *not* happening in this lifetime!' Emmie specified with emphatic bite. 'But what I really can't believe is that you talked of how my photo on that website could bring your company into disrepute and then you went ahead and booked me!'

'I realised that you were the perfect match for my requirements,' Bastian fielded with characteristic cool, noting that with that pink warming her cheeks and her animated expression she was glowingly alive, like a candle that had suddenly been lit for the first time. 'However, if you don't want to do it, return the fee and we'll say no more about it.'

Return the fee? Consternation at that practical suggestion filtered through Emmie's anger because she didn't have a penny in the world, indeed still had an overdraft on her bank account from her student days.

Odette had admitted to having already spent some of the money and Emmie had no way of replacing it, nor was she naïve enough to believe that she had a prayer of persuading her materialistic mother to hand over what remained of that cash. 'I can't believe that you can still look me in the eye…' she said with scorn, side-stepping the money issue.

Bastian strolled forward, lean, darkly handsome features infuriatingly calm and assured. He was disturbingly graceful in motion, not a visible ounce of tension in his big powerful frame as he stepped unexpectedly into her space and without warning whisked the spectacles off her nose to examine them. 'These are clear glass…what do you wear them for?'

'Give me those back!' Emmie snapped, fit to be tied at his cheek.

With a sardonic laugh, Bastian tossed them aside and reached instead for the clip pinning her thick hair to the back of her head.

'What on earth do you think you're doing?' Emmie gasped, overpowered by his proximity and totally disconcerted by his bold approach.

The clip went the same way as the spectacles and released the heavy golden fall of her hair round her taut shoulders. 'Maybe I wanted to see what I was paying for,' Bastian said succinctly, indifferent to whether or not he caused offence. After all, wasn't he hiring her to do a job? Why should he pussyfoot around her sensibilities?

Rampant disbelief gripped Emmie as she focused

on his devastating face, struggling to block out the hard male beauty of his bronzed features, refusing to acknowledge it when he was being so objectionable. 'How *dare* you?' she snapped furiously.

'It's the truth even if you don't like it,' Bastian countered drily, watching her dark pupils dilate in a betraying sign of sexual awareness, emphasising the incredible blue of her eyes all the more. Even up close, she was dazzling, skin luminous, eyes bright, mouth sugar-pink and luscious. Raw hunger pulsed at his groin, the kick of instant and intense arousal taking him by surprise. Yes, she was very beautiful but he was accustomed to beautiful women and repulsed by those who sought payment for their attention. Unfortunately the natural repugnance he had expected to feel around her wasn't working as the barrier he had hoped it would.

'You haven't bought me…you *can't* buy what isn't for sale!' Emmie flung back at him in fierce rejection, reacting to the maddening buzz in the atmosphere that was firing a sensation of uneasy warmth between her thighs and unnerving her.

'Yet I've still managed to buy your time for the whole of one weekend.' Bastian savoured the fact, dark eyes glittering golden as hot sunlight below level black brows.

'No…no way!'

'Then return the fee and we'll forget about the arrangement,' Bastian responded lazily again. 'I'm not in the market for an unwilling escort. In the wrong frame of mind you would be useless to me.'

Emmie backed away from him, pausing to scoop up the clip and the spectacles he had carelessly abandoned on his desk. He was forcing her to accept unwelcome facts. Of course he wanted the money back if she wasn't prepared to deliver the service he had booked and she wasn't *able* to return his wretched money to him! It put her between a rock and a hard place and frustration roared through her. Had Odette won their battle so easily? She could deny all connection to her mother's escort agency and leave Bastian Christou to pursue the return of the money he had paid, but that would undoubtedly plunge Odette into serious legal and financial trouble. And the woman who had financed the surgery that had given Emmie the opportunity to live a normal able-bodied life again deserved better than that from her, Emmie conceded reluctantly. The gift of that life-enhancing surgery truly was a debt that could never be repaid.

'Why the disguise?' Bastian enquired indolently. 'Are you afraid of being recognised in the day job?'

Emmie went pink again. 'Something like that.'

She couldn't tell him the truth, had never told anyone the truth. When Saffy's face had gone global and her twin was constantly pictured in the media, Emmie had no longer felt that her face was her own. Even more awkwardly, people had started mistaking her for Saffy in the street and it had got embarrassing: strangers approaching her asking for autographs and photos, men coming on to her, people getting angry and abusive when she insisted that she wasn't the famous Sapphire because they didn't believe her. The attention had mortified and intimidated her, making her feel like a fake copy of her famous sister, incapable of satisfying people's expectations. She had always been a very private person and could never have put herself on show as her sibling had done to make a living in front of the cameras. She had never had that kind of confidence in her face and body.

Bastian relaxed back against the side of his desk. 'If you make a good job of the role I have for you I'll pay you a bonus,' he told her smoothly. 'This is very much a business arrangement, not a pleasure trip.'

Emmie wondered if this was what he always did when a woman became difficult: offer her more money, clothes, jewellery, *whatever*? Did he often use his wealth as a bribe?

'Are you in the habit of using an escort service?' Emmie enquired flatly.

'You will be the first…and the last,' he informed her grimly.

'And why didn't you tell me what you'd done when you spoke to me yesterday about the photo on the website? Wasn't that complete hypocrisy?' she asked him drily again.

'Common sense. If I take you to my sister's wedding, I naturally don't want your escort identity to still be visible online,' he pointed out coolly. 'And I'm not a hypocrite. What you see is what you get. I'm a very forthright guy.'

'Your sister's wedding? You want me to accompany you to a family occasion?' Emmie prompted in surprise.

'I don't want anything to take the gloss off my sister, Nessa's big day,' Bastian admitted. 'Seeing me with you will persuade her that I have moved on from my broken engagement and that will make Nessa happy. She's a very soft-hearted soul. And as my ex is one of her bridesmaids, it will be more comfortable for everyone present if I have a partner of my own.'

'One of her bridesmaids?' Emmie grimaced at the concept. 'Sticky—'

'But less so with you on my arm,' he confirmed. 'May I assume that you will be accompanying me to my home in Greece?'

Emmie gulped at the prospect, thinking frantically about how she could possibly repay the fee he had paid, knowing that, short of a lottery win, she could not. There was no way out, no convenient escape route. What was one weekend to be spent in the company of family and wedding guests? It sounded innocent, *safe*. She swallowed hard and then nodded in surrender, curling lashes lowering over her angry gaze.

'All that remains is the provision of suitable clothing for you to wear over the weekend,' Bastian remarked.

'That won't be necessary—'

'It *will* be,' Bastian contradicted, derisive eyes dropping to scan her loose shirt and ill-fitting skirt. 'I'll organise a stylist and personal shopper to furnish you with what you will require. Naturally I'll cover the bills. I have your phone number. I'll text you with the details.'

Emmie swallowed hard, dislike and resentment combining in a tangled knot of defiance inside her. He was treating her like an inanimate object to be correctly packaged for public show. He saw her as an escort, a woman for hire and, even though she told herself that she was doing this for her mother's benefit and to repay a debt, it was an utterly humiliating process and not an experience that she would forget in a hurry.

CHAPTER THREE

OUT OF THE corner of her eye, Emmie saw heads turning as she walked through the airport. She was mentally offering up a prayer that that would be all the attention she attracted when a man with a camera stepped right into her path. 'Stop right there, Sapphire!'

Head high, face expressionless, Emmie sidestepped him, not even bothering to pause and contradict his assumption that she was her sister because she had learned that people and the paparazzi in particular refused to credit that she was not who they thought she was. After all, a photo of Sapphire was worth a lot of money and no pap ever wanted to admit that he had made a mistake. Dressed as she was in designer gear, Emmie knew there was even less chance than usual of anyone believing that she was not her twin. The mini wardrobe of new garments packed into the sleek case she was wheeling was not bargain-basement fare by anyone's standards. Indeed Emmie had never in her life worn such expensive clothing and, ironically, knowing that she looked her best had lifted her confidence.

That acknowledged, however, the prospect of a weekend at the Christou family home still had her nerves leaping about like jumping beans. There was a tight hard knot of anxiety in her abdomen as well, for nothing she had since learned about the Greek billionaire had eased her misgivings in the slightest.

Before his engagement Bastian had been a notorious womaniser and her Internet searches had offered her fertile information on his likes and dislikes for, in common with many rich, high-profile men, he had occasionally fallen victim to the kind of lover who sold her story of their intimate dealings to a newspaper for cash. There had been a sordid little tale of a chaotic affair with two sisters, more than one cringe-worthy reference to his penchant for early-morning sex and all the usual fillers about the extravagant gifts he bought, how easily he got bored, how quickly and coldly he severed ties when he lost interest. At the office he was a neat freak with everything in its place and no clutter and definitely on the emotionally detached side of sociable. Emmie had learned nothing else worthy of note and very little about his true nature. He was extremely intelligent but, having studied his career, she had already known that for a fact. He had built his business from the ground up and it had soared to meteoric heights.

Bastian saw Emmie walking towards him and experienced a rare instant of shock. She was a vision of golden loveliness and sophisticated elegance in tailored cropped trousers, sky-high heels and a soft clingy top. He tensed. Perfect for the role, he told himself sharply;

nobody would doubt the veracity of his relationship with a woman who resembled a screen goddess with her simply amazing face, long lazy walk and incredibly shapely legs. OK, shorn of disguise and in the right clothing, Emmie Marshall was absolutely gorgeous, but he was *not* personally affected, he assured himself on the back of the reminder that he had always preferred small, curvy brunettes. But the cut of his trousers still felt too neat and his strong jawline clenched hard. A little reaction was normal, he conceded grudgingly. He would be dead from the neck down if he didn't react to Emmie at all and didn't wonder if that luscious pink-tinted mouth would taste as good as it looked. Only at the last possible moment did he finally appreciate that she was being pursued by a couple of men waving cameras and he could not work out why he had not noticed them first. He signalled his bodyguards to protect her from the intrusion.

'Emmie…' he breathed.

'Mr Christou,' Emmie replied glacially, resisting with all her might the sheer raw charisma of Sebastiano Christou, sheathed in a dark designer suit perfectly tailored to his lean powerful frame, his jawline darkened by faint stubble, heavily lidded dark golden eyes fringed by amazing black lashes resting on her like a gun to a target. Bull's eye, she thought maniacally, a burst of heat warming her pelvis, breasts high and taut, her entire body positively leaping into a terrifying state of electrically charged sexual awareness.

'Bastian…' he traded drily a split second before he reached for her.

Emmie was so startled by the manoeuvre that she froze like a rabbit in headlights. She had convinced herself that she had nothing to worry about with Bastian Christou. After all, he wasn't going to be getting much time alone with her at a big family wedding. Not only was she not his type, being blonde and about a foot too tall, but he also only wanted her on his arm for show. And then he kissed her and her every conviction that she was safe fell at the first hurdle.

He caressed the corner of her mouth with his firm male lips and she tingled all over, every sense awakening. Her lips parted and then he surged in like an invasion force and took shameless advantage. It was an explosive kiss and she was lost in it as unfamiliar excitement blasted through her slender body with every delving dart of his skilful tongue. It was agonisingly intimate, much more so than any kiss had ever been for her. Little tremors of shocked reaction quivered through her, the inner burn at her core exercising an almost unbearable ache as he set her back from him with strong hands, eyes so dark they glittered like polished jet in his hard face. Her legs felt dislocated from the rest of her body and that ache, that ache she dimly recognised as unfulfilled desire, clawed cruelly at her. For a split second she wanted to snatch him back into her arms and conduct a wild experiment on him. It didn't matter that he was her boss or that they were in a public place. All that was driving her in that moment was a fierce need to feel that same wild conscience-free excitement again and see where it would take her.

'I wasn't expecting actual ph-physical contact,' Emmie told him shakily while in the background a man with a camera argued volubly with one of Bastian's security men.

'You can't be that naïve. We're supposed to be lovers. Anyway, what's a kiss worth?' Bastian derided with an elegant shrug of dismissal.

On her terms it had been more than a kiss; it had been the kind of intoxication she felt as if she had been waiting for all her life. But that was a silly immature thought more worthy of a teenage fantasist than a grown-up, she scolded herself, fighting to stay cool and in control. A kiss was just a kiss: he was right. And that he should know how to do it so well was hardly surprising with his reputation. Even less surprising was that she should finally lust after a man in earnest. It was only proof that she was a normal breathing woman, nothing she needed to agonise about…at least as long as she didn't surrender to the temptation.

Bastian was still seething with himself as they boarded his private jet, hostile eyes veiled, jawline clenched, handsome mouth compressed. *Diavelos*, she was a freaking escort, admittedly not a hooker, but he remained deeply suspicious as to exactly what following such a profession entailed. Obviously pleasing men went hand in hand with the role, so was it really a revelation that she turned him on hard and fast? No, to cope with such a job she had to be a practised flirt and seductress and confident she could handle a man. Well, there was no way that she was going to get the chance to handle him! He had principles, standards and hell would freeze over before he went to bed with a hired escort!

Listening to Bastian growl at the steward's efforts to ensure his comfort, Emmie rolled her eyes and picked up a magazine. He was in a bad mood and he wasn't polite enough to keep it to himself. Those lustrous eyes below those thick sooty lashes were positively smouldering, his spectacular bone structure set like granite below his bronzed skin. Why? He was the one who had launched the kissing thing. Men! Who needed them? Odette always had, she reflected unhappily.

Emmie had few happy memories of her childhood years with her mother. Odette had divorced her father when he went bankrupt. It had been a very bitter divorce and when the twins' father had remarried and begun a second family, he had immediately decided to forget that he already had two children. Emmie had last seen her father when she was twelve years old. She knew where he lived, knew what his wife looked like and the names of her half siblings: that was the joy of the Internet, which enabled spying from afar and which had satisfied her curiosity. With her sister, Kat's encouragement she had written to her father when she was a teenager requesting contact but he had never bothered to respond, his silence making his lack of interest clear. His detachment teamed with her mother's lack of affection had hurt deeply.

While she was still getting work as a model, Odette had enjoyed a never-ending stream of men in her life and she had brought every one of those men home. The only one who had even been passably nice and semi-interested in Odette's daughters had been the father of Emmie's youngest sister, Topsy, a South American polo player, whose affair with her mother had died a natural death when he went home again.

Emmie had sworn that she would never *need* a man in her life. Men were demanding and difficult; men took over; men were *selfish*. She watched Bastian help himself to a drink from the built-in bar without offering her anything and suppressed a sigh: he was putting out enough moody bad-tempered vibes to cast a claustrophobic storm cloud inside the spacious cabin.

'You sulk like a girl… Do you throw a tantrum afterwards as well?' Emmie heard herself say without even thinking about what she was saying. But she was fed up, *really* fed up. Here she was dressed up exactly as he had requested, punctual, smiling…well, not perhaps smiling, she conceded reluctantly, but at least she was willing to *try*, which was more than he was.

In astonishment, Bastian swung round and settled outraged golden eyes on her in disbelief. 'What did you say?'

'You're very temperamental and I'm doing the best I can but I suppose I shouldn't have used those particular words,' Emmie responded ruefully. 'If it wouldn't be too much trouble, I'd like a drink as well. A pure orange if you have it…'

The slightest tinge of colour accentuated his carved cheekbones at the unspoken reminder that he had not offered her a drink. He lifted a bottle and uncapped it.

'It's all right, you can relax,' Emmie told him with helpless amusement as he extended the glass to her. 'I already know you don't have any manners.'

'What the hell gives you the idea that you have the right to insult me?' Bastian thundered down at her.

Emmie was not intimidated. 'I didn't think it was an insult to tell you the truth. You never say please or thank you and you walk through every door first. You're a very rich and powerful man, most people you meet are subordinate to you and naturally you have learned to take advantage of that. *Might is right. Money talks.* That's how the world works, so I can't even blame you for it.'

Bastian was stunned by the level of sheer indignation rising inside him, but then he could not remember ever having been attacked in such a way by a woman before. Generally women bored him stiff with their fawning flattery. Who did she, a little office worker going nowhere, think she was to criticise *him*? And if this was 'trying to please', what did she do for an encore? Pull a gun on him?

'I do not take advantage of my employees!' Bastian shot back at her, because although he would very much have liked to say otherwise he could not recall the words 'please' and 'thank you' *ever* figuring much in his vocabulary. But then he was a man of few words, he reminded himself furiously, but he made those few words *count* and issued clear concise instructions that were rarely misunderstood. In addition, for the past two years running his company had won an award for being one of the best to work for, offering as it did un-rivalled working conditions to its employees.

'Well, you certainly take advantage of Marie,' Emmie fielded without hesitation. 'I did her time sheets and I know that for a fact. I'm sure you pay her an excellent salary—'

'I do,' Bastian sliced in grittily on the score of his trusted PA, while wondering how on earth he would tolerate Emmie for an entire weekend without killing her.

'But I doubt if it's enough to warrant keeping a married mother of three working until eight at night on Christmas Eve,' Emmie tossed back. 'Or for taking her abroad to work on her fortieth birthday, so that she had to reschedule her party.'

'I didn't *ask* Marie to work late on Christmas Eve. As for her birthday, as I have no idea when her birthday is I can't comment. But I will point out that if she didn't choose to mention a prior arrangement to me, you can't blame me for it!'

'It was Christmas Eve. You told her the work was urgent and she did it,' Emmie expanded gently. 'Of course she did. She's very diligent. A considerate employer would have appreciated her position on that particular day of the year.'

Bastian ground his even white teeth together. 'Keep

quiet,' he told her harshly. 'I don't want to hear another word out of you for the remainder of the flight!'

Emmie made a teasing zip-up gesture across her lips, which went down like a lead balloon. She veiled her eyes, cloaking the amusement there and then glanced at him again. She knew she was annoying him and she didn't feel the slightest bit guilty. Well, he shouldn't have kissed her, she reasoned, still resenting that breaking down of boundaries. *That* had been a step too far in their pretence. She glanced up again, collided unwarily with burning golden eyes and felt heat surge as if he had lit a torch inside her. Her cheeks burned. Standing there, tall, lean and dark as sin, even with that brooding sardonic slant to his hard chiselled features, he was too gorgeous for words.

'You shouldn't have kissed me,' Emmie said abruptly into the heavy silence.

'And how do you expect to put on a convincing act of being my girlfriend in my home if you can't cope with one little kiss?' Bastian derided.

'There was no need for you to touch me. There were no witnesses at the airport who needed to be convinced of anything,' Emmie pointed out. 'We'll get along better if you respect the ground rules—'

'*What* ground rules?' Bastian demanded grimly.

'Please don't touch me unless you absolutely have to.' Emmie studied him with clear blue eyes and lifted her chin. 'You may have bought my time but don't make the mistake of believing you've bought anything else.'

'Are you saying that you have *never* slept with a client?' Bastian pressed with so much incredulity in his voice that she wanted to slap him hard.

'Never,' Emmie told him vehemently.

'Next you'll be telling me you're a virgin and pure as driven snow!' Bastian exclaimed, throwing his long powerful body down into a seat and flipping open his laptop with an air of purpose.

As that was exactly what she was and little opportunity had recently arisen for her to redress the condition, Emmie compressed her lips and returned her attention to the magazine she had abandoned. She had said what she *had* to say because she needed him to know upfront that sex was not an option. For an instant, she wished she could simply tell Bastian Christou the truth, but the prospect of explaining that her mother ran an escort agency and had virtually blackmailed her into accepting his booking stuck in her throat. It would be too degrading to admit that her mother would do virtually *anything* for money. After all, mud always stuck. He wouldn't believe that she had never worked as an escort before either, and that he was, in fact, her first *and* last client. Anyway, why was she worrying about what he thought of her? Why should that matter to her? Bastian Christou was simply a filthy-rich, domineering and very spoilt male and she wasn't one bit surprised that he had had to hire an escort rather than approach an obliging female friend for assistance. She wouldn't be a bit surprised to discover that he didn't *have* any female friends.

In a state of festering irritation, Bastian watched Emmie sleep, a long slender hand topped with delicate pale pink nails tucked below her cheek, luscious lips parting infinitesimally on every breath, superbly long elegant legs stretched out and crossed at the ankle— very dainty ankles too—golden hair tumbling like a waterfall of glorious silk across her sweater. For an escort, she wasn't very good on the entertainment front, he mused, his full sensual mouth compressing. Of course to be fair if she had chitter-chattered all the way from London, he would have been ready to strangle her by now, but the complete unconcern and indifference to his opinion that had allowed her to fall asleep in his company was almost an insult. If he was honest, he had expected her to flirt like mad and make a move on him, using the opportunity he had given her to get close to him. As a young, extremely rich and presentable man he was accustomed to receiving that attitude from her sex. Women tried to impress him, charm him, seduce him… They didn't just fall asleep as if he were a piece of furniture! Bastian ground his perfect teeth together again, struggling to suppress the suspicion that he was disappointed that she wasn't all over him like a rash.

Emmie slept right up until the jet landed in Athens and stumbled drowsily onto the helicopter that was to convey them the final leg of their journey to the island of Treikos. 'Your own island…I should've expected that, shouldn't I?' she mumbled abstractedly, speaking her thoughts out loud. 'Owning your own island is almost textbook Greek billionaire.'

'Treikos belongs to my grandfather, Theron,' Bastian said flatly.

'I take it…your mood hasn't improved?' Emmie remarked gingerly.

'There is *nothing* wrong with my mood!' Bastian ground out, what little patience he possessed challenged beyond tolerance level.

Eyes flaming gold below sinfully long black lashes, he was moving his hands in a violent arc, suddenly for the first time striking Emmie as thoroughly foreign and exotic. He said more as well but she couldn't hear him because of the noisy ignition of the helicopter. Getting airborne again was a relief while she deliberated on the way she had been reacting to him. Her cheeks reddened on the awareness that she had taken her resentment of her position out on him when it would have been more just to take it out on her mother. She had needled Bastian, criticised him, even scorned him. Right there and then, she was shaken to have to accept that she could behave like that. She swallowed hard. He had paid a small fortune for a pleasant companion and had instead received a venomous and truculent one.

As it would have been quite impossible to communicate with him while they were airborne due to the noise level inside the helicopter, Emmie dug a pen out of her bag and wrote on the back of her hand and then extended it to him so that he could see what she had written.

When it came to women, Bastian considered himself to be incapable of surprise at anything a woman did, but when Emmie printed 'I'm sorry' on the back of her hand and thrust her apology at him, he was strongly disconcerted by her approach. He blinked, looked again and then suddenly he wanted to laugh, but he didn't want to hurt her feelings when he genuinely admired the wholehearted honesty of her admission that she had been challenging company. In answer he caught her hand in his and kissed her fingertips in forgiveness.

Equally startled, Emmie tugged her hand back, fingers tingling from that brief salutation. He had style and he really *didn't* sulk, she conceded guiltily. But it *was* partly his fault that she had been behaving badly. Good grief, that kiss had knocked her sideways and she hadn't been able to cope with that! She had believed that she had made a total fool of herself when she responded to him. She stole a sidewise glance at his bold bronzed profile. But she was undoubtedly dealing with a guy who *always* got a response out of a woman. He was downright beautiful and she could have kissed him for an hour without getting bored, stunned by the bonfire of reaction one kiss could light in her body. Even so, what she was experiencing was only sexual attraction and perhaps she had never felt it so strongly before, she reasoned, wishing she didn't want him to do it again, wishing she were back safe in his office where such temptation had been unknown and he had been a distant figure whom someone as insignificant as her rarely saw, never mind got close to.

'You were right about the manners,' Bastian admitted wryly as he helped her out of the helicopter again, his bodyguard bringing up the rear. 'I have no excuse. I spent years at an exclusive English public school where I learned every courtesy. Then I went to visit my mother in Italy one summer when I was fourteen and…er, lost the habit—'

Surprised by that far from arrogant and generous concession, Emmie turned to look at him. 'Why? What happened?'

'My mother said that every time I opened a door for her it made her feel like an old lady and that all the thank-yous I used made me sound like a waiter.'

'I know some women do believe that a man being courteous to a woman these days is sexist,' Emmie allowed, resisting a strong urge to criticise his parent. 'But I don't think that way.'

'Obviously not.' Dark eyes dancing with raw amusement, Bastian shot her a glance, making her maddeningly conscious of his thick dark eyelashes. 'I was trying so hard to impress my mother, and make her proud of me because I didn't see her very often, but evidently I overdid it.'

Or his mother was an unfeeling shrew, Emmie reflected in pained silence, in much the same way as Emmie had been to judge Bastian on appearances and assume that his wealth and status explained his seeming lack of manners.

'I suppose I was sort of prejudiced about you,' Emmie admitted ruefully.

'Ditto,' Bastian added.

'I'll try very hard not to hold your money against you,' Emmie muttered.

Bastian almost laughed out loud, for it was the very first time it had been suggested to him that his fortune could act as a source of prejudice. 'And I will try equally hard not to cherish misconceptions about your…er, profession outside the office.'

Emmie winced. 'Don't use that word, "profession",' she advised. 'It's misleading when you think of that reference to "the oldest profession of all".'

'You're right. That wasn't tactful.'

Feeling almost in charity with him, Emmie was taken aback when he reached down and closed his hand round hers and her bright blue eyes dropped to their linked fingers in silent question.

'We're in view of the house. We now have those witnesses you said we needed before I could touch you,' he extended in calm justification.

Emmie was tense, intent on the sheer novelty value of Bastian smiling at her, even if it was fake and for public show. Good grief, it was an incredible smile that utterly transformed his face, chasing the detachment she had so often glimpsed there. Reddening, she looked ahead of her and only just managed not to gasp like an overexcited child at the sight of the huge white rambling modern house sprawling along the edge of the beach. 'That's your home?'

'I demolished my father's old house and had this one

built about six years back. Before that I stayed with my grandfather, who lives on the other side of the island…'

It was a massive house. Nervous butterflies leapt in her tummy at the thought of the family occasion she was about to crash in her false identity of girlfriend, not to mention the ex-fiancée, who she assumed would be present the night before the wedding in her role as bridesmaid.

'You know we haven't discussed any sort of cover story,' she pointed out belatedly. 'Where will I say we met?'

'The office. Keep it simple but I doubt if you'll be asked nosy questions. As a rule my relations are afraid of offending me and should be civil and reserved,' Bastian reassured her.

That didn't exactly suggest a warm and friendly welcome to Emmie and she felt more than ever like an intruder on private territory. It wasn't possible to get more personal than seeing someone's home and family. The warmth of his hand on hers was strangely comforting in spite of the fact that it was only part of the masquerade. He had such big hands that her hand felt lost in his. She sucked in a sustaining breath.

'Stop stressing,' Bastian urged. 'You're only here to smooth over any potential unpleasantness on my sister's big day.'

That was not a comment designed to give Emmie a swollen head, she conceded with reluctant amusement. 'Won't your ex resent me being there?' she asked abruptly.

'She doesn't care enough to resent you,' Bastian drawled without expression.

'And *this* is the woman you were planning to marry?' Emmie prompted in a voice of disbelief.

'Some of us don't pin much faith on hearts and flowers.'

And then a private conversation became impossible as they climbed the steps to the front door where the housekeeper, a widely smiling older woman, was already shooting a flood of welcoming Greek to Bastian and he was replying in kind.

'They're all out by the pool,' he explained, releasing her hand to lead the way through a vast echoing hall ornamented with a sweeping staircase.

Emmie breathed in deeply, smoothing damp palms down over her trousered legs and straightening her slender back when she heard the noise of voices, splashing and the shouts of excited children. Bastian strode ahead of her out into the sunshine again and a young blonde woman leapt up with a delighted grin to call, 'Bastian! I thought you were never going to get here!'

As Bastian had momentarily forgotten her presence, Emmie hovered uncertainly by the poolside, infuriatingly conscious that she was the focus of all eyes but *his*. And then someone cannoned into her, knocking her off balance in her high heels and she went flying with a cry of fright into the pool. It happened so fast that she had no way of trying to stabilise herself and her head struck the edge of something hard and blackness claimed her.

* * *

Emmie recovered consciousness to find herself lying flat on a gigantic bed in soaking wet clothes. Pain was pulsing at the back of her head and she moaned, lifting her hand to gently trace the source of the sizeable bump beneath her hair.

'Do you feel sick?' a familiar voice asked and she lifted her swimming head and began to sit up only to find a large hand planted to her midriff to press her down flat again. 'Lie still. You gave your head a hell of a thump,' Bastian told her harshly.

'Yes…' Eyes opening, she focused dizzily on Bastian standing over her, clad only in a towel, a startling enough vision to make her stiffen. 'You're not dressed—'

'Yes, and you're dripping all over my bed,' Bastian informed her.

A sudden shiver took hold of Emmie and she registered the wet cling of her sodden garments and groaned out loud. She was still staring at the most perfect set of masculine abs she had ever seen outside a movie screen. Stripped, Bastian had the musculature of a Greek god—not a very original thought, she conceded abstractedly, considering who and what he was.

'Emmie…the doctor's coming.' Bastian bent down and scooped her up into his arms without warning. A muffled squeak of surprise escaped her. 'What are you doing?'

'I'm putting you in the bathroom so that you can

get out of your wet clothes,' Bastian told her with immense practicality. 'Do you think you can stand up?'

'I'll have to,' she muttered as he very carefully settled her down on her bare feet. 'What happened?'

'One of the teenagers rammed you and you fell in the pool. You were knocked out—'

'My word, I might have drowned,' Emmie framed shakily, her knees buckling under her. 'I'm sorry, I'm feeling dizzy—'

Bastian hauled her up against him and sat down on the side of a raised bath.

'Don't you dare try to help me take my clothes off!' Emmie warned him.

Face taut with frustration, Bastian lowered her limp body down onto the tiled floor. 'Do you really think I'm likely to touch you inappropriately in the condition you're in?' he enquired angrily.

Shivering violently with the chill of her damp clothing, Emmie rested her brow down on her raised knees. 'Just leave me…I'll be OK—'

'You really do have a very low opinion of me, don't you?' Bastian growled like an angry bear.

'Sorry,' Emmie whispered, on the edge of tears because she felt so weak while she was now also being tormented by the disastrous start she had made to her weekend with Bastian. So much for the girlfriend he wanted to use as cover! One minute inside the door she had taken a header into the pool and rendered herself unconscious and a liability.

In answer, Bastian trailed her sweater off over her

head and tossed it aside. He draped a towelling robe round her pale slight shoulders, gazing down at her while wondering why she looked so absurdly vulnerable, fluffy lashes drooping, full lower lip trembling. He didn't get involved with women who looked that breakable and had no idea what to do with her.

Emmie managed to dig her arms into the sleeves of the robe to at least cover her bra. She felt absolutely humiliated as Bastian lifted her upright again, urging her to hang onto the edge of the vanity while he freed her from her trousers with as much seductive intent as he might have used towards a cardboard cut-out. She thought of the surgical scars marring her leg and hoped he wouldn't notice them. Tears stung her eyes. 'I'm sorry about this!'

'Why are you apologising?' Bastian demanded impatiently while he struggled to behave like a man of honour and not sneak a glance at the truly spectacular female figure he had briefly unveiled. Unfortunately his own body was rather less disciplined and was already betraying him with very masculine efficiency. He cursed under his breath, wondering what it was about her that made his hormones react as if she were a rocket attack. She was destroying his self-discipline and he was well aware that experiencing desire while she was feeling wretched was the act of a selfish, unfeeling bastard. Which he was, Bastian fully accepted that, knew he was no candidate for sainthood. Of course, he wasn't going to *do* anything about the inconvenient way she made him respond with every flash of those stunning blue eyes, he reminded himself grimly. But with bleak humour he recalled how he had suspected that she might go out of her way to lure him into having sex with her. It was a suspicion that now struck him as insane. There she was hunched in the robe as though she were in the presence of a ravening beast of masculinity likely to rip it off her; no, there was nothing flirtatious or seductive about her behaviour. When had he got so big-headed that he assumed that every woman wanted him? And why was he even thinking such peculiar things?

'I gather you got me out of the pool.' Emmie guessed the reason for his lack of clothing.

'*Ne*...yes,' he confirmed in English.

Emmie walked back into the bedroom slowly and made for the bed. 'I just want to lie down for a while and then I'll get dressed and come downstairs to join you,' she promised.

'I don't think so. We'll abide by what the doctor advises when he arrives.'

Having settled back against the pillows, Emmie looked at him and turned bright red. He wasn't shy anyway. Poised in what appeared to be the doorway of another room, he had cast off the towel and was pulling on a pair of black boxers. Perhaps he didn't realise that she could see his astonishingly beautiful tawny body rippling with well-honed muscle with every fluid movement. She closed her eyes tight shut. She wanted to apologise again but knew that irritated him and sealed her lips, watching him leave, shock-ingly elegant again in a dark grey suit. Two less suited personalities than she and Bastian had never been born.

A knock sounded on the door and Emmie sat up to see a young blonde woman looking in at her. 'Do you feel well enough for a visitor?' she asked with a smile. 'I'm Bastian's sister, Nessa.'

'Of course, come in,' Emmie encouraged awkwardly, thinking that she would never have known to look at brother and sister that they were even distantly related, for Nessa was small, curvy and blonde.

'I've never seen my brother move so fast in his life as when he dived into the pool.'

'Sorry for all the fuss.' Emmie sighed ruefully. 'Who knocked into me?'

'One of my teenaged cousins. His parents are really embarrassed and they wanted to come up and apologise because it could have been a serious accident,' Nessa pointed out. 'We're very lucky that Bastian realised you'd hit your head going into the water.'

'I'm all right though. Accidents happen,' Emmie responded lightly.

'How's your head?' Nessa asked 'Do you mind if I stay a while?'

'I have a bump, that's all. Of course you can stay,' Emmie answered, charmed by Nessa's smiling friendliness.

'Are you sure you're OK?' Bastian's sister prompted worriedly, touching Emmie's hand. 'My goodness, your skin is icy cold! Get into bed and warm up. I'll get you a drink!'

Emmie scrambled below the duvet and rested her head back on the piled up pillows, very much appreciating Nessa's kind-heartedness because it made her feel less of a nuisance. 'You should be with your guests,' she said guiltily.

'Technically they're Bastian's guests because this is his house but they're all family,' Nessa told her, disappearing through one of the doors and reappearing with a glass, which she thrust into Emmie's hand. 'Drink it. I'm sure I read some place that it's good for someone in shock.'

Emmie drank and then began to cough as brandy burned the back of her throat, for she really hadn't expected to be given an alcoholic drink. The rich liquid raced like a flame though down into her chilled tummy.

'So, tell me about you and Bastian…' Nessa perched on the bed beside Emmie, bright brown eyes leaping with warmth and curiosity. 'I was over the moon when I realised he'd met someone else, and so quickly too… like magic—'

'Oh, yes, pure magic,' Emmie agreed uneasily, thinking how very young and refreshingly unspoilt Nessa seemed.

'You are so beautiful!' Nessa commented with satisfaction. 'Lilah will tear her hair out when she sees you—'

'As long as it's not mine. I don't want to upset anyone—'

'I know she's one of my bridesmaids but she's treated my brother very badly,' Nessa proclaimed, condemnation tightening her pretty face. 'He deserved better and she should have dropped out of my wedding, not insisted on carrying out her role when it's no longer appropriate.'

'Perhaps Lilah didn't want to let *you* down,' Emmie suggested, sipping at the brandy while appreciating that Bastian's sister was not at all attached to her brother's former fiancée.

'No, she wants Bastian back,' Nessa contradicted, her conviction sending a current of alarm through Emmie. 'She doesn't know my brother as well as she thinks she does though. He's tough—'

'I know.'

'He had to be tough. By the time he was eighteen years old he had lived through four divorces and three stepmothers. People don't understand what he went through and what all that did to him,' Nessa declared, fiercely defensive of her half sibling. 'My mother was the only one who didn't treat him badly.'

'That's something to be grateful for,' Emmie soothed, curious but keen to stem the flood of information, which she did not feel entitled to receive because she knew Bastian wouldn't appreciate her knowing such private stuff.

'Bastian's never had a family life. He doesn't know what one is.'

'Childhood can be challenging,' Emmie commented vaguely, touched by Nessa's innocence, comprehending why her brother was prepared to go to such lengths to ensure she wasn't upset on her wedding day.

Nessa grimaced. 'Well, I was lucky. I was spoilt rotten by my mum. But Bastian didn't have an easy time.'

'He's a very confident, *private* man,' Emmie remarked with gentle emphasis.

'That's why I'm telling you this—so that you understand him better. I mean, if you're waiting for him to tell you anything, you'll wait for ever.' Nessa pulled a comic face on the score of her brother's reticence. 'The minute I heard you worked with him I knew you would be a normal woman and that's exactly what I think he needs.'

The two women were interrupted by another knock on the door, telegraphing the arrival of the doctor with Bastian in tow.

'You don't need to stay,' Emmie informed Bastian with a stiff smile.

'I'm afraid I do. Dr Papadopoulos doesn't speak any English.'

Suppressing the suspicion that she would never ever get the last word with Bastian, Emmie nodded agreement, poker-faced. Bastian translated the doctor's questions and then Emmie's head was examined. The older man finally said that he thought that there wasn't much wrong with her that couldn't be cured by a good night's sleep. He then gave her painkillers for her headache and departed.

'I'll get up now,' Emmie told Bastian before he could leave with the doctor.

'You heard the doctor…*rest*,' Bastian spelt out grittily, noting that the mascara streaks on her cheeks suggested that she had been crying and was probably not half as composed as she would like him to believe. 'I would have been happier if he had agreed you needed to be checked out at the nearest hospital.'

'I'm OK…and this household doesn't need all that fuss the night before Nessa's wedding,' Emmie reasoned, knowing that that would carry more weight with him than any other argument.

'You could go home and try to sue me,' Bastian commented grimly.

Emmie groaned out loud. 'I'm not going to sue anyone. I'm not like that.'

His face remained impassive.

Alone again and too warm now in the robe, Emmie took it off, stripped off her damp underwear and slid back naked into the comfortable bed. A little nap would brighten her up, she told herself, but Bastian's remark, his concern that she might try to sue him for her accident, had troubled her. What sort of a life had he had and what sort of experiences that even a minor mishap taking place in his home could make him that cynical and distrustful? After all, she had suffered no lasting injury. Was he so used to being targeted by greedy people? That accustomed to those who tried to take advantage of his wealth?

CHAPTER FOUR

TWO HOURS LATER, Emmie wakened from a restful doze. Her head no longer throbbed and she felt a good deal stronger and calmer. While she slept her suitcase had arrived and she opened it up and pulled out clothes for the evening ahead. Apparently there was to be some sort of a party to which the locals were invited. She showered and washed her tangled hair, drying it carefully and renewing her make-up. The party dress was fuchsia pink with a jewelled neckline and short full skirt that swirled with every step she took in the toning shoes. She was ready for anything and prepared to be a pleasant companion, she told herself staunchly while she walked down the magnificent staircase.

In the hall below, Bastian was engaged in greeting dinner guests with his grandfather, Nessa and her bridegroom, Leonides. He frowned in surprise when he saw Emmie actually up and out of bed. And then ten seconds later, overpowered by one of the curious contradictions that continually afflicted him in her radius, he wanted to sweep her straight back between the sheets with him for company. In all his many years of freedom he had never met a woman who could hold a candle to Emmie Marshall with her golden hair bouncing on her slim shoulders, her big blue eyes bright as stars while a natural smile flashed like sunshine across her succulent pink mouth when Nessa saw her and grinned. Well, his sister certainly liked her; in fact Nessa was behaving rather as though he had got engaged again. It would do no harm to depress his sister's expectations a little after the honeymoon and mention with regret that he had moved on. As he would *have* to move on, he told himself impatiently, and stop fantasising about riding Emmie's perfect body with her legs locked round his waist, her beautiful face aglow with desire. His tall, well-built body already tense, Bastian shifted restively at the charge of unholy lust firing his every hormone to a needy flame. He had never wanted any woman as badly as he wanted Emmie at that moment.

'So, you're Emmie…' A tall white-haired elderly man greeted her with a pleasant smile and a handshake. 'I'm relieved that Bastian didn't succeed in drowning you in his pool on your first visit,' he confided. 'I'm his grandfather, Theron Christou.'

During the meal that followed, Emmie struggled to eat. Nessa had insisted that she sit beside her and Leonides while Bastian was at the head of the table next to his grandfather. Even though she was hungry she was hopelessly on edge, her fingers curving to her wine glass for something solid to hold onto because every time she glanced up she met black-fringed dark golden eyes that sent her thoughts and her speech into a complete loop even as her heart hammered and her mouth ran dry, leaving her thirsty, constantly sipping and yet still overheated. She could not control the slow burn that travelled to her feminine core every time she met Bastian's stunning eyes and, even worse, she could not suppress the sense of intense longing that constantly gripped her. This wasn't her, this was *not* the woman she was, she argued angrily with herself. She had never been the type to get over-excited by a man or whose body yearned for the touch of one. Indeed she had often thought such promptings belonged more to fantasy than reality and now all of a sudden she was finding out how naïve she had been.

After dinner, the guests moved to a large room, furnished with a buffet, a bar and a DJ where many of the islanders were already arriving with gifts and good wishes for the bridal couple. Bastian banded a guiding arm to her waist and introduced her to what seemed like dozens of people. Her head swam with names unattached to faces, and the lush scent of his cologne spiced with clean, warm male set up goose-flesh across her skin. She had never been so aware of a man, of every fluid movement of his lean, hot body, the rich timbre of his dark accented drawl above her head, the ridiculously arousing feel of the long fingers flexing against her hipbone. Her breasts were full and taut below her clothing, the tips swollen and tingling, and down below in a place she rarely thought about she was tender and embarrassingly damp. It was sheer insanity to react that way to Bastian Christou but every time she connected with his lustrous dark eyes, rational thought vanished.

Desire could make anyone stupid, she reasoned as the evening marched on with the bride and groom very much the centre of attention. Bastian was a gorgeous guy and inexperience made her vulnerable to his indescribably potent sexual charisma. Maybe she had set the bar too high before taking a lover because she had wanted to find trust, honesty and caring with one special man. Maybe if she had been a little more sophisticated she could have laughed and ignored Bastian. As it was, she was wickedly, weakly conscious of his every move, every word, every glance and it felt as if she had a bomb ticking down to detonation inside her.

'Let's dance,' Bastian breathed above her head, guiding her onto the crowded floor, and she shivered, feet hesitant to follow because she didn't want to slow dance with him, didn't want to take that risk of getting physically closer. But it was getting late and soon she would be able to retire to bed, duty done, she reckoned, as bendy and inviting as a concrete post when he tilted her hips towards his and closed his strong arms around her.

Momentarily she shivered with reaction, blindsided by the hard muscular steel of him against her softer curves, helplessly intoxicated by that sheer masculinity laced with the intimacy of his evocative scent. He tipped up her head and kissed her before she knew what he was doing, and the kiss from those firm male lips cut through her like a knife blade slashing through butter, burning and arousing wherever it touched. As her nipples constricted into stiff, straining buds a sliding sensation curled low in her pelvis, leaving her knees trembling and an inarticulate sound breaking from her throat.

Bastian lifted his proud dark head. 'I want you, *moraki mou*,' he husked.

The compelling beauty of his face at that instant inflamed her. She didn't feel like herself any more: she felt *wild*, hungry, out of control, all the things she never allowed herself to be. That thought kicked off alarm bells in the back of her head but her body and the unquenchable craving for him that she couldn't fight held her fast, pinned as close to him as his own skin. He was as turned on as she was and that knowledge was strangely soothing. The brutally hard ridge of his erection against her stomach was inescapable and shamelessly thrilling on a level she refused to think about.

'You set me on fire,' he growled almost accusingly. 'I don't do one-night stands—'

'Neither do I,' she sliced in breathlessly.

Dark eyes smouldered brilliant gold over her flushed face. 'Tonight we break the rules—'

'No…' she framed feverishly and then he kissed her again, his hard mouth stealing her protest with a passionate intensity she could not resist.

He guided her through the crush of party-goers with a word here, a wave there, smoothly ensuring that nobody intercepted them and slowed their progress. She mounted the stairs by his side, ever so slightly dizzy, lower limbs a little clumsy and, away from the music, the noise and the bright lights, suddenly conscious that she was not quite sober. How much wine had she drunk? And she had not eaten much at dinner, she recalled vaguely. Drinking on an empty tummy after that huge brandy Nessa had pressed on her—how foolish could a woman be? But the burn of that scorching kiss was still on her swollen mouth, firing an unbearable ache between her legs and destroying her self-discipline.

A lean brown hand closing round hers, he pulled her into the bedroom she had vacated earlier. His hands cradled her face, glittering dark eyes heavily lidded with desire. 'Once we get back to London *this* didn't happen. It will be our secret,' he told her arrogantly.

'It's not going to happen,' she faltered, taken aback by that ruthless assurance that warned her there would be no future beyond the next dawn. 'I'm not cheap—'

His fingertips grazed her delicate jawbone. 'You want me.'

Madly, insanely, *crazily*, she acknowledged, still fighting to think straight.

One night, Bastian was bargaining with himself, one rare night of self-indulgence that smashed his usual boundaries. *She wasn't cheap?* He had got that unsavoury message, wished he hadn't and wanted the strength of mind to evict her from his bedroom but he could no longer fight his devouring hunger for her. He pulled off his jacket with impatient hands and ripped loose his collar before he reached for her and crushed her succulent mouth below his again. Gathering her up to him, he brought her down on the bed, stretching down a hand to flip off her high heels.

His hard, demanding mouth and the plunging stab of his tongue were like a drug Emmie craved, a need as powerful and natural as taking a next breath. In a minute she promised herself that she would stop him, call a halt, assert logic, but with every demanding kiss he demolished her mental misgivings. She was flat on the bed, rejoicing in his weight, which seemed to answer some of the longing clawing at her, when he lifted her up and ran down the zip of her dress.

'Bastian…we—' *mustn't*, she intended to say but he enveloped her in the folds of her dress as he trailed it off over her head.

'We *must*,' he contradicted, second-guessing her words while burying his carnal mouth against the pulse beating raggedly at her collarbone, licking the salt from her skin with a wicked tongue, tracing a trail down to the shallow valley between her small high breasts, fingers already dealing with her bra, everything moving so fast she couldn't keep track of it or call a pause.

'I want to be sensible,' she argued frantically, spooked by the out-of-control feeling she was experiencing.

'Sensible?' he exclaimed with incredulity, straddling her prone length to rip off his shirt with positive violence, buttons flying in all directions. 'There's nothing sensible about feeling like this. Some actions are driven by instinct, *koukla mou*.'

Either instinct or appreciation kept her still, her dazed blue gaze welded to the smooth muscular planes of his magnificent brown torso. Heat hummed at the heart of her and the ache stirred again stronger than ever. Her bra was gone and she hadn't even noticed it going, was suddenly much more aware of the burn of his eyes over her bare breasts, the devastating touch of expert fingers rubbing against the unbearably swollen tips. Her spine bowed, her body reaching upward in a helpless arch as long fingers grazed down her leg and came to a sudden stop to retrace their path over the roughened stretch of skin he had detected.

'What's this?' he breathed, glancing down.

Emmie froze, more naked and vulnerable in that moment than she would have been had she wakened to find herself walking nude down a street, and she turned paper pale. 'I had surgery…years ago…there was something wrong with my leg,' she explained jerkily. 'You see, I've got some ugly scars. I'm not perfect—'

'I don't want or need perfect,' Bastian declared hungrily, running a caressing but unconcerned hand over the marks he had discovered.

'But I do want you,' he breathed thickly, eyes hot gold below sooty lashes. 'I'm as hard as a rock.'

Her pallor receded, her face burning with sudden colour as he sprang off the bed and shed his tailored trousers, the male bulge of arousal prominent in his fitted boxers. Shyness and uncertainty and apprehension engulfed her. She didn't know what to do or how to behave and yet still he was the most beautiful thing she had ever seen and she couldn't take her eyes off him. That lithe tawny body called to hers on a visceral level. Desire, she was discovering, incited much more overwhelming responses than she could ever have guessed. She had never dreamt she could want to touch a man so badly.

Bastian used his mouth to tease her rosy nipples, suckling and lingering to torment while he kneaded the full mounds of her breasts. Little involuntary sounds escaped her throat and when he ran a hand up her inner thigh she literally stopped breathing, the ache stirring again and overriding every other impulse. He raked a finger down over the tight, damp fabric of her knickers and she shuddered, intolerably conscious of the swollen damp flesh pulsing between her splayed thighs. Every reflex and hormonal reaction in her entire body seemed to be centred there.

'A woman has never made me feel this desperate,' Bastian growled in a tone of bemused disbelief as he tugged off the last barrier between them.

Emmie recognised that he was shaken up too and the fierce wanting that drove her no longer seemed quite so shameful. She stared up at him, loving the hard, angular bone structure that gave his features such charismatic strength, the smouldering eyes beneath the lush curling lashes, marvelling that mere days earlier he had still been a stranger. Nobody had ever made her feel the way he made her feel. He touched her where she frantically needed to be touched, a fingertip whispering over the bundle of nerve endings below her mound, and she jerked as if he had burned her, her entire body coming alive with electric reaction.

He snaked down her body with strong supple power and spread her thighs, and her fingers knotted into his luxuriant black hair to stop him before the first breathtaking sensation of his sensual assault engulfed her feverish body. Her teeth chattered together, shock winging through her at the ferocious intensity of her own response. He explored her with his mouth and his fingers and she twisted and arched and gasped over and over again, lost to sensation, lost to the violent need he had incited. Hungry heat spiralled in her pelvis and rose to an excruciating height and she was quivering and moaning and rising closer to the climax she sensed when he rose over her and plunged deep into her.

Pain and pleasure combined with explosive effect. Even as the involuntary ripples of orgasm clenched round his hard shaft and pulsed wildly through her she cried out in pain and he fell still, frowning down with perplexed eyes at her dismayed face.

'Don't stop!' she told him urgently, too mortified by her own cry to be willing to draw such stark attention to what she had just sacrificed. That was not something she was prepared to discuss and she dimly hoped that continuation and a more natural conclusion would stifle comment. She had not known that first time sex would hurt, suspected that she should have warned him in advance but could not imagine what words she might have employed with which to share her deepest secret.

For that reason, she squeezed her eyes tightly shut, her cheeks burning, and tried to concentrate on the extraordinary feel of him inside her as he shifted position.

'Are you all right?' Bastian asked tautly.

'Of course, I am,' she parried, for that fleeting pain had speedily receded, leaving her with only the erotic sense of his alien fullness stretching her and sinking deeper into her receptive body.

'If I was too rough, I'm sorry...you feel *amazing*,' Bastian confided with ragged emphasis, easing back with care before sinking into her again. His movement provoked a melting wave of honeyed heat in her lower body, making her heart thump fast and hard again. The excitement gathered like the eye of a storm inside her chest, every sensation intensified by his fluid rhythm.

Suddenly she was caught up in the same endeavour, fully a partner, no longer an uncertain onlooker. Her heart pounding like mad, she bucked and lifted her hips beneath him, meeting his thrusts, urging him on as the writhing electric excitement and the frenzy of need overwhelmed the last remnants of her control. She could feel herself reaching another height and she plunged over the edge with a startled cry of pleasure, quivering in the waves of ecstasy while he drove into her one last time. He vented a harsh groan of satisfaction and shuddered over her and she felt him spill inside her.

He shifted and pressed his mouth in a brief salutation to her damp brow. 'That was an unforgettable experience, *moraki mou*...'

Unforgettable for her as well, Emmie acknowledged in a daze. Even though their intimacy had begun on a note of pain he had twice brought her to a climax and she was blissfully relaxed and adrift on a fluffy cloud of well-being. She squashed the misgivings already trying to infiltrate her. She wasn't going to turn all girly and silly in the aftermath, she assured herself with determination. He had surpassed her expectations but all they had shared was their bodies, nothing more. Nobody fancied themselves in love, nobody needed to get hurt, least of all her. She was in full control of her emotions.

Bastian rolled back from her and studied her with frowning golden eyes the colour of burning amber. 'So, what's going on here?' he queried, black brows pleating. 'I don't want to misjudge you and assume that this was some bizarre set-up.'

CHAPTER FIVE

TAKEN ABACK BY Bastian's provocative statement, Emmie blinked away her drowsiness and lifted her head up off the pillow. 'A…*set-up*? Bizarre?' she repeated blankly in her confusion. 'What on earth are you talking about?'

'By all means, tell me if I'm wrong,' Bastian urged, wide sensual mouth tense. 'But I believe you were a virgin.'

Emmie sat up, hugging the sheet defensively to her breasts. Suddenly, her face was literally burning with mortification, for she had been hoping that he either hadn't noticed or hadn't guessed what had been amiss with her. 'Yes?' she gritted in a so-what tone of discouragement.

'Then why throw yourself away on me?' Bastian asked flatly. 'I'm not proud that you succeeded in enticing me into bed but I wasn't expecting anything more from you than a typical shag.'

Emmie tensed in sheer shock and anger at his accusation. 'Look, I did *not* entice you!' she snapped back.

'You're so beautiful that you've naturally been enticing me from the moment we met at the airport,' Bastian
extended grudgingly and, recognising his pronounced
discomfiture in the aftermath of his sexual satisfaction,
he labelled himself a total hypocrite and sprang out of
bed to distance himself from her. But he had done what
he should not have done and now he had to deal with
the fallout. She had proved to be a temptation he could
not resist. But what he could not comprehend was that
Emmie Marshall had also been a virgin. That did not
make sense, nor did it match the characteristics of the
adventurous and more experienced woman he had believed she had to be to work as an escort.

'Believe me, it wasn't intentional!' Emmie fired
back, thrusting back the bedding and snatching up the
towelling robe folded over a nearby chair. She dug her
arms into it and tied the sash tight, adjusting the la-
pels to cover every piece of skin that she could for the
last thing she now wanted to be was naked in any way
around Bastian Christou. *A typical shag?* Was that all
her body had meant to him? Could he possibly *be* any
more insulting?

'I wasn't expecting a hired escort to be a virgin. I
don't pay for sex either, I never have and never will,
but I'll naturally compensate you for your…er, generosity—' Bastian selected the word with razor-edged
care '—with diamonds and hope that they meet your
expectations.'

Emmie had honestly believed that she could not feel
any worse but now and without the smallest warning it

was as if the bottom had fallen out of her world, leaving her hovering in sickening limbo. He truly did believe that she would want to be paid in some way for having slept with him! She was shattered and simultaneously cut to the quick by his view of her. Seemingly he saw her as barely one step removed from a hooker. A man didn't normally offer a woman diamonds in reward after sex, at least not in *her* world. And *this* was the male she had chosen to sleep with? She could only despise her blind stupidity.

In the buzzing silence, Bastian noted her pallor and the tightness of her delicate bone structure. 'Have I got this situation wrong? You did say quite plainly upfront that you weren't cheap—'

'But that didn't mean that I put a price on my body like a whore!' Emmie shot back at him wrathfully, a shudder of mortified rage writhing through her tall slender figure as she stood there, stiff with disbelief. 'I meant that I don't do casual sex, that's what I meant! I wasn't talking about money or jewels or *anything* of that nature!'

'Since I've clearly offended you, I apologise,' Bastian fielded curtly. 'But what else was I to think when you made that comment about not being cheap? You're an escort, whose company I paid for. It didn't take a fertile imagination to leap to the conclusion that you would expect some further form of remuneration for including sex in our arrangement...'

And that was the exact instant in which Emmie finally recognised what a dreadful, indefensible mistake she had made in going to bed with him, for not for one moment had he forgotten that she was an escort whose time he had purchased. Not for one moment had he truly buried his suspicions about exactly what being an escort might entail. She was the one who had forgotten the barriers between them; she was the one who had somehow crucially forgotten that he was *paying* for the role she was playing. Humiliation and regret touched her deep.

'I already told you that I wasn't an escort!' she slammed back at him fierily, golden hair tumbling round her flushed cheekbones. 'But you wouldn't believe me!'

'I saw your photo on that website. I phoned up and I booked you. If you weren't an escort, how would that be possible?' Bastian demanded drily, unimpressed, a tall commanding figure for all his state of undress.

'It's not that simple,' Emmie parried, her shoulders bowing as a wave of sudden weariness engulfed her. She sank stiffly down on the sofa by the far wall, as far as she could get from him and still be in the same room. Nothing but the unlovely truth would suffice, she registered dully. She did not have a choice: she had to tell him the truth to clear her name.

Emmie breathed in deep and lifted her head high, refusing to be apologetic about what she could not help. 'My mother owns the escort agency—'

'Your...*mother*?' Bastian said incredulously, striding into the dressing room to tug a pair of jeans and a T-shirt out of the built-in closets that lined the walls.

Her mother ran an escort agency? He was astonished and appalled by that startling piece of information.

'Yes, my mother,' Emmie confirmed between compressed lips and then went on to explain a little about her background and how her elder sister had raised her and her siblings after Odette had put her younger daughters into foster care. 'I hadn't seen Odette since I was twelve and when she rang out of the blue and said I could live with her for free while I worked unpaid for your company, I leapt at the opportunity. It wasn't just that I needed a low-cost place to live…' She hesitated and her cheeks warmed, her eyes veiling to conceal her vulnerability. 'I thought it would be a great way to finally get to know my mother as well.'

Wincing at the troubled note in her voice that she could not hide, Bastian zipped up his jeans. 'Did you know about the agency *before* you moved in with her?'

'Of course not, and the minute I did move in and she told me about it she immediately began nagging at me to work as one of her escorts,' Emmie admitted ruefully, trying not to stare as he hauled on the tee, dragging it down over his amazingly muscular bronzed abdomen. Embarrassed colour stung her face with unwelcome heat. 'She was very annoyed when I took a job as a waitress instead—'

'You work as a waitress as well?' Bastian prompted with a frown of a surprise, his attention lingering on the soft full curve of her delicious mouth, which was still swollen from his kisses. That fast he wanted her again, that fast it was a challenge to concentrate on what she was saying, and he paced restively across the room, exasperated by his overactive sex drive and yet awesomely unfamiliar with the modest art of listening to a woman talk and actually recognising her distress.

'Five nights a week. I needed the money,' Emmie pointed out reluctantly. 'But I suspect that my mother was counting on me agreeing to work as an escort for her when she asked me to move in—in fact that's probably the *only* reason she invited me to live with her in the first place. She took the photo from my camera to put it on her website. I didn't know about it. I would never have agreed to that.'

'So, if you weren't working as one of your mother's escorts, what the hell are you doing here with me?' Bastian demanded bluntly, dark eyes glittering suspiciously as he searched her pale tight face, judging her sincerity, recognising her discomfort in confiding such things about her mother. As a son who had often been embarrassed by parental behaviour, Bastian had sympathy enough with her on that score.

'I'm afraid my mother brought out the big guns to persuade me to accept the booking with you,' Emmie confided with an unamused laugh, her facial muscles locking tight with self-discipline as she broached an even more personal topic. 'You saw the scarring on my leg…'

'*Ne*…yes,' Bastian responded in Greek again, reacting to her clear discomfiture.

Emmie compressed her lips. 'When I was younger, my leg was badly injured in a car crash and I ended up in a wheelchair. Eventually I graduated from the chair on to crutches. I was disabled and if I hadn't had a private and very expensive operation abroad I would probably still be on crutches. That surgery enabled me to walk again and turned my life around. After my mother accepted your booking she told me that *she* had paid for that surgery and that I owed her.'

His face hardened. 'You didn't owe anyone anything, least of all a woman so keen to use you—and possibly your body as well—as a source of profit.'

'I felt I owed her,' Emmie contradicted with quiet dignity. 'That operation meant so much to me. It gave me normality back. When my mother admitted that she was short of money I was willing to be an escort for one weekend for her out of gratitude.'

'Therefore, you've genuinely never worked as an escort before,' Bastian breathed harshly, events finally falling into place and comprehension with it. 'But why did she keep that photo of you on her website?'

'She thought it brought in more business and when her clients asked for me, she simply said I was fully booked,' Emmie advanced heavily.

'*Ne*…yes. She tried that gambit with me until I offered her so much money she was ready to blackmail you into providing the service for my benefit,' Bastian told her with palpable distaste. 'Why didn't you tell me all this from the start? I would never have got mixed up in this nonsense!'

Emmie tensed and stood up. 'I couldn't get the

money back off Odette so what would have been the point?'

'I'm not a complete bastard,' Bastian retorted in a raw driven undertone.

Emmie disagreed but said nothing. *A typical shag*, words for ever etched on her soul to shame and hurt. No, she wasn't so brave and unafraid now, was she? Being forced to confront the image Bastian had of her was the most humiliating experience of her life. That she had impulsively leapt into bed with him and surrendered her virginity was something she was convinced she would regret until the day she died. Now, she badly wanted privacy. She had said what she had to say and had nothing else to add.

'This is your bedroom, isn't it?' Emmie guessed, pushing a heavy hand through her hair. 'I should have realised earlier when you got dressed here but after I bashed my head I wasn't really thinking clearly. Tell me, did you ever plan to respect the ground rules of being with an escort? How could you think it was OK in these circumstances to expect me to share a room and a bed with you?'

Face grim, Bastian strode across the room and flung another door wide. 'Make yourself at home in there,' he urged.

Emmie wasted no time in picking up her suitcase, which was spilling garments, in both arms and stalking through the door. She walked back and entered the bathroom to remove her toiletries, ignoring the spill of her clothing beside the bed. There was just no way she could pick up her knickers without feeling demeaned, she acknowledged wretchedly, shame threatening to overwhelm her.

'What are you planning to do tomorrow?' Bastian enquired coolly.

Emmie turned her head, bright blue eyes equally cool. 'What you paid me to do. I like your sister, Nessa. I'll still act like your partner but strictly in a hands-off way.'

She closed the door, turned the key in the lock with a click and breathed again. Good grief, she *hurt*! But then what had she expected from what could only be a casual sexual encounter? Well, certainly not the level of humiliation that he had unleashed, she replied inwardly. A knock sounded on the door and she froze, lovely face paling again.

Swallowing hard, she unlocked it. Bastian handed her an armful of her clothes and she grasped them, tilting her chin in defiance, refusing to cringe.

'One more thing,' he breathed tightly. 'Are you using any form of contraception?'

Her eyes widened to their fullest extent.

'I gather that's a no?' Bastian prompted. 'Unfortunately I didn't either. I forgot—'

'You...*forgot*?' Emmie exclaimed in disbelief.

'I've been in an exclusive relationship for a long time and precautions were unnecessary,' he stated curtly. 'I had a recent health check and can confirm that I'm free of any infection but there's obviously a risk that you could conceive.'

By the end of that speech, Emmie had lost all her angry colour. She clutched her clothes tightly to her chest. 'Oh, my word…I hope not.'

'If there is a problem, be assured that you will have my full support.' His dark eyes gleamed like polished ebony below his lush lashes and her heart thumped rata-tat-tat in a tattoo below her breastbone. It shamed her that even in that instant of stark fear she could still react like a schoolgirl to his raw dark charisma. 'I don't know if it will be any consolation…but I regret what happened between us as much as you do.'

Emmie nodded, face blank, said goodnight and closed the door, not bothering to lock it again, ESP telling her that she had nothing more to fear from Bastian. So, *he* had regrets…well, bully for Mr Insensitive! *A typical shag*, not a label she would ever forget, not how she would have wanted to remember her first serious sexual experience. She sped into the en suite shower and washed herself thoroughly. There was a dulled ache between her legs and her full mouth turned down at the corners. Suck it up, she told herself angrily. She was the author of her own misfortune but surely she had been punished enough? An unplanned pregnancy would be a disaster for her. Suppressing that concern on the belief that there was no advantage to foreseeing trouble that might not happen, Emmie got into bed and lay in the darkness, tears trickling down her cheeks.

CHAPTER SIX

EMMIE NIBBLED WITHOUT appetite at a piece of toast, no criticism of the truly sumptuous breakfast that had been delivered to her in bed: she simply wasn't very hungry, and when a knock sounded on the door that led onto the corridor, she froze and paled.

'Come in!' she called, stiff as a stick of rock.

Bastian's sister, clad in a dressing gown with her up-swept bridal hairdo gleaming with pearl pins, erupted through the door, her eyes anxious. 'I can't believe you're *still* in bed, Emmie!' she exclaimed.

'Sorry, I slept in. Do you need help with anything?' Emmie asked guiltily, wondering what had happened to etch that worried look on the other young woman's face.

'Lilah arrived first thing this morning and she won't leave Bastian alone!' Nessa relayed with unconcealed resentment. 'You should be down there protecting him!'

'I think Bastian's well able to protect himself,' Emmie replied gently, but she couldn't prevent her facial muscles from tightening at the prospect of meeting Bastian's ex, the day after she herself had slept with him.

Nessa frowned and stared back at Emmie. 'Do you really not care?'

Emmie belatedly recalled the role she was supposed to be playing and registered that she wasn't acting as a concerned girlfriend might. Or at least the sort of girlfriend who let all her feelings hang out in conversation with his sister. 'I'll be downstairs as soon as I'm dressed,' she promised ruefully. 'But stop worrying. I honestly don't think he wants Lilah back.'

'I've known men as clever as my brother trapped by gold-diggers before...not least our father,' Nessa countered with surprising cynicism. 'Lilah will do and say anything to get Bastian back. She's a barracuda and he took her by surprise—she didn't expect him to just let her go when she broke off the engagement!'

Wide-eyed at that information, Emmie gazed back at Nessa. 'Is it wrong of me to admit that she sounds a bit much for me to handle?'

Nessa laughed and sighed. 'Don't let Lilah intimidate you. You're the woman Bastian brought to my wedding.'

The bride's phone buzzed and she pulled it out, muttered something about a make-up session and fled. Emmie pushed away the tray and got out of bed. It was time to do what she had been paid to do...what her mother had been paid for Emmie to do, she adjusted wryly, while recalling Bastian's attitude to what Odette had done. Maybe she should have stood her ground and ignored Odette's efforts to guilt her daughter into doing something so much against her own principles. And if it was true that her weakness had brought down the roof on herself, well, she was paying the price, she acknowledged unhappily, for the prospect of acting like Bastian's girlfriend around the barracuda was not an inviting one. Emmie would have been much happier had she never had to lay eyes on Bastian again but sadly that escape route wasn't open to her, and if she was uncomfortable now, it was also her fault for having allowed their relationship to become embarrassingly intimate, she reflected unhappily.

Bastian watched Emmie descend the stairs in a flowing blue maxi dress that matched her beautiful eyes. Five seconds later he was imagining a necklace of sapphires round her unadorned throat and five seconds after that he was meeting her eyes and registering that she might look like a goddess but she was a goddess of the iceberg variety, not the warm, chatty type. Frustration growled through Bastian, who was not in a good mood. So, he had got it wrong, so he had hurt her feelings, been less than tactful, but did she have to continue to hold that against him? He had apologised, hadn't he? As a male who rarely apologised he attached a great deal of significance to that apology. He watched Emmie's face light up with a sudden warm smile when the parents of the teenager who had knocked her flying into the pool the day before approached her and he noted the effort she was making to put his uncle and aunt at ease. Lilah would still have been complaining and nursing her bruises and making everyone around her feel bad about the accident, but then Emmie, whatever else she was, didn't revel in being the centre of attention. As Bastian sprang upright to go and greet his supposed partner he saw Lilah's face tighten. No, even Lilah hadn't counted on a beauty of Emmie's calibre coming along to distract him, he conceded with a shot of unexpected amusement. And that was all this weird way he was feeling was, all the irrational thinking he had been doing and dwelling on mistakes, which was *so* not his style, Bastian thought impatiently, gritting his teeth. Emmie was simply a distraction, a very pleasant, very sexy distraction in the wake of the weeks of media drama that Lilah had enjoyed whipping up.

Emmie saw Bastian first, breathtakingly handsome in his pearl grey morning suit. Her heart skipped a beat and her mouth ran dry and she really didn't want to meet his eyes and was grateful when his uncle and aunt engaged her in conversation. Over their shoulders, she glimpsed Bastian's ex, Lilah, staring at her fixedly. Lilah was wearing a black and white frothy bridesmaid dress that made her tiny figure look more than ever like a delicate fairy's. Her heart-shaped face and almond brown eyes glowed between the wings of her waterfall-straight dark hair. She was quite exquisite in a dainty doll-like way and suddenly Emmie felt like a great hulking giantess, standing as she did comfortably six feet tall in her heels.

'Emmie…' Bastian murmured, leaning close so that

his breath warmed her cheek and the scent of his cologne brought back a shattering memory of how it had felt to be in his arms the night before when such a recollection was least welcome. He rested a light hand against her spine, a contact that made her bristle like a Rottweiler ready to attack. 'I'm relieved you're here. I'm having a trying morning.'

'Misery loves company,' Emmie remarked, noting the petulant expression Lilah was now sporting. Nessa thought her brother's ex was a gold-digger but right then, her own ego bruised as it was by Bastian's rough treatment, Emmie thought he deserved to fall victim to a gold-digger.

'Never a rose without a thorn,' Bastian quipped in the same style, disconcerting Emmie with the comeback.

'You actually have a sense of humour,' Emmie noted, pleased by her tone of indifference, for he would have had to torture her to get a warmer reaction out of her.

'No, Lilah killed it. She arrived an hour ago and upset Nessa within the first five minutes,' Bastian told her wryly.

'Nessa will be fine. Your sister is worried about you.' Although goodness knows why that would be, said Emmie's inflection.

'All you have to do is act as though we're inseparable,' Bastian informed her half under his breath.

'That's quite a challenge, Bastian.'

A hand closed over her slim shoulder as Bastian

turned her round, forcing her to collide with his glittering dark eyes. 'It wasn't a challenge for you last night, *glyka mou*.'

Last night? The discovery that he fought dirty did not surprise Emmie and mortified colour leapt into her cheeks, her brittle composure splintering at that full-on reminder of her weakness. 'Yes, but then I had drunk a little too much,' she countered in a forced whisper while smiling with determination at a couple walking past them. 'And even a frog could contrive to look like Prince Charming in the condition I was in.'

Bastian flipped her round to face him again. 'You were *not* drunk,' he ground out in an aggressive undertone.

'I don't see why it should bother you so much…you weren't the virgin who ended up with the frog!' Emmie snapped back at him vitriolically.

Smouldering black-lashed golden eyes assailed her, a line of dark colour suddenly accentuating his high cheekbones. His beautiful mouth compressed with iron control. 'I suggest we drop the subject.'

'You mentioned it first,' Emmie reminded him with spirit.

Bastian muttered something in Greek that sounded nasty.

'I'm sorry but I really do hate you,' Emmie confided shakily.

It was dawning on Bastian that the apology had not been worth its weight in gold or indeed in any currency, and he was genuinely quite shocked that he had

not been able to charm Emmie into forgiving him. A
fleet of limousines pulled up to take the bridal party
and her relatives to the village church, and with difficulty Bastian suppressed his roaring sense of annoyance with the world in general to appreciate the pretty
picture his kid sister made as she came down the stairs
in her wedding dress.

Emmie sat silent in the limo driving them at a stately
pace along the picturesque road, which was bounded
by sandy beach on one side and olive groves and hills
on the other. She wished she had not voiced that final
outburst and longed even for better control over emotions that seemed to be operating on a terrifyingly
high-powered level unfamiliar to her. But she had told
Bastian the truth, the absolute truth: she *hated* him
for even briefly thinking that she might be the kind
of woman who sold her body for profit, but she hated
herself for having succumbed to his dubious charms
even more. Nor did she need a brain transplant to appreciate that Bastian Christou was not accustomed to
being handed the frozen mitt—his expectation that his
blue-blooded birth, power, influence and great wealth
entitled him to more flattering treatment fairly shone
from the tension in his bold bronzed profile.

The silence nibbled at her nerves and conscience reminded her that she had promised to deliver the companionship he had paid for. 'Where did Nessa meet
Leonides?'

'She's known him all her life. His father is the island
doctor. Nessa and Leonides started school together,

went to uni in tandem and have been a couple virtually ever since.'

'That's so romantic,' Emmie commented. 'They
must know each other so well.'

'But they're very young to be getting married,' Bastian remarked in a tone of disapproval. 'Nessa's already
talking about starting a family.'

'Sometimes people know what they want at an early
age. What age is she?'

'The same age as you. Have you similar dreams?'
Bastian enquired a shade drily.

'Good grief, no!' Emmie declared with a grimace at
the idea. 'I wouldn't know what to do with a husband
or children. I'm a career girl.'

The pretty little church by the harbour was packed
with well-wishers. Bastian settled Emmie into a front
pew and left her there because he was standing as Leonides' best man. Emmie settled back to enjoy the
unfamiliar Greek wedding ceremony, which seemed
rather more colourful than the English version as the
bearded priest swung his incense burner and chanted.
Nessa looked ravishingly happy and, seeing the way
bride and groom looked at each other, Emmie found
that she was smiling until Lilah cast her a chilling
glance over a bony shoulder that was pure malice. After
posing for photos outside the church in the sunshine
with Lilah moving closer to Bastian at every opportunity while giggling girlishly and clinging to his arm,
Emmie could only think what bad taste in women Bastian had. Lilah was so horribly fake and gushy. Bastian

might be extremely clever in business but he couldn't be the sharpest tool in the box when he had decided to marry a woman as artificial as Lilah.

The reception back at the house followed, caterers moving around with trays of champagne while Emmie stuck masochistically to water and simmered when Bastian raised a fine ebony brow as though mocking her abstinence. That man, she would surely have killed him outright for his audacity had he meant anything to her, which he *didn't*, she assured herself soothingly, taking a seat at the top table while Lilah watched Bastian fan out Emmie's napkin for her with sullen dark eyes.

'To forgive is divine,' Bastian teased.

'Men hate those they have hurt,' Emmie shot back at him thinly.

'But I don't hate you. You know, if you would try to be logical about this instead of emotional—'

'I am not *being* emotional,' Emmie seethed back at him, rage sparkling in her lovely eyes. He infuriated her. That she still thought he was gorgeous, found her gaze absently lingering on his spectacular bone structure or compelling eyes, only added fuel to her furious resentment.

'I think you're a *very* emotional individual,' Bastian returned with a derisive edge to his dark drawl.

'Better than having about as much feeling in me as a block of wood!'

Bastian watched his sister take to the floor with her new husband. Nessa was wreathed in smiles. The job was done and his sister was content, he told himself grimly. Why was he bothering to even try mending fences with the most challenging woman he had ever met? He had always avoided difficult, demanding personalities. His sister caught his eye and swivelled her gaze towards Lilah, and Bastian stood up to lead the chief bridesmaid onto the floor.

Emmie watched in consternation as Bastian led the tiny brunette onto the dance floor. Lilah behaved like a light that had been switched on full beam, all animation, smiles and chatter. Emmie's mouth folded down at the corners. Maybe he *was* going to end up back with his ex. They had been together a long time and ties that close weren't easy to break. Maybe Emmie had simply been a face-saving piece of arm candy on Bastian's terms, retaliation because Lilah had broken off their engagement. And Lilah *was* exquisite, there was no denying that. Emmie watched the tiny brunette nestle intimately into Bastian's tall powerful frame and her hands knotted into fists below the table and her teeth ground together. Typical guy, he had told her to stick to him like glue to keep Lilah at bay and now he was encouraging the other woman. Feeling hot moisture sting her eyes, Emmie was dismayed enough to slide out of her chair and head for the powder room off the main hall.

What on earth was the matter with her? She wasn't jealous, had never been jealous of a man in her life. No, all that was wrong with her was that she felt foolish and ashamed and humiliated that she had had sex with Bastian. Satisfied with that explanation, Emmie returned to the hall and found Lilah squarely planted in her path.

'You're Emmie,' Lilah remarked with her cut-glass laugh.

And Emmie cringed, thinking, Good grief, he's told her he was with me last night! There was something so knowing and nasty about Lilah's scornful smile. 'And you're Lilah,' Emmie responded flatly.

'Bastian picked you up at the office, I believe—how sweet but how *lazy* of him. Men can be such bastards,' Lilah trilled like the evil fairy as Emmie stared down at the brunette feeling sick with embarrassment, guilt and discomfiture. 'He's using you to get at me. Don't you have any pride?'

'Don't you?' Emmie dared. 'We're not having this conversation.'

And Emmie swept on past, with her head held high, pale and trembling a little and grateful to have escaped Bastian's shrewish former fiancée. If the brunette had really cared for him would she ever have risked losing him in the first place? As Emmie crossed the room to Bastian's side she was seethingly conscious of his stunning dark golden gaze clinging to her. She mightn't like him but she *adored* his eyes. Suddenly it was hard to drag oxygen into her lungs and a flock of butterflies were dive-bombing her tummy. He reached out and closed a hand over hers to draw her close with an ease she resented. He seemed to feel no discomfiture at all over what had happened between them the night before.

Colour crawled up Emmie's cheeks, her nostrils flaring on the hot evocative scent of him that close to her, memory dragging her down and down so deep and fast she was lost within seconds. Her heartbeat quickened as she recalled the driving intensity of his body over and inside hers and an instant surge of heat snapped her nipples painfully tight and mushroomed in her pelvis.

'We need to talk, *glyka mou*,' Bastian breathed in a roughened undertone, but it was the very last thing he wanted to do. Her slender body was trembling infinitesimally beneath his arm and that close to the warmth of her he had an instant erection. Hunger was raging through him like a bush fire and all he wanted to do was drag her back to his bed and keep her there fully occupied until he felt normal again, cool again, *himself* again. Instead he thrust open the door into the conservatory and walked her in there.

'What are you doing?' Emmie demanded thinly. 'I don't want to be alone with you. The show of togetherness is only for public viewing!'

Smouldering golden eyes fringed by lush black lashes zeroed in on her. 'Stop fighting with me. It's childish. I apologised—'

'The man *apologised*!' Emmie scorned. 'I'm impressed.'

'You really do know how to press my buttons,' Bastian growled, golden eyes bright with anger as he hauled her into his arms. 'We start again afresh now—'

'No,' Emmie cut in, face uncertain and hectically pink as she looked up at him, fiercely resisting temptation. He had made a fool of her once; she wouldn't let him do it to her twice.

'I want you to be the same way you were with me last night,' Bastian admitted darkly.

'A tipsy stupid pushover?' Emmie snapped. 'Not a chance!'

He brought his hot devouring lips down on hers and it was like a lethal rocket attack on her treacherous body, sending a wave of melting heat to her feminine core with a kiss so boldly sexual and exciting that it left her head swimming and her knees weak. Her hands clutched at his shoulders to keep her upright, a drowning, quivering, overwhelming awareness engulfing her like a tide as her every skin cell lit up like a traffic light. He kept on kissing her, his tongue delving hungrily, one lean hand massaging the pouting curve of her breasts, releasing a whimper of sound from her throat as he rubbed her straining nipples through the fabric. His fingers reached down to yank up the skirt of her dress, trailed along her thigh and she froze, dragging her mouth free in desperation.

'No, Bastian.'

'Maybe some guys get off on rejection—I don't!' he bit out angrily.

The ache between her slender thighs hurt along with the knowledge that she could not satisfy her outrageous craving for him. 'Monday I'll be back at work for two short weeks and we pretend none of this ever happened…OK?' she pressed in desperation.

'If that's what you want,' Bastian framed between gritted teeth.

Emmie simply nodded. It *had* to be what she wanted. After all, no relationship between her and Bastian could go anywhere but the bedroom. He was a billionaire businessman, for goodness' sake, way out of her league and right now he was at a loose end and probably frustrated because he had a high-voltage libido and he was just out of a long relationship. All he could possibly want from her was sex and she refused to lower herself to that level. *A typical shag,* she reminded herself doggedly of his comment about his expectations of her the night before, which represented all too clearly how he saw her: as an escort for hire, an easy little office girl, surprising only in her lack of experience and currently the only available sexual option below his roof because most of his guests were his relatives.

He freed her and Emmie returned to the ballroom, shaken but determined to stay in control. She followed everyone else out to the big hall where Nessa stood on the upper landing of the stairs, posing for the hovering photographer to throw her bouquet. Twenty seconds later, the bouquet pitched down into Emmie's startled arms and Nessa whooped with satisfaction.

'I don't think so,' Lilah Siannas derided, treating Emmie to a contemptuous appraisal.

Emmie ignored the brunette and was literally watching the clock to calculate how soon she could excuse herself and retire to her room for the night. After all, once the bride and groom had departed, her role was surely at an end.

His simmering gaze pinned to Emmie's retreat up the stairs, Bastian knocked back a brandy without respecting the vintage and gritted his teeth: Emmie had thrown in the towel while Lilah was behaving like a demented stalker. Suddenly, Bastian was out of all patience with the entire female sex and he crossed the room to join his grandfather and make a suggestion about how they could best spend what remained of the night. Theron's lean weathered face lit up in surprise and pleasure.

'No, I don't want to talk about it,' he told the old man grimly.

Emmie wakened when a maid brought her breakfast. She had slept like a log, exhausted by the strain of keeping up a front on Nessa's wedding day. In the warmth of the sunlight now filling the room, she felt stronger and brighter, and she took a quick shower to freshen up before sitting down at the table out on the balcony where her breakfast awaited her. The view of the empty beach and the turquoise sea arched over by a clear blue sky was fantastic. A text beeped on her cell phone and she lifted it.

'Be ready to leave at nine. I will not be travelling with you. Thank you for your assistance.'

It was from Bastian, no *x* at the end, nothing personal. A sharp sense of disappointment pierced Emmie and she questioned her response. After all, her role was at an end and as she had refused Bastian the night before he naturally saw no point in further contact with her. She was once again the woman he had hired to do a job and the job was done, she reminded herself painfully, disconcerted that her eyes were filling with stinging tears. What the heck was wrong with her? This was how the cookie crumbled when he was a billionaire and she was an office worker…unless she fell pregnant, a little voice whispered in the back of her mind, sending a cooling shiver of consternation through her. With that possibility in mind it might be more sensible to be a little less aggressive in her attitude to him, she reasoned unhappily, and she stood up, wondering if Bastian was still in his room. Not even sure of what she planned to say, she went to the door between their rooms on impulse and knocked. She was shocked when the door jerked open to reveal Lilah.

'Oh…' Emmie breathed, losing colour and falling back a step.

A complacent smile on her lips, Lilah preened in the doorway, making the most of Emmie's surprise at her being in Bastian's bedroom.

'You're being sent straight back to London,' Lilah pointed out as though her presence in Bastian's room and Emmie's travel itinerary were connected, which very probably they were, Emmie reflected with a sinking heart and a despondent sense of humiliation. If Bastian was back with his ex, Emmie was too much of an embarrassing extra to keep below the same roof.

'Yes,' Emmie agreed with no expression at all, too

proud to betray her mortification to the other woman but feeling vindicated in her decision not to take Bastian's apparent interest in her seriously the night before. Evidently he was back in the arms of his ex. That hadn't taken long. Bastian had been on the rebound; that was the only reason he had come after her but, clearly and understandably, it was Lilah whom he had *really* wanted. For no reason that she could comprehend, Emmie felt gutted, absolutely gutted by that obvious fact.

The door closed. Dry-eyed, facial muscles locked tight, Emmie packed her case. She had better hope she wasn't pregnant for, in this situation, what a disaster such an unwelcome development would be!

CHAPTER SEVEN

THREE WEEKS LATER, Emmie ripped open a pregnancy-testing kit during her break at the café and pulled out the instruction leaflet. Her heart was beating as fast as a drum, sheer tension slicking her taut face with a sheen of perspiration. After all, she was already homeless and pretty much jobless and she most definitely did not need to be pregnant into the bargain. Admittedly, she had sore breasts and was feeling sick round the clock. But so what? It was a bug she had picked up some place, a stupid bug, she told herself frantically.

At the same time, in the considerably greater comfort of his office in the City, Bastian was tossing aside his phone after contacting Emmie's mother, Odette Taylor. That had proved to be a fruitless call. Evidently Emmie had moved out without leaving a forwarding address and her fond parent neither knew nor cared where she had gone. That was the point when Bastian realised that he had hit a brick wall. Of course, he hadn't expected to learn that Emmie had already left his employ when he arrived back in London but he still *had* to see her, had to check she was all right. He owed her that consideration at least, Bastian reasoned grimly, and as far as he was aware his PA, Marie, was the only member of his staff who had got to know Emmie in any depth. He called the efficient brunette in and after a couple of going-nowhere minutes of tactful probing lost patience and simply admitted that he wanted to contact Emmie.

Back in the tiny café staffroom, Emmie scanned the test wand again with swimming eyes. She wanted to sob and scream like a little child for the pregnancy test had proved positive and for a couple of shameful minutes nothing less than terror controlled Emmie. A *baby*…she was going to have a *baby* and the pregnancy was already making her as sick as a dog! She felt awful, truly awful! And yet she couldn't contemplate a termination because she was all too well aware that had Odette had that option, neither she nor her sisters might ever have been born. Didn't her baby deserve love and appreciation? She could not reject her child simply because the timing didn't suit, the pregnancy was unplanned and she had no supportive man in the picture. Emmie released her breath on a dismissive hiss on that latter score. With the single exception of Kat, neither Emmie nor her siblings had enjoyed the advantage of a caring father in their lives.

'It's getting busy out here!' her boss called through the door to bring her break to an early conclusion.

Emmie straightened her overall, locked her bag away again and returned to work. She had no choice now but to go home to her sister, Kat, she reflected guiltily. At present she was sleeping on a friend's sofa and she wasn't earning enough at the café to pay rent and eat at the same time. Kat ran a guesthouse in the Lake District and would probably be glad to have help with the cleaning and catering, Emmie thought, striving for a more positive angle than a daunting image of herself being forced to run home like a helpless teenager, who couldn't cope with the adult world. Of course she could have approached her sister Saffy for assistance: Saffy owned an apartment in London. But the prospect of asking for help from her very much more successful twin was too humiliating for Emmie. She could not imagine the shrewd and worldly-wise Saffy ever making such a basic mistake as to fall accidentally pregnant. In short Emmie literally cringed at the idea of having to admit to her twin how very badly her own move to London had gone for her.

Bastian was able to pick Emmie out from across the café. She wore a candy-pink overall that was a little too short for such a leggy young woman and she looked incredibly pale. Maybe she just wasn't wearing make-up, he reasoned, taking a seat in a booth while still studying her tall slender figure. Her head turned, treating him to a flash of dazzling blue eyes, luscious pink lips parting to show a glimpse of the oddly enticing gap between her two front teeth. His body, recently proven to be woodenly impervious to the charms of more available women, reacted with an instant arousal that set his teeth on edge. Emmie saw him and stilled in obvious dismay. Bastian smiled regardless, shifted lean brown fingers in fluid invitation, mentally willing her to move in his direction.

The potent pull of Bastian in the flesh was so powerful that Emmie felt as if she were being yanked across the floor by a force stronger than she was. She approached him reluctantly, notepad in hand, mouth dry, every muscle strained taut. 'What are you doing here?' she asked breathlessly.

'When do you finish?'

Emmie collided with dark golden eyes as compelling as chains snaking out to entrap her body. She supposed there was no avoiding what had to be faced. He had a right to know about the pregnancy. His preference for Lilah did not enter the equation because that was personal, *his* personal business. All that should really matter to Emmie was that she was carrying his child; however the shock of that discovery was still rippling through her like the aftermath of an earthquake. 'My shift ends at ten.'

'I'll be waiting.' Without further ado, Bastian sprang up and strode outside: decisive, impatient, stubbornly practical, she affixed ruefully. She knew he would have demanded she leave right now in the middle of her shift had he believed he could bully her into doing so.

When she emerged from the café at closing time a limousine was parked by the kerb.

'Miss Marshall?' the driver asked out of the window before getting out to whip open the passenger door for her. Emmie swallowed hard, struggled to suppress the nausea in her stomach, and climbed in. She was disconcerted by the discovery that the limo was empty and asked Bastian's driver where he was taking her.

'I'm to drive you back to Mr Christou's apartment.'

Emmie pushed her weary head back against the headrest. She didn't care at the moment where she was going, was only grateful that she did not have to walk there. If she had to make her big announcement, it was better to do so where they would not be overheard or interrupted. How would he react? Would he be angry, resentful, bitter? Would he offer to pay for a termination or even suggest adoption as an alternative? The driver escorted her into a luxury block of apartments and, tucking her into a lift, pressed the correct button for her.

Bastian impatiently paced the wooden floor of his elegant lounge. He was convinced that he knew what she was going to tell him: he had suspected the truth the minute her strained eyes had met his. Three weeks ago, Emmie had been considerably more cheerful and calm and he could not credit that escaping her harpy of a mother had left her in such low spirits. Now Bastian, who was confident that he excelled at solving problems, was bent on working out how he could best turn an apparent negative into a positive.

A man in a suit had the door of Bastian's apartment standing open for her arrival when she stepped out of the lift into a stylishly decorated hallway. Crossing it, Emmie tightened the sash on her raincoat and dug her nervous hands into her pockets, pushing her shoulders back as she entered the dimly lit apartment, noting the long expanses of window that denoted a penthouse, the clean lines of sleek contemporary furniture and the same lack of clutter that distinguished Bastian's office. Even on that level they didn't suit each other, Emmie mused, for she was a great hoarder of sentimental bits and pieces.

Bastian strode forward. 'Take your coat off. Make yourself comfortable,' he urged huskily.

Emmie flicked a glance at his lean, darkly handsome face and the lustrous brilliance of his dark, thickly lashed eyes and turned pink and uncomfortable. He was spectacularly good-looking and had the most colossal impact on her every time she saw him. Heat flickering like an uneasy flame low in her pelvis, she undid her coat, shrugged it off, sat down, and pressed her knees and her hands together like a child urged to be on her very best behaviour. 'It's not good news,' she told him awkwardly.

Bastian's gaze roamed across her flawless face and down over the elegant lines of her willowy figure with instinctive appreciation. There was something special about her and he still didn't know what it was but it was a quality that shouted at him every time he saw her. 'That depends on how you look at it.'

'I'm pregnant,' Emmie delivered curtly. 'And no matter how you look at it, it's a problem. I don't want a child right now when I'm only at the start of my career and yet I couldn't live with having an abortion just because it's a case of bad timing—'

'*I* could take the baby,' Bastian interrupted.

Thoroughly taken aback by that suggestion, Emmie lifted her head and stared back at him with bright blue eyes of disbelief. 'You can't be serious?'

'Why not? I was prepared to get married to have a family. How is this situation different?'

'If you had married, you would have had a wife—'

'Don't be prejudiced. I would make an excellent single father. Certainly, I know all the things a father *shouldn't* do,' Bastian proffered with brutal honesty. 'My father was an appalling role model.'

'So was mine…er—'

'All I'm saying is that if you don't want the baby, I *do*—'

'I didn't say I didn't want it!' Emmie protested, dismayed by his attitude and suddenly feeling ridiculously protective of the new life forming inside her. And yet on another level, she respected him for his unexpected willingness to get involved and take responsibility. 'I think it's just that I don't know what to do *now*.'

'We don't have to make any serious decisions for months yet,' Bastian pointed out soothingly.

'I *do* want my baby,' Emmie started to confide but her tummy was rolling about like a ship on a stormy sea and she was forced to leap back upright. 'Where's the cloakroom?' she gasped in dismay.

Luckily, she made it there in time and was sick for the second time that evening. Afterwards, limp and drained, she leant across the vanity unit to freshen up and peered at her bloodshot eyes and extreme pallor in the mirror. She looked like death warmed over, she conceded painfully.

'Should I call a doctor?' Bastian greeted her right outside the door, which embarrassed her. 'Take you to a hospital?'

'No, I assume this is what the books call morning sickness, only it seems to strike me at all hours of the day,' Emmie told him morosely, rubbing her cheeks on the recollection of how pale she had looked and then wondering why she was bothering…as if *that* were going to make a difference and transform her from a humble waitress clad in an ugly overall into a sexually appealing woman! Why on earth would she even want to appeal to him now?

'I didn't think you would be affected by anything of that nature this early,' Bastian remarked.

'That makes two of us, but I already feel pretty sick most of the time.'

'Where are you staying at the minute?' Bastian asked.

Emmie reddened and sat down again. 'How did you know I'd moved out of my mother's flat?'

'I tried to contact you there.'

'She was still trying to get me to accept bookings from her clients,' Emmie admitted reluctantly. 'I had no choice but to leave.'

'I thought she would continue to put you under pressure. Where are you currently staying?' he asked again.

Emmie admitted she was sleeping on a sofa at a friend's house. 'There's not much else I can do. I'm not earning enough to pay rent,' she admitted stiffly, mortified by the difference in their financial situations but determined to be as honest as she could be.

Bastian's face tensed, his wildly sensual mouth compressing into a taut line. 'That *is* something I can help with. I own several apartments for the use of employees flying in from abroad. You can move into one of them.'

Emmie frowned. 'I couldn't possibly—'

'Of course you can,' Bastian cut in firmly. 'I'm responsible for the situation you're in. It's the least I can do.'

Emmie swallowed hard on the pride threatening to choke her. The prospect of sleeping on a sofa for another night had little appeal and she couldn't possibly inconvenience her friend by staying with her for much longer. Being homeless was frightening, Emmie acknowledged wretchedly. The security of a roof over her head would give her a much-needed breathing space, which she could use to decide what to do next. 'OK, but I'm only agreeing because I don't have any other option.'

Bastian pulled his phone out and spoke to someone at length in his own language. 'The place will be fully stocked for your use by the time we arrive,' he asserted. 'Give me the address where you have been staying and I will arrange to have your belongings conveyed to the apartment for you.'

He made everything sound so easy. Although she could not help being impressed she also knew that nothing could have better illustrated the vast gulf between them—the extent of his wealth and power versus her poverty and lack of influence. Only that did not mean she had to be weak or meek, she reflected, tilting her chin. But sometimes accepting a helping hand when life was tough was the most sensible move.

Two hours later, Bastian gave Emmie a tour of the apartment he had offered her. It contained every luxury she could think of, from a stock of DVDs and a power shower to a fridge freezer stocked with every necessity. 'I'll be very comfortable here,' Emmie remarked carefully. 'But you have to promise to tell me when you need it for someone who works for you.'

Dark golden eyes accentuated by luxuriant black lashes focused on her intently and her heart hammered hard beneath her breastbone. 'Right now, your needs are more important. Let's face it, that's *my* baby you're carrying,' he traded levelly. 'Naturally you're my first priority.'

The possessive note of that comment about the baby disconcerted her. Her soft pink lips parted. 'Is that really how you feel? Do you like children?'

'Never really thought about it. I don't *dislike* them,' Bastian declared pensively. 'But the child you have, whether it's a boy or a girl, will be my heir.'

'Even though we're not married?'

'It will still be my child with my blood in its veins.'

There was something rather basic and territorial about that statement and Emmie was even more surprised. She recognised that he had not only adapted to the idea of becoming a father but had also warmed to the prospect.

'To be blunt, I've never been in a hurry to get married,' Bastian admitted drily. 'Watching my father screw up matrimonially four times over soured me on the institution.'

'I can understand that. So you think that having a child without having to tie yourself down to marriage might actually suit you better?' Emmie queried, keen to understand his point of view.

'Only time will answer that question. In the morning I'll make enquiries and organise an obstetrician for you,' Bastian continued. 'You must have proper medical care.'

'You can be very…bossy.' Emmie selected the label with care, because in spite of the shock news she had given him he had been remarkably kind and considerate and she didn't want to seem ungrateful.

A wicked grin that was the very essence of masculine charisma sliced across Bastian's beautifully shaped and stubborn mouth. 'You could say that being dominant comes naturally to me, *glyka mou*. Or even beware of Greeks bearing gifts,' he teased.

'Needs must when the devil rides,' she quoted, her gaze compulsively welded to that grin, and she was as short of breath as if all the oxygen had been sucked out of the atmosphere.

'I'm not the devil. I only want to do what's best for you,' Bastian told her thickly, staring down at her with smouldering golden eyes.

Emmie felt her treacherous body react to his proximity and the husky, sexy note in his deep voice. Her nipples tingled, awareness washing through her in an exhilarating overload of sudden sexual energy. But this time, Emmie fought what she was feeling to the last ditch. She stepped hurriedly back from him, her cheeks burning as she deliberately turned her head away from him to avoid eye contact. She was hugely attracted to him but could not forget his renewed intimacy with Lilah on the night of his sister's wedding. Although there had been no reference in the gossip columns to a reconciliation between Bastian and his former fiancée, Emmie didn't want to risk getting more deeply involved with a man already entangled with another woman. Wasn't it worrying enough that she was pregnant by him? The last thing she needed now was to let her overwrought emotions persuade her that she was in some way attached to Bastian Christou.

'Emmie...' he breathed thickly, stroking a fingertip very lightly over the back of her hand, making her quiver and long to twist round and hurl herself into his arms like a lovesick fool. But she *wasn't* lovesick and she *wasn't* a fool, she told herself fiercely.

'Let's not complicate things,' Emmie pleaded in a charged undertone. She found him almost impossible to resist but there was such a thing as common sense and it was way past time she exerted it over her more self-destructive promptings. And going to bed with Bastian again would definitely come under the heading of destructive, she thought painfully.

Bastian closed a strong hand to her shoulder and turned her back to face him. Diamond-bright dark eyes locked to hers enquiringly. 'We're already complicated.'

'Exactly, and you're helping me out here, which I'm very grateful for,' she said shakily. 'But—'

His winged black brows drew together. 'Just as you didn't expect diamonds, I'm not expecting any kind of reward for helping out,' he told her drily.

Discomfited at the way he had interpreted her statement, Emmie reddened. 'That wasn't what I meant.'

Bastian had her cornered in the hall, his lean, powerful body squarely planted between her and the front door. 'Then what did you mean?' he pressed.

Emmie jerked an awkward shoulder in the tense silence that had fallen. 'I know you slept with Lilah the night of the wedding—'

Bastian lifted a frowning black brow, dark eyes widening in surprise. 'No, I didn't—'

'She was in your room the next morning.'

'But I *wasn't*,' Bastian riposted with hard emphasis. 'I spent the night at my grandfather's and we sat up playing poker until the early hours. I lost a packet to the wily old buzzard too. If Lilah was in my room she was there uninvited. Think about it, Emmie. Do you think I'm such a fool that I would hire you to keep her at bay and then get back into bed with her again?'

Emmie didn't know what to think. 'She even knew that I was leaving the island—'

'Anyone in the house could have given her that information as I made the arrangements for your departure with my staff before I left the night before.' Bastian frowned down at her and slowly shook his handsome head. 'Obviously Lilah would have wanted you to think that I had been with her and she knew that I was spending the night at Theron's. I can't believe you fell for it.'

Mortified by that assessment, Emmie said nothing. The doorbell buzzed and Bastian yanked the door open. The suitcase she had taken to her friend's house was carted over the threshold. 'Is this all that you have?' Bastian asked in surprise.

'No, I left some stuff boxed up at my mother's,' Emmie admitted wryly.

'I'll sort that out for you as well,' Bastian declared, carrying the case into the bedroom and then striding back to the front door with an air of relief. 'I'll phone you tomorrow...check that you're all right.'

And that fast he was gone and Emmie was left blinking at the space he had occupied and guiltily suppressing a strong sense of disappointment. Her bringing up the subject of Lilah and falsely accusing him had evidently stifled any desire on his part to make their relationship more intimate, she registered ruefully. Had he truly spent that night at his grandfather's house?

'There are two heartbeats,' the obstetrician informed Emmie. 'You're carrying twins.'

'Twins?' Emmie listened transfixed to the galloping pace of her babies' heartbeats. She was only eight weeks into her pregnancy and was amazed at how much could already be seen on a scan.

'I think this is why you've been feeling so sick. Severe nausea is more common with a twin pregnancy,' the older man informed her.

Emmie rested her head back down and wondered how Bastian would react to the news. The prospect of two babies unnerved her, raised as she had been on horror stories of how hard her mother had found it to cope with twins. Her heart sank as a rather more practical concern struck her: how many years would it be before she could hope to earn enough to afford childcare for *two* children? And if she couldn't earn enough, how would she ever get her independence back? Was she destined to live off Bastian's largesse for years to come?

For the present, Bastian was keeping her and Emmie wasn't comfortable with that arrangement, no matter how often he pointed out that the baby that was putting her out of commission with nausea was as much his responsibility as hers. During the past two weeks while Emmie struggled to cope with the almost constant sickness, which even medication had failed to banish, Bastian had become a surprisingly regular visitor. He would call in to check up on her on his way home, sometimes he would order in food for them both and stay a while and on two occasions he had sent the limo to pick her up and bring her back to his penthouse to enjoy a meal cooked by his housekeeper. The new relationship they had forged had limits though, Emmie acknowledged tautly. Bastian would ask her how her visit to the obstetrician he had engaged had gone but he wouldn't accompany her or make his questions too personal. In the same way he had made no further attempt to renew the intimacy they had so briefly enjoyed.

Spending time with Bastian on a platonic basis, however, was torture for Emmie and she was thoroughly ashamed of that truth. It was as though, having been programmed to react to him once, her body could not learn how to block the signals of attraction. She had to consciously will herself not to stare at him, not to lean closer, indeed not to touch him in any way. It disconcerted her that even feeling unwell couldn't stifle the strong sexual feelings Bastian still awakened in her.

Before she could lose her nerve she texted her news to Bastian, reasoning that that was less emotional than telling him face to face.

'Had scan. We're having twins,' ran her text.

And the text was sent before she could think better of using that royal 'we' as if they were a couple, rather than two very different people attempting to find common ground as potential parents on the strength of an accidental pregnancy.

Twins? An unholy grin of satisfaction illuminated Bastian's lean dark features in the midst of the meeting he was chairing. He totally forgot what he had been saying while texting back a one-word response. Emmie was having two babies and he thought that was terrific news. He had been a lonely only child for more

years than he cared to count but *his* child would have
company and a sibling to play with. He left the meeting to instruct Marie to send Emmie flowers. He saw
the flash of surprise in his PA's face when she heard
the name and realised where Emmie was living and
frowned, wishing he could bring the relationship out
of the closet. Unfortunately, Emmie didn't want people
gossiping about them and preferred to stay in the background of his life while totally ignoring the reality that
a child could not be hidden indefinitely.

Bastian, however, didn't want to stage an argument
with Emmie and lay down the law. How could he when
she was getting so thin he would do almost anything to
persuade her to eat a decent meal? Her doctor had given
her medication but it had yet to provide a cure. Before
his very eyes the constant sickness was wearing her
health down, stripping away her delicate curves, giving her face a pinched look. Concealing his concern,
respecting the boundaries set by someone else went
against the grain with Bastian, but he continually told
himself that it would all be worth it for the end result.

After all, all his life he had dreaded the idea of getting married, fearing that he would somehow repeat his
father's mistakes. He had deemed Lilah a safe choice,
only realising what a nightmare she could be *after* they
had parted. Conversely, Bastian choosing to stay single and childless would devastate his grandfather, who
was obsessed with the continuation of the family tree.
But, quite unexpectedly, Emmie was giving Bastian
the best of both worlds: a child without the risk and the

restrictions of marriage. Theron would be shocked that Bastian's children were illegitimate but Bastian was convinced that however he felt the old man would not ignore his great-grandchildren's arrival into the world.

'Fantastic...' ran Bastian's text and it came back too fast in response to Emmie's announcement to be a polite fiction.

CHAPTER EIGHT

EMMIE SMILED WITH pleasure at Bastian's very positive reaction and on impulse texted him back again inviting him to join her for dinner. She wasn't a versatile cook but she could manage a decent steak. She was even more pleased when Bastian's flowers arrived. Having set the table in the alcove off the lounge, she changed into the dress she had worn the night before Nessa's wedding. Although it was a much tighter fit over her enlarged breasts, the rest of her was as slender as ever and the zip went up easily.

Bastian was punctual and she hurried to answer the door. His brilliant dark-lashed eyes roamed over her leggy figure in the fuchsia-pink dress and she blushed furiously, embarrassed that she had gone to so much trouble to make the most of her appearance.

'Are we celebrating?' Bastian enquired, studying her with hungry intensity. 'I love that dress.'

'You seemed pleased about the twins,' Emmie pointed out awkwardly, feeling painfully self-conscious with his full attention trained to her. Her nipples prickled and lengthened, the sensitive tips scraping against the lace cup of the bra cupping the full mounds. A clenching sensation low in her pelvis made her press her thighs together and squirm with shame. Without even trying Bastian lit her up like a bonfire inside, she acknowledged in fierce mortification.

Something primal flamed and smouldered in the depth of Bastian's dark deep-set eyes and without warning he reached for her, pulling her into the hard, unyielding heat of his lean, powerful body. His mouth plunged down in hot, urgent demand on hers. Excitement exploded through Emmie and she couldn't breathe for the wild clamour of her thundering heart and the heightened effect on her senses.

'Tell me yes…' Bastian growled into her hair as she snatched in a quivering breath, struggling not to shudder in reaction as he ran lean fingers up a slender thigh below the hem of her dress, roving tantalisingly close to the source of the intimate ache making her so tense. '*Yes*, you want this as much as I do.'

The solid ridge of his arousal was potent and compelling against her stomach, and that he could hunger for her that much made desire leap inside her while moisture gathered in readiness at the heart of her. Weak as a newborn as that wild surge of yearning engulfed her, her fingers biting into his shoulders, she leant into him. 'Yes…' she whispered, no longer able to suppress her natural inclinations, frantic to feel him moving inside her again, awakening her to a level of sensation she had never known possible. 'Yes…'

And Bastian required no further invitation. He lifted her up into his arms and carried her through to the bedroom, sinking down on the mattress with her across his lap as he unzipped her dress. 'I feel like I've waited for ever for you, *glyka mou.*'

Emmie lifted her fingers to rest them gently against his stubborn, wilful and utterly beautiful mouth, trembling as he parted his lips and sucked on her fingertips. 'You're not used to waiting, I'm not used to giving.'

And it was true, for she had too often played safe simply to protect herself from the risk of hurt and rejection, but something about Bastian destroyed her defences, blew her heart wide open, made her want to *give* instead. She met eyes ablaze with sexual hunger and marvelled that she had the power to make him feel that way. Another kiss and he was stripping off her dress, peeling away her bra to curve gentle caressing fingers to her swollen nipples, his every touch sending fire to her aching core.

Emmie twisted against Bastian, fingers clenching into his luxuriant hair to hold him close while she kissed him with all the passion she had repressed for so long. Quick to get the message that speed could be an advantage, Bastian kissed her fervently back while also hauling off his jacket, ditching his tie and embarking on his shirt buttons. She spread reverent fingers across his hard-muscled bronzed torso, appreciating the lithe strength and raw masculinity of his powerful body. He lifted her off him, disposed of his well-cut pants and stretched out beside her on the bed, but he lay still for barely a second before he sat up again to study her semi-naked length with burnished eyes of appreciation.

'I want you so much it's painful to hold back,' Bastian groaned, a fingertip toying teasingly with the shallow indentation of her belly button, and then straying down over her mound to more responsive territory and skating over the taut, damp triangle of material stretched beneath.

Emmie's back arched and her hips writhed as he touched her, fierce hunger pounding through her like a pagan drum beat that filled her ears and her thoughts so that she was aware of nothing beyond the wicked skill of his hands on her unbearably tender flesh. He whisked away the last barrier and, parting the delicate pink folds, he thrust a finger into her aching core. She gasped, twisted and turned, wanted him so much it physically pained her to withstand such teasing.

'I want to watch you come this time,' Bastian confided thickly, sliding down the bed to caress the engorged buds of her nipples with his mouth and his tongue while at the same time he drove her crazy with every plunge of his fingers.

Emmie couldn't stay still. She was on fire for him, quivering with excitement and a level of need that came close to torment. 'Bastian, *please*,' she whimpered.

And he lifted her up and sank into her so hard and deep and fast that she cried out with excitement.

Bastian groaned with sensual satisfaction. 'Hot… wet…tight, *khriso mou*, my every dream come true.'

Emmie was on a high of rapturous sensation. He rode her with abandon, pleasuring her with hard rapid strokes that stoked her excitement to feverish heights. She was out of control, her heart thundering as she flew high on his erotic rhythm, her body rising to meet his. At the apex of her climax she convulsed around him, shattering in the devouring waves of pleasure that consumed her.

'On a scale of one to ten that was an eleven, *khriso mou*,' Bastian breathed raggedly, releasing her from his weight only to snake an arm round her and hold her captive to his long lean length.

His comment jarred, slicing like a blade through the cosy cocoon of relaxation Emmie's body was embracing, because she was too well aware that in bed she had nobody she could compare him to. It made her feel cheap to think he might be comparing her to past lovers and she stiffened defensively.

Her movement made Bastian look down at the arms he still had wrapped round her restless body. Faint colour accentuating his high cheekbones because he was uncomfortable with his own unfamiliar behaviour, he freed her abruptly, but not before he had dropped a kiss on her furrowed brow.

'So where do we go from here?' Emmie prompted.

Bastian hated questions like that and he thought it was typical that Emmie would put him on the spot and want immediate answers. 'It's just sex,' he parried very drily. 'Let's not get too worked up about it.'

Face burning in receipt of that demeaning response, Emmie froze and gritted her teeth together.

Bastian knew he had said the wrong thing but he was too arrogant to take it back. He also didn't know the answer to her question and was already mentally sidestepping all the many complications he imagined lay ahead of them. She was carrying his kids and that made her much more than a lover. He tensed, not in the mood to think about that reality and suddenly very keen to be distracted from such troublesome and confusing thoughts.

'Let's go out to eat,' he suggested abruptly.

'I was going to make a meal.'

Bastian didn't want to share an intimate meal in the apartment because he foresaw more difficult questions hovering like storm clouds on his horizon. 'I can't stay long,' he told her, sliding out of the bed with fluid grace. 'I'm flying to Australia tomorrow and moving on into Asia to check our operations there. I'll be away for a while.'

Taken aback by this first reference to his imminent departure, Emmie sat up, feeling ridiculously lonely and lost. *It's just sex.* His bronzed profile was hard and taut, his tension palpable to her. He didn't want her attaching fancy labels to their lovemaking or attaching strings of commitment to him. She might be pregnant with his babies and he might still want to have rampant sex with her, but he was not prepared to offer her a more serious relationship. Had she really expected anything else? All over again she had tumbled into bed with Bastian without thinking about what she was doing, without worrying about how he thought of her or wondering about where it would lead.

Bastian's silence, his patent eagerness to leave gave her an answer she really didn't want. A hard lump filled her throat and she couldn't swallow. She felt hurt, desperately hurt and rejected. Obviously she wanted more from Bastian than she was currently receiving. Equally obviously she had been in proud denial of what he could make her feel. Yet again she had ignored the clear limits of their association, for she dared not call it a relationship.

'If you don't feel like going out, I'll order food in,' Bastian volunteered, buttoning his shirt, grabbing up his jacket.

In that moment she hated him more than any man alive. 'I've already eaten,' she lied.

'You know you need to be eating more when you're being so sick,' Bastian reminded her darkly.

Sensing his impatience, Emmie simply nodded agreement. 'You order,' she advised, snaking out of bed to snatch up her dressing gown and vanish into the bathroom.

She had never felt less hungry in her life, she acknowledged wretchedly. *It's just sex*. Those three words had ripped her apart and forced her to re-examine the consequences of allowing Bastian to pay her bills and maintain a roof over her head. Did he see her as something less now? Had he ever had any respect for her? *It's just sex*. Even worse, did he now think of her as his mistress? How did a very rich man regard a woman whom he was already keeping? Certainly not as an equal. Emmie knew she had a big nasty decision to make but she would have to handle that later when Bastian had gone. Right then the bravest thing she had ever done in her life was shelve all her messy emotions, walk back out of the bathroom, throw on the only jeans that still fitted her and join him in the lounge where he was already ensconced watching the business news.

Korean food was delivered. While he watched she nibbled, chased the food round her plate, drank a lot of water. 'You need to eat more,' Bastian told her again and he leant out of his chair to close a big hand round her thin forearm. 'You're getting ridiculously skinny.'

Hot colour splashed her cheeks and then receded again as she wondered if he found that thinness unattractive. Her bright blue eyes rested on his handsome features, lingering on the spiky black lashes shading his dark golden gaze, the strong blade of his nose, the hard cheekbones and the beautifully modelled mouth. She swallowed hard, taking a mental snapshot of him because she already knew it would be a long time, if ever, before she saw him again.

'I'll phone when I can,' Bastian told her at the front door, looking down at her, wondering how she could look so beautiful and yet so painfully vulnerable at the same time, wishing he could take her abroad with him to give him something to look forward to at night other than an empty hotel suite. She needed looking after though, not foreign travel, he acknowledged grudgingly, and he had never looked after anyone before and didn't quite know where or how to begin.

Tears trickled down Emmie's face as she checked the train times online to plan her journey home to the Lake District. It would be madness to stay where she was when she and Bastian wanted such different things. She wanted more than sex from Bastian but she suspected that he still saw her as little more than the escort he had hired at such great expense to attend his sister's wedding with him. How on earth had she contrived to fall in love with him? He might be great in bed but he had to be the most insensitive man alive! And yet Bastian's constant phone calls and visits had still become ridiculously precious to Emmie in recent weeks. She blinked back the tears, ashamed of her weakness, her wanton desire to stay on in London and settle for whatever he was offering. Bastian was being as supportive as he knew how because it was his fault she was pregnant. Beyond that did he feel anything for her but basic sexual attraction? And how long would that last once she began to resemble a blimp? No, Emmie told herself angrily, she had to cut the connection and leave while she still had her pride. Sleeping with Bastian again had been a serious mistake but staying on in an apartment he owned would be an even worse mistake.

'Emmie's moved out…are you sure?' Bastian growled down the phone at his PA. After months of unanswered calls and considerable concern on his part he had finally caved in and asked Marie to check Emmie's apartment for him.

'Well, the wardrobe and the drawers are empty but she's left her teddy collection behind in a box on the bed,' Marie told him, working tactfully at keeping the amusement out of her voice. 'Oh, wait a minute, there's an envelope here with your name on it. Looks like she's left you a note.'

Bastian wanted to know very badly what was in the note but he refused to ask his PA to open it and read it to him over the phone. Some things were private. On the other side of the world he stared blankly at the wall of his hotel suite: *Emmie had walked out on him*. Rage momentarily electrified him. *Diavelos*, she was expecting his kids, she had no right to stage a disappearance when he had been doing everything possible to make her feel happy and secure! Well, possibly not *everything*, conscience bade him admit, discomfiture infiltrating his angry sense of betrayal.

In the following months since Emmie had travelled to visit her sister Kat, everything had turned out very differently from what Emmie had initially expected, she reflected wryly, while conceding that different didn't necessarily mean bad.

Firstly, her plan to help her sister run her guesthouse had died the very first day when Kat admitted that business was very poor and she was actually on the brink of bankruptcy. Luckily, a very wealthy Russian had come out of the woodwork to save the day for her sister. Mikhail Kusnirovich had invited Kat to stay on his mega yacht and act as hostess to his guests. While Kat was away Emmie stayed on in the farmhouse to keep her youngest sister, Topsy, company during the school holidays. A few weeks later, Kat admitted that she and Mikhail had fallen in love and that she was moving into his Georgian country mansion, Danegold Hall, to live with him as his partner. Within months Mikhail and Kat were married.

Denied her elder sister's company aside of occasional weekends spent in the lap of luxury at Danegold, Emmie had been thrown very much on her own resources. She had taken a temporary job as a shop assistant in a local supermarket but was currently engaged in looking into the possibility of opening a gift shop/café in a property available for rent in the village. Her new brother-in-law, Mikhail, had blithely offered her unlimited funds with which to start up her own business.

'I don't care what it costs me. Kat's worried sick about you. If she sees that you're making a new start in life on a decent income, she'll stop worrying about you being a single parent,' Mikhail had told Emmie cheerfully, not even trying to hide the reality that his main motivation was to make her sister happy.

As the months passed and her pregnancy advanced, Emmie had suffered less from nausea, and holding down a job and working regular hours had become a good deal easier. Yet when her twin, Saffy, had announced that she was remarrying her first husband,

Zahir, Emmie had used her health as an excuse not to attend the wedding and she was still ashamed of that. Her sister was now the wife of the King of Maraban and a future queen. And as Saffy had always enjoyed a good deal of natural dignity and assurance, Emmie believed her sibling would be a stunning success as a royal. Unfortunately, Emmie's own deep unhappiness had persuaded her that she would be a sad spectre at the feast if she attended her twin's wedding and that she would only cast an unwelcome pall of gloom over her sister's big day. When all was said and done, after all, her sisters already pitied her for being pregnant and alone, and Emmie had been equally quick to notice that even Kat was shy of expressing her love and affection for Mikhail in her sister's inhibiting presence. No, the unmarried pregnant sister had been wiser staying at home when she had the excuse.

To avoid such negative thoughts, Emmie had spent every spare moment researching local craftspeople to supply merchandise for the gift shop while also checking out the strict requirements for running a café. That project had kept Emmie extremely busy. Although she had little time to mope she often lay awake late into the night picturing a lean, darkly handsome face and aching unbearably as though she had lost a limb. In spite of the fact that she had found it impossible to envisage a feasible future with Bastian, walking away from him had still hurt like hell. But it would have been crazy, she reasoned, to hang around on the outskirts of Bastian's life, sleeping with him in the forlorn hope that he would eventually want to take their relationship to another level or assume a regular paternal role once the twins were born. She needed to get over him and she needed to do it fast, she told herself impatiently. And in her opinion seeing too much of Saffy's and Kat's deliriously happy marriages to the men they loved was unlikely to help her to recover from her own unrequited love any more quickly. Indeed her sisters' success and contentment on that front only made Emmie feel like a total failure in the love stakes.

For the second time in as many weeks, Bastian drove up to the Lake District. A glossy celebrity magazine lay open on the passenger seat beside him and every time he noticed it he gritted his teeth, a ferocious sense of injustice assailing him. On this occasion, Bastian needed no directions to reach his destination because he knew exactly where he was going as he nosed his Ferrari into the driveway of the farmhouse, parked it, dug the magazine into his pocket and sprang out to stride impatiently to the front door.

Emmie groaned as the doorbell buzzed because she was in the middle of making pastry and her hands were covered with flour. She wiped her hands on the front of her apron, surprised as she always was to feel the firm swell of her pregnant stomach arching out in front of her. She was the size of a small house, which, according to the local doctor, was only to be expected with twins on the way. She trundled to the front door and pulled it open, lashes fluttering up on startled blue eyes as she focused on the tall black-haired male on the doorstep.

Sheathed in a dark suit and a cashmere overcoat, Bastian surveyed her with brooding intensity, narrowed dark eyes glittering like polished jet. 'Surprise… surprise…'

CHAPTER NINE

EMMIE STEPPED BACK and Bastian stalked through the front door, slamming it shut in his wake with an imperious hand.

'I wasn't planning to invite you in,' Emmie snapped.

'Given enough rope you really will hang yourself, won't you?' Bastian riposted with derision. 'Perhaps you'd like to explain why I only qualified for one sentence of explanation when you staged your disappearing act. In fact, what exactly was "This isn't working for me" supposed to convey?'

Emmie stiffened, acknowledging that while she hadn't wanted to go emotionally overboard in her goodbye note she had perhaps tried a little too hard to play it cool. 'I don't want to discuss it.'

Bastian threw back his wide shoulders and stared down at her with blistering force, his handsome mouth a hard ruthless line. 'We're going to discuss a lot of things before I leave here, *glyka mou*.'

Emmie stared at him, unwillingly captivated by the sheer gorgeous potency of Bastian in the flesh. Radiating masculine energy and buckets of authority, Bastian towered over her, scanning her appearance in a red roll-neck sweater, apron and jeans. 'You've put on weight…'

'Duh! You noticed?' Emmie shot back at him witheringly, turning on her heel to march back towards the kitchen.

As she stood briefly sideways Bastian focused on the swell of her pregnant belly pushing out the apron and stared, taken aback by the size of her. 'I meant… you haven't lost any *more* weight, so I assume the sickness wore off—'

'Weeks ago,' Emmie confirmed, turning back to face him again with open reluctance, blonde hair tumbling round her flushed cheeks.

'And yet you didn't think to get in touch with me and tell me that?' Bastian fired back at her furiously. 'Didn't it occur to you that I'd be worried about you? When I last saw you, you were far from well!'

'I thought with you it would be a case of out of sight, out of mind,' Emmie admitted truthfully, straightening her slender shoulders and standing her ground in the kitchen doorway lest he get the idea that she was intimidated by him.

'Those babies are half mine!' Bastian launched back at her wrathfully. 'When did I ever give you the impression that I was so irresponsible?'

Emmie pretended to think deeply. 'Oh, maybe it was when you warned me not to get worked up about having sex with you…I *didn't*, by the way.'

A feverish veil of colour highlighted his spectacular

cheekbones and his dark golden eyes blazed like the heart of a hot fire. 'Maybe I was playing safe.'

'Playing safe?' Emmie queried, all at sea.

His beautiful wilful mouth hardened. *'Ne...*yes, you blow hot, you blow cold, and you run away. That's twice you've done that to me now.'

Emmie took an angry step forward. 'I do not blow hot and cold and I do *not* run away!'

'You do,' Bastian contradicted with maddening assurance. 'I offended you the night before Nessa's wedding and you went from hotter than hot to cold as charity and ran away from the attraction between us. You may be an adult but you suffer from the same emotional overreactions as a teenager!'

'How dare you?' Emmie snapped, fit to be tied at that slur being cast on her maturity.

'I dare because I'm honest and I have *always* been honest with you,' Bastian declared with impressive emphasis. 'We had a disastrous misunderstanding the very first night we were together—I apologised—you refused to accept my apology. But at least I was willing to admit that I had made a mistake but was still attracted to you. We would never have been apart had you had the courage to be equally honest with me...'

'It's not about honesty, it's about sensitivity, and you are the guy who told me that what we had was just sex!' Emmie slammed back at him emotively.

'At the end of the day, sex is only sex and I stand by that statement!' Bastian growled back at her unapologetically. 'But in every way that mattered I demonstrated that I cared about what happened to you and I cared about the welfare of those babies you carry.'

Emmie struggled to be fair while her deep sense of having been insulted still rankled. 'Yes, you did,' she allowed, tight-mouthed at having to concede that point.

'I didn't deserve that you walked out on me and didn't tell me where you were going.'

'I would have got in touch with you *after* the birth,' Emmie protested.

'I want to be a lot *more* involved than that,' Bastian informed her with unconcealed hostility.

Emmie lifted her chin, refusing to back down. 'Well, I'm sorry if you don't like it but perhaps I didn't feel that you being more involved in my pregnancy was appropriate in the circumstances.'

'If that's how you felt you should have discussed it with me,' Bastian argued fiercely. 'Walking out and vanishing the minute I was safely out of the country was childish and cowardly!'

'I wanted to avoid a big confrontation like this!' Emmie pointed out.

'How are you doing with that ambition?' Bastian derided, making her teeth grind together in frustration.

'I am not childish and I am not cowardly,' Emmie returned resentfully to his determination to blame her for walking away from a difficult relationship.

'No? Well, at the very least you have some strange hang-ups,' Bastian condemned, interrupting her without hesitation as he dug a magazine out of his pocket and slapped it down aggressively on the hall table.

'She's your sister, your twin, and presumably the reason you go around dressed in a frumpy disguise most of the time! But did you think to mention her existence to me even once?'

Emmie froze in consternation as she found herself gazing down at a magazine photo of Saffy and Zahir's wedding day. Laughing and smiling with happiness, Saffy looked fantastic and Emmie's heart constricted at the sight, regret belatedly stabbing her that she had avoided playing a role at her sister's nuptials. 'How did you find out?'

'Nessa saw it and put it in front of me. I couldn't believe what I was seeing,' Bastian admitted with angry dark eyes. 'At first I thought it was you marrying royalty and then I saw her name...she's Sapphire, you're Emerald, so it was obviously no coincidental likeness. I did some research and that's when I realised how much you had been hiding from me.'

'There was no need for you to know.'

'I couldn't believe *she* was your sister.'

Emmie lost colour at that admission. 'I understand that. We may be identical twins but she still looks very different from me.'

'Yes, even though it was only photos I was merely fooled into thinking it was you for about five seconds,' Bastian spelt out.

Unsurprised by the assertion but dreading the comparison he had to be making between her and her gorgeous sister, Emmie lowered her head, her face shadowing. 'Yes—'

'You have a beauty spot on one cheekbone and your eyes are a lighter blue,' Bastian contended, sharply disconcerting her for few people were that observant. 'I also suspect that you're smaller—'

'By at least an inch. Even after the surgery on my leg I never quite caught up with Saffy in height,' Emmie conceded. 'I don't wear a disguise though—you don't understand…I just don't like being mistaken for Saffy and, believe me, it happens a lot if I dress up and go out and about in London. She's a celebrity, after all. I've also found it's just easier not to mention that she's my sister to the people I meet.'

'I can imagine that but you're not the same—you're not carbon copies of each other.'

'You don't think so?'

'I don't quite understand it but when I look at her, she does as much for my libido as a blank canvas on the wall, but when I look at you I have an instant reaction,' Bastian confessed in a husky undertone.

Emmie wasn't quite sure she could believe that, for she was much more accustomed to thinking of her sister as a vastly superior, more sophisticated and sexier version of herself—in every way a supermodel-perfect creature. But then Saffy had always been the prettier, livelier, more talented twin, Emmie the sickly, shy one, who was boringly academic, not that she had had much choice on that score when her disability had meant she couldn't go out and about like her twin. She glanced up at Bastian, her lovely face pink with self-consciousness, wondering if it could possibly be true that he found her more sexually appealing than her sister. After all, all her life she had been second-best to Saffy.

'It happens *every* time I look at you,' Bastian imparted thickly, his dark deep drawl vibrating down her spine, his stunning dark golden eyes hotly pinned to her in a smouldering look that created an atmosphere of shocking intimacy. 'Because while I know it's just sex, it's still the most freakin' fantastic sex I've ever had with a woman!'

A surge of responsive heat flooded Emmie's pelvis, swelled her breasts, tightened her nipples and no matter how hard she tried she couldn't suppress that wave of physical awareness. Bastian was attempting to turn an insult into a compliment and failing abysmally, she told herself firmly. She wasn't going to pick him up on it; she wasn't going to go there at all. Talking about sex with Bastian was a bad idea because talking about it made her think about it and she was determined to keep the door closed on that kind of misleading intimacy.

Breathing in deep, she turned her head away to duck his direct gaze and said tautly, 'So how did you find out where I was living?'

'Once I had linked you to your celebrity sister I had enquiries made and discovered this place,' Bastian told her, his handsome mouth compressing with annoyance. 'I drove up here straight away but you weren't here and the house was locked up.'

'Oh…' Emmie was surprised he had come to the farmhouse on a previous occasion and couldn't hide it.

'Did you come here at the weekend? I must have been staying with Kat.'

Bastian was frowning down at her. 'Your eldest sister? The one married to the rich Russian, who owns this house?'

Emmie studied him in surprise at the level of his knowledge. 'You have been doing your homework about my family.'

'Enough to know that you shouldn't be living here, forced to rely on the generosity of another man.'

'That other man happens to be my brother-in-law—'

'It doesn't matter. You're in this situation because of me and I'm the one who should be taking care of you.'

Emmie threw her head high, her lovely face taut with strain as she shifted her weight onto her one leg while rubbing at the thigh of the other. 'I don't need anyone taking care of me when I can do that for myself.'

'But I *want* to do it,' Bastian grated in a raw undertone, watching her massage her leg. 'Your leg's hurting you right now. Why don't you sit down? I want to look after the mother of my children. Is that so wrong?'

Emmie was disconcerted by that blunt declaration and that he had actually noticed that her leg was beginning to bother her. 'No, not wrong, but maybe a little surprising after some of the things you've said.'

'Why don't you forget what I've said in the past and look to the future instead? I think right now that would be a lot more useful,' Bastian countered with ringing confidence, striding into the cosy living room where a log fire had burned low in the grate.

Emmie followed him at a slower pace. 'What future?'

'Yours and the twins',' Bastian specified, gazing back at her with challenging intensity. 'I want you to come back to Greece with me and meet my family.'

Her eyes widened in astonishment. 'Er...I've already met your family,' she protested.

'Not as the future mother of my kids. You can't keep us in the closet with two babies on the way,' Bastian informed her with dark eyes glittering with amusement. 'You're part of my life now and that's not going to change.'

'I still don't think that there's any need for you to take me back to Greece with you and make some sort of formal announcement,' Emmie contended.

'I think it's important.' Bastian's stubborn jawline clenched his face taut as he stared back at her. 'Family connections mean a great deal to me. It'll be easier for you to make that connection now *before* the twins are born.'

'I'm not interested in visiting Greece right now,' Emmie declared, throwing her shoulders back.

'I want the time to see if we can work this relationship out,' Bastian admitted in a driven undertone. 'I shouldn't have to spell that out to you.'

Her troubled eyes widened a little and remained glued to his stunning dark eyes as if she was seeking answers there. 'Oh, I think you do…speaking as the guy who told me that all we had going for us was sex.'

'Are you ever going to let me forget I said that?' Bastian slammed back at her furiously.

'Probably not,' Emmie admitted waspishly. 'It's still screaming in my memory banks. Now all of a sudden you've changed your tune and you're talking about us working out this relationship when before you wouldn't even admit we *had* a relationship!'

In thunderous silence Bastian ground his teeth together. Like salt on an open wound she picked up every mistake he made and flung it at him with an aggression he was unaccustomed to meeting with in a woman. 'So I'm not perfect,' he bit out grudgingly.

'And you have hang-ups too,' Emmie added sweetly. 'Particularly when it comes to commitment.'

'I was engaged,' Bastian reminded her darkly.

'But funnily enough you never made it to the altar,' Emmie remarked.

'Lilah took offence at the pre-nuptial contract she was presented with and I wouldn't marry her without it.'

'I don't *want* your money,' Emmie told him baldly.

Bastian flattened his passionate mouth into a hard line and lowered his attention to her stomach. 'But your children will be entitled to a good deal of my money. That's a fact of life.'

Emmie coloured uncomfortably, not knowing what to say to that that wouldn't sound facetious, for in all likelihood when the babies she carried grew up they *would* want and expect access to their father's privileged lifestyle.

'I'll stay here tonight. We'll leave in the morning,' Bastian told her forcefully.

'You can't just bully me into travelling to Greece with you!' Emmie exclaimed, not knowing whether to laugh or cry at his attitude.

'I'm not trying to bully you. I'm asking you to put the needs of our children first. At the very least we need to establish a more civilised connection.'

There was a lot of truth in that statement, Emmie acknowledged uneasily. Having a contentious relationship with the father of her children was a very bad idea but she did not know if she could change the way she felt about Bastian or forgive him for not feeling the same way about her. She wanted too much and he wanted too little, she conceded unhappily.

'All right, I'll think about Greece,' Emmie muttered tightly.

'I'll make the arrangements—'

'Look, when the heck did "I'll think about it" turn into agreement?' Emmie stormed back at him, out of all patience with his arrogance.

Bastian stared broodingly back at her, the full intensity of his aggressive temperament in that charged appraisal. Electric heat sizzled through Emmie and she flushed, mortified by the way he affected her even when he was demonstrating his least attractive traits. On the other hand maybe if she gave a little, he would as well, because she didn't think that with the twins on the way it was wise to be at odds with him. After all, mightn't her attitude have a bad effect on his future relationship with her children? That, she acknowledged hollowly, was a major responsibility to carry, particularly when she was all too well aware how wounding she had found her own father's indifference to her existence. She definitely didn't want her children to undergo the same paternal rejection because she had created a problematic relationship with Bastian. Hadn't her mother done that with her father? Her parents had had a very bitter breakup and divorce and that reality had poisoned her father's attitude to his daughters as well. He had found it easier to walk away from *all* of them, not only his ex-wife.

'OK, I'll go to Greece,' Emmie agreed abruptly on the back of that final depressing thought. 'I'll show you up to your room.'

His room, *not* hers. Bastian watched the ripe curve of Emmie's hips going up the stairs, unwillingly allowing that his hopes of an immediate dropping of all barriers had been rather too optimistic. She wanted him to work at things, relationship things, and Bastian had never worked at anything like that in his whole life. Women had always worked to please him, to fit *his* expectations, not the other way round. He gritted his even white teeth at what seemed like a memory from the far distant past for he could see that pleasing him was not even on Emmie's agenda. It bothered him that he didn't even know what she wanted from him. He was doing his best but so far he had not got any points for trying, he reflected angrily. She hadn't noticed one blasted positive thing he had done so far, so why was he bothering? The answer to that question came fast: he didn't *know*, he just knew he couldn't leave her alone.

Emmie showed Bastian into one of the guest rooms her sister Kat had always kept prepared for guests. She studied his bold bronzed profile from below her lashes, reckoning there was no escape from feeding him as well while wondering why he brought out such a mean streak in her. Did she want him to go hungry? After all, it wasn't his fault that he hadn't fallen madly in love with her, was it? That was something that either happened or didn't happen. And unlike her estranged father, Bastian was already determined to make a major effort to be a parent from the start, well, before the twins were even born.

'There's hot water if you want a shower,' Emmie told him, belatedly wondering if she was trying to be hostess of the year a little too late. 'You can join me for dinner in an hour. It'll be a change to have company. My younger sister is only here for school holidays. She stays with Kat and Mikhail in London now if she leaves school to come home for the weekend.'

Bastian supposed she was offering him an olive branch of sorts and had a sudden recollection of that written apology on her hand way back at the start of their acquaintance. He almost smiled but the strained look in her bright blue eyes made him tense up instead.

* * *

'What did you say?' Emmie prompted Bastian in a nervous whisper, her cheeks burning after he had finished addressing his household staff, who had assembled in the big hall to greet their arrival. The official line-up struck her as incredibly Edwardian in style and thoroughly intimidated her. To be fair, she thought unhappily, it was embarrassing enough to reappear on the island on Bastian's arm while toting an enormous pregnant stomach, but it was even worse when absolutely everyone else was pointedly avoiding looking in that direction.

'Why?' Bastian asked shortly as he guided her up the main staircase with a firm hand at her back. Emmie wondered if he feared that she was so big upfront that she might over-balance and fall over backwards like a beached whale, and then scolded herself for being so self-critical. *You're very pregnant with twins, get over it,* she told herself in exasperation.

'I'm curious,' Emmie admitted.

'I told them that you're in charge here now—'

'You did...*what*?' Emmie stopped dead to exclaim in astonishment.

Bastian frowned. 'I didn't want anyone wondering about what your status was here and I want you to receive the very best attention possible from my staff.'

'But I'm not the mistress here...or wife or whatever!' Emmie argued.

'Do we need a label for you? To all intents and purposes you are the most important woman I've ever had in my life,' Bastian countered. 'You're expecting my children.'

'I can't possibly be the *most* important woman…I mean, what about your mother?'

'Apart from the fact that I'd have a problem if she was still the most important woman at my age,' Bastian quipped, 'what about her?'

'Is she still alive?'

'Yes. She lives in Italy and I only see her if she wants money.'

Emmie's brow furrowed. 'That's sad, Bastian. Are you sure you're not misjudging her?'

'Remind yourself of what your mother was willing to do to you in the name of profit,' Bastian commented with considerable cynicism. 'As the son of a woman even more mercenary than Odette, I know what I'm talking about.'

That reminder about Odette's greed struck home but Emmie gave him a troubled look, dismayed by his outlook. 'Why do you think your mother's like that?'

Bastian sighed as he threw wide the door of the room where Emmie had stayed on her previous visit to his home. 'Why are you interested?'

Emmie thought fast and hard, desperate to come up with an unemotional angle to conceal her revealing hunger for every detail she could glean about Bastian and his background. 'Your mother will be my children's grandmother.'

'But Cinzia will never visit your children. Even when I was a little boy she found the idea of being seen with a child as "too aging",' he retorted drily. 'She's very vain and will never accept being a grandparent. She was a film star when my father met her but her earning power was fading because she was getting older. She married him because she needed a meal ticket and when she got tired of him, she divorced him in a process that took half of everything he possessed.'

Emmie winced as a servant settled her cases down in the beautifully appointed bedroom and withdrew. 'Nasty.'

'His ego battered, my father found comfort in the arms of his secretary instead,' Bastian continued even more drily. 'The secretary got pregnant and he married her within weeks of his divorce from my mother being granted.'

'Oh dear,' Emmie remarked a good deal less securely as she wondered if he saw a dangerous parallel in that development between past and present: his father had married a woman because she fell pregnant by him and clearly it hadn't worked out.

'She was Nessa's mother and the only decent woman my father ever married,' Bastian explained wryly. 'But because my father wasn't in *love* with her…' contempt edged his tone as he voiced that particular word '…he thought it was acceptable to start an affair with the woman who became his third wife.'

'Then I gather that Nessa's mother didn't last long?'

'Two years.'

Emmie recalled Nessa telling her that her mother had been the only stepmother who was kind to Bastian and, considering his own mother had not set a good example of maternal affection, she found it sad that his father's marriage to Nessa's mother had been so brief. 'And wife number three?'

'Had one affair after another. My father hit the bottle hard before he finally got shot of her.'

'He sounds—'

'Foolish?' Bastian scorned.

'I was going to say vulnerable. I mean, he kept on trying so hard to find a happy relationship.'

'Only the grass on the other side of the fence was always greener and he couldn't content himself,' Bastian completed grimly. 'Wife number four spent most of her time trying to get *me* into bed because younger men gave her a buzz.'

That revelation made Emmie turn pink. 'That must have been ghastly.'

'While that marriage went on, I spent a lot of time at my grandfather's house—I was only eighteen,' Bastian admitted flatly, staring out of the bedroom window, broad shoulders rigid. 'Tragically my father's fourth marriage literally killed him. He came home unexpectedly one day and overheard his wife trying to seduce me. He got back into his car and crashed it into a tree a few miles down the road. The happy widow got what was left of my father's estate, which wasn't much. His marriages had virtually bankrupted him.'

'With a family history like that I'm surprised you were even considering getting married,' Emmie confided truthfully.

Bastian turned away from the window, tall, darkly handsome and intensely charismatic. His dark eyes glittered like gleaming gold ingots in sunlight. 'But unlike my father I didn't have any stupid ideas about love having anything to do with marriage…'

Emmie was relieved to think that Bastian had not been in love with Lilah, but his words and his attitude certainly didn't offer *her* much room for hope that he might develop such feelings for her in the future. 'Have you ever been in love?' she asked baldly, reasoning that subtlety was wasted on Bastian.

'In lust many times,' Bastian quipped. 'In love… never. I'm probably too practical.'

So, at the very least he must have been in lust with Lilah, Emmie assumed uneasily, and she certainly couldn't blame him for that because his ex-fiancée was exquisitely easy on the eye. 'I fell in love when I was at university,' she heard herself admit.

Unaccustomed to such personal conversations with a woman, Bastian dealt her a disconcerted look.

Emmie compressed her lush mouth. 'It turned out that Toby was only with me because he had a poster of my sister the supermodel on his bedroom wall—she was his fantasy and I was just the closest he could get to her,' she related ruefully.

'What a fool when you're even more beautiful,' Bastian breathed huskily.

'I'm not more beautiful than Saffy,' Emmie protested.

'I think you are,' Bastian admitted, his dark gaze

roaming over her lovely face. 'You're more natural, not all made up and artificial like your sibling.'

Without warning and for the first time in her life, Emmie found herself laughing at a comparison being made that could not leave her feeling inadequate. 'Well, I'm certainly not anywhere near as well groomed as my sister,' she conceded with a smile. 'She always looks perfect.'

Bastian rested lean brown hands on her slim shoulders, gazing down at her with smouldering heat in his heavily fringed dark golden eyes. 'I don't want or need perfect, *khriso mou.'*

Emmie stiffened, suddenly unsure of what should happen next, wanting him with every skin cell in her treacherous body but conscious that intimacy would plunge her deeper into a relationship that had no safe boundaries to protect her from hurt. 'Bastian…er—'

Long brown fingers brushed her cheekbone in a lazy caress and he kissed her with hungry driving urgency. Her heart hammered so fast she was scared it would burst out of her chest. The glorious swell of emotion and sensation that only he could give her was waiting in the wings like a terrible temptation, making nonsense of her firm conviction that she could take care of herself. For a split second she wanted Bastian so much it was terrifying, her body kindling like dry twigs touched by a flame, senses awakening with a surge of slumberous intensity. Her breasts stirred beneath her clothing, full and swollen and ripe for his touch, an ache biting deep in her pelvis to leave a sense of hollowness in its wake.

'I should unpack,' she said breathlessly, drawing back in a movement that demanded every atom of her self-discipline while her glance briefly skimmed over the door that led into Bastian's bedroom, and she wondered how long she could possibly keep her distance from him.

In a rare act for a male in the grip of fierce arousal, Bastian backed off several steps, lean, strong face taut and flushed. Emmie was in Greece, on the island of Treikos, safely beneath his roof, and that was enough for one day, he reflected ruefully, apprehensive for the first time ever of making a wrong move with a woman.

Conscious of the tension in the air, Emmie coloured and turned aside to her luggage. Her legs were shaking, her rebellious body screaming with tight, strained nerve endings and she was ashamed of her weakness. Somehow it had not occurred to her that Bastian might still exert that much physical power over her even when she was several months pregnant. Where he was concerned, she badly needed an off switch.

Four days later, Nessa arrived for the weekend and mortified Emmie straight away by walking out to the terrace where Emmie and Bastian were having lunch and saying cheerfully, 'So, when's the wedding?'

Bastian frowned. 'What wedding?' he queried, standing up to pull out a chair for his sister.

Nessa simply laughed. '*Your* wedding, of course,'

she said teasingly, studying the pair of them with amused brown eyes.

'We're not getting married,' Emmie declared with red cheeks hot enough to fry eggs on.

Nessa raised a brow as though that was an extraordinary statement and responded, 'Grandpa is going to be very disappointed.'

Initially relieved by Nessa's arrival because the presence of a third person would surely stifle the shocking level of sexual tension Bastian roused inside her, Emmie could now only feel appalled at the brunette's lack of tact.

'I don't think so,' Bastian countered smoothly, seemingly unembarrassed, Emmie noted with some relief.

'Trust me.' Nessa grinned. 'Grandpa's expecting to hear wedding bells and just waiting on you making the announcement. Don't say you weren't warned.'

'Excuse me,' Emmie breathed, rising to her feet.

'Where are you going?' Bastian demanded as if he was entitled to know her every move.

'It's hot and I'm a little tired...thought I'd lie down for a while,' Emmie told him disjointedly, taking refuge in being pregnant in her eagerness to escape sitting in on a humiliating dialogue between brother and sister.

Upstairs she lay down on her bed, dully recalling what entertaining company Bastian had been since their arrival. They had picnicked on the beach, wandered through olive groves on lazy walks and eaten in the taverna down by the harbour where Emmie had suspected that all the other diners were staring at her.

Even so, apart from that one kiss on the first day, Bastian hadn't touched her again. She was never going to understand Bastian, she reflected in frustration. Why had he kissed her if he had no plans to follow up on it? And *why*, when she knew that intimacy would only fire them into dangerous territory again, was she even wondering?

Her cell phone pinged on a message and she snatched it up, surprised to see that it was from Saffy, who rarely made direct contact with her.

'I'm in the pudding club too,' Saffy texted jokily, and Emmie gasped and before she could even consider what she was doing she was phoning her twin. It struck her as extraordinary that both of them should contrive to be pregnant at the same time.

Saffy was audibly disconcerted to hear Emmie's voice on the line but the warmth of her response soothed any awkwardness Emmie might have felt. When Saffy startled Emmie by freely admitting that she had conceived her baby *before* marrying Zahir, Emmie was captivated and touched by her honesty and the barriers really came down between the sisters as Emmie shared the history of her relationship with Bastian.

At one point, Saffy interrupted her twin. 'Odette lied to you. She *didn't* pay for your surgery, Kat did!'

'Are you sure? But where did Kat get the money from?' Emmie questioned in amazement.

'Kat took out a loan to cover the cost. Our mother is a dreadful liar.' Saffy groaned. 'As for this escort agency stuff, we'll have to prevent Topsy from visiting her or she'll be trying to set her up next! Topsy's *so* trusting and I bet Odette milked our kid sister for every bit of useful info about us that she could get.'

'Probably,' Emmie conceded, shocked at the news that her mother had deceived her but at the same time semi-stunned that she was managing to have such a friendly conversation with her twin when they had been estranged for so long. 'I'm sorry I didn't come to your wedding, Saffy. It's no excuse but I was feeling pretty down and I just couldn't face it.'

'I'll forgive you if you promise…to stay in touch with me,' her sister responded hesitantly.

Her heart lifting at that request, Emmie was quick to agree.

'You said you were in Greece—what's happening between you and Bastian right now?' Saffy finally asked.

'I think that for the sake of the future, we're trying to be friends,' Emmie told her heavily.

'And you want more?' Saffy asked perceptively. 'I felt the same way with Zahir. I didn't want him to stay with me only because I was pregnant.'

Emmie's eyes stung at the depth of her twin's understanding. She blinked back tears and a little while after that the groundbreaking conversation concluded with Saffy promising to phone again the next day. Afterwards, Emmie sat still dumbfounded by the discovery that she could talk easily again to her twin and she was so grateful that neither of them had dared to broach any topic that might be controversial. That both sisters were pregnant, however, had provided them with a bridge that spanned the challenges of their shared past. In addition, Emmie acknowledged wryly, Bastian had somehow contrived to lift Emmie's confidence so that she no longer felt that she was a poor, disappointing copy of her glamorous and vibrant twin.

'You should invite Saffy and her husband to visit,' Bastian remarked when she volunteered the news over dinner that she and her sister were talking again. Nessa had gone to visit her in-laws, who lived in the village.

Emmie tensed. 'That's very kind of you but obviously I don't know how long I'll be staying here in your home.'

Bastian raised an ebony brow, brilliant dark eyes bright as diamonds in his handsome face. 'At least until the twins are born,' he supplied without hesitation. 'I want you to stay, and when I return to London to work, I'll want you to accompany me there as well.'

Taken aback by that sweeping statement, Emmie studied him with shaken blue eyes. 'I had no idea that's what you were planning. I thought I was only here for a short visit.'

Across the table, Bastian stared steadily back at her. 'Naturally you're free to do whatever you want and live where you choose…but speaking on my own behalf *I* want you to *stay* with me.'

Emmie was hugely touched by that assurance even though she still had no real idea of what he meant by his words. Did he believe that simply being pregnant was so hazardous that he had to keep a careful watch over her? Did he feel guilty that he had got her pregnant? Was that why he was so determined to look after her? Or was there a more personal element than that? As she bent over her delicious dessert, she was insanely conscious of his attention locking to the rather low neckline of her top. She glanced up quickly and tracked the path of his hot golden gaze locked to the plump swell of her cleavage. She reddened and thought, *Yes, it's definitely personal.*

'Does that invite of yours include sharing a bed?' Emmie enquired baldly.

A sudden grin flashed across Bastian's stubborn mouth. 'I'm yours any time you want me, *khriso mou*. I don't play hard to get.'

Emmie didn't know where to look because when she met his stunning eyes after that admission she felt intoxicated and dizzy. Unable to think straight, she savoured the sweetness of her dessert, the tip of her tongue sliding out to lick a drop of chocolate mousse from her full bottom lip.

Following that process, his attention locked to her succulent pink mouth, Bastian groaned out loud. 'You're killing me.'

Emmie froze. In the condition she was in she found it quite impossible to view herself as seductive in any way, but when she looked across the table to see Bastian's molten golden gaze welded to her, her heart skipped a startled beat. He thrust back his chair and sprang upright, approaching her to stretch down a lean brown hand and grasp hers to tug her to her feet.

'Bastian…?' Emmie framed uncertainly.

'I want you so much,' he growled. 'I've been working so hard to keep my hands off you.'

Emmie had only felt her own tension and had not appreciated that he was exercising restraint as well. 'You find me attractive like this?' she murmured wonderingly.

Bastian looked down at her with smouldering dark eyes. 'I don't really understand it but I find your pregnancy an amazing turn-on.'

'OK,' Emmie marvelled while nodding dumbly, entranced by the hunger etched in his face and the very slight yet revealing tremor in his hands as he raised them to gently cup her cheekbones.

And then there was no more talking and the last barrier crashed down between them while he kissed her breathless. He took her upstairs to lift her into his bed, where he made slow sensual love to her until she cried out her pleasure in wondering wanton delight.

A long time later, he lay with his arms wrapped round her and the most glorious sense of peace settled over Emmie. She loved it when he held her close and wanted to swarm all over his long, lean, powerful body like a flock of bees savouring pollen. Self-discipline, however, kept her still and unadventurous because she was terrified of revealing too much emotion or enthusiasm. Sex was sex, as Bastian had told her unforgettably, and she didn't want to begin kidding herself that it was anything more. While they were living together, they might as well be sharing a bed, she bargained desperately with herself. She didn't have to have a relationship all set out in stone steps in front of her to be happy, did she? And why shouldn't she settle for being happy for now and letting the future take care of itself?

'I have a charity ball to attend in Athens tomorrow evening,' Bastian told her when she had almost drifted to sleep. 'You're welcome to accompany me.'

'Nothing to wear, *truly* nothing to wear!' Emmie exclaimed, eyes flying wide in dismay in the darkness. 'But thanks for asking…er, appearing in public this pregnant with you would be kind of making a really loud statement, wouldn't it?'

'It would,' Bastian agreed with a curious lack of expression. 'Perhaps you're right and it's too soon.'

Emmie hadn't said or meant that but she didn't argue, reasoning that he would have tried harder to persuade her to go with him if her presence had really mattered to him. Thirty-six hours later those same thoughts came home to haunt her with a vengeance.

The morning after the Athens ball, Bastian had still to return to the island and Emmie was having a leisurely breakfast on the terrace overlooking the beach when the morning newspapers were brought out and settled on a nearby table for her convenience. Emmie got up to browse through the pile of papers, automatically flipping past the Greek editions only for her fingers to falter as she stiffened in consternation at the sight of a photograph adorning the front page of one of the local tabloids.

It was a photo of Bastian and Lilah drinking champagne and laughing together. Lilah looked tiny and ravishing in a romantic pink chiffon gown, like one half of a matched couple on intimate and friendly terms, while Bastian smiled down at her. The bitter hurt of jealousy pierced Emmie deep. In fact Emmie felt as sick as though she had been punched because she was already recalling that Bastian really hadn't made that much effort to persuade her that he wanted her with him in Athens. And was this why? Had he known beforehand that Lilah would be attending the same event? And was it any wonder that the papers were probably speculating as to whether or not the formerly engaged couple had reconciled?

Feeling shaken, scared and angry with herself for being scared, Emmie sank back down on her chair, eyes blank as she stared out unseeingly at the beautiful view she had been admiring only minutes earlier. Was Bastian still attracted to Lilah? To be fair, what man wouldn't be? And what could Emmie possibly do about it, if he was? Retreating with dignity when she was already virtually living with Bastian would be a challenge in the circumstances, she thought painfully.

CHAPTER TEN

EMMIE WAS CONVINCED that she could only blame herself for her predicament. Clearly, it was all her *own* fault, an argument her mother had been prone to making every time anything went wrong in Emmie's life when she was a child.

Here she was, after all, decidedly the author of her own destruction: pregnant and having an affair with Bastian in a relationship that had neither rules nor safe boundaries. How sensible was that? Emmie had always liked to know where she stood, only she never had known that when it came to Bastian. That was why she was reluctant to trust him and even more reluctant to risk relying on him. And there would soon be no room for self-respect either if she was forced to start questioning him about Lilah.

The helicopter flew in low and fast and began to land. Emmie didn't move a muscle. She did try to cross her legs casually beneath her white cotton sundress but her large tummy got in the way and she had to forget that pose. Bastian leapt from the helicopter into view, black hair ruffled by the breeze, lean powerful body taut as he strode across the lawn to join her, his striking black-fringed dark golden eyes seeking Emmie out where she sat in the shade. As always, he was gorgeous, she conceded helplessly. She had only to look at his tense bone structure to guess that he knew about the photograph and was in an understandably wary frame of mind.

'You look so serene and beautiful sitting there, *khriso mou*,' Bastian imparted huskily, his attention lingering to take in the rich golden gleam of her hair and the glow of her delicate English-rose complexion in contrast to her bright blue eyes.

'Appearances can be deceptive,' Emmie quipped.

'I flew straight back when I saw that photo…I gather you've seen it?' An ebony brow quirked enquiringly.

Emmie nodded, reluctantly impressed that he had jumped right into the issue without trying to avoid it or fake an innocence that she would never have believed.

'Aside of the fact that Nessa was with me throughout the evening, the photo was a definite stitch-up,' Bastian complained with a sardonic look. 'Probably set up by Lilah and taken by one of her friends. Lilah revels in provoking press attention and speculation.'

Emmie parted stiff lips, her hands clasped together tightly below the level of the table. 'You do look happy to be with her,' she remarked flatly.

'After the way Lilah behaved when we broke up I no longer even like her,' Bastian countered drily. 'But I have too much respect for her family to cut her dead in public and I see no reason to embarrass myself or her by parading our differences. If I'm happy now it's because I have *you* in my life.'

'I'd never have guessed I mattered that much to you,' Emmie confided uncomfortably, sitting very still and unconvinced, her shoulders as rigid as her spine.

A rueful smile briefly curled Bastian's wide sensual mouth. 'I'm so terrified of losing you again you wouldn't believe it.'

Emmie blinked. 'I don't believe it…you, *terrified*?'

'Totally,' Bastian confirmed, staring down at her from his considerable height with steady, dark, serious eyes. 'When you went missing while I was still abroad I went crazy. I couldn't eat, I couldn't sleep, I couldn't think of anything but you. And when I did get back to London I couldn't believe that stupid note you left was all you had to say to me.'

'I didn't think I had anything to say to you that you had enough interest to want to hear,' Emmie admitted uneasily. 'I wasn't going to hang myself out on a limb for you after you said that all we had going for us was sex.'

'I didn't mean that…I very much *regret* saying that,' Bastian emphasised on the back of a groan. 'But to be frank, I didn't really appreciate what you meant to me until you vanished.'

'Oh?' Emmie was glued to every word falling from his lips, scarcely breathing while she listened.

Bastian leant back against one of the supporting stone pillars that held up the roof over the terrace, his gaze veiled, his lean muscular length taut with tension. 'Then I didn't feel anything like I should have felt for Lilah. I know that now. I shouldn't have even considered marrying her when I felt nothing for her, but for a long time I honestly thought that that was the best way to be in a relationship.'

'If you're an inanimate object and not a person,' Emmie suggested wryly.

'I thought if there was no emotion involved I would see more clearly and choose a wife more wisely,' Bastian confessed and then frowned, black brows lacing together. 'And we know how well that turned out! Lilah may have wanted me mainly for my status and wealth but even she deserved better than a fiancé who couldn't have cared less when she broke the engagement and took up with another man.'

'But she must have known that it was more a…er practical marriage than a meeting of souls,' Emmie commented tightly, thinking what a hypocrite she could be, for she had been wonderfully reassured by Bastian's assurance that he didn't even like Lilah any more and it was obvious that he could no longer see what virtues he had once assumed the other woman possessed.

'I was never really happy with her…I didn't stop noticing other women either,' Bastian admitted reluctantly. 'I didn't *do* anything about it, I was faithful while I was still with her but I imagine that I would have strayed eventually.'

'Then you weren't right for each other.' Emmie

sighed. 'What would have been the point of getting married?'

'Exactly,' Bastian agreed, shooting her a smouldering smile. 'I'm so different with you. I don't like other men looking at you and I certainly have no desire to look at other women. I can't stand not knowing where you are and what you're doing. I want to be sure you'll answer your phone when I call. I want to know you're living in my home and that you'll raise our children there with me. I also want to know that you're truly *mine*.'

'*Yours?*' Emmie questioned. 'In what way do you want me to be yours?'

'In the most basic way that a man and a woman can belong to each other,' Bastian retorted, digging into his pocket to produce something, which he extended.

Emmie blinked at the spectacle of the huge diamond solitaire ring that he was offering her. 'Er… what's this?'

'You're bright enough to work it out,' Bastian teased. 'But it's going to be the shortest engagement on record because I intend to add a wedding ring to your finger as soon as possible.'

Emmie stiffened, facial muscles setting tight. 'I don't want you to feel you *have* to marry me because it's what your family expect of you,' she told him squarely.

'I knew they'd stick their oar in if they could but this has nothing to do with my family. This,' Bastian declared, lifting her slender hand to thread the diamond ring onto her engagement finger, 'is all about me and you and how I feel about you. I can't stand you being away from me.'

'Maybe you're just possessive,' Emmie remarked.

'I can't sleep when you're not there.'

'It's sex you miss,' Emmie contended heavily, refusing to be convinced by his transformation.

Bastian swore under his breath and lifted her up to face him. 'Stop being grumpy and difficult,' he instructed. 'Somehow I fell madly in love with you and now you've become so much a part of my life that I can't imagine it without you. It's got nothing to do with you being pregnant either—that's simply a wonderful added extra.'

'An added extra?' Emmie repeated in astonishment.

'I love you,' Bastian murmured intently, dark golden eyes locked strongly to hers. 'And I finally understand how much that emotion can enrich my life.'

'But you only hired me as an escort,' Emmie protested. 'If it hadn't been me, it would have been someone else.'

'No. You were never an escort and I've never been with one and now I never ever will be, *khriso mou*,' Bastian declared emotively. 'You were special and you dug your way into my heart and taught me to feel stuff I never thought I would or could experience.'

A great bubble of happiness was swelling inside Emmie and making her feel light-headed. 'Seriously?' she pressed.

'Seriously,' Bastian confirmed levelly.

'Pride comes before a fall,' Emmie teased with a huge grin.

'Slow and steady wins the race,' Bastian muttered, nuzzling his passionate mouth against her throat so that she shivered in the circle of his arms. 'But I'm sorry I was such a slow learner.'

'I'll forgive you because I love you too,' she whispered. 'But I didn't admit it to myself until it was almost too late because I was scared of getting too involved with you and getting hurt.'

'I will never hurt you,' Bastian swore huskily. 'My ambition is to marry you and spend my life ensuring that you and our children are happy.'

Emmie linked her arms round his neck and gazed up at him with adoring eyes and a sunny smile. 'I'm not going to complain about that. You're going to be a fantastic father as well,' she assured him with loving confidence.

'Even though I've got no manners?'

'Says the guy who opens doors for me all the time?' Emmie riposted as he did exactly that with the door in front of them.

'So you actually noticed that change in my behaviour?' Bastian quipped. 'Why didn't you mention it then?'

'Didn't want to give you a swollen head!' She gasped, breathless with excitement as he paused to kiss her.

'You have to notice to encourage me, *khriso mou*,' Bastian informed her raggedly, holding her tightly to him, ensuring that she was fully aware of the effect she was having on him.

'My word, Bastian, the last thing you need from me is encouragement!' Emmie laughed at the idea, joy sparkling through her as she wrapped her arms round him and clung to stay upright.

EPILOGUE

FOUR YEARS LATER on her wedding anniversary, Emmie strolled down to the beach where Bastian was playing ball with their toddler sons, Dmitri and Stavros, Saffy's husband, Zahir, and their son, Karim. In Emmie's arms snuggled her baby daughter, Appollonia, cute as a button at six months old with her mother's hair and her father's eyes.

For a pleasant change the usually empty stretch of beach below the house was downright crowded. Bastian's grandfather, Theron, was sharing one of the tables on the sand with Nessa, Leonides and their infant daughter, Olympia. A family BBQ was organised for later that evening. Kat and Mikhail, Topsy and their twins were due to arrive on Mikhail's fabulous yacht before nightfall. Emmie knew it would be a fantastic, noisy celebration with kids running wild and sisters talking nineteen to the dozen to catch up on the latest news and she could hardly wait.

'Give me that beautiful baby,' Saffy urged, reaching for Appollonia, who gave her aunt a gummy smile.

'Trust you to get it right. I'm having another boy when I was convinced I was carrying a little girl this time,' she lamented, patting the rounded contours of her stomach.

'Maybe the next time,' Emmie said with a grin.

'I told Zahir there wasn't going to be a next time.'

'You said that after Karim's birth as well,' Emmie reminded her twin, loving the closeness of the bond reborn after their long estrangement from each other.

'Did I?' Saffy sighed. 'Zahir is mad about kids, almost as bad as Bastian.'

A black-haired squirming bundle of lively toddler tucked under each muscular arm, Bastian lowered his twin sons to the ground and doled out cold drinks from the cool box.

Bastian strode across the sand to lift his daughter out of Saffy's arms and hold her high above him. The baby chuckled like mad, arms and plump little legs waving in frantic excitement. She was a cheerful baby with a wonderfully infectious laugh while her brothers were live-wire kids, who kept both parents on their toes.

Sometimes, Emmie could barely believe that years had passed since their quiet wedding on the island, which had only been attended by family. They had held a terrific party afterwards and just six weeks later their twin boys had been born early. One of their devoted nannies retrieved Appollonia from her father and Bastian crossed the sand to close an arm round Emmie's slim shoulders.

'Happy anniversary, *pethi mou*,' he husked, brushing his sensual mouth gently across her temples.

In the sunlight, Emmie touched the perfectly matched pearls that gleamed at her throat with appreciative fingertips, Bastian's gift to mark the occasion. As a wedding present he had given her an outrageously extravagant sapphire necklace, confiding that the first time he had watched her walking down the stairs in his island home he had pictured her sporting sapphires that matched her eyes. Her husband's generosity had ensured that her jewellery collection and her wardrobe were pretty special. Never again would Emmie be able to use the excuse that she had nothing suitable to wear, for she owned a wonderful selection of clothes. Indeed anything she wanted, Bastian ensured she received and Emmie loved being spoilt and valued for the first time in her life.

'Happy anniversary, my love,' Emmie whispered, gazing up at her darkly handsome husband with smiling warmth and love. 'Has marriage lived up to your expectations?'

Bastian tugged her close to his big sun-warmed body. 'Life with you has exceeded my every expectation.'

'I know you never dreamt until I came along that you might enjoy three rug rats round your feet,' Emmie teased fondly, watching approvingly as she saw Zahir pull Saffy close with the quiet assurance of a firmly bonded couple. Emmie had never dreamt that falling in love could give her so much happiness.

'The more the merrier,' Bastian quipped, stunning dark golden eyes welded with sensual intent to her blushing face. 'We could head back into the house to check the catering arrangements.'

Her lovely face heated even more in the sunlight, hunger stirring as she looked up at him, a hunger laced with an excitement that had yet to fade. 'Whatever you like,' she told him breathily.

'Oh, I like…I like you very much,' Bastian growled raggedly, his arm tightening round her as he walked her back off the beach.

Her husband's desire for her never failed to make Emmie feel like the most exciting woman alive and she no longer remembered what it felt like to feel second best. She smiled, full of love and lust, happy and relaxed and grateful for the security and continuity of her tight-knit family circle.

* * * * *

"You should leave."

Another primal sound of anger came out of Demyan before he crossed the small distance between them and yanked Chanel's body against his with tender ruthlessness. "I'm not going anywhere. Not tonight. Not ever."

"You can't make promises like that." His breaking them was going to destroy something inside her that her parents and ex had been unable to touch.

The belief that she was worth *something*.

"I can."

"What? You're going to marry me?" she demanded with pain-filled sarcasm.

"Yes."

BY HIS ROYAL DECREE

At his command and in his bed!

Crown Prince Maksim Yurkovich and his royal cousin
Prince Demyan know exactly the price of duty.

Having already sacrificed so much,
what is one more thing?

Tied to women by necessity, it's hard to say who is
more surprised by the fiery strength of their desire—
the Princes or their brides.

But when the sheets cool on the marriage bed
who will win…Queen or country?

Last month you read Prince Maksim's story
in
ONE NIGHT HEIR

This month discover how far Prince Demyan
will go to do his duty in
PRINCE OF SECRETS

PRINCE
OF SECRETS

BY
LUCY MONROE

MILLS
& BOON

First published in Great Britain 2013
by Mills & Boon, an imprint of Harlequin (UK) Limited.
Harlequin (UK) Limited, Eton House, 18-24 Paradise Road,
Richmond, Surrey TW9 1SR

© Lucy Monroe 2013

ISBN: 978 0 263 90031 6

Printed and bound in Spain
by Blackprint CPI, Barcelona

Lucy Monroe started reading at the age of four. After going through the children's books at home, she was caught by her mother reading adult novels pilfered from the higher shelves on the bookcase... Alas, it was nine years before she got her hands on a Mills & Boon® Romance her older sister had brought home. She loves to create the strong alpha males and independent women who people Mills & Boon® books. When she's not immersed in a romance novel (whether reading or writing it), she enjoys travel with her family, having tea with the neighbours, gardening, and visits from her numerous nieces and nephews.

Lucy loves to hear from her readers:
email LucyMonroe@LucyMonroe.com,
or visit www.LucyMonroe.com

Recent titles by the same author:

ONE NIGHT HEIR *(By His Royal Decree)*
NOT JUST THE GREEK'S WIFE
HEART OF A DESERT WARRIOR
FOR DUTY'S SAKE

Did you know these are also available as eBooks?
Visit www.millsandboon.co.uk

For Debbie, my sister and my friend.
God blessed our family immeasurably when
He brought you into it. And for Rob, a dear brother
of the heart. Together, you have brought so much
generosity, love, faith and joy to our family and to me
personally. Much love to you both, now and always!

PROLOGUE

"WHAT AM I looking at?" Demyan asked his uncle, the King of Volyarus.

Spread before him on the behemoth antique executive desk, brought over with the first Hetman to be made Volyarussian king, was a series of photos. All were of a rather ordinary woman with untamed, curly, red hair. Her one arresting feature was storm-cloud gray eyes that revealed more emotion in each picture than he would allow himself to show in an entire year.

Fedir frowned at the pictures for several seconds before meeting Demyan's matching espresso-dark gaze.

Those who mistook Demyan for Fedir's biological son could be forgiven—the resemblance was that strong. But Demyan was the king's nephew and while he'd been raised in the palace as the "spare heir to the throne," three years older than his future king, he'd never once gotten it confused in his own mind.

Fedir cleared his throat as if the words he needed to utter were unpalatable to him. "That is Chanel Tanner."

"Tanner?" Demyan asked, the coincidence not lost on him.

"Yes."

The name was common enough, in the United States, anyway. There was no immediate reason for Demyan to

assume she was related to Bartholomew Tanner, one of
the original partners in Tanner Yurkovich.

Except the portrait of the Texas wildcatter hanging in
the west hall of the palace bore a striking resemblance to
the woman in the pictures. They shared the same curly
red hair (though Bartholomew had worn it shorter), high
forehead and angular jaw (though hers was more pleas-
ingly feminine).

Her lips, unadorned by color or gloss, were a soft pink
and bow-shaped. Bartholomew's were lost beneath the
handlebar mustache he sported in the painting. While his
eyes sparkled with life, hers were filled with seriousness
and unexpected shadows.

Bartholomew Tanner had helped to found the company on which the current wealth of both Volyarus and
the Yurkovich family empire had been built. At one time,
he had owned a significant share in it as well.

"She looks like Baron Tanner." The oilman had been
bequeathed a title by King Fedir's grandfather for his
help in locating oil reserves and other mineral deposits
on Volyarus.

Fedir nodded. "She's his great-great-granddaughter and
the last of his bloodline."

Relaxing back in his chair, Demyan cocked his brow
in interest but waited for the king to continue rather than
ask any questions.

"Her stepfather, Perry Saltzman, approached our office in Seattle about a job for his son." Another frown,
which was unusual for the king, who was no more prone
to emotional displays than Demyan. "Apparently, the boy
is close to graduating university with honors in business."

"Why tell me? Maks is the glad-hander on stuff like
this." His cousin was also adroit at turning down requests
without causing diplomatic upset.

Demyan was not so patient. There were benefits to not being raised a Crown Prince.

"He is on his honeymoon." Fedir's words were true, but Demyan sensed there was more to it.

Otherwise, this could have waited. "He'll be back in a couple of weeks."

And if Mr. Saltzman was looking for a job for his son, why were there pictures of his stepdaughter all over the conference table?

"I don't want Maks to know about this."

"Why?"

"He will not agree to what needs to be done." Fedir ran his fingers through hair every bit as dark as Demyan's, no strands of gray in sight. "You know my son. He can be unexpectedly...recalcitrant."

For the first time in a very long while, Demyan had to admit, "You've lost me."

There was very little his cousin would not do for the country of his birth. He'd given up the woman he wanted rather than marry with little hope for an heir.

Fedir stacked the pictures together, leaving a candid shot on top that showed Chanel smiling. "In 1952, when Bart Tanner agreed to help my grandfather find oil on or around the Volyarussian islands, he accepted a twenty-percent share in the company in exchange for his efforts and provision of expertise, a fully trained crew and all the drilling equipment."

"I am aware." All Volyarussian children were taught their history.

How Volyarus had been founded by one of Ukraine's last Hetmans, who had purchased the chain of uninhabited and, most believed, uninhabitable islands with his own personal wealth from Canada. He and a group of peasants and nobles had founded Volyarus, literally meaning free from Russia, because they'd believed it was only a matter of time before Ukraine fell under Russian rule completely.

They had been right. Ukraine was its own country again, but more people spoke Russian there than their native tongue. They had spent too many years under the thumb of the USSR.

Hetman Maksim Ivan Yurkovich the First had poured his wealth into the country and become its de facto monarch. By the time his son was crowned King of Volyarus, the House of Yurkovich's monarchy was firmly in place.

However, the decades that followed were not all good ones for the small country, and the wealth of its people had begun to decline, until even the Royal House was feeling the pinch.

Enter wildcatter and shrewd businessman Bartholomew Tanner.

"He died still owning those shares." Fedir's frown had turned to an all-out scowl.

Shock coursed through Demyan. "No."

"Oh, yes." King Fedir rose and paced the room, only to stop in front of the large plate glass window with a view of the capital city. "The original plan was for his daughter to marry my grandfather's youngest son."

"Great-Uncle Chekov?"

"Yes."

"But…" Demyan let his voice trail off, nothing really to say.

Duke Chekov had been a bachelor, but it wasn't because Tanner's daughter broke his heart. The man had been gay and lived out his years overseeing most of Volyarus's mining interests with a valet who was a lot more than a servant.

In the 1950s, that had been his only option for happiness.

Times had changed, but some things remained static. Duty to family and country was one of them.

King Fedir shrugged. "It did not matter. The match was set."

"But they never married."

"She eloped with one of the oilmen."

That would have been high scandal in the '50s.

"But I thought Baron Tanner left the shares to the people of Volyarus."

"It was a pretty fabrication created by my grandfather."

"The earnings on that twenty percent of shares have been used to build roads, fund schools… *Damn*."

"Exactly. To repay the funds with interest to Chanel Tanner would seriously jeopardize our country's financial stability in the best of times."

And the current economic climes would never be described as that.

"She has no idea of her legacy, does she?" If she did, Perry Saltzman wouldn't bother to ask for a job for his son—he'd be suing Volyarus for hundreds of millions. As one of the few countries in the world that did not operate in any sort of deficit, that kind of payout could literally break the Volyarussian bank.

"What's the plan?"

"Marriage."

"How will that help?" Whoever she married could make the same claims on their country's resources.

"There was one caveat in Bartholomew's will. If any issue of his ever married into the Volyarussian royal family, his twenty percent would revert to the people less a sufficient annual income to provide for his heir's well-being."

"That doesn't make any sense."

"It does if you know the rest of the story."

"What is it?"

"Tanner's daughter ended up jilted by her lover, who

was already married, making their own hasty ceremony null."

"So, she still could have married Duke Chekov."

"She was pregnant with another man's child. She'd caused a well-publicized scandal. He categorically refused."

"Tanner thought he would change Great-Uncle Chekov's mind?"

"Tanner thought *her* son might grow up to marry into our family and link the Tanner name with the Royal House of Yurkovich for all time."

"It already was, by business."

"That wasn't good enough." King Fedir sighed. "He wanted a family connection with his name intact, if possible."

"Family was important to him."

"Yes. He never spoke to his daughter again, but he provided for her financially until she remarried, with only one caveat."

"Her son keep the Tanner name." It made sense.

"Exactly."

"And he presumably had a son."

"Only one."

"Chanel's father, but you said she was the only living Tanner of Bart's line."

"She is. Both her grandfather and father died from dangerous chemical inhalation after a lab accident."

"They were scientists?"

"Chemists, just like Chanel. Although they worked on their own grants. She's a research assistant."

The woman with the wild red hair in the pictures was a science geek?

"And no one in the family was aware of their claim to Tanner's shares?"

"No. He meant to leave them to the people of Volyarus. He told my grandfather that was his intention."

"But he didn't do it."

"He was a wildcatter. It's a dangerous profession. He died when his grandson was still a young boy."

"And?"

"And my grandfather provided for the education expense of every child in that line since."

"There haven't been that many."

"No."

"Including Chanel?"

"Yes. The full ride and living expenses scholarship she received is apparently what gave Perry Saltzman the idea to approach Yurkovich Tanner and trade on a connection more than half a century old."

"What do you want me to do? Find her a Volyarussian husband?"

"He has to be from the Yurkovich line."

"Your son is already married."

"You are not."

Neither was Demyan's younger brother, but he doubted Fedir considered that fact important. Demyan was the one who had been raised as "spare to the throne," almost a son to the monarch. "You want me to marry her."

"For the good of Volyarus, yes. It need not be a permanent marriage. The will makes no stipulations on that score."

Demyan did not reply immediately. For the first time in more years than he could remember, his mind was blank with shock.

"Think, Demyan. You and I both know the healthy economy of Volyarus sits on a precarious edge, just like the rest of the world's. The calamity that would befall us were we to be forced to distribute the funds to Miss Tanner would be great."

"You are being melodramatic. There's no guarantee Maksim the First's duplicity would ever be discovered."

"It's only a matter of time, particularly with a man like Perry Saltzman in the picture. His kind can sniff out wealth and connections with the efficiency of ferrets."

"So, we deny the claim. Our court resources far exceed this young woman's."

"I think not. There are three countries that would be very happy to lay claim to Volyarus as a territory, and the United States is one of them."

"You believe they would use the unclaimed shares as a way to get their hands on a part of Volyarus."

"Why not?"

Why not, indeed. King Fedir would and, come to it, Demyan wouldn't hesitate to exploit such a politically expedient turn of events himself.

"So I marry her, gain control of the shares and dump her?" he asked, more to clarify what his uncle was thinking than to enumerate his own plans.

He would marry one day. Why not the heir to Bartholomew Tanner? If she was as much a friend to Volyarus as her grandfather had been, they might well make an acceptable life together.

"If she turns out to be anything like her grasping stepfather, yes," Fedir answered. "On the other hand, she may well be someone you could comfortably live with."

The king didn't look like he believed his own words.

Frankly, Demyan wasn't sure he did, either, but his future was clear. His duty to his country and the well-being of his family left only one course of action open to him.

Seduce and marry the unpolished scientist.

CHAPTER ONE

DEMYAN SLID THE black-rimmed nonprescription glasses on before pushing open the door to the lab building. The glasses had been his uncle's idea, along with the gray Armani cardigan Demyan wore over his untucked dress shirt—no tie. The jeans he wore to complete the "geeky corporate guy" attire were his own idea and surprisingly comfortable.

He'd never owned a pair. He'd had the need to set the right example for his younger cousin, Crown Prince to Volyarus, drummed into Demyan from his earliest memory.

He'd done his best, but they were two very different men.

Maksim was a corporate shark, but he was also an adept politician. Demyan left politics to the diplomats.

For now, though, he would tone down his fierce personality with clothes and a demeanor that would not send his prey running.

He knocked perfunctorily on the door before entering the lab where Chanel Tanner worked. The room was empty but for the single woman working through her lunch hour as usual, according to his investigator's report.

Sitting at a computer in the far corner, she typed in quick bursts between reading one of the many volumes spread open on the cluttered desktop.

"Hello." He pitched his voice low, not wanting to startle her.

No need to worry on that score. She simply waved her hand toward him, not even bothering to turn around. "Leave it on the bench by the door."

"Leave what, precisely?" he asked, amused in spite of himself by her demeanor.

"The package. Do you really need to know what's in it? No one else ever asks," she grumbled as she scribbled something down.

"I do not have a package. What I do have is an appointment."

Her head snapped up, red curly hair flying as she spun her chair to face him. "What? Who? You're Mr. Zaretsky?"

He nodded, impressed by the perfect pronunciation of his name.

"You aren't expected for another half an hour." She jumped to her feet, the pocket of her lab coat catching the edge of a book and knocking it to the floor. "And you're going to be late. Corporate types interested in funding our research always are."

"And yet I am early." He crossed the room and picked up the book to hand to her.

Taking it, she frowned, her small nose scrunching rather charmingly. "I noticed."

"Eventually, yes."

Pink stained her cheeks, almost washing out the light dusting of freckles. "I thought you were the delivery guy. He flirts. I don't like it, so I ignore him if at all possible."

The woman was twenty-nine years old and could count the number of dates she'd had in the past year on less than the fingers of one hand. Demyan would think she might welcome flirting.

He did not say that, of course. He gave her the smile

he used on women he wanted to bed. "You have no filter, do you?"

"Are *you* flirting with me?" she demanded, her gray eyes widening in shock.

"I might be." Awkward and this woman were on very friendly speaking terms.

Her brows furrowed and she looked at him with evident confusion. "But why?"

"Why not?"

"I'm hospitably inept, not desperate."

"You believe you are inept?"

"Everyone believes I'm *socially awkward,* particularly my family. Since not one of them has trouble making friends and maintaining a busy social life, I bow to their superior knowledge in the area."

"I think you are charming." Demyan shocked himself with the knowledge that he spoke the truth.

An even bigger but not unwelcome surprise was that he found the geeky scientist unexpectedly attractive. She wasn't his usual cover model companion, but he would like very much if she would take off her lab coat and give him the opportunity to see her full figure.

"Some people do at first, but it wears off." She sighed, looked dejected for a few short seconds before squaring her shoulders and setting her features into an expression no doubt meant to hide her thoughts. "It's all right. I'm used to it. I have my work and that's what is really important."

He'd learned that about her, along with a great deal else from the investigation he'd had performed on top of the dossier his uncle had provided. "You're passionate about your research."

"It's important."

"Yes, it is. That is why I am here."

The smile she bestowed on him was brilliant, her gray

eyes lighting to silver. "It is. You're going to make it possible for us to extend the parameters of our current study."

"That is the plan." He'd determined that approaching
her in the guise of a corporate investor was the quickest
way to gain Chanel's favor.

He'd obviously been right.

"Why are you here?" she asked.

"I thought we'd been over that."

"Most corporations donate without sending someone
to check our facility over."

"Are you offended Yurkovich Tanner did not opt to
do so?"

"No, just confused."

"Oh?"

"How will you know if this is a good setup or not? I
mean, even the most fly-by-night operation can make their
lab look impressive to a layman."

"The University of Washington is hardly a fly-by-night
operation."

"No, I know, but you know what I mean."

"You really have no filter, do you?"

"Um, no?"

"You as good as called me stupid."

"No." She shook her head for emphasis.

"The implication is there."

"No, it's not. No more than I consider myself stupid
because I could stare at my car's engine from dawn to
dusk and still not be able to tell you where the catalytic
converter is."

"It's under the engine."

"Is it?"

"Point taken, but you knew your car exhaust system
has one. Just as I know the rudimentary facts about lab
research."

"I know about the catalytic converter because my mother's was stolen once. I guess it's a thing for young thugs to steal them and sell them for the precious metal. Mom was livid."

"As she had a right to be."

"I suppose, but getting a concealed weapons permit and storing a handgun in her Navigator's glove box was taking it about sixty million steps too far. It wasn't as if she was in the car when they stole the thing."

Demyan felt his lips twitching, the amusement rolling through him an unusual but not unwelcome reaction. "I am sure you are right."

"Is English your second language?"

"It is." But people rarely realized that. "I do not speak with an accent."

"You don't use a ton of contractions either."

"I prefer precise communication."

Her storm-cloud gaze narrowed in thought. "You're from Volyarus, aren't you?"

He felt his eyes widen in surprise. "Yes."

"Don't look so shocked. My great-great-grandfather helped discover the oil fields of Volyarus. Did you really think I wouldn't know that the Seattle office of Yurkovich Tanner is just a satellite? They paid for my university education. It was probably some long-ago agreement with Bartholomew Tanner."

She was a lot closer than was comfortable to the truth. "He was bequeathed the title of baron, which would make you a lady."

"I know that, but my mom doesn't." And from Chanel's tone, she didn't want the older woman finding out. "Besides, the title would only pass to me if I were direct in line with no older sibling."

"Do you have one?" he asked, knowing the answer but following the script of a stranger.

"No."

"So you are Dame Tanner, Lady Chanel, if you prefer."

Her lovely pink lips twisted with clear distaste. "I prefer just Chanel."

"Your mother is French?" he asked, continuing the script he'd carefully thought out beforehand.

Demyan was always fully prepared.

"No. She loves the Chanel label, though."

"She named you after a designer brand?" His investigators had not revealed that fact.

"It's no different than a parent naming their child Mercedes, or something," Chanel replied defensively.

"Of course."

"She named me more aptly than she knew."

"Why do you say that?" he asked with genuine surprise and curiosity.

He would have thought it was the opposite.

"Mom loves her designers, but what she never realized was that Coco Chanel started her brand because she believed in casual elegance. She wore slacks when women simply did *not*. She believed beauty should be both effortless and comfortable."

"Did she?"

"Oh, yes. Mom is more of the 'beauty is pain' school of thought. She wishes I were, too, but well, you can see I'm not." Chanel indicated her lab coat over a simple pair of khaki slacks and a blue T-shirt.

The T-shirt might not be high fashion, but it clung to Chanel's figure in a way that revealed her unexpectedly generous curves. She wasn't overweight, but she wasn't rail thin either, and if her breasts were less than a C cup, he'd be surprised.

That information had not been in her dossier, either.

"You're staring at my breasts."

"I apologize."

"Okay." She sighed. "I'm not offended, but I'm not used to it. My lab coat isn't exactly revealing and the men around here, well, they stare at my data more than me."

"Foolish men."

"If you say so."

"I do."

"You're flirting again."

"Are you going to try to ignore me like the delivery man?"

"Am I going to see you again to ignore you?"

"Oh, you will definitely see me again."

As hard as Chanel found it to believe, the gorgeous corporate guy had meant exactly what he said. And not in a business capacity.

He wanted to see *her* again. She hadn't given him her number, but he'd called to invite her to dinner. Which meant he'd gone to the effort to get it. Strange.

And sort of flattering.

Then he'd taken her to an independent film she'd mentioned wanting to see.

Chanel didn't date. She was too awkward, her filters tuned wrong for normal conversation. Even other scientists found her wearing in a social setting.

Only, Demyan didn't seem to care. He never got annoyed with her.

He didn't get offended when she said something she shouldn't have. He didn't shush her in front of others, or try to cut off her curious questioning of their waiter on his reasoning behind recommending certain meals over others.

It was so different than being out with her family that

Chanel found her own awareness of her personal failings diminishing with each hour she spent in Demyan's company.

She'd never laughed so much in the company of another person who wasn't a scientist. Had never felt so comfortable in a social setting with *anyone*.

Tonight they were going to a dinner lecture: *Symmetry Relationships and the Theory of Point and Space Groups*. She'd been wanting to hear this particular visiting lecturer from MIT for a while, but the outing had not been her idea.

Demyan had secured hard-to-come-by tickets for the exclusive gathering and invited her.

She'd been only too happy to accept, and not just because of the lecture. If he'd invited her to one of the charity galas her mother enjoyed so much, Chanel would have said yes, too.

In Demyan's company, even she might have a good time at one of those.

Standing in front of the full-length mirror her mother had insisted Chanel needed as part of her bedroom decor, she surveyed her image critically.

Chanel didn't love designer fashion and rarely dressed up, but no way could she have been raised by her mother and *not* know how to put the glad rags on.

Tonight, she'd gone to a little more effort than on her previous two dates with Demyan. Chanel had felt the first two outings were flukes, anomalies in her life she refused to allow herself to get too excited over.

After all, he would get that glazed look at some point during the evening and then not call again. Everyone did. Only, Demyan hadn't and he had—called, that is.

And maybe, just maybe, she and the corporate geek had a chance at something more than the connection of two bouncing protons.

He understood what she was talking about and spoke in a language she got. Not like most people. It was the most amazing thing.

And she wanted him. Maybe it was being twenty-nine or something, but her body overheated in his presence big-time.

She'd decided that even if their relationship didn't have a future, she wanted it to have everything she could get out of it in the present.

Both her mother and stepfather had made it clear they thought Chanel's chance of finding a lifelong love were about as good as her department getting better funding than the Huskies football program.

Nil.

Deep inside, Chanel was sure they were right. She was too much like her father—and hadn't Beatrice said she'd married him only because she was pregnant with Chanel?

Chanel wasn't trapping anyone into marriage, but she wouldn't mind tripping Demyan into her too-empty bed.

With that in mind, she'd pulled out the stops when dressing for their dinner tonight. Her dress was a hand-me-down Vera Wang from her mother.

It hadn't looked right on the more petite woman's figure, but the green silk was surprisingly flattering to Chanel's five feet seven inches.

The bodice clung to her somewhat generous breasts, while the draping accentuated her waist and the line of her long legs.

It wasn't slutty by any stretch, but it was sexy in a subtle way she trusted Demyan to pick up on. She would usually have worn it with sensible pumps that didn't add more than an inch to her height.

But not tonight. Demyan was nearly six-and-a-half feet

tall; he could deal more than adequately with a companion in three-inch heels.

Chanel had practiced wearing them on and off all day in the lab.

Her colleagues asked if she was doing research for a physics experiment. She'd ignored their teasing and curiosity for the chance to be certain of her ability to walk confidently in the heels.

And she'd discovered it *was* like riding a bike. Her body remembered the lessons her mom had insisted on in Chanel's younger years.

The doorbell rang and she rushed to answer it.

Demyan stood on the other side, his suit a step up from his usual attire on their dates, too.

He adjusted his glasses endearingly and smiled, his mahogany gaze warm on her. "You look beautiful."

Her hand went to the crazy red curls she rarely did much to tame. Tonight she'd used the full regimen of products her mother had given her on her last birthday, along with a lecture about not getting any younger and looking like a rag doll in public. "Thank you."

"Do we have time for a drink before we leave for the dinner?" he asked, even as he herded her back into the small apartment and closed the door behind him.

"Yes, of course." Heat climbed up her neck. "I don't keep alcohol on hand, though."

The look in his eyes could only be described as predatory, but his words were innocuous enough. "Soda will do."

"Iced green tea?" she asked, feeling foolish.

Her mother often complained about the food and drink Chanel kept on hand, using her inadequacies as a hostess to justify the infrequent motherly visits.

Demyan's eyes narrowed as if he could read Chanel's thoughts. "Iced tea is fine."

"It's green tea," she reiterated. Why hadn't she at least bought soda, or something?

"Green tea is healthy."

"Lots of antioxidants," she agreed. "I drink it all the time."

He didn't ask if the caffeine kept her up, but then the man drank coffee with his meals and had gotten a large-size fully caffeinated Coca-Cola at the movie.

"I keep both caffeinated and decaf on hand," she offered anyway.

"I'll take the caffeine. I have a feeling we'll be up late tonight." The look he gave her was hot enough to melt magma.

Suddenly, it felt as if all the air had been sucked out of her apartment's cheerfully decorated living room. "I'll just get our tea."

He moved, his hand landing on her bare arm. "Don't run from me."

"I'm not." How could two simple words come out sounding so breathless?

His hand slid up her arm and over and down again, each inch of travel leaving bursts of sensation along every nerve ending in its wake, landing proprietarily against the small of her back. "I like this dress."

"Thank you." Somehow she was getting closer to him, her feet moving of their own volition, no formed thought in her brain directing them.

"You're wearing makeup."

She nodded. No point in denying it.

"I didn't think you ever did."

"I stopped, except for special occasions, after I moved away from home."

"An odd form of rebellion."

"Not when you have a mother who insists on image

perfection. I wore makeup from sixth grade on, the whole works."

"And you hated it."

"I did."

"Yet you are wearing it now." The hand not resting on her back came up to cup her nape. "For the visiting MIT professor?"

"No."

"I didn't think so." Then Demyan's head lowered, his mouth claiming hers with surprisingly confident kisses.

And she couldn't think at all.

Sparks of pleasure kindled where their lips met and exploded through her in a conflagration of delight. It was only a kiss. He was barely touching her, just holding her, really. And yet she felt like they were in the midst of making love.

Not that she'd actually done the deed, but she'd come close and it hadn't been anything as good or intimate as this single kiss. She'd been naked with a man and felt less sensation, less loss of control.

Small whimpers sounded and she realized they were coming from her. There was no room for embarrassment at the needy sounds. She wanted too desperately.

She'd read about this kind of passion, but thought it was something writers made up, like werewolves and sentient beings on Mars. She had always believed that this level of desire wasn't real.

Before meeting Demyan.

Before this kiss.

The hands on her became sensual manacles, their hold deliciously unbreakable. She didn't *want* to break it. Didn't want to take a single solitary step away from Demyan.

Their mouths moved together, his tongue barely touching hers in the most sensual kind of tasting. He used his hold on her nape to subtly guide her head into the position he wanted and she found it unbearably exciting to be mastered in this small way.

Demyan was one hundred percent in control of the kiss, and Chanel reveled in it with every single one of her sparking nerve centers.

The hand on her waist slid down to cup her bottom. He squeezed. The muscles along her inner walls spasmed with a need she'd never known to this intensity.

She'd been tempted to make love before, but never to the point of overcoming the promise she'd made to herself never to have sex—only to ever make love. In her mind, that had always meant being married and irrevocably committed to the man she shared her body with.

For the first time, she considered it could well mean giving her body to someone she loved.

Not that she loved Demyan. How could she? They barely knew each other.

The feelings inside her had to be lust, but they were stronger than anything she'd ever considered possible.

He kneaded her backside with a sensual assurance she could not hope to show. She tilted her pelvis toward him, needing something she wasn't ready to give a name to. Her hip brushed the unmistakable proof of his excitement; they moaned into one another's mouths, the sounds adding to the press of desire between them.

The knowledge he wanted her, too, poured through her like gasoline on the fire of her desire.

Her hands clutched at his crisp dress shirt as she rocked against him, wanting more, needing something only he could give her. He rocked back against her, the sounds coming from him too feral and sexy for the "normal corporate guy" he was on the outside.

The disparity so matched her own newly discovered

sexual being inside the science geek, the connection she felt with him quadrupled in that moment.

Without warning, he tore his mouth from hers and stepped back, his breathing heavy, his eyes dark and glittery with need. "Now is not the time."

Her own vision hazy with passion, all that she saw in focus was his face, the expression there an odd mixture of confusion and primal sexual need that could not be mistaken.

Even by someone as socially inept as she was.

Why was he confused? Didn't he realize how much she wanted him, too?

"We don't have to go to the dinner." She stated the obvious.

CHAPTER TWO

"No. We will go." He took a deep breath, like he was trying to rein in the passion she so desperately wanted him to let loose.

On her.

What would it be like to be the center of the storm she could see swirling in his intent gaze?

Shivering, she knew with absolute certainty that was one query she wanted answered.

"Do not look at me like that," he ordered.

"Like what?"

"You want to be naked," he gritted out as if it was an accusation.

Though how could it be? With the erection pushing so insistently against his dinner trousers, there could be no question his body was on board with hers in the desire department.

More to the point, *she* wanted *him* naked, but she didn't have the moisture in her mouth to say so. She simply nodded a hazy agreement.

"No. We have the dinner. Sex…" He shook his head as if finding something difficult to comprehend. "Sex will come later."

"Please tell me you aren't into delayed gratification." She'd found her voice and cringed at how blunt she'd been, not to mention needy sounding. "It's just that I don't get a lot of gratification at all. I don't want to put it off."

She snapped her mouth shut, biting her lips from the inside to stop any more untoward words from escaping.

Instead of reassuring her that it would be perfectly okay to miss the lecture, and dinner, and anything else that stood between them and making love, he seemed amused by her words. Darn it.

Demyan's mouth curved slightly and the need in his eyes receded a little. "Rest assured when we make love, you will not feel in any way ungratified."

Chanel usually objected to the euphemism of lovemaking for what was essentially a physical act between two people. An act she had heretofore refused to indulge in completely. They weren't in love, so how could they make love?

Only, she found the words of objection stuck in her throat. In fact, she could do nothing but agree with his assertion. "I'm sure."

He might be something of a corporate geek, but his confidence in his sexual prowess was too ingrained not to be well based.

Demyan helped Chanel into her seat, his head still reeling from how quickly he'd lost control with her back at the apartment.

He'd very nearly taken her right there in the living room. No finesse. No seduction. Just raw, consuming, *needy* passion.

Demyan did not do consuming. He did not do need.

Raw exposure of desire was for other men. He didn't hold back, but he didn't lose control either. He was known for showing maximum restraint in the sexual realms, bringing his partners to levels of pleasure they showed great appreciation for.

He did not lose it over a simple kiss.

His tongue had barely penetrated Chanel's mouth. With two layers of clothing between them, their bodies had not been able to touch intimately. He'd still been so close to coming, he'd had to pull away before he shamed himself with a reaction he'd never even evinced in adolescence.

The plan had been to give *her* a small taste of passion before leaving the apartment, to flirt with Chanel in subtly sexual ways over dinner and then leave her after a make-out session that left her wanting more.

Gaining her acquiescence to a hasty marriage with the prenuptial agreement the royal family's lawyers had already drawn up required strict adherence to his carefully thought out strategy.

The plan was to keep her reason clouded by emotion, unfulfilled lust built into consuming desire being the primary element.

He didn't plan to consummate their relationship for another week, at least. He wanted her blinded by her own physical wants, ready to commit to him sexually and emotionally.

Instead, he felt like an untried boy gasping for the chance to feel up under her skirt.

"Are you okay?" Chanel asked, worry in her tone.

Shaking off the disturbing thoughts, he gave her his most winning smile. "Of course. I am here with you, aren't I?"

"Don't say things like that." Her frown was far too serious for his liking.

"Why not, when they are true?"

"They don't *sound* true." There was too much knowing

in her gray eyes for his comfort. "That smile you give me sometimes, it's just like a plastic mannequin."

How odd that she should claim to know the difference. No one doubted his sincerity.

A smile was a smile. Except when it wasn't. As he well knew but had not expected his less-than-socially-adept companion to. Taken aback, he sat down, noting as he did so the interested looks of their neighbors.

He turned the smile on them. "What do you say? Am I sincere?" he asked an older woman wearing something he was sure fit a lecture hall better than a formal dinner hosted in the Hilton ballroom.

Her returning smile was the besotted one he was used to getting from women. Even academics. "Very. Perhaps your companion can't help her insecurities. Women like us don't usually snag such lovely escorts."

Chanel made a small, almost wounded sound next to him.

Before he could respond to it, the short, rather round man beside the older woman puffed up like a rooster. "Is that meant to imply that I am not as imposing?"

The woman looked at her date, and the smile she gave him shone with the kind of emotion Demyan found incomprehensible. "No, you are not, and that's exactly the way I love you. I would not have married you nearly forty years ago and stayed this long otherwise."

Feathers suitably smoothed, the man relaxed again in his chair, even deigning to give a somewhat superior smile to Demyan before turning to his wife. "Love you, too, m'dear."

The older couple became obviously lost in a moment Demyan felt uncomfortable witnessing. He turned his attention to Chanel, only to find her frowning, her expression sad and troubled.

"What is it?"

"She's right. You don't belong with me."

"That is not what she said, Chanel." He put his hand on the green-silk-clad thigh closest to him. "I would say there is great evidence to the contrary."

"What do you mean?"

He did not answer, but his expression was as meaningful as he could make it.

He could tell the exact moment all the tumblers clicked into place in Chanel's scientific brain.

Her eyes widened, color surging up her neck into her face. "That's just chemistry. A kiss hardly constitutes a claim."

On that, he could not agree. Loss of control or not, their kiss had been a definite claim-staking on his part. "I'm surprised a woman of your education would declare there was anything *mere* about chemistry."

"We're *here*."

"And?"

"And if the chemistry was so amazing, we wouldn't be."

He couldn't believe she'd said that. He'd damn near ruined a pair of Armani trousers because of the heat between them.

They were not back at her apartment making love for two important reasons only, and neither had a thing to do with how much he'd wanted what she offered so innocently.

Making love tonight wasn't according to plan. Even if it had been, Demyan would have changed the plan because he'd needed the distance from his passion.

He couldn't tell her that, though. Not even close. "I thought you wanted to hear this lecture."

"I did."

He let one brow quirk.

"I do," she admitted with the truculence of a child, made

all the more charming because he was fairly certain she had not been a truculent child.

Just a very different one than her mother had expected her to be.

From everything he'd learned about her, both from the investigative dossier and herself, Chanel Tanner took after her father, not her mother. Not even a little. Mrs. Saltzman had clearly found that very trying when raising her daughter.

An hour later, Chanel looked up from the furious notes she'd been taking for the past twenty minutes on her smartphone. "I'm enjoying myself. Thank you."

A genuine smile creased his lips. "You're welcome."

He liked seeing her like this, enthusiastic, clearly in her element.

"Dr. Beers has made at least two points I hadn't considered before. They're definitely worth additional consideration and research." Chanel glowed with satisfaction Demyan found oddly enticing.

He liked this confident side of her.

Afterward, Demyan made sure she got the opportunity to talk to not only the visiting lecturer but also the head of the university department overseeing her lab's research.

Her boss, who had attended the dinner as well, kept shooting her accusing glances from across the ballroom.

Demyan observed, "The head of your research is not happy to see you here."

"He doesn't like any of his assistants to make connections outside the department." Chanel didn't sound particularly bothered by that fact.

"That is very shortsighted."

"He's a brilliant scientist, but petty as a human being." She shrugged. "I have no aspirations to run my own lab."

"Why not?"

"Too much politics involved." She looked almost guilty. "I like the science."

That sounded like what Demyan knew of her father. "Why the frown?"

"My mother and stepfather would be a lot happier if I had more ambition, or any at all, really."

"Yes?"

"When Yurkovich Tanner offered my schooling scholarship, they made it clear I could attend any school I wanted to."

This was not news to Demyan, but perhaps she would explain why she'd opted for a local state school when she'd had the brains, the grades and the SAT scores to attend MIT, or the like.

"You graduated from Washington State University."

"It was close to home. I didn't want to move away."

Pity. It might have done both Chanel and her mother a world of good. "You were still looking for a relationship with your mother."

He understood that, though he'd never told another soul. His parents had given him up in everything but name, but he'd never cut ties completely with them.

He'd spent his angst-ridden teen years waiting for them to wake up and realize he was still their son. It hadn't happened and by the time he left to attend university in the States, he'd come to accept it never would.

"I think I still am," Chanel answered with a melancholy he did not like.

"You are very different people."

"I'm the odd one."

"You are not odd." Unique, but not in a bad way.

"I wasn't the daughter she wanted. My younger sister is the much-improved model."

"That's ridiculous. You are exactly as you should be."

"Sometimes even I think you're being sincere."

Once again, she'd startled him. Because she was right. In that moment, he'd been speaking nothing but the truth with no thought of his final agenda.

Chanel wasn't sure of the proper way to go about inviting a man up to her apartment for sex.

Demyan wasn't making it easy, either. She wasn't entirely sure, despite the kiss earlier, that he would accept. He'd been attentive over dinner, made sure she enjoyed herself to the fullest. She'd even caught him giving her that look, the one that said he wanted her.

Only, she got this strange sense that he was holding back.

And not for the same reason she was so uncertain about this whole sex thing. No way was Demyan a virgin.

She couldn't help it—no matter how much her body was clamoring for sexual congress with this man, there was still a part of her that insisted that *act* was supposed to be a special one. Not very scientific of her, she knew.

Everyone from her mother, who had given up on Chanel's nonexistent love life, to friends who could not comprehend her "romanticized view of sex," agreed on one thing. Chanel's virginity was just another sign of how she did not fit into the world around her.

But making love was supposed to be something more than two bodies finding physical release, she was sure of it.

Chanel had never wanted just sex. Wasn't sure what effect it would have on her sense of self if she indulged in it now.

Things looked different at twenty-nine than they had at nineteen, though.

She should be more relaxed about the prospect of casually sharing her body with another person. She wasn't.

If anything, the older she got the more important she realized each human connection she made was. Sex was *supposed* to be the ultimate act of intimacy.

She had to admit she'd never felt the bone-deep connection with the few men in her past that she'd felt in that single kiss with Demyan.

She wasn't stupid. She knew losing the two people in her life who had loved her unconditionally at the tender age of eight had made her reticent about opening up to others, particularly men.

Her father and grandfather.

Chanel's stepfather hadn't loved her at all, never mind without limits. As for her mother, Chanel was twenty-nine and the jury was still out on that one.

Which, as an adult woman, had nothing to do with the question of if and how Chanel should offer her invitation to Demyan.

His car slid to a halt by the curb outside her apartment building. He cut the engine, reaching to unclip his belt in one smooth move.

Maybe she wouldn't have to figure it out, after all.

"You're coming up?"

"I will see you to your door."

"It's not necessary." She could have smacked herself. "I mean, only if you want to."

Oh, that was so much better.

One dark brow lifted as he pushed his door open. "Have I ever left you to see yourself inside?"

"It's only our third date." Hardly enough time to set a precedent in stone.

Her own words hit her with the force of a solid particle mass traveling beyond the speed of light. What was she thinking? *Sex with him when they'd barely spent more than a minute in each other's company?*

Still remembering the pleasure of his kiss earlier, her body screamed *yes* while her mind sounded a warning Klaxon of *nos*.

No closer to a verdict about how to handle the rest of the night, she stalled in frozen indecision.

Her door was opened and Demyan bent toward her in his too-darn-sexy dinner suit, his hand reaching toward her. "Are you coming?"

She fumbled with her seat belt, getting it unbuckled after the second try.

The knowing look in his dark eyes said he knew why she was so uncoordinated.

"Don't," she ordered.

The knowing glance turned into a smirk. "Don't?"

"You're smug," Chanel accused as she climbed from the car, eschewing the help of his hand.

Ignoring her attempt to keep her distance, he put his hand around her waist, tucking her body close to his as they approached her building. "I am delighted by your company."

Heat arced between them and, that quickly, she remembered why after only three dates she was ready to break a lifetime habit of virginity.

"I'm still not sure why we're here."

"You live here?" Amusement laced his voice as he led her into the unsecured building.

The lack of a doorman was a bone of contention between Chanel and her mother. If the older woman had been concerned for her safety, Chanel might have considered moving, but the issue was in how it *looked* for her to live in an unpretentious, entirely suburbanite apartment complex.

"I do not like the fact that the entrance to your home is so accessible. This dark cove outside your door is not entirely secure, either," Demyan complained as he took her keys and unlocked the door.

She hadn't quite decided if the action was some throwback to old-world charm or simply indicative of his dominating nature when he ushered her inside.

They moved into the living room and he shut the door behind them. There was meaning in that, right? The shut door. If he'd wanted only to see her inside, he could have left her on the landing.

"Would you like a drink or something?" Like her?

Was she really going to do this? Chanel thought maybe she was.

"Not tonight." The words implied he planned to leave, but the way he stepped closer to her gave an entirely different meaning.

She didn't reply, his proximity stealing her breath just that fast. For the first time in her life, she began to understand *how* her mother, Beatrice, had ended up pregnant by a man so very different from herself.

Sex *was* a powerful force. "Body chemistry is so much more potent than I ever believed." She sounded every bit as bewildered as she felt.

"Because you have never felt it so strongly with someone else." There was no question mark at the end of *that* sentence.

Chanel would take umbrage at the certainty in his tone if Demyan didn't speak the absolute truth.

"I'm sure *you* have."

Something strange moved across his features. Surprise? Maybe confusion. "No."

"You stopped earlier, not me."

"It was not easy."

Was that supposed to make her feel better about the fact he'd been more determined to go to the lecture than *she'd* been? Sarcasm infused her voice as she said, "I'm glad to hear that."

His eyes narrowed, a spark of irritation showing before it disappeared. She wasn't surprised. Demyan might not be the corporate shark her stepfather was, but he was not a man who liked to lose control, either.

Not that he had. Now, *or* earlier.

He had stopped after all, and right now, as much as she could read desire in his dark gaze, he wasn't acting on it.

She, on the other hand, was seconds away from kissing him silly. She, who had never initiated a kiss in her life.

"Do you want to stay?" she asked baldly.

Subtlety was all well and good for a woman who found the role of flirt comfortable, but that woman wasn't Chanel.

He smiled down at her. "Do you want me to?"

"I don't know."

Shock held his face immobile for the count of three seconds. *"You don't know?"*

She shook her head.

"You didn't seem unsure about what you wanted earlier tonight." Disbelief laced his voice.

She nodded, making no attempt to deny it. Subterfuge was not her thing. "I barely know you."

"Is that how it feels to you?"

She experienced that strange sense of disparity she'd had with him before. The words were right, the expression concurrent and yet, she felt the lack of sincerity.

Only, unlike at the dinner, there was a vein of honesty in his words that confused her.

"You already know you could take me to bed with very little effort."

"I assure you, the effort will not be minimal." Sensual promise vibrated in every word.

Chanel felt his promise to her very core and her thighs

squeezed together in involuntary response, not because she feared what he wanted but because it made her ache with a need she'd never known.

"That's not what I meant." Her voice cracked on the last word, but she pretended not to notice.

The slight flaring of his nostrils and the way his eyes went just that much darker said he had, though. "What did you mean then, *little one?*"

"I'm hardly little." At five foot seven, she was above average in height for a woman.

"Do not avoid the question."

"I wasn't trying to." She'd just been trying to clarify, because that was familiar territory.

The rest of this? Was not.

Only he knew how tall she was, so if he wanted to call her *little one,* maybe that was okay. "I suppose I do seem kind of short to you. You're not exactly average height for a man in North America, though maybe I should be comparing you to Ukrainians, as that's your country's formative gene pool."

In fact, he was well above average height, certainly taller than most of the men in her life, and that gave her a peculiar kind of pleasure. Which, like many things she'd discovered since meeting him, surprised her about herself.

She'd never thought she would enjoy feeling *protected* when she was with a man, or that the difference in their height would even succeed in making her feel that way. Maybe it wasn't just that difference but something else about Demyan entirely.

Something intangible that didn't quite match his casual designer sweaters and dark-rimmed glasses.

"You do not seem *short.*" He tugged at one of her red curls, a soft smile playing about his lips as if he could read her thoughts and was amused by them. "You are just right."

This time there was no conflict between the words and sincerity in his manner.

But it put the times there was in stark relief in her mind. "I can't make you out."

"What do you mean?" He looked surprised again and she got the definite impression that didn't happen a lot with him.

"Sometimes I think you mean everything you say, but then there are times, like at dinner tonight, when it seems like you're saying what you think I want to hear."

"I have not lied to you." Affront echoed through his tone.

"Haven't you?"

"No." Dead certainty, and then almost as if it was drawn from him without his permission, "I have not told you everything about myself."

"I didn't expect you to bring along an information dossier on our first date." Of course she didn't know everything about him; that was part of the dating process, wasn't it? "You don't know everything about me, either."

His gaze turned cold, almost ruthless. Then he adjusted his glasses and the look disappeared. "I know what I need to."

Sometimes there was a glimmer of another man there—a man that even a shark like Perry would swim from in a frantic effort to escape. Then Demyan would smile and the impression of that other man would dissipate.

CHAPTER THREE

DEMYAN DIDN'T SMILE now, but she knew the man in front of her wasn't a shark.

Not like the overcritical Perry, and definitely not like someone even more ruthless than her stepfather. There was too much kindness in Demyan, even if he was wholly unaware of it, as Chanel suspected he was.

"What did you mean earlier?" he asked, pulling her back to the original question.

Oh, yes…right.

"It's just…you must realize I'm a sure thing. Even if I'm not sure I *want* to be."

"Why aren't you sure?" he asked, deflecting himself this time.

Or maybe he just really wanted to know. Being the center of someone else's undivided attention when she wasn't discussing her work wasn't something Chanel was used to.

When she was with Demyan, he focused solely on her, though, as if nothing was more important to him. He wanted to know things others reacted to with impatience, not interest. It was a heady feeling.

Even so, peeling away the layers to reveal her full self to him wasn't easy. "You'll laugh."

"Is it funny?"

"Not to me." Not even a little.

"Then I will not laugh."

"How can you be so perfect?"

"So long as I am perfect for you, that is all that matters."

"Do you mean that?"

"Yes." There could be no doubting the conviction in his tone or handsome features.

"Why?"

"Are you saying you feel differently?" he asked in a tone that implied he knew the answer.

"Love at first sight doesn't happen."

"Maybe for some people it does."

All the breath seemed to leave the room at his words. "Are you saying…" She had to clear her throat, suck in air and try again. "Are you saying you feel the same?"

"I want to be your perfect man."

"You mean that." And maybe it was past time she stopped doubting his sincerity.

How much of her feeling he was saying what she wanted to hear stemmed from her own insecurities? Why was it so hard for her to accept that this man didn't need her to be something or someone different to want to be with her?

The answer was the years spent in a family she simply didn't fit, the daughter of a mother and stepfather who found constant fault with a child too much like her own father for their comfort.

"I do."

She nodded, accepting. Believing. "I've never had sex."

Once again she'd managed to shock him. And this time she didn't have to look for subtle signs.

His whisker-shadowed jaw dropped and dark eyes widened comically. "You are twenty-nine."

"I'm not staring retirement in the face, or something." She had eleven more years of relatively safe childbearing, even.

Not that she thought she was going to marry and have children. She'd given up on that idea when she realized that even in the academic world, Chanel was a social misfit.

"No, I didn't mean that." But his voice was still laced with surprise and his superior brain was clearly *not* firing on all cylinders. "You're educated. *American.*"

"So?" What in the world did her PhD in chemistry have to do with her virginity?

"Are you completely innocent?"

Man, did he even realize how that sounded?

And people thought she was old-fashioned. "Even if I'd had sex, I would still be innocent. Sex isn't a crime."

"You know that is not what I was referring to."

"No, I know, but *innocent?* Come on."

The look he was giving her was way too familiar.

"I'm awkward," she excused with a barely stifled sigh. "I told you." Had he forgotten?

"You are refreshingly direct." That wasn't disappointment in his tone and the look she thought she recognized.

Well, it wasn't. He almost looked admiring. If she believed it, and hadn't she diced to do just that? "Mother calls it ridiculously blunt."

"Your mother does not see you as I do."

"I should hope not."

They both smiled at her small joke that did nothing to dissipate the emotional tension between them.

He put his big hands on her shoulders, his thumbs brushing along her collarbone, the hold possessive like before. And just like earlier, she found a new unexpected part of her that liked that. A lot.

"Demyan." His name just sighed out of her.

She didn't know what she meant by it. What she wanted from him.

He didn't appear similarly lost, his gaze direct and commanding. "You say you've never had sex. I want to know what that means."

It took two tries to get words past her suddenly constricted throat. "Why does it matter?"

"You can ask that?"

"Um, yes." Hadn't she just done?

"You are mine."

"Three dates," she reminded him.

"Love at first sight," he countered.

"You… I…"

"We are going to make love. What I want to know is what you have done to this point." His thumbs continued the sensual caress along her collarbone. "You are going to tell me."

"Bossy much?"

"Only in bed."

She wasn't sure she believed him, was even less sure if it mattered. She wasn't worried about standing up for herself. She'd never conformed when it counted, no matter how much easier it would have made her life—especially with her family.

Right now she found she wanted to answer his question, needed to. Still, she kept it general. "Heavy petting, I guess you'd say."

"Be more specific."

"No." Heat crawled up her neck.

He shouldn't care, should he? Virginity wasn't an issue for modern men. *Or modern women,* her inner voice mocked her, *and yet you are a virgin.*

He bent so close their lips almost touched. "Oh, yes."

Thoughts came and went, no words making it past her lips until she made a sound she'd never heard from her own vocal cords before. It was something like surrender, but more.

It was sexual.

The air between them grew heavy with the most primal kind of desire, pushing against her, demanding her acquiescence.

In a last-ditch desperate bid for space, she shut her eyes, but it did no good. She could feel his stare. Could feel his determination to get an answer.

She was super sensitive to his nearness, too, her body aching to press against his, her lips going soft in preparation for his kiss.

The kiss didn't come.

"Tell me," puffed across her lips.

The sound of his voice whispered through her, increasing the sensual fire burning through her veins.

"It wasn't anything."

"Were you naked?"

"Once."

"Good." He kissed her, his lips barely there and gone before she could lose herself in the caress she wanted more than air or research funding. "When?"

"In college."

He just waited.

"He told me he loved me." She'd wanted to be loved so badly, she realized later.

"You didn't let him into your body."

"No."

"Why?"

"It didn't feel right." Old pain twisted through her heart.

She turned her head away, stepping back when a few seconds before she would have said she wasn't capable of moving at all, much less away from him.

"He hurt you." The growl in Demyan's voice made Chanel's eyes snap open, her gaze searching for him, for visual proof of what had been in his tone.

The anger in his eyes wasn't directed at her, but it still made Chanel shiver. "He broke up with me."

Her ex had called her a dried-up relic, a throwback woman who belonged in a medieval nunnery, not a modern university. Chanel had a lot of experience with disappointing her family, so her ex-boyfriend's words should not have had the power to wound.

She should have been inured.

But they'd cut her deeply, traumatically so.

She'd never shared with another person the experience that had left her convinced her mother and stepfather were right, had never admitted her ultimate failure.

"I'm hopeless with men." What was she doing here, wanting to give her body to a man destined to eviscerate her heart?

He wasn't ever going to stay with her. He said they were going to make love, but they couldn't. He didn't love her, no matter what his words had implied. He couldn't.

She wasn't that woman.

Chanel wasn't a bubbly blonde beauty like her sister, Laura. She wasn't a cool sophisticate like her mother. Chanel was the awkward one who could make perfect marks in chemistry courses but utterly fail at the human kind.

She shook her head, her hands cold and shaking. "You should leave."

Another primal sound of anger came out of him before he crossed the small distance between them and yanked her body into his with tender ruthlessness. "I'm not going anywhere. Not tonight. Not ever."

"You can't make promises like that." His breaking them was going to destroy something inside her that her parents and ex had been unable to touch.

The belief that she was worth *something*.

"I can."

"What? You're going to marry me?" she demanded with pain-filled sarcasm.

"Yes."

She couldn't breathe, her vision going black around the edges. Words were torn from her, but they came out in barely a whisper. "You don't mean that."

He cupped the back of her head, forcing her gaze to meet his. "I do."

"You can't."

"I am a man of my word."

"Always?" she mocked, not believing.

No one kept all their promises. Especially not to her. Hadn't her father told her he'd always be there for her? But then he'd died. Her mother had promised, in the aftermath of Jacob Tanner's death, that she and Chanel would always be a team, that she wouldn't leave her daughter, wouldn't die like her husband.

Beatrice *hadn't* died, but she'd abandoned Chanel emotionally within a year of her marriage to Perry, making it clear from that point on that the only team was the Saltzmans'. Chanel Tanner had no place on it.

"Try me," Demyan demanded, no insecurity about the future in *his* words.

"You'll destroy me."

"No."

"Men like you…" Her words ran out as her heart twisted at the thought of never seeing him again.

"Know our own minds." There was that look in his eyes again.

As if he was a man who always got what he set out to, no matter what he had to do to get it. As if she might as well give in because he *never* would.

"I wanted to wait until I got married. I didn't want to trap someone into a lifetime they would only resent."

"There are such things as birth control."

"My mom was on the Pill when she got pregnant with me. I was not part of her future plans. Neither was my father."

"She didn't have to marry him."

"She loved him. At first." Chanel didn't know when that had changed.

She'd been only eight when her dad died, but she'd believed her parents loved each other deeply and forever. It was her mother's constant criticism and unfavorable comparisons later that made Chanel realize Beatrice had not approved of her husband any more than she did their daughter.

"They were not compatible." Demyan said it like he really knew—not that he could.

"I thought they were, when I was little. I was wrong," she admitted.

"We aren't them. We are compatible."

"You don't know that."

"I know more than you think I do. We belong together." There was a message in his words she couldn't quite decipher, but his dark gaze wasn't giving any hints.

"I told you I was a sure thing." Though she wasn't sure that was true. Part of her was still fighting the idea of total intimacy, especially at the cost of opening herself up like this. "You don't have to say these things."

"I am not a man who makes a habit of saying things I do not mean."

"You never lie." He'd as good as said so earlier.

Something passed across his handsome features. "I have not lied to you."

His implication was unbelievable. "You really plan to marry me. After three dates?"

"Yes." There was so much certainty, such deep conviction in that single word.

She could not doubt him, but it didn't make sense. Her scientific brain could not identify the components of the formula of their interaction that had led to this reaction.

In her lab she knew mixing one substance with another and adding heat, or cold, or simply agitation resulted in identifiable and documented results.

Love wasn't like that. There was nothing predictable about the male-female interaction, especially for her.

But one thing she knew—a man could not hide his true reaction to a woman in bed. It was why she'd refused her ex back at university. He hadn't been completely into it.

Oh, he'd wanted to get off, but she could tell that it didn't matter it was *her* he was getting off with.

"Show me," she challenged Demyan now. "Make me believe."

His eyes narrowed, but he didn't pretend not to understand what she wanted.

Demyan could not let Chanel's challenge go unmet.

Whatever the cretin who had turned her off sex had done to her, at least part of her thought Demyan would do the same thing. He could see it in the wary depths of her gray eyes.

"You will see, *sérdeńko*. I am not that guy."

"You keep calling me little." She didn't sound as if she was complaining, just observing.

He noticed she did that when the emotions got too intense. She retreated behind the barrier of her analytical mind.

When this night was over there would be no barriers between them.

"You speak Ukrainian." Her dossier had mentioned she studied the language, but not how proficient she was.

To translate the endearment, which was a diminutive form of heart, implied a far deeper knowledge of his native tongue than the investigative report had revealed.

"I studied it so I could read scientific texts by notable scientists in their native tongue."

"And *sérdeňko* came up in a scientific text?" he asked with disbelief.

"No." She sighed as if admitting a dark secret. "I like languages. I'm fluent in Ukrainian, Portuguese and German."

"So you could read scientific texts."

"Among other things." She blushed intriguingly.

"What things?" he asked, his mouth temptingly close to hers.

He wanted to kiss her. She wanted the kiss, too—there could be no doubt.

"Erotic romance."

"In Ukrainian?" he asked, utterly surprised for the third time that night.

This woman would never be a boring companion.

"Yes."

"I am amazed."

"Why?"

"If you like reading about sex so much, how are you still a virgin?"

"I like reading murder mysteries, too, but I haven't gone out and killed anybody."

He laughed, unable to remember the last time he'd been so entertained by a female companion.

This marriage he had to bring about would not be a hardship. Chanel Tanner would make a very amiable wife.

With that thought in mind, he took the first step in convincing her that they belonged together.

He kissed her, taking command of her mouth more gently than he might have before her revelation.

She couldn't know it, but her virginity was a gift to him in more ways than one.

First, that he was the only man who would ever share her body in this way was not something to take lightly. Not even in this modern age.

But second, and more important to his efforts on behalf of Volyarus, once Demyan had awakened her passions for the first time, Chanel would be more likely to accept his proposal of marriage.

It meant adjusting his schedule up for her seduction, but he wasn't leaving her tonight. Doing so might cause irreparable harm to the building of trust between them. She needed to know he wanted her, and he did.

Unlikely as he would have considered it, he desired this shy, bookish scientist above all other women.

She didn't want to believe in forever with him, but she would learn. He had spoken the truth earlier. Prince Demyan of Volyarus did not break his promises.

And he had promised King Fedir that Demyan would marry Chanel Tanner.

She whimpered against his lips, her sexual desire so close to the surface he thought she needed her first climax to come early so she could enjoy the lead-up to the next one.

With careful precision, he built the kiss until the small sounds of need were falling from her lips to his in a steady cascade. Control starting to slip, he deepened the kiss, wanting more of her taste, more of her response...more of everything Chanel had to give.

A small voice in the back of his mind prompted that the time had come to pull back and lead her into the bedroom.

Only, his lips didn't want to obey, and for the first time in memory Demyan found himself lost in a kiss, his plans for a suave seduction cracking under the weight of his more primitive need.

He had just the presence of mind to move her backward toward the sofa. Unbelievably, *neither* of them was going to be able to stay vertical much longer.

Demyan maneuvered them both so Chanel sat sprawled across his lap, her dress hiked up, her naked thighs pressing against his cloth-covered ones.

He never let her lips slide so much as a centimeter away from his.

Demyan liked sex. According to Maks, he'd had more than his fair share of partners. Some of them were very experienced in the art of seduction, women who knew exactly how to use their bodies for maximum effect. None of them had turned him on as much as the uncalculated and wholly honest way Chanel responded to his kiss.

She moved with innocent need against him, her body undulating in unconscious sensuality that drove him insane with the need to show her what those types of movements led to.

He brought his hand down and cupped her backside, guiding those untutored rolls of her hips into something that would give them both more pleasure and fan the flames of desire between them into an all-out inferno.

She jolted and moaned as her panty-clad apex rubbed over his trapped hard-on. He couldn't hold back his own sounds of raw sexual desire and keep from arching his hips to increase the friction.

The kiss went nuclear and he did nothing to stop it, demanding entrance into her mouth with his tongue and getting it without even a token resistance.

This woman did not play the coquette. Her honest passion was more exciting than any practiced seduction could be. She couldn't know, though; she was too unused to physical intimacy. For that ignorance, at least, he could be glad.

She could not take advantage of a weakness she did not recognize in him, and damned if he would point it out. He might not be able to control himself completely this first time with her, but no doubt that was a big part of the reason why.

It *was* her first time and he found that highly erotic.

The one benefit was that it was clear Chanel was completely out of control and definitely imprinting on him sexually.

Equally important, after what she'd revealed, was for her to realize *he* wanted *her*.

As she'd demanded, he would show her.

She would never again doubt her feminine appeal to him, not after tonight. And perhaps that, even more than her virginity, would lead her to accept his speed-record-breaking proposal when it came.

That it might no longer be completely about his duty to country was a thought he dismissed as unimportant.

He would have her. She would have him and whether she knew it or not, she needed him. He was good for her.

It started with now, giving her what she hadn't realized she was missing.

After insuring she kept the rhythm that made her body shake, he mapped her body with his hands through the soft green silk of her dress, caressing her in ways reserved for a lover.

He enjoyed this part of sex, touching a woman in ways no one else was allowed and, in Chanel's case, never had been.

Knowing a woman had put her body in his very-capable-to-dole-out-pleasure hands turned him on. Demyan liked *that* control, too. For reasons he didn't feel the need to dwell on, that knowledge was even more satisfying with Chanel than it had been with other women.

She might not realize it, but the kind of response she gave meant she would let him do *anything*. That acknowledgment came with a heady kind of enjoyment destined to undermine his self-control further if he wasn't very careful.

It was important for her pleasure, particularly this first time, that he not let that happen. He had to maintain some level of premeditation, or he could hurt her.

That reminder sobered him enough to think—at least a little—again.

Touching her was good, though. Too damn good.

He cupped her breasts, reveling in the catch of her breath as his thumbs brushed over turgid nipples. He wanted to feel them naked, but even this was incredible.

His sex pressed against the placket of his trousers in response to the feel of her in his hands.

He pinched, knowing the layers of silk and her bra would be no true barrier between those buds and the sensation he gave her.

She tore her mouth from his, her eyes opening, pupils blown with bliss almost swallowing the stormy irises. "I... That..."

"Is good." He did it again, increasing the pressure just enough to give maximum pleasure that might border on pain but would never go over. "Say it."

CHAPTER FOUR

CONFUSION FLITTED ACROSS the sweet oval of Chanel's face. "What?"

"Say it feels good."

She didn't have to speak her refusal—it was there in the way her body stiffened and she averted her gaze.

"Look at me," he demanded, his fingers poised to give more pleasure but not offering it. "Look at me and say it."

Her storm-cloud gaze came back to his, her mouth working, no words coming out.

"You are a woman. You can acknowledge your own pleasure, Chanel. I believe in you."

"It's not that." The word cut off as if her air had run out. She took a deep breath and let it out, her tongue coming out to wet her lips. "I know sex is supposed to feel good."

"Do you?"

"I've read books."

"Erotic books."

"Yes."

"So, say it."

"You want to strip me bare," she accused.

He saw no point in denying it. "Yes."

"Why?"

"You have to let go."

"You never let go."

"I am the experienced one here. If I let go of my control, we'd both be in trouble."

"That doesn't make sense."

"Only because you haven't done this before."

She didn't deny his words. "I like it."

"I know." He pressed just slightly, giving her a taste of what was to come.

She moaned, her head falling back, her eyelids sliding down to cover the vulnerability in her gaze. "So, why do I have to say it?"

"For me. Say it for me."

"It feels good." The words came out in a low, throaty whisper infused with sincerity.

Oh, yes, this woman would learn to hold nothing back.

He rewarded her with more pleasure until she was rocking against him with gasping breaths. "Demyan!"

"What, *sérdeńko?*"

"You know! You have to know."

"This?" he asked as he pushed up to rub his hardness against her, pinching her nipples at the same time.

"Yes."

He did it again, making sure to continue the friction against that bundle of nerves through the damp silk of her panties. "Let go, Chanel."

"I…"

He didn't want arguments. He wanted her surrender. "Come for me, Chanel. You are mine."

And unused to this level of pleasure, she came apart, her body arching into a stiff contortion of delight while a keening wail sounded from her throat.

Oh, yes, this woman belonged to him. Her body knew it, even if her mind was still in some doubt.

He let the shivers of aftershock finish, concentrating on gaining his own breath and a measure of mental fortitude. When he was sure he could do it without his own limbs giving way, he tucked one arm under her bottom and the other against her back and stood with her secure in his hold.

Her head rose from where it had come to rest against his shoulder, her face still flushed with pleasure, her gray gaze meeting his. "What... Where?"

"Your first time will not happen on a sofa, no matter how comfortable."

"It already did."

He shook his head. "That was not sex."

"But it was my first orgasm with another person."

Perhaps that small fact helped to explain why she was still a virgin, too.

He didn't repeat his shock at her age, or his disgust with her previous partners. "It will be the first of many, I promise you."

She swallowed audibly, but nodded with appreciative enthusiasm.

He felt his mouth curve into a very rare and equally genuine smile.

How had she remained untouched so long?

This woman was sweetly sensual and engagingly honest. Far from socially inept. Demyan found her fascinating.

It did not bother him at all, though, that she would be giving her body to him and only him. He would honor the gift and she would find no reason to regret it.

He made the vow to himself, and Demyan never broke his word. Chanel was still trying to catch her breath when Demyan laid her oh so carefully on the bed after yanking back the covers.

Sexual demand radiated off him like heat from a nuclear reactor. Yet there was no impatience in the way he handled her.

The bedding? Yes. It lay in disarray on the floor, his powerful jerks pulling the sheet and blanket that had been tucked between the mattress and box spring completely away.

But her?

He settled with a gentle touch that belied his obvious masculine need.

"I was going to wait." He shrugged out of his suit jacket, letting the designer garment drop to the floor without any outward concern about what that might do to it.

"Why?"

"It seemed the thing to do."

"Because things are moving so fast between us," she said rather than asked.

He only loosened his tie and undid the top buttons on his shirt before pulling the whole thing over his head in one swift movement. "We will not be waiting."

His torso was chiseled in that way really fit men with natural strength were. Dark curls covered his chest, narrowing into a V that disappeared into the waistband of his trousers. She wanted to see where that trail of sexy hair led.

She might be a virgin, but she was pretty sure she wasn't a shy one.

"You are beautiful," she breathed.

"Men are not beautiful." But his eyes smiled at the compliment.

"The statue of David is beautiful."

"That is art."

"So are you."

He shook his head, his hands going to his trouser button. "I am a flesh-and-blood man, never doubt it."

How could she, with all that flesh staring her in the face?

His trousers slid down his legs, revealing CK black knit

boxers that conformed to every ridge of muscle and the biggest ridge of all. His erection.

Her mouth went dry, the moisture going straight to her palms. "You're big, aren't you?"

"I've never compared myself to other men." With that he shucked out of his boxers, leaving his very swollen, very rigid length on display.

"According to scientific studies, the average penile length is five to five-point-seven inches in length when erect." And Demyan was definitely longer, unless her eyes were deceiving her.

But Chanel was a scientist who had conducted enough measurements she could usually guess within a centimeter's accuracy.

He frowned and stopped at the side of the bed, his erection bobbing with the movement even as it curved upward toward his belly. That wasn't usual, either, she'd read. Most men erected perpendicularly with a slight leaning toward one side. Some even had a small downward angle.

For Demyan's hardness to be curving upward, it had to be *extremely* ready for intercourse.

"How do you know that?" he demanded with amusement in his voice.

"I read. A lot."

"You cannot believe everything you read in your Ukrainian erotica."

"Of course not."

His brow rose, the mockery there.

"I read that particular fact in a scientific journal."

His dark gaze pinned her to the bed, though he had yet to join her with his incredibly gorgeous naked body. "We have better things to do than discuss frivolous scientific research."

"It isn't frivolous to the tens of thousands of men who

have been feeling inadequate because of the supposed average lengths gleaned from self-measurement."

"What you are telling me is that men measure themselves as larger than they are?" He definitely sounded amused now.

"I don't think *you* would."

"I would not measure myself at all." From his tone, he found the idea of doing so absolutely ridiculous.

"I think I'd like to measure you."

"No."

"With my hand."

The erection in question jumped at her words and it was her turn to smile.

"Do not tease," he warned.

"I'm not teasing."

"You are smiling."

"I'm just really happy that you react to me so strongly." So strongly in fact that despite the fact she'd led them down one of the conversational byways that always annoyed others, his visible response to her had not dimmed in the least.

"You are a very sexy woman."

She couldn't help laughing at that assertion, but she didn't accuse him of lying. Honest desire burned in the brown depths of his eyes.

"It is time I did something about your lack of focus." He didn't sound mad about it, though.

She just nodded, wanting more of what they'd done in the living room, more kisses, more touching, more of that amazingly intimate connection.

"First we need to get you naked, too."

She'd already kicked her heels off in the living room and she wasn't wearing panty hose. That didn't leave much to get rid of.

She started tugging her skirt up, only to have his hands

join her in the effort. Only somehow he made the slide of silk up her body into a series of sensual caresses, so she was shivering with renewed passion by the time he pulled the green fabric over her head.

He tossed it away.

"My mother would be very annoyed if she saw you treating clothes the way you do." Especially high-end designer ones.

"Your mother has no place in our bedroom."

"It's not *our* bedroom."

"You belong to me. This room belongs to you. Therefore, it is ours."

She couldn't push a denial of his claim through her lips. There was too much truth to it.

It was almost scary, but she wasn't afraid.

In fact, that part of her that had felt alone in the world since her mother's marriage to Perry Saltzman warmed with an inexplicable sense of belonging.

"She's still my mother," was all Chanel could think to say.

"And she always will be, but her views and opinions about you are skewed by grief and a lack of understanding. Therefore, they have no place in our life together."

"We don't have a life together," she said with more vehemence than she felt.

But it was insane, this instant connection, his claim he planned a future with her. It just wasn't real. Couldn't be.

"We do. It starts with this." His hands reached behind her to unhook her bra clasp, sight unseen.

Her nipples, already tightened into hard points from his earlier manipulations, contracted further from the cooled air brushing across them.

There was no stifling the shiver that went through her in response to the extra stimulation.

His smile was predatory. "You have very sensitive breasts."

"Nipples," she couldn't help correcting. It wasn't her entire boob responding, was it?

He brushed his fingertips along the side of her breast, sliding forward, but not touching the nipple.

Desire coiled low in her belly, her body arching toward his.

He did it again. "Very responsive."

"You don't like to be wrong, do you?" she asked in a voice that hitched every other syllable with her gasping breaths.

"It is a rare occurrence."

"Arrogant."

"Certain."

"Same thing."

"It is not." Then he kissed her, preventing any more words.

It was a sneaky way to end an argument, but she couldn't make herself mind. Not when it felt so wonderful. It might be only their lips that were connected, but she felt as if he was touching her to the very depths of her soul.

He pulled back, their breath coming in harsh gasps between them. "One thing left."

"What?" she asked, nothing but his lips making any sense in that moment.

"Your panties."

Were surplus to requirements. She got the picture but found she was hopeless in the face of doing something about it.

It was okay, though. His long masculine fingers were sliding between her hips and the silk and then it was being tugged down, baring the last bit of her to him.

"There will be nothing between us," he growled, as if he could read her mind.

She looked up at him, their gazes locking, and what she saw in his left her in no doubt he *wasn't* just talking about clothing.

He'd pushed her in the living room, demanding she acknowledge her own pleasure, her own desires, this crazy thing happening between them.

He was going to push her further now.

"It's just sex," she claimed with a desperate attempt to believe her own words.

"We are making love, locking our lives together."

"This isn't real."

"It is very real."

"Please…"

He cupped her face, the move one she was becoming quite familiar with and incidentally learning to love. "Please, what?"

"Just tonight? Can it just be about tonight?"

He lowered his head until their lips almost brushed. "No."

This time, she kissed him. Couldn't help herself and was glad she hadn't when he took control and drew forth a response from her body that shouldn't have been possible. Not after she'd just climaxed.

Only it was.

It was as if they were connected by live electric current, energizing, transforming every synapse in its wake, so that her body was uniquely tuned to him. The way that big body blanketed hers, his hardness rubbing against the sensitive curls at the apex of her thighs indicated he was being tuned to the same frequency.

A frequency she thought would rule her body's responses for the rest of her life.

And if she could believe his words, it would.

The kiss pulled her out of time, suspending them in an intimacy that had no limits, not in hours and minutes, or in emotional connection.

It was beyond anything she thought two people could feel together.

His hands were everywhere, bringing pleasure, teaching her body his touch, making that indescribable pleasure spiral tighter and tighter inside her again.

She touched him, too, letting her fingertips learn his body, and just doing that gave her a level of delight she'd never known. She could caress this man, touch his naked skin and he wanted it, wanted *her* touch. Not just any woman's. *Hers.*

An empty ache started, making her body restless for what it had never known.

As if he knew exactly what she needed, he nudged her thighs apart and adjusted his body so the head of his erection pressed against the opening to her body. However, he made no move to enter her.

The moment felt so momentous that tears washed into her eyes and trickled down her temples. He broke the kiss, lifting his head, his expression knowing.

He touched the wetness, wiping at the tears with one finger. "It is not just about tonight."

"It's not supposed to be this big."

"You have waited twenty-nine years, *krýxitka.*"

She wasn't a baby, not by any stretch, but having him call her one didn't feel wrong. "But women don't, anymore."

"You had your reasons."

"I want this."

"I know."

"You do, too."

"Yes."

"With *me*," she confirmed, maybe needing a little more reassurance than she'd realized.

"Only *you* from this point forward."

"You do not believe in infidelity?" A lot of businessmen thought it was their right when they flew out of town to leave their wedding ring in the bedside drawer of their hotel rooms.

Or so she'd read. Honestly, as awful as Perry might be toward Chanel, she couldn't imagine him cheating on her mother. It was one of the reasons she respected him, even if she didn't like the business shark.

She could never respect a man who didn't understand and adhere to the true meaning of loyalty and faithfulness.

"It is too damaging to everyone involved." There was something about Demyan's tone that said he knew exactly what he was talking about.

She would have asked about it, but right now all she could really focus on was how much she needed him inside her. "It's time."

"Not yet."

Unexpected anger welled up. "You're not going to get bossy about this. I'm not begging."

"I don't want you begging. Tonight."

"But—"

He smiled down at her, indulgence and tenderness she wasn't even sure he was aware of glowing in his dark gaze. "You are a virgin. A certain amount of preparation will make the difference between a beautiful experience and one you never want to have to remember."

"You make it sound so dire."

"It can be."

"Much experience deflowering virgins?" she asked with sarcasm and maybe just a hint of jealousy.

"Tonight is not the time for discussing past sexual encounters."

"That isn't what you said earlier."

His jaw hardened but he said, "Fine. She was young. I was young. It was a disaster."

"Did you love her?"

"Not even a little."

"Did she love you?"

"No." No doubt there.

"You decided to figure out how to fix the problem." She could so see him doing that.

She might not know everything there was to about this man, but some of his basic characteristics she understood very well.

He nodded even as he shifted again so there was room for his hand to get between them. A single finger gently rubbed along her wet folds.

"That feels good," she whispered.

"It is supposed to."

The touch moved up, circling her clitoris. It felt so delicious she gasped with the pleasure of it.

He kissed her and then lifted his head. "Touching you is such a pleasure. You hide none of your responses from me."

"Am I supposed to?"

"No." Very definite. Unquestionably vehement.

"You're kind of a control freak in bed, aren't you?"

"Giving you pleasure takes a lot of concentration. Why would you try to hinder my efforts by lying to me?"

"I never..." She gasped as his fingers moved a certain way. "Didn't say I would."

"Never?" he asked.

She could have accused him of taking unfair advantage, but really? It wouldn't have mattered if he'd asked her in the middle of the street standing ten feet away.

Her answer to that question would always be the same. "Never."

"Thank you." Demyan continued to touch her until she was moving restlessly beneath him.

"Please…" She wasn't even sure what she was asking for.

Intercourse? Maybe, but what she really wanted was resolution to the storm building inside her and Chanel didn't really care how she got it.

Even so, she was shocked when he shifted down her body, his intention clear. She'd read about this. Of course she had. Her ex-boyfriend had even wanted to do it to her, but he'd told her she'd have to shave her hair off first.

She'd refused.

Demyan didn't seem in the least put off by the damp curls between her legs, his tongue going with unerring accuracy right to where his finger had been.

She cried out, her hips coming off the bed. His mouth followed, his ministrations with lips and tongue never pausing.

This was oral sex? This intimate kiss that led to feeling so close to someone else that there was nothing embarrassing about it?

She always thought it would bother her to have a man's mouth *there*. She hadn't refused to shave her nether region just because she was a prude back then.

Only it didn't bother her. Not at all.

It felt so good, so perfect.

Demyan's fingers came back to play, this time with one of them sliding just inside her as his tongue swirled over her most sensitive spot. He moved the finger in and out, going a little deeper each time until he pressed gently against her body's barrier.

It didn't hurt; it was not too much pressure, but it would be different when he was inside her. Wouldn't it?

He would have to break through the barrier then. With his longer-than-average erection. That's what had to happen next.

Only, he didn't seem to have the script, because he kept licking, sucking and nibbling at her clitoris until she was on the verge of climax. His finger inside her continued sliding in and out of her channel, pressing just a little bit harder against the thin barrier every few times.

His other hand came up to play with her breasts and tease at her nipples, increasing the sensations below by a factor of ten. It was incredible. Amazing.

And she felt that precipice draw closer and closer. She didn't think she was supposed to climax again before they were joined, but she didn't worry about it. He knew what he was doing and wouldn't let her.

Only, he didn't seem concerned when she warned him it was getting to be too much. He only renewed his efforts, sucking harder on her clitoris and nipping it ever so gently with his teeth.

Without warning, her body splintered apart in glorious pleasure again, this time so intense she couldn't even get enough air to scream. He didn't stop the intimate kiss, but he gentled it, bringing her prolonged ecstasy that went on and on even as his finger pressed more insistently against that thin membrane of flesh inside.

Until, as she floated on a cloud of sensual bliss, she felt the sharp sting of pain and realized he'd broken through the barrier of her body. With his finger.

"What? Why?" she asked, the hazy peace cracking a little.

"It hurts less." He gently withdrew his finger before placing a single soft kiss against her nether lips.

It felt like a benediction.

He moved off her and she saw him grab a corner of the sheet from the floor to wipe his face and hand before he rejoined her on the bed.

Demyan pulled her body into his still-very-aroused one, his expression very satisfied. "You are beautiful in your passion, Chanel."

"We… Aren't you going to…"

"Oh, yes. But only when you are ready to begin building toward climax again."

She didn't know what he meant, but he showed her, after cuddling her and telling her how amazing and lovely she was. After his touch and nearness once again began to draw forth need to be joined with him.

When he finally pressed inside her, she cried for the second time that night. He didn't look in the least worried he'd hurt her, though. In fact, his expression was one of understanding overlaying utter male satisfaction.

She didn't begrudge him one iota of it, either.

He might have had a debacle with his first virgin, but he'd made this one's initiation into intimacy unbelievably good.

Once she started to move against him, his control slipped its leash and his passion turned harsh and exciting. She screamed her pleasure this time even as his body pounded into hers, and his shout was loud enough to make her ears ring.

Afterward he was quiet, his expression impossible to read. "You'll want a shower."

"Couldn't we shower together?" she asked.

"Your bathroom isn't meant for shared intimacies."

She hadn't been propositioning him, couldn't believe he thought she had any energy left for *that,* but she didn't say so.

While she was in the shower she tried to go over what had happened, but couldn't figure out why he'd withdrawn and wondered if he'd even still be there when she came out.

CHAPTER FIVE

He was, though, and he'd remade the bed with fresh sheets.

"Thank you," she said, feeling unsure.

"We will be more comfortable sleeping on clean bedding."

That one small word washed through her like life-giving oxygen. *We.* He'd said *we.*

Before she could remark on it, or say anything at all, he started toward the bathroom. "I'll have my shower now. Get in bed."

"You said you were only bossy in the bedroom."

He stopped at the doorway to the bath and looked at her over his shoulder. "We are in the bedroom."

"Why don't you just admit you have oldest-child syndrome?"

His expression turned somber, though she didn't understand why. "Noted."

She would have teased that wasn't an admission, but Demyan disappeared into the bathroom.

Chanel didn't understand what was going on with him, but he wasn't leaving. She'd take that as a good sign.

Did he regret the implications toward the future he'd made before they had sex? Was he realizing now that he'd gotten his rocks off how ludicrous they'd been?

Maybe he thought she'd try to hold him to his words as if he'd made promises. She wouldn't.

Perhaps she needed to tell him that.

She crossed the room, but when she tried the door to the bath, it was locked.

She let her hand drop away. Okay, then.

Maybe she just needed to go to bed. Any talking could happen in the morning.

After only a few moments' deliberation, she opted to wear pajamas to bed. The mint-green jersey knit wasn't exactly sexy, but it was comfortable.

She was still awake when he joined her some indeterminate time later.

He didn't pause before pulling her into his arms, though he made a sound of surprise when his hands encountered fabric. "Why are you wearing this?"

Because she'd needed a barrier between them, a level of armor, even if it was just her favorite pair of pj's. "Why not?" she answered rather than admit that, though.

"Because I prefer naked skin and I think you do, too."

"I wouldn't know. I've never slept with another person," she replied a tad acerbically.

"Perhaps it is for the best tonight. You will be too sore tomorrow if we make love again in the night."

"Oh." He still wanted her?

That was good, right?

"Do not sound so disappointed. We will make love again. Many times."

As promises for the future went, that was one she could live with. "I'm glad."

They were silent for several seconds before she offered, "Thank you for making my first time so special."

"I lost control." And there it was.

What was bothering him. She *knew* it.

"I liked it."

"I could have hurt you."

"But you didn't and I think it *would* have hurt me if you hadn't lost yourself just as badly as I did."

"Yes?" he asked, as if the concept was foreign to him.

"Absolutely."

"I am very glad to hear it." He'd turned out the light, but she could still hear the smile in his voice.

"Go to sleep."

"Your wish is my command."

She would have said something sarcastic about that blatant fabrication, but her mouth didn't want to work and she slipped into sleep, comforted by their banter.

Chanel was astonished by how easily she grew used to sleeping with someone else.

Not to the sex, though. She wasn't sure she'd ever grow *used to* the level of pleasure she and Demyan found in one another's bodies.

He *was* bossy in bed, just like he'd told her, but it was all targeted toward her enjoyment. Every directive, every withholding of one instant gratification for something more was so that her final satisfaction was so incredibly overwhelming, she lost her mind with it.

But the sleeping together, that was different. That was all-night-long intimacy of another sort.

She, who had never even cuddled a bear in bed, found it difficult to sleep now when Demyan's arms weren't wrapped around her, his heartbeat a steady, comforting sound against her ear.

Hence her yawning this morning as she crunched the new data, despite three cups of coffee made in the new Keurig machine Demyan had gotten her.

He liked to buy her things, she'd noticed. Things *she* would like.

Her entire life, gifts had come with a subtle message to her to become something different. Designer clothes in a style unlike the one she favored, athletic shoes that were supposed to encourage her to take up running when she was perfectly happy with her tae kwon do training. Golfing gear, though she hated the game, a tennis racket despite the fact she'd never played.

But Demyan's pressies were different. They were all targeted to the woman she was now, with no eye to making her into someone else. He showed an uncanny ability to tap in to her preferences, even when she'd never shared certain things with him.

Like her addiction to flavored coffees in direct opposition to her frustration over the complicated business of making a good cup of the beverage. So Demyan had found a way to feed the one while minimizing the other.

And the coffee? Delicious. And so darn easy.

She couldn't mess it up even when she got sidetracked by a new algorithm she wanted to try.

Even when she was sleepy from waking every couple of hours, reaching for him in the bed only to find empty space.

Demyan had left Seattle in the wee hours of the previous morning for what Chanel assumed was a business trip. She hadn't asked what it was about and he hadn't offered the information.

What she did know was that he wouldn't be back for two more days and an equal number of nights. Forty-eight more hours without him.

In the time line of life, it was hardly a blip.

So why did it feel longer than a particularly depraved man's purgatory to her?

Chanel already missed him with an ache that made absolutely no sense to her scientific brain. Okay, so they'd been dating a month now, not just three days. Making love and sleeping together every single night of the past three weeks of that month.

Still. How could she have become more addicted to his company than caffeine?

Because Chanel knew without any doubts she could go without coffee a heck of a lot more easily than she was finding it to be without her daily dose of Demyan.

She didn't know if she'd fallen in love at first sight like he'd hinted at three weeks ago, but she was in love with him now.

And that scared her more than a weekend at the spa with her mother.

"How close are you to closing the deal?" Fedir asked without preamble once he and Demyan were alone in the king's study.

Demyan's cousin and Gillian had returned from their honeymoon, and Queen Oxana wanted *family time*. That meant everyone in their small inner circle had come to the palace for a few days of "bonding."

Since his own parents would cheerfully go the rest of their lives without seeing Demyan, he never took Oxana's desire to spend time as a *family* for granted.

Though on this particular occasion, his mother and father and siblings were also staying at the palace in order to get to know their future queen, Gillian, better.

His father wouldn't make any effort to spend one-on-one time with Demyan, though. For all intents and purposes, Demyan's younger brother was his acknowledged oldest son.

Pushing aside old wounds Demyan no longer gave the

power to hurt him, he answered his uncle's question. "She's emotionally engaged."

"When will you propose?"

"When I return."

Fedir nodded. "Smart. The time apart will leave her feeling vulnerable. She'll want to cement your bond. Women are like that."

Demyan didn't reply. His uncle was the last man, bar none, he would ask for advice on women.

"She'll sign the prenuptial agreement?"

"Yes." The more Demyan had gotten to know Chanel, the more apparent it had become that money was not a motivating factor for her.

She'd sign even the all-contingency prenuptial agreement Fedir's lawyers had drawn up simply because the financial terms would not matter to her.

"Good, good."

"I'll want changes made to some of the provisions before I present her with it, though."

Fedir frowned. "What? I thought the lawyers did a good job of covering all the bases."

"I want more generous monetary allowances for Chanel in the event our marriage ends in divorce or my death."

"What? Why?" Fedir's shock was almost comical. "Has a woman finally gotten under the skin of my untouchable nephew?"

Of course his uncle would immediately assume an emotional reason behind Demyan's actions. His sense of justice was a little warped by his all-consuming dedication to the welfare of Volyarus.

"I will do whatever I need to in order to protect this country, but I will do it with honor," Demyan replied.

"Of course, but your integrity is in no way compromised by your actions to insure the healthy future of our country."

Demyan wasn't sure he believed that. Regardless, he would minimize how much tarnish it took. "The terms will be changed to my requirements, or I won't offer the document to Chanel to sign."

As threats went, it wasn't very powerful. Baron Tanner's will had been clear and airtight. Chanel lost all claim to the baron's shares in Yurkovich Tanner upon marriage to any direct relation to the king.

"And without a prenup, there will be no wedding," Demyan added after several seconds of silence by his uncle.

"You don't mean that."

"When have you ever known me to bluff?" Demyan asked.

Fedir frowned. "She really does mean something to you."

"My integrity certainly does."

He was a ruthless man. Demyan knew that about himself. He could make the hard choices, but he was an honest man, too. And he didn't make those choices without counting the cost.

"A man has to make sacrifices, even in that area for the greater good."

Demyan shrugged. "I'll contact the lawyers with the changes I want made to the agreement."

He wasn't going to debate his uncle's choices. The other man had to live with them and their consequences. It might be argued that everyone in the palace did, too, but Demyan wasn't a whiny child, moaning how his uncle's decisions had cost him his family.

The truth was, his own parents and their ambition were every bit as culpable.

"I'll trust you to be reasonable in your demands."

"I appreciate that."

"Demyan, you will never be king, but you are no less a

son to me than Maksim." Fedir laid one hand on Demyan's shoulder and squeezed.

The words rocked through Demyan. His uncle was not an emotionally demonstrative man, in word or deed. Nor was he known for saying things he did not mean, at least not to family.

However, Demyan's cynicism in the face of life's lessons drove his speech. "A son you call nephew."

"A son I and all of Volyarus call prince."

"You never adopted me." According to Volyarussian law, which the king could change should he so desire, doing so would have made Demyan heir to the throne, not the spare.

He understood that, but it was also a fact that if he were truly every bit as much a son to Fedir, his place in the right of succession wouldn't have been a deterrent.

"Your parents refused."

Was Fedir trying to imply he'd asked? "I find that difficult to believe. They gave me up completely."

"But so long as you were legally their son, your father had leverage for his interests. He and your mother categorically refused to give that up."

His uncle's words rang true, particularly when weighed against how few of Demyan's father's efforts had met with support of the king since he'd become an adult. "I get my ruthlessness from him."

"But your honor is all your own. You are a better man than either of your fathers, the one by birth and the one by choice."

Fedir was not a man who gave empty compliments. So, Demyan couldn't help that the older man's words sparked emotion deep inside, but he wasn't about to admit that out loud.

"Oxana feels the same. She is very proud of both of her sons."

He thought of the excitement the queen had shown when Demyan had warned her that he'd found the one. "She wouldn't be proud of me if she knew why I'm pursuing Chanel."

"You're wrong. I am very proud of you." Oxana came into the room from the secret passageway entrance. "You have put the welfare of our people and your family ahead of your own happiness. How can I be anything but proud of that?"

Fedir started, clearly shocked his wife had been listening in.

"She's a special woman. She deserves a real marriage." It wasn't a sentiment Demyan would have expressed to Fedir without prompting, but this was Oxana.

She'd sacrificed her entire life for their country and her family. Yet she was not a bitter woman. She loved them all deeply, if not overtly. She deserved to know that Demyan wasn't going to play Chanel for the sake of her inheritance.

"So, give her one." Oxana smiled with the same guarded approval she'd given him since he was a boy, though as he'd grown older he'd learned to look deeper for the true emotion. It was there. "She is a very lucky woman to have you."

Since he wasn't about to comment on the latter and the former was Demyan's plan, he merely nodded.

"That's not a reasonable request," Fedir said forcefully.

"For you, we all know that is true. But Demyan is a different man. A *better* man, by your own admission."

Fedir scowled at his wife of more than three decades. "He is our son. How can you demand he sacrifice the rest of his life for the sake of this girl's feelings?"

"How can you ask him to sacrifice his personal integrity to save our country?" Oxana countered, deigning to look at Fedir.

"He is not being dishonest."

"Oh, so you've told Chanel about her inheritance?" Oxana asked Demyan.

But he knew she wasn't talking to him, not really, so he didn't answer with so much as a shake of his head.

"How do you know about it?" Fedir asked Oxana, with shock lacing his usually forceful tones.

"It is in the historical archives for anyone to read."

"Anyone with access to the private files."

"I am queen. I get access."

Fedir opened his mouth and then shut it again without a word being uttered, his face settling into a frown.

Oxana turned to face Demyan, effectively cutting Fedir out of the conversation. "Promise me one thing."

"Yes." He didn't have to ask what it was. He trusted Oxana in a way he didn't trust anyone besides Maks.

If she wanted a promise, he would give it to her.

"Don't tell this woman, Chanel Tanner, that you love her unless you mean it. Love isn't a bartering tool."

"She loves me." Chanel hadn't said so, but he was sure of it.

It's what he'd been working toward since he'd first walked into her office.

"No doubt. You are an eminently lovable man, but you owe it to her and to your own sense of honor not to lie about something so important."

"I never lied to you," Fedir inserted.

"Nothing has ever hurt as much as realizing Fedir had only said the words to convince me to give him the heir he needed for the throne."

"I did love you. I do love you."

Oxana spun to face her husband, but *not* her lover. "Like

a sister. The few times you shared my bed, you called out *her* name at the critical moment."

This was so much more than Demyan wanted to know, but he saw no way of extricating himself from the situation. He could walk out easily enough, but he wouldn't leave Oxana to face the aftereffects of the emotional bloodletting that had been decades in the making.

"You knew about Bhodana from the beginning."

"You told me you loved me. I thought that meant you were going to let her go."

"I never promised you that."

"No, you were very careful not to."

"Oxana."

She waved her hand, dismissing him and his words as she turned back to Demyan. "You promise me, be the better man. Do not make declarations you don't mean."

"You have my word."

"I look forward to meeting her."

"I didn't plan to bring her here before the wedding."

"You don't want to scare her away."

"No." Unlike many women, Chanel was less likely to marry a prince than a normal man. "I've taken great care not to frighten her off."

"Does she know the real you?" Oxana asked.

He thought about their time in bed, intimacy during which his plans flew straight to heaven in the face of his body's response to Chanel. He'd try to convince himself that it would only be the first time, but subsequent sessions of lovemaking had proven otherwise.

"Yes," Demyan said. "She may not realize it, but definitely."

"Then all will be well. She is marrying the man you are at your core, Demyan, my son, not your title or the corporate shark who runs our company's operations so efficiently."

He hoped once Chanel saw his true persona and position, she would agree with her future mother-in-law. It was the one element to his plan that he could not be absolutely sure about.

With another woman, maybe, but with Chanel...learning he was a de facto prince could turn her right off him.

Excited anticipation buzzed through Chanel as the limousine taking her to meet Demyan rolled through the wet streets of Seattle.

His flight had arrived that morning, but he'd had a full day of meetings. Thankfully he'd told her about them before she offered to take a vacation day to spend with him.

Needy much?

She cringed at how much she'd missed him and was fairly certain allowing him to see the extent of it might not be the best thing to do. Even someone as socially inept as Chanel realized that.

Still, it had been hard to play it cool and agree to let him send a driver for her without gushing over the idea of seeing him tonight and not having to wait until tomorrow.

They were attending an avant-garde live theater production downtown. No dinner. Demyan's schedule had not permitted.

Chanel was just glad he hadn't put off seeing her, but he'd seemed almost as eager to be with her as she felt about seeing him again. Considering the number of times their short phone call had been interrupted, she knew he'd had to force a slot into his schedule for her.

Knowing she was going to see him had made focusing on her work nearly impossible. Chanel had ended up taking the afternoon off and calling her sister for a last-minute shopping trip. Laura had helped Chanel pick out an outfit that was guaranteed to *drive the guy crazy.*

The sapphire-blue three-quarter-length-sleeve top was deceptively simple. With a scoop neckline outlined by a double line of black stitching and mock tuxedo tucking in the front, it was tailored in along her torso to emphasize her curves. The semi-transparent silk was worn over a bra in the same color. Not overtly slutty with the pleats in front, it still did a lovely job of highlighting Chanel's femininity.

The black silk trousers appeared conservative enough. Until she sat down, bent over or walked. Then the slit from midthigh to ankle hidden by the tuxedo stripe when she was standing gave intriguing glimpses of naked skin.

She'd never worn anything so revealing, but Laura insisted the peek-a-boo slit was interesting and not cheap. At the prices Chanel had paid for each piece of the outfit, she supposed *cheap* would not be a term that would ever apply to the clothing.

It had looked sophisticated in the boutique's full-length mirror, a little more scandalous in her own.

Laura had insisted on styling Chanel's ensemble as well, adding a demure rope of pearls knotted right below her breasts in an interesting juxtaposition that drew attention to the curves as effectively as the blue silk.

Her heels were strappy black sandals with what Laura called a *do-me-baby* heel. Chanel hadn't bothered to admonish her sister about the description.

She'd decided years ago that Laura was light-years ahead of Chanel in the girl-boy department. She didn't know if her baby sister was still a virgin like Chanel had been when she met Demyan, and honestly she had absolutely no desire to know.

The limousine slid to a halt and Chanel took a calming breath that did exactly no good.

She resisted the urge to pull at the carefully styled curls her sister had worked so hard to effect and waited for the driver to open the door.

It wasn't the chauffeur's hand reaching in to help her out of the limousine, though.

It was Demyan's, and his dark eyes glittered with lust as he took in her exposed thigh before meeting her gaze. "Hello, *sérdeńko*. I am very happy to see you."

She made no effort to stifle the smile that took over her features as she surged forward to exit the limo. If he hadn't been there with a steadying hand and then his arm around her waist, she would have fallen flat on her face.

But he *was* there and part of her heart was beginning to believe maybe he always would be.

He tucked her into his body protectively before leaning down to kiss her hello, right there in front of the crowd making their way into the theater.

She responded with more enthusiasm than probably was warranted, but he didn't seem to mind.

The kiss ended and he smiled down at her. "You look beautiful tonight. Very sexy."

"Laura played stylist."

"Your younger sister?"

"Yes. She's got even more acute fashion sense than Mom."

"Tell her I approve."

"She said you would."

His gaze skimmed her body. "Though I am not sure how I feel about everyone else seeing your body."

"They're just legs."

"Nice ones."

"It's the tae kwon do." Chanel's mother had heard somewhere that taking martial arts could improve Chanel's grace.

It hadn't done much for her poise and composure, but Chanel had discovered she *enjoyed* the classes. She'd insisted on continuing when her mother would have preferred she take a dance class.

Just one of many arguments between her and Beatrice during Chanel's formative years marked with parent-child acrimony.

"Then I am very grateful for your interest in Korean martial arts."

"You've never asked what color belt I am," she observed as he led her into the theater.

His thumb brushed up and down against her waist as if he couldn't help touching her. "What color?"

"Third-level black belt."

"Sixth-level black in judo," he said by way of reply.

"Want to spar?" she teased breathlessly.

The silk of her shirt transmitted the heat from his skin to hers and she wondered if she was the one who was going to end up teased to distraction by her outfit tonight.

"I spar with my cousin. I prefer less competitive physical pursuits with you."

She looked up into the side of his face, loving the line of his jaw, the way he held himself with such confidence. "Me, too."

He groaned.

"What?"

He stopped in the lobby and pulled her around so their gazes locked.

His was heated. "How can you ask what? You are dressed in a way guaranteed to keep my thoughts off the play and on what I plan to do to you once we get back to my condo."

CHAPTER SIX

HE SHOOK HIS HEAD as if trying to clear it. "What do you think has me groaning? It has been three nights."

She tried not to look as pleased as she felt, but was afraid she wasn't doing a very good job.

So she averted her head and met the envious gaze of another woman. Chanel ignored it, the envy having no power to pierce the bubble of happiness around her.

Demyan was with her and showed zero interest in being with, or even looking at, another woman.

She looked up at the sound of his laughter. He was watching her.

"I'm funny?" she asked.

"You are very pleased with yourself."

"I am happy with life, and you most of all," she offered.

She wasn't one to share her feelings easily, but Laura hadn't spent the afternoon just coaching Chanel on fashion choices. Her little sister had told Chanel that if she really liked this man, she needed to open up to him.

"You can't do that thing you do with Mom and Dad and everyone else besides me and Andrew," Laura had said.

Even though Chanel thought she knew, she'd asked, "What thing?"

"The way you hold the real you back so no one can hurt her."

"You're pretty insightful."

"For a teenager, you mean."

"For anyone." Their mother was nearly fifty and Beatrice had less understanding of her oldest daughter's nature.

Demyan's hand slid down her hip, his fingertips playing across her exposed flesh through the slit.

Chanel gasped and jerked away from the touch.

His look was predatory. "I don't like to be ignored."

"I wasn't ignoring you."

"You weren't thinking about me."

"How can you tell?"

"I know."

"You're arrogant."

"So you have said, but you know I do not agree."

And the more she knew of him, the less she believed the accusation herself. There was a very hard-to-detect strain of vulnerability running through the man at her side. You had to look very closely to see it, but she watched him with every bit of her formidable scientist's brain focused entirely on one thing. Deciphering the data that made up Demyan Zaretsky.

"I'm thinking about you now," she promised.

"I know."

She laughed, feeling a light airiness that buoyed her through the crowd.

"Demyan!" a feminine voice called.

There was no mistaking the way his body tensed at the sound, not with him so close to Chanel as they walked.

He was coiled tightly, even as he turned them toward the woman who had called his name, with one of those fake smiles Chanel hadn't seen since their very first dates on his face. "Madeleine."

Madeleine's fashion sense and poise was everything Chanel's mother wished for her daughter.

Unfortunately, Chanel refused to make it a mission in life to live up to such hopes. She'd learned too young that nothing she did would ever be enough; therefore, what would be the point in trying to be someone she was not?

Madeleine's blond hair probably wasn't natural, but there were no telltale indicators. She wore her Givenchy dress with supreme confidence, her accessories in perfect proportion to the designer ensemble.

Chanel couldn't tell the other woman's age by looking at her but guessed it was somewhere between thirty and a well-preserved forty-five.

The look she gave Demyan said *he* knew her age, intimately.

If this had happened a month ago, Chanel would have withdrawn into herself and given up the playing field.

But what she'd denied on their third date was a certainty now. She was head over heels in love with Demyan Zaretsky, though she hadn't had a chance to tell him yet. Wasn't sure exactly when she wanted to.

While he'd never said the words, either, he hinted at a future together almost every time she saw him.

That love and his commitment to their future gave her strength.

Drawing on a bit of her mother's aplomb, Chanel stepped forward and extended her hand. "Chanel Tanner. Are you an *old* friend of Demyan's?"

Madeleine didn't miss Chanel's slight emphasis on the word *old,* her eyes narrowing just slightly with anger but no righteous indignation. So, she was older than she looked.

"You could say that." Madeleine put her hand on Demyan's sleeve. "We know each other quite well, though I admit I *didn't* know he wore glasses."

Demyan adroitly stepped away from the touch while keeping a proprietary arm around Chanel. "Is your husband here tonight, Madeleine?"

Stress made Chanel's body rigid. Had Demyan and this woman had an affair? He'd said he didn't believe in infidelity.

Had he been lying?

"He couldn't get away from the Microsoft people. I'm quite on my own tonight." Madeleine smiled up at Demyan, her expression expectant.

It was clear she was angling for an invitation to join them, though Chanel wasn't sure how that was supposed to happen.

Their tickets had assigned seats.

Demyan ignored the hint completely. "The cost of being married to a man with his responsibilities."

The older woman frowned again, this time genuine anger lying right below the surface. "Does your little friend here know that? Or is she still in the honeymoon phase of believing you'll make her a priority in your life?"

"She is a priority." He pulled Chanel closer.

She didn't know if the move was a conscious one, but Madeleine noticed it, too.

That made Madeleine flinch and Chanel felt unexpected compassion well up inside her. "I'm sure you're a priority to your husband. He works to make a good life for you both."

That's what she remembered her father saying to her mother.

"I knew what I was getting when I married him." Madeleine gave a significant look to Demyan. "And what I was giving up. I liked my chances with Franklin better."

"He married you. You read the situation right." There was a message in Demyan's voice for the other woman.

He was telling her *he* wouldn't have married her, and her words had put Chanel's mind at rest about the affair. Oh, it was clear the two had shared a bed at one time, but it was equally obvious that circumstance had ended before Madeleine married Franklin.

"How long were you two together?" Chanel asked with her infamous lack of tact but no desire to pull the question back once it was uttered.

It might be awkward, but it struck her how very little she really knew about Demyan.

"Didn't he tell you about me?" Madeleine asked, her tone just this side of snide.

And still Chanel couldn't feel anything but pity for her. She didn't look happy with her choices in life.

"No."

The other woman didn't seem happy with the answer. Maybe Madeleine had thought she'd made a bigger impact on Demyan's life than she had. "You're a blunt one, aren't you? Did your mother teach you no tact?"

"To her eternal disappointment, no."

That brought an unexpected but small smile to Madeleine's lips.

Demyan leaned down and kissed Chanel's temple, no annoyance with her in his manner at all. "She is refreshingly direct," he said to Madeleine while looking at Chanel. "There is no artifice in her."

"So, she does not see the artifice in you," Madeleine opined, sounding sad rather than bitter.

"He holds things back," Chanel answered before Demyan could, but she did the older woman the courtesy of meeting her gaze to do so. "But if I know that, he's not hiding anything. I understand how hard it can be to share your true self with someone else."

"Heavens, don't you have *any* filters?" Madeleine demanded.

"No."

It was Demyan's turn to laugh, the sound genuine and apparently shocking to the other woman. Madeleine stared at him for a count of five full seconds, her mouth agape, her eyes widened comically.

Finally, she said, "I've never heard you make that sound."

"He's just laughing." Okay, so he didn't do it often, but the man had an undeniable sense of humor.

"*Just,* she says. This young thing really doesn't know you at all, does she?" Madeleine was the one looking with pity on Chanel now.

"It was a pleasure to run into you, but we need to find our seats. If you will excuse us," Demyan said, his tone brooking no obstacles and implying the exact opposite to his words.

Madeleine said nothing as they walked away.

When they reached their seats Chanel understood how the other woman had thought she might be included in their evening. Demyan had a box.

Although there was room for at least eight seats in it, there were only two burgundy-velvet-covered Queen Anne-style chairs. A small table with a bottle of champagne and two-person hors d'oeuvres tray stood between them.

Demyan led her to one of the seats, making sure she was comfortable before taking his own.

He looked out over the auditorium, stretching his long legs in front of him. "She's wrong, you know."

"Madeleine?"

"Yes."

"About what?"

He turned his head, looking at her in that way only he

had ever done. As if she was a woman worthy of intense desire, of inciting his lust. "You know the man at the base of my nature."

"I hardly know anything about you." The words came from the scientist's nature even as her heart knew he spoke the truth.

That man who lost his control when he tried so hard not to, that man was the real Demyan.

Demyan shook his head, his dark eyes glowing with sensual lights she now recognized very well. "You know the most personal things about me."

"So does she."

"No."

"You had sex with her." And even though she now knew that Madeleine hadn't been married at the time, Chanel realized it still bothered her a little.

She knew he'd been with other lovers. Probably lots of them, but she really didn't want to keep running into them.

"She never saw the more primal side of my nature. No other woman has seen it."

"You think I know you better than anyone else because you don't show absolute control in the bedroom?" It's what she'd thought only seconds before, but saying it aloud made the very concept seem unreal.

"Yes."

"I want to know about your past. Not names of every woman you've been with. I hope I never meet another one, but I don't know *anything* about you." Except that to him, she was special.

She kept that to herself. She wanted more.

"It's the future that counts between us."

"But without a connection to the past, there is no basis for understanding the future." Historians made that claim all the time and scientists knew it to be true as well, for different reasons.

"I thought scientists were all about progress."

"Building on the discoveries of the past."

"Not making something entirely new?"

"Nothing is new, just newly discovered."

"Like your sexy fashion sense?" he teased.

"That's all Laura."

"I don't see Laura here now."

"I'd like you to meet her." If they had a future, they had to share their present lives.

Even the less-than-pleasant bits, which meant he'd have to meet her mother and Perry, as well.

"I would enjoy that very much."

"You would?"

"Naturally. She is your sister."

"A part of my past."

"And your present and your future."

"Yes, so?" she prompted.

He gave her a wary look she didn't understand. "You want to meet my family?"

"Very much. Unless… Do you not get on?" Maybe his relationship with his parents was worse than hers with Beatrice and Perry.

"I get on very well with the aunt and uncle who raised me."

"What happened to your parents?"

"Ambition."

"I don't understand."

"They gave me to be raised by my aunt and uncle to feed their own ambition."

There had to be more to the story than that, but she understood this was something Demyan didn't share with everyone. "Do you ever see them?"

"My aunt and uncle? Often. In fact, that's where I spent the last three days."

"I thought it was business."

"I did not say that."

"You didn't say anything at all."

"You did not ask."

"Do I have the right to ask?"

"Absolutely."

That was definitive and welcome. "Okay."

"My parents come to family social occasions," he offered without making her ask again, proving he'd known what she meant the first time around.

"And?"

"They do not consider me their son."

"Or their beloved nephew."

"Not beloved anything." His expression relayed none of the hurt that must cause him.

"I am sorry."

"You don't have it much better with your mother and Perry."

"I'm not sure I have it better at all," she admitted.

"Your parents do not understand you."

"They don't approve of me. That's worse, believe me." It would have been so much easier for her if her mother and Perry simply found her an enigma.

Instead, they considered her a defective model that needed constant attempts at fixing.

"I approve of you completely."

"Thank you." She grinned at him, letting her love shine in her eyes. She had a feeling the words weren't far from her lips, either. "I approve of you, too."

"I am very glad to hear that." He picked up the champagne bottle and poured them each a glass.

"Why champagne?" she asked.

If it was his favored wine of choice, she wouldn't ask, but he'd shared with her he drank champagne on only very special occasions.

He handed her a glass. "I'm hoping to have something to celebrate in very short order."

Goose bumps broke out over Chanel's skin, her heart going into her throat. "Oh?"

He reached into his pocket and brandished a small box that was unmistakable in size and intent.

"Isn't this supposed to happen after a five-course dinner and roses, and…" Her breath ran out and so did Chanel's words.

"I am not a man who follows other people's dictated scripts."

She had no trouble believing that. "Just your own."

Something passed through his eyes, almost like guilt, but that didn't make any sense. He might be bossy outside the bedroom a bit, too, but it was nothing to feel guilty about.

Chanel was no shrinking violet that she couldn't stand up to him if need be.

He moved, and suddenly he was on one knee in front of her, the ring box open and in his palm. "Marry me, Chanel."

"You… I… This… How can you want… It's only been a month…"

"Is longer than three dates. I knew I wanted to marry you from the beginning." There could be no questioning the truth of that statement.

It was there in his eyes and voice. Nothing but honesty. He'd known he wanted her, had never wavered in that belief.

"What about love?"

"Do you love me?" he countered.

She nodded.

"Say it."

She glared. "You first."

"I may never say the words. You will have to accept that."

"If I want to marry you."

"Oh, you want to."

She did, but she didn't understand. "Why can't you say the words?"

"I can promise you fidelity and as good a life together as it is within my power to make for us. Is that not enough?"

The syntax change was odd and then she realized that as a native Ukrainian speaker, he was using the sentence structure of his first language. Did that mean he was nervous despite how calm and assured he appeared?

She looked at him closely and saw it, that small strain of vulnerability she knew he'd rather she never witnessed. "I do love you."

"And I will always honor that."

"I don't know."

He flinched, uncertainty showing in his expression for a brief moment before his face closed. "You need time to consider it. I understand."

He stood up, pocketing the ring. "Lights will be going down momentarily for the play."

The gulf between them was huge, but she didn't know what to do to bridge it. She couldn't say *yes* right then. She didn't know if it was enough to never hear the words. Did not saying them mean he didn't feel the sentiment?

Maybe if he'd tell her *why* he couldn't say them, but clearly he didn't want to.

Still. He wanted to marry her. "Tell me why."

"Why, what?"

Was he playing dense, or did he really not know? "Why you won't say the words."

"I made a promise."

"To who?"

"The mother of my heart."

Chanel tried to understand. "She doesn't want you to get married?"

"Of course she does. She's very eager to meet you."

"But she doesn't want you to love me?" That didn't sound promising.

"She does not want me to use the words to convince you to marry me. It must be your decision entirely."

"Is this a Ukrainian thing?"

"We are not Ukrainian. We are Volyarussian."

Unlike their Ukrainian brothers, the Volyarussians had not been subject to Russian rule and loss of identity. Their ties to the old ways of doing and thinking from their original homeland were probably stronger than in the current Ukraine, but she understood what he was saying.

"Okay, a Volyarussian thing."

"It is a Yurkovich family thing."

"Your last name is Zaretsky."

"My parents never gave up legal rights."

"You could change your name now." He was an adult. There was nothing stopping him.

He jolted as if the idea had never occurred to him. Then he smiled. "Yes, I could."

"Maybe you should."

"Maybe if you agree to share it, I will change my last name to the one of my heart."

Those words played through Chanel's mind as the lights dimmed and the play began. She couldn't follow what was happening on the stage; she was too busy trying to figure out what was going on in Demyan's mind.

He'd asked her to marry him. He'd as good as told her he planned to, but she hadn't let herself believe.

She cast one of many glances in his direction, but his attention seemed riveted by the performance. He'd backed off so quickly, given up so easily.

That wasn't in character for him. Her certainty on that matter pulled her thoughts short. She'd claimed not to know him. He'd said she knew the man he was at his most basic nature. And she'd taken that to mean sexually.

But the truth was she knew him well in a lot of areas. He was a man driven by his own agenda, even ruthless in achieving it. The way he brought her pleasure, withholding both hers and his own until they'd reached *the* place indicated as much.

Demyan didn't give up easily, either. He pushed for what he wanted. Like convincing her to try making love while her hands were tied with silk scarves. She'd been leery and unwilling to do it, but he'd convinced her.

And it had been amazing.

Which begged the question: Did he not want her badly enough to fight, or was he sitting in that chair right now plotting how to get her while pretending to watch the actors on the stage?

She was pretty sure she knew the answer and it wasn't a disheartening one, though it was kind of alarming.

He was plotting, but she *wasn't* ready to give him an answer. Which meant she had to orchestrate a preemptive strike to prevent whatever it was he was planning. Probably to make love to her until she was an amenable pile of happy goo who would say *yes* to anything.

Not letting herself think about it too long and lose her nerve, Chanel scooted off her chair and onto the floor. Demyan's head snapped sideways so he could see her, proving he was highly attuned to what she was doing.

Definitely plotting.

"What are you doing?" he whisper-demanded.

She knee-walked the couple of feet between her chair and his. "You know, you could have opted for a more romantic setting. This would be easier if you'd had a settee brought in."

He stared at her, shock showing with flattering lack of artifice on every line of his handsome face. "What?"

"This." She reached for his belt.

He grabbed her wrist. "What are you doing?"

"You're repeating yourself and I would have thought it was obvious."

"Here?" he demanded, not sounding like himself at all.

She liked that. Very much.

In answer, she tugged her wrist free so she could undo the buckle on his belt. Once it was apart, she unbuttoned the waistband and then slowly and, as quietly as she could, she began to lower the zipper on his trousers in the darkened theater box.

No one could see her, though there were literally hundreds of people mere feet away.

The backs of her fingers brushed over an already erect shaft and a small laugh huffed out of her.

"What is funny?"

"I was wrong."

"About?"

"I thought you were over here plotting, but the truth is, you were thinking about sex, weren't you?"

"Yes."

"Or were they one and the same?" she asked, realizing belatedly the one did not necessarily preclude the other.

He didn't answer, which was answer enough.

"We've done a lot of things."

His head nodded in a jerky motion.

"But not this."

"No."

"Why?"

"I did not know if you wanted to."

"You decided I wanted a lot of other things I wasn't sure about."

"This is different."

Maybe it was. Maybe this had to come at her instigation. "This is me, instigating."

"I do not understand."

She smiled at the confusion in his tone. "Here I thought you could read my mind."

"Not even I can do that."

Not *even* him. She almost laughed. "But you're not arrogant."

CHAPTER SEVEN

"CONFIDENT, NOT THE SAME." His words came out gritty and chopped, not at all like him.

Understandable and welcome in the circumstances.

"No, maybe it's not." She worked his hot shaft out through the slit in his boxers, thankful they were made from stretchy fabric. "I've never done this before."

"Do whatever you want. I promise to enjoy it."

She smiled. She believed him. There was one area of their relationship she was absolutely certain about and that was the amount of pleasure he took from their physical intimacy.

The man could not get enough of her.

So she didn't let herself worry if she was doing it right when she bent forward and licked around the head of his erection. It was wide and she knew she'd have to stretch her lips to get him inside. No way was much of him going to fit into her mouth, though.

She didn't worry about that right now, but concentrated on enjoying the taste of him. It was salty and kind of bitter, but sort of sweet, too. His skin was warm and clean and hot against her lips and tongue.

She liked it. A lot.

He didn't try to rush her, though a steady stream of pre-ejaculate was now weeping from his slit and his thighs were rock-rigid with tension. She jacked the bulk of his shaft with her hands while sucking on the end.

He made small, nearly nonexistent noises, letting her know he was enjoying this as much, or more, than she was.

Suddenly he grabbed her head and pulled it back, messing up the curls Laura had taken such effort to tame. "You have to stop."

"No."

"I'm going to come," he said fiercely.

"That's the point," she whispered back.

He shook his head. "You're not swallowing your first time. You don't know if you'll like it."

"You're being bossy again and this is not the bedroom."

Ignoring her less-than-stern admonition, he pulled her into his lap, maneuvering her so she could continue to touch him. Then he handed her a napkin from the table.

She grinned and almost asked what it was for to tease him, but the light in his eyes had gone feral. And really, she wasn't looking to get arrested for public indecency, which might well happen if his control slipped his leash completely.

So she finished him with her hand, catching his ejaculate with the napkin and his shout with a passionate kiss.

When he was done, he slumped in the chair, though his hold on her remained tight. "You did that on purpose."

"To give you pleasure?"

"That, too."

She snuggled into him. "I'm not giving you an answer tonight."

"Okay."

"Really?" She kissed under his chin, a little startled by the reality of his suit and tie still pristinely in place.

"Yes, but that will not stop me taking you back to my condo and showing you what our married life will be like."

"I've got no doubts about the great sex."

"We will make sure of that by morning."

"Should I call in at work tomorrow?" She didn't want to try to do the complicated calculations for their current phase on no sleep.

And the look in his dark eyes said while she might get to know his bed very well, she wasn't going to be doing a lot of resting there.

"I think perhaps you should."

She did. In the early hours of the morning after he made love to her through the night in his condo that turned out to be a penthouse taking up the entire top floor of one of the more historic Seattle buildings.

Demyan woke her with kisses and caresses a few hours later.

Their lovemaking was slow and almost torturous in its intensity. He seemed set on proving something to her, but Chanel wasn't convinced it was what she needed to know to agree to marry him.

When she was once again sated and relaxed, he informed her he'd called her sister and arranged to invite Chanel's entire family, including Andrew, whom he was flying up for the weekend in his private jet, for dinner the following evening.

"My parents are coming here?" Postcoital bliss evaporated like water pooled on a rock in the desert as she jumped out of his king-size bed and started pacing the darkly masculine bedroom. *Tomorrow?*

"Yes."

"Didn't you think you should ask me first?" she demanded.

Looking smug and certain of his answer, he said, "You were asleep."

"You could have waited until I woke up."

"I was bored."

"Right. And you had nothing else to occupy your time but calling my sister. How did you even get her number?" Had he gone snooping through her phone?

He averted his gaze without answering.

She sighed. "You got sneaky and underhanded, didn't you?"

It wasn't exactly a challenging conclusion to draw. As if there was any other way to get her sister's private cell number without waking and asking Chanel.

"The prospect does not make you angry?" he asked with a cautious look.

Nonplussed, she stared at him. "You aren't worried about how annoyed I am that you made plans with my family, just how irritated I am about your method for getting my sister's number?"

He shrugged.

"News flash—I find it a lot less upsetting that you scrolled through my phone's contacts while I was sleeping than the fact you used said contacts to set up a dinner with my family." She shook her head. "Well, this ought to be interesting."

With that, she went into the bathroom for a shower. It was her turn to lock the door.

Being the sneaky, underhanded guy he was, Demyan found his way inside regardless. Chanel hadn't expected anything else.

So she didn't jump when his hand landed on her hip and his big body added to the heat behind her from the shower. "You told me you wanted me to meet your family."

"I said my sister," Chanel gritted out.

The man was far too intelligent not to have made the distinction.

He turned her in his arms, his expression more amused than concerned. "You know I will have to meet all of them eventually. Why not now?"

"Because I'm not ready!" She made no effort to control her volume, but she wasn't a yeller by nature, so the words came out sounding only about half as vehement as they did in her head.

The argument might have escalated, but he had the kissing-to-end-conflict technique down to a fine art.

They made love, moving together under the cascading water, his body behind hers, his arms wrapped around her so his hands could reach her most sensitive places.

As he brought her the ultimate in pleasure, he promised, "It will be all right, sérdeńko."

She desperately wanted to believe him, but a lifetime of experience had taught her otherwise. "You'll see me through their eyes."

"Or I will teach them to see you through mine."

Maybe, just maybe, his supreme self-confidence would guide his interactions with her family down that path.

She could hope.

The following night, her entire family showed up at Demyan's condo right on time.

Chanel was so happy to see Andrew and Laura that her stress at seeing her mother and stepfather didn't reach its usual critical levels instantly. That might also be attributed to the way Demyan kept one comforting arm around her throughout introductions and the launch into the usual small talk.

He'd brought in catering with servers so Chanel didn't have to cook or play hostess getting drinks. Somehow he'd known that those domestic social niceties had always been a source of criticism and failure with her family in the past.

She hadn't invited her parents to her apartment since moving out as a fresh-faced nineteen-year-old. Chanel had thought that having her own place would make a difference in how Beatrice and Perry responded to her efforts at cooking.

She'd learned differently quickly enough when they'd made it clear she fell short in every hosting department. The meal was too simple, the drinks offered too narrow in choice and even her bright stoneware dishes from a chain department store were considered inferior.

As could be inferred by her mother's gift of appropriate understated chinaware on Chanel's next birthday. She'd donated it to Goodwill and continued using her much less expensive, bright and cheerful dishes.

Since then, Chanel had assiduously avoided her mother's inferences and even direct suggestions that Chanel might like to host one of the smaller family get-togethers over the years. In the ten years since that first debacle, Chanel had made sure there were no situations in which she'd have to invite her mother or stepfather into her home for so much as a drink of water.

Perry was clearly impressed by Demyan as a host, though, the older man's expression shining with approval over the high-end penthouse and being offered his high-ball by a black-clad server.

Demyan kept them occupied with small talk, redirecting the conversation any time it looked like it would go into the familiar *let's-criticize-Chanel* direction. He was also overtly approving, verbalizing his appreciation for Chanel in ways that could not be mistaken or overlooked by her parents.

His protective behavior touched her deeply and Chanel found herself relaxing with her family in a way she could not remember doing in years.

"So, you work for Yurkovich Tanner?" Perry asked Demyan over dinner.

"I do."

Chanel added, "In the corporate offices."

A vague answer never satisfied her stepfather and she
wasn't sure her addition would, either, but she could hope.
She didn't want to spend the rest of the evening listening to Perry grill Demyan about his connections and job
prospects.

She realized moments later that she needn't have worried.

Demyan adroitly evaded each sally until Perry gave up
with a rather confused-sounding "Well, maybe you can put
a good word in for Andrew. I tried contacting them on his
behalf, you know, because of Andrew's connection to one
of the original founders."

Andrew wasn't the one connected to Bartholomew Tanner. That was Chanel and her connection was tenuous at
best, but trust Perry to dismiss her blood relationship to
the founder and receipt of a Tanner Yurkovich university
scholarship as unimportant altogether.

"I haven't heard back." Perry shrugged. "It was a long
shot, but business is all about contacts."

Demyan nodded and then looked away from Perry to
smile at Chanel. "I'm always happy to put a good word
in for family."

Oh, the fiend. Chanel kicked Demyan's ankle under
the table, but he didn't even have the courtesy to flinch.

So, that's why the dinner tonight. He'd said he was okay
with waiting for her answer on his proposal, but really he
had every intention of getting her family on his side. He
had to realize it wouldn't take much.

Beatrice Saltzman had given up hope her oldest daughter would ever marry, and had never had any that it would

be advantageously. She would be Demyan's biggest sup-
porter once she realized the plans he wanted to make.

Chanel was going to kill him later, but right now she
had to deal with the fallout of his implication.

It wasn't her mother or Perry who picked up on it, either. They wouldn't

"You're getting married?" Laura gasped, her eyes shining. She grinned at Chanel. "I told you that outfit was
going to hook him."

"I wasn't looking to *hook* anybody. We're not engaged."

"But I have asked Chanel to marry me."

Chanel's mother stared at her agape. "And you haven't
said *yes?* No, of course you haven't." She shook her head
like she couldn't expect anything else from her socially
awkward eldest.

"I'm thinking about it." Chanel glared daggers at Demyan, but he smiled back with a shark's smile she was
now convinced was *not* her imagination.

"Don't think too long. He's likely to withdraw the offer,"
Perry advised in serious, almost concerned tones. "You're
not likely to do better."

"It's not a business deal." Chanel ground out the words,
refusing to be hurt by her stepfather's observation.

Because it was true. She couldn't imagine anyone *better* than Demyan ever coming into her life, but that wasn't
what was holding her back, was it?

"No, it's not," Andrew chimed in, giving his dad a fierce
scowl. "Leave her alone about it. Demyan would be damn
lucky to have Chanel for a wife and he's obviously smart
enough to realize it."

Their mom tut-tutted about swearing, but Andrew ignored her and Chanel just gave her little brother a grateful
smile. He and Laura had never taken after their parents'

dim view of Chanel. Their extended family, other friends and colleagues of the Saltzmans might, but not her siblings.

For that, Chanel had always been extremely thankful. Because she loved Andrew and Laura to bits.

Instead of looking annoyed by Andrew taking Chanel's part, Demyan gave him an approving glance before turning a truly chilling one on Perry. "Neither of us is likely to do better, hence my proposal."

"Well, of course," Perry blustered, but no question—he realized he'd erred with his words.

Chanel wanted to agree to marry Demyan right then, but she couldn't. There was too much at stake.

Chanel was sitting down to watch an old-movie marathon on A&E when her doorbell rang the next evening.

She'd turned down Demyan's offer of dinner and a night in at the penthouse, telling him she wanted some time alone to think.

He hadn't been happy, insisting she could think as easily in his company as out of it. Knowing that for the fallacy it was, she'd refused to budge. No matter how many different arguments he brought to bear.

Chanel had taken the fact she'd gotten her way as proof she could withstand even the more forceful side of his personality. *And* that he respected her enough to accede to her wishes when he knew she was serious about them.

If he was the one ringing the bell, both suppositions would be faulty and that might be the answer she needed.

As painful as it might be to utter.

It wasn't Demyan through the peephole, though. It was Chanel's mom.

Stunned, Chanel opened the door. "Mother. What are you doing here?"

"I wanted to talk to you. May I come in?"

Chanel stepped back and watched with some bemusement as her mother entered her apartment for the first time since she'd moved in years ago.

Beatrice sat down on the sofa, carefully adjusting the skirt of her Vera Wang suit as she did so. "Close the door, Chanel. The temperature has dropped outside."

"Would you like something to drink?" Chanel asked as she obeyed her mother's directive and then hovered by the door, unsure what to do with herself.

"No, thank you." With a slight wave of her hand toward the other end of the sofa she indicated Chanel should sit down. "I... You seemed uncertain about your relationship with Demyan last night. I thought you might want to talk about it."

"To you?" Chanel asked with disbelief as she settled into her seat.

Her mother grimaced, but nodded. "Yes. I may not have been the best one these past years, but I am your mom."

"And he's rich." His penthouse showed that even to someone as oblivious as Chanel could be. Beatrice would have noticed and probably done a fair guesstimate of Demyan's yearly income off it.

"That's not why I'm here."

"He has corporate connections Perry and Andrew might find useful, too. I suppose that might carry even more weight with you." After all, scientists could be rich, but Beatrice had never made any bones about not wanting another one in the family.

Her mom sighed. "I am not here on behalf of your brother or my husband, either."

"You're here for my sake," Chanel supplied with full-on sarcasm.

But her mother nodded, her expression oddly vulnerable and sincere. "Yes, I am. The way you two are together. It's special, Chanel, and I don't want you to miss that."

"We've only been dating a month," Chanel said, shocking herself and voicing her biggest concern.

Beatrice nodded, as if she understood completely. "That's the way it was for me and your dad. We knew the first time we met that we would be together for the rest of our lives."

"You stopped loving him." What would Chanel do if Demyan stopped wanting her?

Her mother's eyes blazed with more emotion than Chanel could ever remember seeing in them. "I never did."

"But you said…" Pain lanced through Chanel as her voice trailed off.

There were too many examples to pick only one.

"He was *it* for me."

"You married Perry."

"I needed someone after Jacob died."

"You had me. You promised we would always be a team." That broken promise had hurt worst of all.

"It was too hard. You were too much like him. I tried to make you different, but you refused to change." Her mother sighed, looking almost defeated. "You are so stubborn. Just like him."

For the first time, Chanel heard the pain in those words her mother had never expressed.

Some truths were just as hurtful to her. "Perry hates me."

"He's a very jealous man."

"He wasn't jealous of me. You weren't affectionate enough to me to make him jealous."

Sadness filled Beatrice's eyes. "No, I haven't been. He was jealous of Jacob."

"Because you never stopped loving him." Despite all evidence to the contrary.

"How do you stop loving the other half of your soul?"

Finally Chanel understood a part of her childhood she'd always been mystified by. She'd tried with Perry at first. Really tried. "Perry blamed me. He took his jealousy out on me."

"Your father wasn't around to punish."

"You let him."

Beatrice looked away and shrugged. As if it didn't matter. As if all that pain was okay to visit on a child.

"You let him," Chanel said again. "You knew and you let him hate me in effigy of my father."

Her mom's head snapped back around, her expression dismissive. "He doesn't hate you. He wanted you to be the best and all you wanted was your books and science."

"It's what I love. Didn't that ever matter to you?"

"Of course it mattered!" Beatrice jumped up, showing an unfamiliar agitation. "Science stole your father from me. Do you for one second believe I wanted it to take you, too?"

"So, you pushed me away instead."

"That wasn't my intention."

"I don't fit with the Saltzmans."

Beatrice didn't deny it, but she didn't agree either. Should Chanel be thankful for small mercies?

"I did fit with the Tanners."

"Too well, but they're all gone, Chanel. Can't you see that?"

"And you think I'll die young like Dad did because of my love for science?"

"You're too much a Tanner. You take risks."

"I don't!" She'd been impacted by the way her father and grandfather had died, too. "I'm very careful."

"If you are, then I've succeeded a little, anyway."

"You succeeded, all right. You succeeded in picking away at our relationship until there wasn't one anymore." Chanel nearly choked on the words, but she wouldn't hold them back anymore. "You couldn't handle how much having me around reminded you of Dad, so you pushed me away with both hands."

"And now you can barely bring yourself to see me even once a month."

"Visits with you are too demoralizing."

"Your sister and brother see you more often."

Even Andrew. He was away at university, but Chanel went to visit her brother at least once a term. She always made sure she got time with him when he was home. While she'd done her best to nurture her relationships with her siblings, Chanel had avoided her mother with the skill of a trained stunt driver.

"You have your sister date with Laura every week, but somehow you manage to avoid seeing me or Perry."

"Can you blame me?" Chanel demanded and then shook her head. "It doesn't matter if you do, or don't. I know whose fault it is we don't have a relationship and it's *not* mine."

Finally, she truly understood that. It wasn't that Chanel wasn't lovable. Unless she'd been willing to become a completely different person, with none of her father's passions, mannerisms or even affections, Chanel had been destined to be the brunt of both her mother's grief and Perry's jealousy.

There was no way she could be smart enough, well behaved enough or even pretty enough to earn their approval.

Not with hair the same color as her dad's and eyes so like his, too. Not with a jaw every Tanner seemed to be born with and her bone-deep desire to grow up and be a scientist.

Beatrice's eyes filled with grief that slowly morphed into resolution. "No, it's not. You deserved better than either Perry or I have given you. You deserve to be loved for yourself and by someone who isn't wishing every minute in your company you would move just a little differently, speak with less scientific jargon…"

"Just be someone other than who I am."

"Yes. You deserve that." Her mom's voice rang with a loving sincerity Chanel hadn't heard in it since she was eight years old and a broken vulnerability she *never* had. "That's why I'm urging you with everything in me not to push Demyan away because how you feel about him scares you. I wouldn't trade the years I had with your father for anything in the world, not even a life without the constant pain of grief that never leaves."

"You think Demyan loves me like Dad loved you?"

"He must." In a completely uncharacteristic gesture, Beatrice reached out and took both Chanel's hands in her own. "Sweetheart, a man like that, he doesn't offer you marriage when he could have you in his bed without it, not unless he wants all of you, but especially the life you can have together."

Her mother hadn't called her sweetheart in so long that Chanel had to take a couple of deep breaths to push back the emotion the endearment caused. "He's really possessive."

And bossy in bed, but she wasn't going to share that tidbit with her mom.

"He needs you. For a man to need that deeply, it's frightening for him. It makes him hold on tighter."

"Did Dad hold on tight?"

"Oh, yes."

Chanel had a hard time picturing it. "Like Perry?"

"Nothing like Perry. Jacob wasn't petty. Ever. He wasn't jealous. He trusted me and my love completely, but he held on tight. He wanted every minute with me he could get."

"He still followed his passion for science."

"Yes. I used to love him for it."

"You grew to hate him, though, didn't you?" That made so much sense.

Chanel hadn't just spent her childhood as scapegoat to Perry for a man who couldn't be reached in death. Her mom had punished her for being too like her father, too.

"I did." Tears welled and spilled over in Beatrice's eyes. "I betrayed our love by learning to hate him for leaving me."

Chanel didn't know what to do. Not only had she not seen her mother cry since the funeral, but they didn't have the kind of relationship that allowed her to offer comfort.

"He doesn't blame you." Chanel knew that with every fiber of her being. Her dad's love for her mom had had no limits.

"For hating him? I'm sure you're right. He loved so purely. But if he were here now to see the damage I've done to you, to our bond as a family, he'd be furious. He *would* hate me, too."

CHAPTER EIGHT

CHANEL COULDN'T RESPOND.

Her throat was too tight with tears she didn't want to shed, but her mom was probably right.

Jacob Tanner had loved his daughter with the same deep, abiding emotion he'd given his wife. He'd expected a different kind of best from both of them than Perry ever had.

The good kind. The human kindness kind.

Beatrice sighed and swiped at the tears on her cheek, not even looking around for a tissue to do it properly. "I wish I could say I would do it all differently if I could."

"You can't?" Chanel asked, surprised at how much that hurt.

"As I have grown older and watched your brother and sister mature, had the opportunity to observe the way you are with them, it's opened my eyes to many things. I have come to realize just how weak a person I am."

"If you see a problem you have the power to fix and do nothing to change it, then yes, I think that does make you weak."

"So pragmatic. Your father would have said the same thing, but you both would have assumed I had the power to change myself. If I did, do you think I would have worked so hard at changing you?"

"So, that's it? Things go on like always?"

"No," Beatrice uttered with vehement urgency. "If you'll give me another chance, I will do better now."

"So, you *have* changed." Could Chanel believe her?

"I've acknowledged the true cost of my weakness. The love and respect of my daughter. It's too much."

"I don't know if I can ever trust you to love me."

"I understand that and I don't expect weekly mother-daughter dates."

"I don't have time." Chanel realized how harsh that sounded after she said the words, and she winced.

Her mom gave her a wry smile. "Your time is spoken for, but maybe we could try for more often than once every couple of months."

"Let's see if we can make those visits more pleasant before we start making plans for more." Words were all well and good, but Chanel had two decades of her mother's criticisms and rejections echoing in her memories.

Beatrice nodded and then she did yet another out-of-character gesture, opening her arms for a hug. When Chanel didn't immediately move forward to accept, her mother took the initiative.

Chanel responded with their normal barely touching embrace, but her mom pulled her close in a cloud of her favorite Chanel No. 5 perfume and hugged her tight. "I love you, Chanel, and I'm very proud of the woman you've become. I'm so very, very sorry I wasn't a better mother."

Chanel sat in stunned silence for several seconds before returning the embrace.

"You don't think I'm too awkward and geeky for Demyan?" she asked against her mother's neck.

Still not ready to see the older woman's expression in case it wasn't kind.

But Beatrice moved back, forcing Chanel to meet her

eyes. "You listen to me, daughter. You are more than enough for that man. You are *all* that he needs. Now *you* need to believe that if you're going to be happy with him."

"It's only been a month, Mom."

"Your dad proposed on our third date."

The synergy of that took Chanel's breath away. Demyan hadn't proposed on their third date, but he'd told her then that they were starting something lifelong, not temporary. "I thought you got married because you were pregnant with me."

"I was pregnant, yes, but we'd already planned to get married. Only, our original plan was to do it after he finished his degree."

"You said…"

"A lot of stupid things."

Chanel's mouth dropped open in shock at her mother's blunt admission.

Beatrice gave a watery laugh. "Close your mouth. You'll catch flies."

"I love you, too, Mom."

"Thank you. That means more than you'll ever know. I know I don't deserve it."

"I didn't say I liked you," Chanel offered with her usual frankness and for once didn't regret it.

Their relationship was going to work only if they moved through the pain, not try to bury it.

"You will, sweetheart. You loved your daddy, but I was your favorite person the first eight years of your life."

"I don't remember." She didn't say it to belabor the point. She just didn't.

"You will. I'm stubborn, too. You didn't get it all from Jacob."

"What about Perry?"

"I'll talk to him. I guess I never realized how bad it was

in your mind between you. He really doesn't hate you. He's even told me he admires you."

Chanel made a disbelieving sound.

"It's true. You're brilliant in your field. I think it intimidates him. He's a strong businessman, but if he had your brains he'd be in Demyan's position."

With a penthouse with a view of the harbor? Her parents lived in the suburbs and she couldn't imagine them wanting anything different.

Her mother left soon thereafter, once she'd promised again to change and make sure Perry knew he had to alter the way he interacted with Chanel, too.

No one could have been more shocked than Chanel when she got a call from the man himself later that night. He apologized and admitted he'd thought she had always compared him unfavorably to her dad, just like her mom did.

Chanel didn't try to make him feel better. Perry did compare unfavorably with Jacob Tanner. Her dad had been a much kinder and loving father, but Chanel agreed to try to let the past go if the future was different.

How had Demyan affected such change in her life in so little time? She wasn't going to kid herself and try to say it was anything else, either.

Somehow Demyan had blown into her life and set it on a different path, one in which she didn't have to be lonely or rejected anymore.

If she could let herself trust him and the love she felt for him, the rest of her life could and would be different, too.

She picked up the phone and called him.

"Missing me, little one?" he asked without a greeting.

"Yes." There was a wealth of meaning in that one word, if he wanted to hear it.

"*Yes* as in yes, you miss me, or *yes* as in you will marry me?" he asked, sounding hopeful but cautious.

"Both."

"I will be there in ten minutes."

It was a half-hour drive from his penthouse, but she didn't argue.

Demyan knocked on Chanel's door with a minute to spare in the ten he'd promised her.

What he hadn't told her when she called was that he was already in the area.

The door swung open, and Chanel's eyes widened with disbelief. "How did you get here so fast?"

"I was already on the road." Had been for the better part of an hour, driving aimlessly, with each random turn taking him closer and closer to her apartment complex.

She frowned. "On your way here?"

"Not consciously." He'd argued with himself about the wisdom of calling or stopping by after she'd told him she wanted the night to think.

So far, respecting her wishes had been winning his internal debate.

"Then what were you doing over here?"

He gently pushed past her, not interested in having this discussion, or any other, on the stoop outside her door. "I was out for a drive."

"On this side of town?" she asked skeptically.

"Yes."

"But you weren't planning to come by."

"No." And that choice had clearly been the right one, though more difficult to follow through on than he wanted to admit.

"Do you go out for drives with no purpose often?" she asked, still sounding disbelieving.

"Not as such, no." He went through to the kitchen, where he poured himself two fingers of Volyarussian vodka before drinking half of it in two swallows.

He'd brought the bottle with him one night, telling her that sometimes he enjoyed a shot to unwind. She'd told him he could keep it in the freezer if he liked.

He did, though he rarely drank from it.

"Are you okay, Demyan?" she asked from the open archway between her living room and kitchen. "I thought you'd be happy."

"I didn't like the emptiness of my condo tonight." He should have found the lack of company peaceful.

A respite.

He hadn't. He'd become too accustomed to her presence in the evenings. Even when she only sat curled up with one of her never-ending scientific journals while he answered email, having her there was *pleasant*.

Had almost become necessary.

"I missed you, too."

"You wanted your space. To think," he reminded her, the planning side of his facile brain yelling at him that his reaction wasn't doing his agenda any favors.

"It was fruitful. Or have you forgotten what I told you on the phone?"

He slammed the drink onto the counter, clear liquid splashing over the sides, the smell of vodka wafting up. "I have not forgotten."

Her gray eyes flared at his action, but she didn't look worried. "And you're happy?"

"Ecstatic."

"You look it." The words were sarcastic, but an understanding light glowed in her lovely eyes.

"You are a *permanent fixture* in my life. It is only natural I would come to rely on your companionship to a certain extent." He tried to explain away his inability to remain in his empty apartment and work, as he'd planned to.

A small smile played around her mobile lips. "So, you considered me a permanent fixture before I agreed to marry you?"

"Yes." He was not in the habit of losing what he went after.

"I see. I wasn't nearly so confident, but I missed you like crazy when you were in Volyarus."

"And yet you refused my proposal at first."

"I didn't. I told you I had to think."

"That is not agreement."

"Life is not that black-and-white."

"Isn't it?"

"No." She moved right into his personal space. "I think you're even more freaked out by how fast everything has gone between us than I am."

"I am not." It had all been part of his plan, everything except this inexplicable reaction to her request for time away from him.

"You're acting freaked. Slamming back vodka and driving around like a teenager with his first car."

"I assure you, I did not peel rubber at any stoplights."

"Do teens still do that?"

"Some." He never had.

It would have not been fitting for a prince.

"I said yes, Demyan." She laid her hands on his chest, her eyes soft with emotion.

His arms automatically went around her, locking her into his embrace. "Why?"

Her agreement should have been enough, but he needed to know.

"My mom came by to talk. She told me not to give up on something this powerful just because it scares me."

"Your mother?" he asked, finding that one hard to take in.

"Yes. She wants to try again, on our relationship."

"She does realize you are twenty-nine, not nineteen?"

Chanel smiled, sadness and hope both lurking in the storm-cloud depths of her eyes. "We both do. It's not happy families all of a sudden, but I'm willing to meet her partway."

"You're a more forgiving person than I am."

"I'm not so sure about that, but one thing I do know. Holding bitterness and anger inside hurts me more than anyone who has ever hurt me."

A cold wind blew across his soul. Demyan hoped she remembered that if she ever found out the truth about her great-great-grandfather's will.

She frowned up at him. "You were driving without your glasses?"

"I don't need them to drive." He didn't need them at all but wasn't sure when he was going to break that news to her.

"You always wear them, except in bed."

"They're not that corrective." Were in fact just clear plastic.

"They're a crutch for you," she said with that analytical look she got sometimes.

"You could say that."

"Do you need them at all?"

He didn't even consider lying in answer to the direct question. "No."

He expected anger, or at least the question, *why did he wear them?* But instead he got a measured glance that implied understanding, which confused him. "If I can step off the precipice and agree to marry you, you can stop wearing the glasses."

The tumblers clicked into place. She saw the glasses

as the crutch she'd named them for him. Being who she was, it never occurred to her that they were more a prop.

"Fine." More than. Remembering them was a pain.

She grinned up at him and he found himself returning the expression with interest, a strange, tight but not unpleasant feeling in his chest.

"Want to celebrate getting engaged?" she asked with an exaggerated flutter of her eyelashes.

The urge to tease came out of nowhere, but he went with it. "You want a shot of my vodka?"

He liked the man he became in this woman's presence.

"I was thinking something more *mind-blowing* and less about imbibing and more about experiencing." She drew out the last word as she ran her fingertip across his lips, down his face and neck and on downward over his chest, until she stopped with it hovering right over his nipple.

He tugged her closer, his body reacting as it always did to her nearness. "I'm all about the experience."

"Are you?" she asked.

He sighed and admitted, "Not usually, no. My position consumes my life."

"Not anymore."

"No, not anymore." He hadn't planned it this way, but marrying Chanel Tanner was going to change everything.

He could feel it with the same sense of inevitability he'd had the first time he'd seen her picture in his uncle's study. Only now he knew marrying her wasn't going to be a temporary action to effect a permanent fix for his country.

And he was glad. The sex *was* mind-blowing, but that didn't shock him as much as it did her. What *he* hadn't anticipated was that her company would be just as satisfying to him, even when it came without the cataclysm of climax.

Right now, though? He planned to have both.

* * *

Chanel adjusted her seat belt, the physical restraint doing nothing to dispel the sense of unreality infusing her being.

Once she'd agreed to marry Demyan, he'd lost no time setting the date, a mere six weeks from the night of their engagement. He'd told her that his aunt wanted to plan the wedding.

Chanel, who was one of the few little girls in her class at school who had not spent her childhood dreaming of the perfect wedding, was eminently happy to have someone else liaise and plan with her mother. Beatrice was determined to turn the rushed wedding into a major social event.

And the less Chanel had to participate in that, the better. If she could have convinced Demyan to elope, she would have, but he had this weird idea that she *deserved* a real wedding.

Since she'd made it clear how very much she *didn't* want to be the center of attention in a big production like the type of wedding her mother would insist on, Chanel had drawn the conclusion the wedding was important to Demyan.

So, she gave in, both shocked and delighted to learn that her mom had agreed to have the wedding take place in Volyarus with no argument.

Beatrice had been vague when Chanel had asked why, something about Demyan's family being large and it only being right to have the wedding in his homeland. Chanel hadn't expected that kind of understanding from her mom and had been glad for it.

She'd even expressed genuine gratitude to Beatrice for taking over the planning role with Demyan's aunt. Chanel had spent the past weeks working extra hours so she could leave her research in a good place to take a four-week honeymoon in Volyarus.

She hadn't been disappointed at all when Demyan had

asked her if she'd be willing to get to know his homeland
for their honeymoon.

She loved the idea of spending a month in his company
learning all she could about the small island country and
its people, not to mention seeing him surrounded by family and the ones who had known him his whole life.

There was still a part of Chanel that felt like Demyan
was a stranger to her. Or rather a part of Demyan that she
did not know.

Her mother had flown out to Volyarus two weeks before to finalize plans for the wedding with Demyan's aunt.
Perry, Andrew and Laura were on the plane with Chanel
and Demyan now.

Perry *had* made a determined effort not to criticize her,
but Chanel couldn't tell if that was because of her mother's
talk with him or out of deference for Demyan. She'd never
seen her stepfather treat someone the way he did Demyan,
almost like business royalty, or something.

It made Chanel wonder.

"What is it you do at Yurkovich Tanner?" she asked as
the plane's engines warmed up.

Demyan turned to look at her, that possessive, content
expression he'd worn since the morning after she agreed
to marry him very much in evidence.

"Why do you ask?"

"Because I realized I don't know."

"I am the Head of Operations."

"In Seattle?" she asked, a little startled his job was such
a high-level one, but then annoyed with herself for not realizing it had to be.

Only, wasn't it odd for the corporate big fish to personally check out the recipients of their charitable donations?

"Worldwide," he said almost dismissively. "My office
is in Seattle."

"I knew that, at least." Worldwide, as in he was Head of Operations over all of Yurkovich Tanner?

She'd done a little research into the company after they gifted her with a university education. It wasn't small by any stretch. They held interests on almost every continent of the world and the CEO was the heir apparent to the Volyarussian throne.

That Demyan was Head of Operations meant he swam with some really exalted fish in his tank.

"You are looking at me oddly," Demyan accused.

"I didn't realize."

He brushed back a bouncy curl that had fallen into her eye, his own expression intent. "Does my job title matter so much?"

"I know your favorite writer, the way you like your steak and how many children your ideal family would have, but I don't know anything about your job."

"On the contrary, you know a great deal. You have sat beside me while I took conference calls with our operations in Africa and Asia."

"I tuned you out." Corporate speak wasn't nearly as interesting as science…or her erotic readings.

Now that she had practical experience, they were even more fascinating.

He smiled with a warm sincerity she loved, the expression almost common now. At least when directed at her. "You did not miss anything that would interest you."

"I figured." She sighed. "I just feel like I should understand this side of your life better. You work really long hours."

So did she, but it occurred to her that maybe his long hours weren't going to go away like hers now that she'd caught up on work for her extended honeymoon.

"It is a demanding job."

"Do you enjoy it?"

"Very much."

"Will you continue working twelve- to sixteen-hour days after we get back from Volyarus?"

"I will do my best to cut my hours back, but twelve-hour days are not uncommon."

"I see. Okay, then."

"Okay, what? You have that look you get."

"What look?"

"The stubborn one." His brows drew together. "The same one you got when you insisted on buying your wedding dress without your mother's or my aunt's input."

Demyan's aunt, Oxana, had offered a Givenchy gown. Chanel had turned her down. Demyan hadn't been happy, wanting to save Chanel the stress and expense of searching for the perfect dress. He knew clothes were not usually her thing, but Chanel refused to compromise on this issue.

While she couldn't really care less about the colors for the linens, what food would be served or even the order of events at the reception, there were two things Chanel did care about.

What she wore and who officiated.

On the officiate, she'd agreed to have Demyan's family Orthodox priest perform the service so long as the pastor from the church she'd attended since childhood, a man who had known and respected both her father and grandfather, led them in their personally written vows and spoke the final prayer.

Her dress she wasn't compromising on at all. Chanel and Laura had spent three weeks haunting eBay, vintage and resale shops, but they'd finally found the perfect one.

An original Chanel gown designed by Coco herself.

Because while her mother had named Chanel after her favorite designer, she'd also named her after the designer she'd been wearing when Chanel's dad proposed. Chanel had wanted a link to her dad on her wedding day and wearing the vintage dress was it.

The rayon lace overlay of magnolia blossoms draped to a demure fichu collar. However, the signature Coco Chanel angel sleeves with daring cutouts gave the dress an understated air of sexiness she liked.

The dress was designed to enhance a figure like Chanel's. Clinging to her breasts, waist and hips only to flare slightly from below the knee, the gown made her look and feel feminine without being flouncy and constrictively uncomfortable.

Buying it had nearly drained Chanel's savings account and she really didn't care. Her job paid well and Demyan wasn't exactly hurting for cash.

Demyan's mouth covered Chanel's and she was kissing him before she was even conscious he'd played his usual *get-Chanel's-attention-when-her-mind-is-wandering* card. She had to admit she liked it a lot more than the sharp rebukes she got from others because of her habit of getting lost in thought.

After several pleasurable seconds, he lifted his head.

Dazed, she smiled up at him even as she was aware of her brother making fake gagging gestures in his seat across the aisle.

Perry shushed him, but Chanel paid neither male any heed.

She was too focused on the look in Demyan's eyes. It was so warm.

"That's better," he said.

"Than?"

"You thinking about something else. You're only thinking about me, now."

She laughed softly. "Yes, I am."

CHAPTER NINE

"WHAT PUT THAT stubborn look on your face before?"

She had to think and then she remembered. "You said you worked twelve-hour days, usually."

"I did and you said that was okay."

"No, I said *okay* in acknowledgment."

"You do not approve of twelve-hour days."

She shrugged. "That's not really the issue."

"It's not?"

"No."

"What is the issue?"

"Children."

His brows drew together like he was confused about something. "We agreed we wanted at least two."

He'd figure it out. He was a smart man.

"We also agreed that because of health considerations and family history, I wouldn't get pregnant after thirty-five."

"So?"

"So, we may have to adjust for an only child, or no children at all."

"Why?" he asked, sounding dangerous, the expression on his gorgeous face equally forbidding.

"Children need both parents' attention."

"Not all children have two parents."

"But if they do, they deserve both of those parents to make them a priority."

"I will not shirk my responsibility to my children."

"A dad does more than live up to responsibilities. He takes his kids to the beach in sunny weather and attends their soccer games. You can't do that if you're working twelve-hour days five days a week."

Something ticked in his expression.

Her heart sank. "You work weekends."

"Thus far, yes."

Was this a deal breaker? No.

But she didn't like figuring it out now, either. "I'll volunteer with after-school programs," she decided. "I don't have to have children to have a complete life."

"You are threatening not to have children if I do not cut my hours?"

"I'm not threatening. I'm telling you I'm not bringing any children into this world who are going to spend their childhoods wondering how important they are to their dad, if at all."

"And you accuse me of seeing the world in only two colors."

"I see lots of shades and shadows. That doesn't mean my children are going to live under one or more of them."

"Have you never considered the art of compromise?"

"I suck at it." Hadn't he realized that already?

She gave in on what didn't matter, and on what did? Well, she could be a bit intransigent.

"This may be a problem. I am not known for giving in on what matters to me." He said it like she might not know.

"It's a good thing we agree on this issue, then."

Demyan didn't look comforted. "How is that?"

"You said you wanted to be the best father possible,

that you never wanted your children to doubt their place in your life."

"Yes."

"Then you agree it is better not to have them if your work schedule isn't going to change."

He looked tired suddenly, and frustrated. "It is not that simple."

"It can be."

"What do you suggest? That I let Yurkovich Tanner run into the ground?"

"I suggest you hire three assistants, one for each major market, men and women who know the company, who care about it and that you trust to make minor decisions. They're the first line for policy and decision making, leaving you open to spend your time on only the most high-level stuff."

"And if that's all I work on already?"

"It's not."

"You told me you tuned out my calls."

"That doesn't mean I can't access the memories."

"You're scary smart, aren't you?"

She shrugged, but they hadn't even bothered finishing her IQ test in high school after she completed the first three exercises before the tester even got the timer going. The teacher hadn't wanted her to feel like a freak.

If only he'd been able to coach her parents.

"You just found out what my job is and you're already giving advice on it." Far from annoyed, Demyan sounded admiring.

"I'm a quick thinker."

"You'd be brilliant in business."

"No interest." Much to both her mother's and Perry's distress.

"I'll talk it over with my uncle."

"Is he your business mentor?"

"He's my boss."

"He works for Yurkovich Tanner?"

"He's the King of Volyarus."

She waited for the rest of the joke, only it didn't come, and the look Demyan was giving her said it wasn't going to.

She knew that ultimately the ownership of Yurkovich Tanner resided with the monarchy of that country. However, the thought that Demyan's uncle and the king were one and the same person had never entered her mind.

"Your uncle is a king."

"Yes."

"Oxana?"

"Queen."

"She told me to call her Oxana."

"That is her privilege."

Chanel felt like she was going to be sick. "You never said."

"I didn't want to scare you off."

"Holding back important information is like lying."

"I'm called Prince Demyan, but I'm no knight in shining armor. At heart I am a Cossack, Chanel. You must realize that. Any armor I have is tarnished. I am a human man with human failings." He said it as if admitting a darkly held secret.

Another time, she would have teased him about his melodrama and the arrogance behind it. Right now? She needed to think.

"I wasn't expecting this. You're this corporate guy who wears sweaters." Only, he hadn't been wearing them, or the jeans, so much lately.

She hadn't really noticed, until now. Clothing didn't matter much to her. She wasn't her mother, or even Laura in that regard. But looking back, she realized there had been a lot of subtle changes over the past six weeks.

He dressed in suits so sharp they could have come out of the knife drawer. She hardly ever saw the more casual attire he'd been wearing when they first met. Sometimes in the evenings, but he never left the house in the morning wearing a sweater.

She never noticed him reaching to adjust glasses that weren't there anymore, either.

Which meant what? That he was a lot more confident than she'd thought.

Okay, anyone who thought Demyan Zaretsky lacked confidence needed to take a reality check. Her included.

She didn't know why he'd worn the glasses, but they weren't a crutch for some deep-seated insecurity.

And honestly, did that matter right now?

"Chanel," he prompted.

She stared at him, trying to make the difference between *who* he was and *what* he was make sense through the shock of his revelation. "You're a prince."

"It's a nominal title only."

"What does that even mean?" What she knew about royalty wouldn't fill a page, much less a book.

"Officially, I am a duke, but I am called prince at the pleasure of my uncle, the king."

"The one who raised you?" Still not making sense, and getting cloudier rather than clearer.

"He and Oxana raised me as a brother to Maksim, the Crown Prince. I was spare to the throne."

"Was?"

"My cousin's wife is expecting their first child."

"Next in line to the throne now?"

"Yes."

"It's just all so strange."

She looked around the plane, which had taken off at

some point but she couldn't have said when. Her family were all staring, making no effort to hide their interest.

Perry didn't look surprised at all, but Andrew's and Laura's eyes were both saucer wide.

"Mom and Perry knew," she guessed.

"Yes."

"They never said."

"They agreed my position might scare you off me. I wanted time to show you *I* am the man you promised to marry."

"But *you* are a prince."

"Does that change how you feel about me?" he demanded, no give for prevarication in his voice.

There were a lot of conflicting things going on inside Chanel, but this wasn't something she was in any question about. "No. I love you, not what you are."

"I am glad to hear it." The relief in his tone couldn't be faked.

"This is so cool," Andrew said, reminding Chanel of their audience.

She frowned at her little brother. "You might think so."

"I do, too," Laura said.

"The only thing that matters is what you think," Demyan said from beside her.

"The jury is still out on that one."

"Don't be flip."

She glared up at him. "I'm not. I mean it. Give me some time to process."

"Chanel—"

"No. I don't want to talk about it right now."

She didn't want to talk at all, and shut down every attempt either he or her family made on the rest of the flight, going so far as to feign sleep to get them all to just leave her alone for a bit.

Life had changed so fast and she'd thought she'd come to terms with that, but Demyan was still throwing her curveballs and Chanel had never been good at sports.

Their arrival in Volyarus was less overwhelming than she might have expected given Demyan's position.

Thankfully, there was no fanfare, no line of reporters with oversize cameras. Of course if there had been, she would have shown them all just how she'd gotten her black belt in tae kwon do, with Demyan as her unwitting assistant in the endeavor.

However, other than some official-looking men who looked like they were straight off the set of *Men in Black,* there were only two other people—Chanel's mother and a beautiful woman with an unmistakable regal bearing. Queen Oxana.

Demyan guided Chanel toward the two women with his hand on the small of her back. He stopped when they were facing his aunt and he introduced them all.

The queen put her hand out to Chanel. "It's a pleasure to meet you. Demyan speaks very highly of you, as does your mother."

Chanel did her best not to show her surprise.

She knew Beatrice was trying, but the idea she had actually *complimented* Chanel to the other woman was still too new to be anything but startling. Oxana had spent the past two weeks in Beatrice's company. In the past, Chanel would have been sure the results would be catastrophic for any hopes she might have of gaining the queen's regard.

From the look of both women, that wasn't something she had to worry about anymore.

Unexpected and warm pleasure poured through Chanel's heart, filling it to the brim, and she smiled at her mother before squeezing the queen's hand. "Thank you for making Demyan a part of *your* family. Someone taught him how to protect the people he cares about and I think that was you."

The lovely dark eyes widened, Oxana's mouth parting in shock and then curving into an open smile. "I believe he will be in very good hands with you, Chanel."

The king was waiting at the palace when they arrived, his manner more reserved and less welcoming to Chanel. She didn't mind.

She thought she understood.

Everyone else was acting as if it was perfectly normal for a prince to get engaged after a month and married six weeks later.

Obviously, King Fedir had his qualms about it.

Since Chanel still had her own fears, she had no problem with the fact he might have some, as well.

Wedding plans made it impossible for Chanel and Demyan to have any time alone for the rest of the day. She was not surprised to find him in her room late that night after she left her mother and the indefatigable Oxana still discussing seating charts.

Demyan pulled Chanel into his arms and kissed her for several long seconds before stepping back. "That is better."

"You missed me."

"I spend all day without you at work."

"But it was different here."

"Yes."

"Worried the mom of your heart would let slip too many of your secrets?" she teased, unprepared for the clearly guilty look that crossed his features. "What?"

He shook his gorgeous head. "Nothing."

"Demyan?"

"She is the mother of my heart."

"Have you told her and the king you filed for an official name change?"

"They will hear when the priest names me during the ceremony."

"You're a closet romantic, aren't you?"

"I am no romantic, Chanel."

"You just go on thinking that." Then a truly horrific thought assailed her. "Are people going to call me Princess after we are married?"

"Are you going to refuse to marry me if I say yes?" he asked, sounding way too serious.

"I'm not going to refuse to marry you, but Demyan, it's not easy, this finding-out-you're-royalty thing."

He nodded, as if he understood, but how could he? He'd grown up knowing what he was.

"So, about the princess thing…" She wasn't willing to let this go. Chanel wanted an answer.

He'd left enough out up to this point.

"That depends on my uncle."

"If he calls me princess…"

"Then others will."

"Oh." Considering the cool reception she'd received from King Fedir, she didn't think he was going to call her princess anytime soon.

"You look relieved."

"I'm not a princess in his eyes." As she said the words, she knew them to be absolute truth. And she didn't blame King Fedir for feeling that way. "I'm not nobility."

"You are. You inherited the title from your great-great-grandfather—you are a dame. Marrying me will make you a duchess."

"So?"

"So, even if you are not called princess, most will call you by your title." His expression and tone said he was perfectly aware she wasn't going to see that truth as a benefit to marriage.

"That's medieval."

"No. Trust me, the nobility system is alive and well in many modern countries."

"But…" She didn't want to be called duchess.

"The correct term is Your Grace."

"That makes me sound like, like… What do they call them, a cardinal or something in the Catholic church."

He laughed, like she'd been joking.

She wasn't, "I'm… This is…"

He didn't let her keep floundering. Showing he knew exactly what Chanel needed—him—Demyan pulled her into his arms and kissed her.

All thoughts of unwanted titles and unexpected ties to royalty went flying from her head in favor of one consuming emotion. Love for the man so intent on making her his wife.

Over the next few days, Chanel hardly saw Demyan—except when he came to her room at night and made passionate, almost desperate love to her.

She didn't understand, but it felt like he was avoiding her. Not sure that wasn't her old insecurities talking, she refused to voice her concerns aloud.

He didn't seem inclined to anything serious for pillow talk either, but she understood that. Chanel certainly didn't want to talk about the wedding and its never-ending preparations and plans. Nor was she interested in discussing her fledgling closer relationship with her mother and stepfather.

Beatrice was in her element planning a wedding for her daughter to a prince. A cynical part of Chanel couldn't help wondering how much of her mother's newfound approval stemmed from this unexpected turn of events.

Perry wasn't nearly as overtly critical as he had been in the past, but he didn't go out of his way to extend even pseudo fatherly warmth, either.

As they had been for the majority of her life, Laura and Andrew were two bright beacons of sincere love and affection for Chanel. Their steady presence reminded her that no matter how her life might change by marrying royalty, some things—the truly important things—remained.

Though she saw little of him during the day, Demyan arrived in her room every night—sometimes very late and clearly exhausted. Apparently when he was in Volyarus, his duties extended beyond the company business into the family business: the politics of royalty.

Sometimes they didn't make love before falling into exhausted slumber, but those nights he woke her in the wee hours in order to bring amazing pleasure to her body.

He'd found time to sit with her today, though, while she and her stepfather's lawyer went over the prenuptial agreement. Perry had offered his expertise as well, but honestly?

Chanel trusted Demyan to watch out for her best interests more than her stepfather.

Once she'd read it through, though, she didn't think she needed anyone else's interpretation. For a legal document, the language was straightforward and to the point.

There was some serious overkill in her opinion, but nothing that bothered Chanel to sign.

Upon her marriage, she and her heirs gave up any and all rights they might have in Volyarus, its financial and political endeavors and anything specifically related to the business enterprises of the Yurkovich family.

The fact that particular paragraph was followed by one giving any children she had with Demyan full interest as *his* heirs, she felt was particular overkill.

Clearly, the royal family was very protective of their interests, though. King Fedir's influence, no doubt.

The man had not warmed up to her at all, but he'd never been unkind, either. After her years with Beatrice and Perry, Chanel was practically inured to anything less than overt hostility.

Even with what she was sure were the king's stipulations, the terms of the agreement were very generous toward Chanel, considering the fact she wasn't bringing any significant accumulated wealth to the marriage. The agreement guaranteed an annual sum for living expenses that Chanel couldn't imagine spending in five years, never mind one.

Unless it was on research, but she didn't see Demyan approving using their personal finances to fund her scientific obsessions. Yurkovich Tanner had been generous in that regard already.

One thing the prenup spelled out in black and white, oversize and bolded print to her heart was that Demyan wanted their relationship to be permanent. If she'd been in any doubt.

Which she wasn't.

The financial provision did not decrease in the event of his death. The annual income was Chanel's and her children's for her lifetime and theirs.

There were some other pretty stringent requirements that would insure she didn't divorce Demyan or be unfaithful to him, though. Not that she would ever do either.

But the agreement spelled out quite clearly that any children born of a different father had absolutely no financial interest through her or any other source in the Yurkovich, Zaretsky or Volyarussian wealth.

Oddly, if she divorced Demyan, or he divorced her for anything other than *her* infidelity, she would still be well taken care of. Until she remarried. If she were ever to marry someone else, or have irrefutable evidence of infidelity brought against her, she lost all financial benefits from her marriage to Demyan.

It wasn't anything less than she expected, but having it spelled out in black and white sent a shiver along her spine that was not exactly pleasant.

Demyan laid his hand over hers before she signed. "You are okay with all the terms?"

"They are more than generous."

"I will always make sure you have what you need, no matter what the agreement says."

"I believe you." And she did. With everything in her.

CHAPTER TEN

The morning of Chanel's wedding was every bit as tediously focused on beauty, fashion and making an impact as she'd feared it might be with Beatrice in charge.

Strangely, for the first time in her life, Chanel found she didn't mind her mother's fussing over her appearance.

For once, going through the paces of having her legs waxed, her hair done and makeup applied resonated with an almost welcome familiarity in this strange new situation that had become her life.

It had been years since Chanel had sat through one of her mother's preparation routines for a social function, but the sound of Beatrice's voice giving instruction to the stylists resonated with old memories.

Memories were so much easier to deal with than the reality of the present. She was marrying a prince.

It was beyond surreal.

"Your fingers are like ice." The manicurist frowned as she took Chanel's hand out of the moisturizing soak. "Why did you say nothing? The water must be too cold."

Beatrice was there in a second, testing the water with her own finger and giving Chanel a look filled with concern. "Are you all right, sweetheart?"

Chanel nodded.

Her mom did not look comforted. "The argan oil solution is warm enough, but the manicurist is right. Your hands feel like they've been wrapped around an icicle."

Chanel shrugged.

"Mom, she's marrying a prince. That's not exactly Chanel's dream job," Laura said in that tone only a teenager could get just right. "She's stressed out."

"But he's perfect for you."

"You've barely seen us together. How would you know?" Chanel asked, with little inflection.

"You love him."

Chanel nodded again. There was no point in denying the one thing that would prompt her to marry a man related to royalty.

"He adores you."

Laura grinned at Chanel, her eyes filled with understanding. "I agree with Mom on that one, at least."

"I think he does," Chanel admitted. Demyan acted like a man very happy with his future.

Beatrice reached out and put her hand against Chanel's temple, frowning at whatever she felt there. "You're in shock."

"Sheesh, Mom, way to state the obvious." Laura didn't roll her eyes, but it was close.

Beatrice frowned. "I do not appreciate your tone, young lady."

"Well, you're acting like Chanel should be all excited and happy when it's probably taking everything in her not to run away. She's a scientist, Mom, not a socialite."

"I am well aware of my daughter's chosen profession." Beatrice was careful not to frown—that caused wrinkles— but her tone conveyed displeasure.

The interaction fascinated Chanel, who hadn't realized her mother and Laura had anything less than the ideal mother-daughter relationship.

Beatrice looked at Chanel. "Do you need some orange juice to bring up your blood sugar?"

Chanel shook her head. "It just doesn't feel real."

"Believe it or not, I threw up twice before walking down the aisle to your father," Beatrice offered with too much embarrassment for it not to be sincere.

Laura snorted. "You were preggers, Mom. It was probably morning sickness."

"I was not morning sick. I was terrified. I nearly fainted when I was getting ready for my wedding to *your* father."

Chanel couldn't imagine her mother agitated to that level. "Really?"

"It's a huge step, marriage. No matter how much you love the man you're marrying."

"I don't know what the big deal is. If it doesn't work out, they can get divorced," Laura said with the blasé confidence of youth.

Their mother glared at her youngest daughter. "That is not the attitude women of this family take into marriage."

"You and Chanel can get all stressed about it, but I'm not going to. If I get married at all. It all seems like a lot of bother over something that ends in divorce about fifty percent of the time. I think living together makes a lot more sense."

Chanel almost laughed at the look of absolute horror crossing their mother's features. She would have, if she could feel anything that deeply.

Right now the entire world around her was one level removed.

"Stop looking like that, Mom. You and Chanel take everything so seriously. I'm not like you."

It was a total revelation to Chanel that Laura considered her like their mother.

"You're more like us than you realize, young lady. Regardless, there will be no more talk of divorce on your sister's wedding day."

Chanel had never heard her mother use that particular tone with her golden-child sister.

And Laura listened, but her less-than-subdued expression implied she *had* heard it before and didn't find it all that intimidating.

How much had Chanel missed about the world around her? She hadn't realized Demyan was a corporate king, much less a real-life prince. She'd had no idea her mother still loved her father and she'd been sure Beatrice no longer loved *her*.

Chanel had been wrong on all counts.

It was a sobering and hopeful realization at the same time.

Nevertheless, she continued through the rest of her personal preparations for the wedding in the fog of shock that had plagued her since waking without Demyan in her bed.

As the makeup artist finished the final application of lip color, a knock sounded at the door.

"The driver is here. Are you both ready?" Beatrice asked, managing to the look the part of the mother of the bride for a prince, anyway.

Laura looked like a blond angel in her ice-blue Vera Wang maid-of-honor dress that was a perfect complement to Chanel's vintage designer gown.

Chanel hoped her mother had worked some kind of magic and she looked her part, as well. She hadn't looked in the mirror since the hair stylist had shown up.

"It's not the driver," Laura announced after opening the door. Then she dropped into a curtsy and Chanel's throat constricted.

Had the king come to tell her he didn't want Chanel

marrying his quasi-adopted son? No, that was an irrational thought.

But…her thoughts stopped their spin out of control in the face of the majesty that was Queen Oxana in full regalia. The Queen of Volyarus swept into the room, making the huge chamber feel very small all of a sudden.

"Good morning, Chanel. Beatrice." The queen gave Chanel's mother a small incline of her head and then a smile to Laura. "Laura, you look lovely."

"Thank you, Your Majesty," Laura replied with her irrepressible smile.

"And you, my dear," the queen said as she focused her considerable attention on Chanel. "You look absolutely perfect. That's an original by Coco Chanel herself, is it not?"

"Yes."

"She was a brilliant and innovative designer who changed the face of female haute couture almost single-handedly. I find your choice to dress in one of her gowns singularly appropriate as I am sure you will be equally as impacting in your field."

It was the first time anyone who mattered to Chanel emotionally had made such a claim. Bittersweet joy squeezed at her heart, even through the layer of numbness surrounding that organ. "Thank you."

Oxana smiled. "You are very welcome." She offered Chanel a medium-sized dark blue velvet box meant for jewelry. "I would be honored if you would wear this."

Expecting pearls, or something of that nature, Chanel felt her heart beat in a rapid tattoo of shock at the sight of the diamond-encrusted tiara. It wasn't anything as imposing as the crown presently resting on the queen's perfectly coiffed hair, but it *was* worthy of a princess.

"I'm not... This is..." Chanel didn't know what to say, so she closed her mouth on more empty words.

"Part of my own wedding outfit," the queen finished for her. "It would please me to see it worn again."

"Didn't Prince Maksim's wife wear it?" Laura asked, managing to verbalize at least one of the questions swirling through Chanel's brain.

"King Fedir gave her his mother's princess tiara. It was decided between us that mine would be reserved for the wife of our eldest."

Chanel's heart warmed to hear Demyan referred to as the eldest child of the king and queen.

Somehow, though the stylist had been unaware that a tiara would be added later, the updo she had designed for Chanel lent itself perfectly to the diamond-encrusted accessory.

Or so her mother told Chanel.

"Here, see for yourself," Oxana insisted.

Both Laura and Beatrice gave her a concerned look. So, they had noticed she hadn't looked in the mirror since that morning.

But Chanel didn't want visual proof that she didn't look like a princess.

"I trust your judgment," Chanel hedged.

"Then you will trust my instruction to look at yourself, my soon-to-be daughter." Oxana's expression did not invite argument.

Oh, gosh...she'd never even considered this woman would truly consider herself Chanel's mother-in-law.

"You look like a princess," Beatrice said with far more sincerity than such a trite statement deserved.

"You're going to knock Demyan on his butt," Laura added with a little less finesse, but no less certainty.

Far from offended, the queen laughed and agreed. "Yes, I do believe you will."

Taking a breath for courage, Chanel turned to face the impartial judge that could not be gainsaid. The mirror reflected only what was—it made no judgments about that image.

The woman staring back at Chanel with wide gray eyes did not look like a queen. No layers and layers of organza to look like any princess bride Chanel had ever seen in the tabloids, either, but in this moment she *was* beautiful.

The vintage Coco Chanel design fit her like it had been tailored to her figure, the antique lace clinging in all the right places. The single-layer floor-length veil and tiara added elegance Chanel was not used to seeing when she looked in a mirror.

The makeup artist had managed to bring out the shape and pink tint of Chanel's lips while making her eyes glow. Her curls had been tamed into perfect corkscrews and then pinned up so that the length of her neck looked almost swanlike.

This woman would not embarrass Demyan walking up the aisle.

Chanel turned to her mother and hugged Beatrice with more emotion than she'd allowed herself to show in years with the older woman. "Thank you."

"It was my pleasure. It has been a very long time since you allowed me to fuss over you. I enjoyed it." Beatrice returned the embrace and then stepped back, blinking at the moisture in her eyes.

Chanel and her mother would probably never agree on what it meant to *fuss* over someone else, but she began to see that, in her own way, her mother hadn't abandoned Chanel completely as a child.

* * *

Wearing the gold-and-dark-blue official uniform of the Volyarussian Cossack Hetman, Demyan waited at the bottom of the palace steps, as it was his country's royal tradition that he ride with Chanel in the horse-drawn carriage to the cathedral.

His dark eyes met hers, his handsome face stern and unemotional. Yet despite wearing what she'd come to think of as his "corporate king" face, there was an unmistakable soul-deep satisfaction glimmering in his gaze.

He put his hand out toward her. The white-glove-covered appendage hung there, an unexpected beacon. He wasn't supposed to take her hand yet; he wasn't supposed to touch her at all. They had been instructed to enter the carriage separately. She was to sit with her back toward the driver and he was to face the people on the slow procession to the Orthodox cathedral.

According to the wedding coordinator and royal tradition, she and Demyan were not supposed to touch so much as fingertips until the priest proclaimed them man and wife.

So this one gesture spoke volumes of her prince's willingness to put Chanel ahead of protocol.

Without warning, the mental and emotional fog surrounding Chanel fell away, the world coming into stark relief for the first time that day. Though it was early fall, the sun shone bright in the sky, the air around them crisp with autumn chill and filled with a cacophony of voices from the crowds lining the palace drive that were suddenly loud.

Love for Demyan swelled inside Chanel, pushing aside worry and doubt to fill her with a certainty that drove her forward toward the hand held out to her.

Their fingers touched, his curling possessively and decisively around her cold ones. He tugged her forward even as electric current arced between them despite the barrier of his glove.

Devastating emotion shuddered through her, completely dispelling the last of the strange, surreal sensations that had plagued her since waking.

His eyes flared and then he was pulling off the cape from his uniform and wrapping it around her. Several gasps sounded around them and the king said something that Chanel had no doubt was a protest.

She couldn't hear him, though, not over the blood rushing in her ears. The long military cloak settled around her shoulders. She didn't argue that she wasn't really cold, because it carried the fragrance of Demyan's cologne and skin, making her feel embraced by him.

He helped her into the open landau carriage, further eschewing protocol to sit beside her.

Cameras flashed, people cheered and while all of it registered, none of it really impacted Chanel. She was too focused on the man holding her hand and looking at her with quietly banked joy.

"It's just you and me," she said softly, understanding at last.

"Yes."

He didn't relate to her as a prince, though he was undeniably that. Demyan related to her as the man who wanted to share his life with her.

That life might be more complicated because of his title, but at the core, it was the life she wanted. Just as at the core, she knew this man and connected to him soul to soul.

The deep happiness reflecting in his gaze darkened to something more serious. "Always believe that, no matter what else might come up, our marriage is about you and me. Full stop."

"Period," she finished, her heart filled to bursting with such love for this man.

It didn't have to make sense, or be rational, she realized. She had fallen for him immediately and she was wholly and completely *in love* with him now.

They could have waited another year to marry and she wouldn't be any surer of him than she was right now.

As her mom had said, this man was *it* for Chanel, the love of her life, and he felt the same. Even if he hadn't said the words.

Even if he never did.

"I love you," she said to him, needing to in that moment as much as she needed to breathe.

"I will treasure that gift for the rest of my life, I promise you."

He made the vow official less than an hour later when he said it in front of the filled-to-capacity cathedral as part of the personal vows they'd agreed to speak. He also promised to care for her, respect her and support her efforts to make the world a better place through science.

Chanel, who never cried, felt hot tears tracking down her cheeks—thank goodness for her mother's insistence on waterproof makeup—as she spoke her own personal promises, including one to love Demyan for the rest of her life.

It wasn't hard to promise something she didn't think she had a choice about anyway.

His name change was also acknowledged for the first time publicly during the wedding ceremony, when the Orthodox priest led them in their formalized vows before pronouncing them married.

A murmur rippled through the crowd, but Demyan seemed oblivious, his attention wholly on Chanel.

The king's expression was filled with more emotion than Chanel thought the rather standoffish King of

Volyarus capable of as he made his official acknowledgment of his *son's* new married state.

Crown Prince Maksim and his wife were both gracious and clearly happy about the name change when Chanel finally met them for the reception line after the ceremony.

She'd thought it odd she hadn't yet met Demyan's *brother* and was relieved when Princess Gillian remarked on it, as well.

It had been clear from several remarks Demyan made that the two men were close. The fact Chanel hadn't been introduced before had had her wondering if maybe the Crown Prince had disapproved of the wedding.

Only now it was obvious he hadn't even known about the upcoming nuptials until he'd been summoned back to Volyarus by his parents. Chanel didn't understand it, but she was the first person to admit that most politics of social interaction and even family relationships went right over her head.

Prince Maksim seemed nice enough and quite willing to accept Chanel into the family. His own wife wasn't royalty or even nobility, so he had to have a fully modern view of marriage within his family.

Though a comment, or two, made by his wife implied otherwise.

Once they'd finished greeting those allowed into the formal reception line, the entire Yurkovich family addressed the people of Volyarus from the main balcony at the front of the palace. The king gave a speech. They all waved and smiled for what felt like hours before everyone but she and Demyan retreated inside.

He addressed the crowd, telling them how honored he was that Dame Chanel Tanner had agreed to be his wife, that he knew her ancestor Baron Tanner would have been very happy, as well.

Then he kissed Chanel.

And it wasn't a chaste, for-the-masses kiss. Demyan took her mouth with gentle implacability, showing her and everyone watching how very pleased he was she was now officially *his*.

Chanel found herself separated from Demyan during the reception, but she wasn't surprised.

He'd prepared her for the way the formal event would unfold, during which they would have very little time together. He had promised to make up for that on their wedding night and the extended honeymoon that was to follow.

What did surprise Chanel was to find herself completely without any of the people who had seemed intent on making sure she was never on her own in the highly political gathering.

Queen Oxana was occupied talking to Princess Gillian. Chanel's mother had been waylaid by an elderly duke, while Andrew flirted with the man's granddaughter under the watchful and not-very-happy gaze of the teen's eagle-eyed mother. Perry was talking business in a corner somewhere—not that he was one of Chanel's self-appointed minders.

Even Laura had lost herself in the crowd.

Chanel thought now would be the ideal time to find a quiet place to regroup a little. The crush of people was overwhelming for a scientist who spent most of her days in the lab, the mixture of so many voices sounding like a roar in her ears.

Seeing a likely hallway, she ducked out of the huge ballroom. The farther she walked along the hallway, the more muted the cacophony of voices from the ballroom became and the more tension drained from her until even her hands, which had been fisted unconsciously at her sides, uncurled.

Only as her fingers straightened did she realize how very hard she'd been holding them.

She could hear voices ahead, one whose tones she recognized with a smile. Demyan.

Delighted by the opportunity to see him amidst the chaos of her wedding day, she quickened her steps, only slowing down when she realized who he was with.

King Fedir.

The one person who intimidated Chanel and brought out her barely resolved and all-too-recent insecurities. There were two other voices as well, a woman and a man.

They were all speaking Ukrainian, thinly veiled anger resonating in at least two of the speakers' tones.

As Chanel slowed her progress, their conversation resolved itself into actual words she could understand.

The unknown woman demanded, "How dare you humiliate us this way?"

"My actions were not intended as an insult toward you." Demyan did not sound particularly worried the woman had taken whatever he'd done as such, though.

"How could they be taken any other way?" a man who was not the king said. "You have repudiated us before all of Volyarus."

"I didn't repudiate you. I aligned myself with my true family."

"I gave you birth," the woman said in fury.

And the identity of the other two people became clear to Chanel: Demyan's birth parents.

"You also *gave* me to your brother, abdicating any responsibilities and all emotional connections to me. I am no longer your son."

"You are not a child." The man speaking had to be De-

myan's biological father. "You know why that was necessary."

"I know that you traded your son for the chance at leverage over your brother-in-law, the king. I know that Fedir
and Oxana needed a secondary heir to the throne, but they
have always treated me as more than an expedience."

"I'm very pleased you took our house's name, Demyan," the king said with sincerity. "Your parents could
have avoided this surprise today by allowing Oxana and
me to adopt you as a child. It was their choice not to, as
you said...for their own expedience. I, for one, was joy-
fully surprised and I know your mother feels the same."

Chanel smiled, pleased the outwardly cold man so obviously cared about his adopted son. Demyan said something she did not catch.

"You think you are more than an expedience to the
king and queen?" Duke Zaretsky sneered. "He has just
ensured you sacrificed the rest of your life for the sake
of his family's wealth. You are far more his tool than you
were ever mine."

Chanel didn't understand what the duke meant by his
words, but there was no question they were intended to
wound. And she wasn't about to stand by while anyone
tried to hurt Demyan.

She pushed open the door to what turned out to be a
very impressive masculine study and crossed to Demyan's side quickly.

His dark gaze flared with something that looked like
worry before pleasure at her presence sparked to life, as
well. "Hello, *sérdeńko.*"

"What are you doing here?" the king asked with his
usual less-than-warm attitude toward her.

"The reception was getting too loud."

"You cannot abandon your responsibilities as a hostess on a whim."

"Really? Then what are you doing back here?" she asked with enough sarcasm to be mistaken for her sister. "Correct me if I'm wrong, but wasn't it *your* name on the invitation listed as host of this party?"

Demyan laughed, taking her hand and pulling her to his side. "You make an excellent case, little one."

Everyone in the room except Chanel showed differing levels of surprise at his humor. The king recovered first, giving her a grudging look of respect when she'd expected a frown and polite dressing-down.

She had a lot of experience with both and a lifetime realizing she was no good at taking the path of least resistance, even if it meant avoiding them.

"Point taken," King Fedir said. "We should *all* be getting back."

"Does she know yet?" the duke asked, his expression calculating, his tone undeniably malicious.

CHAPTER ELEVEN

CHANEL DIDN'T ASK what he meant, or even acknowledge the man had spoken.

He'd done it in Ukrainian. Somehow she doubted Demyan had been into sharing confidences with the older man, which meant the duke had no idea she understood the language. That made his choice to converse in it pointedly without courtesy.

"You will be silent," the king replied in the same language to his brother-in-law, his tone harsh.

Ignoring both posturing men, Chanel smiled up at Demyan. "I missed you."

"Oh, how sweet," Princess Svitlana said in a tone that made it clear she thought it was anything but.

Demyan's expression was an odd mixture of tenderness and a strange underlying anxiety as he looked down at Chanel. "I am very proud of you. Not many science geeks would do so well at an affair of state with so little training."

"You assigned a very potent group of babysitters."

His nostrils flared as if her words surprised him.

"You didn't think I realized you'd asked them to watch over me?" Once she had, she'd felt very well cared for.

Demyan would never leave Chanel to sink or swim in the shark-infested waters of his life.

"I could not be with you the entire time," he said by way of an explanation.

Not that she'd needed one. "Because you're a prince."

"It's a nominative title only," his birth mother said with more venom, in English this time. "He's no more a prince than you are a well-bred princess."

Chanel gave the older woman a measure of her attention, but kept her body and clear allegiance toward Demyan. "I am not a horse and I wasn't born in a breeding program. While I won't claim to be a princess, Demyan is definitely a prince."

"He won't inherit. Not now that Princess Gillian is carrying the next heir to the throne."

"But he is the king and queen's son. That makes him a prince."

"I gave birth to him," the duchess said.

Chanel found it odd that the duke never verbalized his claim at fatherhood. "Congratulations."

"Are you mocking me?"

"No. I don't know what your other children are like. Hopefully more like their older brother than their parents, but I do know you gave birth to an amazing man in Demyan. I'm sure you are very proud of that accomplishment, but you aren't his mother any more than I am a princess."

"Oxana is my mother," Demyan asserted with absolute assurance.

"And you would do anything for her and the man you consider your father, even marry some socially backward American *scientist* to protect the Yurkovich financial interests." She said scientist as if it was a dirty word.

Chanel almost smiled. She'd never considered her vocation as beyond the pale before.

"That is enough, Svitlana." The king's tone was again harsh, his expression forbidding.

"Oh, so you *haven't* told her?" Duke Zaretsky asked snidely, clearly ignoring his king's evident wrath and this time taking evident pleasure in speaking English. "I could almost feel sorry for her. She gave up hundreds of millions of dollars by marrying you and she doesn't even know it."

There could be no doubt the duke was talking about Chanel, but the words made absolutely no sense.

"I didn't give up anything and gained everything marrying Demyan," she fiercely asserted.

The duchess looked at her pityingly. "You have no idea, but no matter what kind of prenuptial agreement these two convinced you to sign, until you spoke your vows three hours ago, you were a twenty-percent owner in Yurkovich Tanner."

"I wasn't. My great-great-grandfather left his shares to the Volyarussian people." He'd told her great-grandmother so in a letter still in Chanel's possession, along with the family Bible.

"And they have been used to finance infrastructure, schools and hospitals since then," the king assured her.

She smiled at him, holding no grudge for his unwelcoming demeanor. "I know. I did some research when I got the scholarship. Your country is kind of amazing for its progressive stance on the environment and energy conservation."

"I am glad you think so."

"That money was yours," the king's sister insisted. "Until you married my son."

The claims were starting to make an awful kind of sense, but Chanel had no intention of allowing the two emotional vultures in front of her to know about the splinters of pain slicing their way through Chanel's heart.

She simply said, "He's not your son."

"Would you like to see your grandfather's will?" the duke asked, clearly unwilling to give up.

Two things were obvious in that moment. The first was that there had to be some truth to what the duke and his wife were saying. If there wasn't, Demyan and the king would have categorically denied it.

Also, they were both way too tense now for the claims to be entirely false.

Second, whatever the duke and Princess Svitlana's motives for telling Chanel, it had nothing to do with helping or protecting *anyone*. Her least of all.

In fact, she was fairly certain their intention was to hurt the son who had finally made a public alliance with the family who had raised him.

She turned away from the duke and duchess to face Demyan. "Tell me your siblings don't take after your egg and sperm donors."

Duplicate sounds of outrage indicated the Zaretskys had heard her just fine.

Demyan didn't respond, an expression she'd never seen in his eyes. Fear.

She wasn't sure what he was afraid of. Whether he was afraid she would mess up whatever plan he'd made with King Fedir, or worried she would go ballistic at their very politically attended reception, or something else really didn't matter.

Whatever Demyan felt for her, Chanel loved him and she wasn't going to let the two people whose rejection had already caused him a lifetime of pain hurt him anymore.

"I think it's time we all returned to the reception." She couldn't quite dredge up a smile, but she did her best to mask her own hurt.

He spoke then, the words coming out in a strange tone. "We need to talk."

She didn't want him showing vulnerability in front of the Zaretskys. Chanel wasn't giving them the satisfaction of believing they'd succeeded in their petty and vindictive efforts.

She reached up and cupped his face, like he did so often with her, hoping it gave him the same sense of comfort and being cared for it had always done her, no matter how much of a lie it might have been at the time. "Later."

"You promise?"

"Yes."

"She is a fool," the duke said in disgusted Ukrainian.

Chanel looked at him over her shoulder, her expression a perfect reflection of her mother's favorite one for disdain. "The only fool here is you if you think for one second you have the power to influence my prince's life for good or ill today, or any time in the future. You simply don't matter."

She had also spoken in his native language and enjoyed the shock that produced in the overweening nobleman.

The duchess gasped. "You're American."

"Which does not equate to uninformed, stupid or uneducated." Chanel met eyes so similar in color but different in expression from Demyan's. "My heritage in this country may not be royal, or as long-standing, but when it comes to the welfare of Volyarus, it is equally as important as yours."

Her grandfather had helped this nation stay afloat financially three decades ago and his efforts were still benefitting the Volyarussians.

"You already knew," the duchess said, almost as if she admired Chanel's acumen. "But then why did you marry him?"

"Because she loves me," Demyan said, his voice gravelly.

Chanel turned back to him without agreeing or giving his parents another single solitary moment of her time. She hadn't known about the will being different than what her great-grandmother had believed, or what that had to do with Chanel's marriage to Demyan, though she could make a pretty educated guess based on the prenuptial agreement.

She wasn't about to admit that to the Zaretskys, though.

Demyan was searching her face as if trying to read Chanel's thoughts. So far in their relationship, she'd been an open book. She had little hope of hiding what was going on in her head right now.

But she didn't have to talk about it. Especially in front of the older generation of the royal family.

"Leave," the king said to his sister and brother-in-law.

The Zaretskys started for the door of the study.

"No," the king instructed. "Out through the secret passage. You will not return to the reception and you will be out of the palace within the hour."

"What? You cannot be serious. How would that look?" his sister demanded.

"Like you threw a temper tantrum when your son chose to change his name to reflect his true parentage," the king replied, his tone arctic.

Princess Svitlana crossed her arms, but stopped just shy of stomping her feet. "I won't do it."

"You will. Do not presume to forget that this is not a nominal King of Volyarus. I hold the power to revoke your citizenship and deport you. Do not tempt me to use it."

The duke and his wife both paled at the king's words, Princess Svitlana doing a fair imitation of a gasping fish, though no words passed her lips.

The expression in her brother's eyes suggested she keep it that way.

Showing she was marginally more intelligent than evidence might suggest, the princess left without another word. Through the secret passageway. Her husband followed close behind her.

Chanel stepped back from Demyan, intending to return to the reception. The crowds of people and litany of voices that fifteen minutes ago had seemed so overwhelming now called like a beacon for escape from the thoughts that were multiplying by the second in her head.

And with every new thought came a shard of pain Chanel had no idea how long she could contain.

The king blocked her exit, his gaze searching hers as much as his adopted son's had done. However, the level of ruthlessness behind his perusal chilled her; she'd felt only confusion mixed with hurt at Demyan's look.

She said nothing, simply waited for the King of Volyarus to move.

He frowned. "You will not return to the reception only to cause a scene."

She was doing her best to hold back an emotional devastation she hadn't experienced since her father's death. Did he really think his display of bossiness was helping the situation?

"Let me give you a small piece of advice, Your Majesty."

His brows rose in obvious shock at her tone.

She went on, "Right this second, all I see when I look at you is a man who would use whatever underhanded means are necessary to rob a woman and her family of a legacy they knew nothing about."

"There was nothing underhanded about your marriage to my son. It is legal in every sense. You cannot undo it."

She said a word that rarely passed her lips, but called the lie for what it was. Oh, he might be correct in that she could not undo whatever legality the wedding had wrought, but as for nothing about it being devious?

That was an ugly bit of nonsense. "All I've done so far is tell you my opinion, not offered my advice. If you're smart, you will take it."

"Chanel, you cannot speak to him like that," Demyan said, sounding tired rather than corrective. "He is your king."

"Not *my* king." Any more than Demyan was *her* prince.

King Fedir asked before Demyan could reply to that claim, "What is your advice?"

"Do not attempt to tell me what to do. Because though my intention is *not* to embarrass my family, or Queen Oxana who has been nothing but kind to me, your very instruction not to cause a scene is nearly overwhelming impetus to do so."

"You love my son."

She didn't deny it. What would be the point? Everyone in that room knew the truth about her emotions. And his now, no matter how misled she'd been that morning.

"But I don't even like you," she told Demyan's adopted father very succinctly.

The king flinched, his face slackening in shock as if he'd never had anyone speak to him in such a way before. Maybe he hadn't.

"Chanel…" That was Demyan, the tone in his voice not one she wanted to hear or could even begin to trust right then.

Definitely not admonishment for her rudeness to his father, but what it was, she refused to name.

She spun to face him, her heart in a vise that brought pain with each indrawn breath. "Don't. Just *don't,* Demyan. However horrible their intentions, the duke and duchess were more honest with me than you've been."

"No." He lurched forward, as if he'd been yanked by a string attached to his chest.

She stepped back quickly, sure of one thing. She could not allow him to touch her right now. "Stop. I said later. I meant *later*."

"Perhaps you two should speak *now*," the king said, sounding less certain than he had to this point.

Chanel made no attempt to hide the utter dislike she felt when she faced him. "You're doing it again. You say maybe we should talk and all I can think is how much more certain I am that there isn't going to be any more talking."

"You are a contrary woman."

"You have no idea how contrary I can be, but spend a few minutes talking with my stepfather and he'll fill you in."

"I have spent some time in his company already."

And heard an earful, Chanel was sure. For the first time in her life, she simply didn't care if Perry had managed to turn someone right off her. "I'm sure he enjoyed that."

"He's an opportunistic man."

"He is." Something clicked in her mind, two memories coming together to form a single conclusion. "He's the one, isn't he, the reason you had to act now?"

The king's face smoothed over into an emotionless mask, but not before she saw the flare of surprise at her guess.

Because she was right.

"My great-great-grandfather Tanner died, apparently with a very different will to the one my great-grandmother believed to have been in existence. Yet no one from your family has approached mine in four generations to secure Baron Tanner's shares in your precious company."

"It is not just a company—it is the financial cornerstone of an entire country."

"Your country."

"Yours now, too."

"That remains to be seen."

"Chanel—" Demyan tried to say something.

She put her hand up. "No. Not you. Not now. Trust me when I tell you it is better for everyone if you show that ruthless patience you are so well-known for in business."

"How do you know about that?"

"I've spent six weeks learning you." Too bad he hadn't done the same.

He would have realized there was no worse way she could have learned of his subterfuge than to be told by an outside party. But then maybe he had realized and it simply didn't matter.

He wouldn't risk upsetting whatever scheme he and his father had set in motion to protect their precious wealth and thereby their country.

She focused on the king again. "My stepfather approached your company trying to trade on connections he didn't really have, but it got you all worried."

"He is a resourceful man."

"He's a shark, though I think maybe Demyan is a bigger, and much meaner, one."

"Without doubt." The king sounded proud.

But then he would be, wouldn't he? His son's ruthless resourcefulness had netted him full interest in Yurkovich Tanner for the first time in four generations.

She didn't know how, or what the details were, but that much she had gleaned from what had and had not been said in this room tonight.

"There are half-a-dozen moderately accessible chemical compounds that would eat the flesh from a shark's body in less than a minute, did you know that?"

The king shook his head, his expression almost bemused.

"I did. I know every single one of them."

"Are you threatening him?"

"I am reminding you that even sharks get eaten if they aren't careful and it doesn't always take a bigger shark to do it."

"I believe there is a strand of ruthlessness in you, too."

"Would you like to find out?"

The king opened his mouth and then closed it, giving Demyan a look of concern before his expression turned thoughtful. "No."

"Good."

"What do you plan to do?"

"Throw the bouquet."

"You know that is not what I meant."

"I care?"

The king's mouth tightened, but he stepped aside, having seemingly finally gotten the message that his admonitions were more effective goads to bad behavior than preventers of it.

Chanel threw the bouquet.

She even managed to dredge up a photo-op-worthy smile when Laura caught it and tossed it away again immediately. Her sister's attitude toward the institution of marriage couldn't have been more obvious.

Chanel had to wonder if the teenager had caught the bouquet just so she could throw it away again. The entire ballroom erupted into laughter and even Beatrice was smiling.

She should be.

Her disappointment of a daughter had managed to land a prince. No wonder she'd come to Chanel's apartment with stories of undying first love.

Chanel couldn't believe she'd thought her mom was

finally showing a vested interest in her oldest daughter's happiness.

But then she'd let herself be convinced that Demyan *wanted* to marry *her*. Not Bartholomew Tanner's only surviving heir.

Smile still fixed firmly in place, Chanel looked out over the ballroom full of people. Her gaze settled on Queen Oxana. The older woman looked pleased, her normally controlled expression filled with unmistakable happiness.

Was that because she knew the Yurkovich fortune was secure, or was she happy at what she thought was her son's marriage to someone she believed was his one true love?

Another memory clicked into place and the smile fell away from Chanel's face. Oxana was the one who had made Demyan promise not to use protestations of love to convince Chanel to marry him.

The queen knew about the will. She must, but she had scruples where her husband and son did not. She might be the only person Chanel could trust to tell her the truth.

She was tempted to leave the reception early, but every time she let her gaze find Demyan, he was watching her. He would only follow her, but she wanted a chance to talk to his mother, to get some answers on her own first.

She got her chance unexpectedly when Oxana came up to her and laid a hand on her arm. "Are you all right, Chanel?"

Chanel looked toward Demyan. He returned her regard, his dark-eyed expression unreadable, but something in the way he watched Chanel and his mother told Chanel he had sent the older woman to her.

"You know," Chanel said instead of answering.

"That you and my husband had something of an altercation earlier? Yes."

Interesting that the queen considered the argument to

be between Chanel and the king, not Chanel and Demyan. "Did he tell you?"

"Demyan did."

Even the sound of his name on Oxana's lips hurt Chanel in some indefinable way. "You were aware of their plans because of my great-great-grandfather's will."

Oxana nodded.

"You made him promise not to lie about loving me. Thank you." She wasn't sure how much worse the pain inside her would be if she'd believed false words of love. "I want to read the will."

"If you ask Demyan, he will tell you everything."

"I don't want to hear from him. He had his chance to tell me. He chose not to."

"He was trying to protect our nation."

Chanel couldn't help mocking. "Because I'm such a huge security risk."

Oxana looked around them, obviously concerned someone might overhear. No one was in range of their subdued tones, but that could change any second.

"I don't want to be here," Chanel admitted hopelessly.

There was nowhere else she could be without someone she didn't want to talk to following her, which included pretty much everyone but Oxana at the moment.

The queen sighed, looking at her sadly. "He cares for you."

Maybe Oxana wouldn't be the best company either. Chanel just shook her head, moving to turn away.

But Oxana's hand on her arm stopped her from putting distance between them. "Come, I will take you someplace away from the scrutiny and company of others."

Chanel thought it a bit obvious when the queen led her to the retiring room for the ladies, but they didn't stop in the outer room as she expected. The queen led her into one of the three small chambers with toilets, closing the door behind them.

While the room was larger than the usual commode stall, it wasn't exactly meant for two people and Chanel didn't think talking about sensitive subjects with only a door between them and anyone who walked into the lounge was a good idea.

But Oxana did not ask any questions, or make any attempts at comfort. She simply pushed up on a section of wainscoting and then the wall behind the commode swung backward.

Oxana put her hand out to Chanel. "Come, I'll take you to the private papers library for the House of Yurkovich. Your great-great-grandfather's will has been stored there."

CHAPTER TWELVE

DARKNESS SURROUNDED CHANEL as she stood on the balcony overlooking the now-silent grounds of the palace. The reception was long over, the last guest's car having left the drive thirty minutes before.

Temperatures had dropped since that morning and she shivered in the cold air, but she did not go back inside.

Before leaving her to read over the will and relevant places in Bartholomew Tanner's diaries the queen had marked for Chanel, Oxana had told her that her favorite place for solitude was this balcony.

"The bedrooms do not have security cameras in them, but they do have infrared monitoring. The public rooms and hallways are all covered with video feed, though. The only two places in the palace where you can relax unmonitored in any way are the public address balcony and the one outside Fedir's rooms."

"Isn't that a security risk?" Chanel had asked.

But Oxana had shaken her head. "The walls and every approach are covered."

Which meant that Demyan would eventually find her because Chanel's path to the balcony would have been tracked by video monitoring once she left the secret passageway.

She could have left the palace completely. Chanel was

a resourceful woman and there had been dozens of cars departing the grounds over the past few hours.

But she wasn't a coward and she'd never hidden from the truth, no matter how much it might hurt to face.

What that truth was, however, wasn't entirely clear. Not after reading the will. Not after remembering Demyan's words in the carriage that morning.

Not after having Oxana tell Chanel exactly what promise she'd extracted from her son over the *love* thing.

Not until Chanel asked Demyan the only question that really mattered.

"Chanel."

She turned at the sound of her name on Demyan's lips.

He stood framed by the light from the hall. He reached and flipped a switch. More golden light flooded the balcony.

"Turn it off," she said, angling her head away so he could not see the damage tears had done on even the indelible makeup job her mother's professional artist had applied.

"No. We do not need more shadows in our relationship."

She swung back to face him head-on, anger making her muscles rigid with tension. "The shadows are all you."

He nodded, his expression as tortured as she felt, if she could believe the evidence of her eyes.

She wasn't sure she trusted her own perceptions at all, though, not after how easily he'd taken her in. However, she didn't think he could fake the parchment-pale of his complexion, the way his black pupils nearly swallowed the espresso irises or the way he breathed in what she would consider panicked gasps in anyone else.

"That day in my lab. It was planned."

"I needed to meet you. You are not a social person."

"So Yurkovich Tanner donated five million dollars to my department for research. That's an expensive introduction." Though nothing in comparison to what the Yurkovich fortune stood to lose if she had made her claim on the Tanner shares in the company.

"It also ensured you were predisposed to look on me favorably."

"Your idea, or the king's?"

"Does it matter?"

"No."

"You've read the will."

"Oxana told you."

"I saw you go into the personal archives library on the video monitor feedback."

"Oh."

"I spent two hours watching the tapes, trying to find you."

"We used the secret passages."

"Yes. You only showed up for brief periods on the video monitors and there were too many extra people in the palace to track you with the infrared body counter and placement."

"Poor you."

"Cha…" Her name choked off and he stepped forward, stumbling, though she knew the stone floor was smooth with no hindrances.

"You never needed your glasses." For anything.

He stopped a couple of feet from her. "I told you that."

"But I thought you needed them as an emotional crutch."

"I do not use crutches."

"No. A man without emotions doesn't need crutches for them, does he?"

"I am human, damn it, not a puppet. I have emotions."

"I bet it was the king's idea to approach me looking like a corporate geek to match my science-nerd personality."

"He believed I would be too intimidating in my usual way."

"That man, the corporate shark, he's part of you."

"Yes."

"But he's not all of you."

"I thought he was."

"Until when?" she pushed.

"Until I met you."

"You don't mean that."

"I've never meant anything more."

"You lied to me."

"I am ruthless when it comes to protecting my country and those I love."

"I noticed."

"There is little hope that will change."

"No. It's part of your nature. You would have made a very good Cossack."

"We still have the elite in our army. As tradition dictates, I spent two years training with them before going to university."

"Wasn't that Prince Maksim's job?"

"He wasn't the oldest son to the king."

"But he is heir to the throne."

"Yes."

"Does that bother you?"

"No. I hate politics."

"I hate being deceived."

"I will not do it again."

"Can you really promise that, with your ruthless nature?"

"Yes."

"Why?"

"I don't understand."

"I think you do."

If anything, his face paled further. "Don't, Chanel."

"Don't what? Make you admit your vulnerabilities. If you have any, that is."

"I do."

"I'm not stupid by any stretch, you know. Legalese may not be science speak, but I understand it well enough."

"Yes?"

"Yes. Bartholomew Tanner's will is unambiguous. My marriage to you negated all claim I, or any of my children, had to Yurkovich Tanner."

Demyan nodded.

"The prenuptial didn't need to spell that out at all."

"No."

"You had that paragraph added as a kind of warning to me, didn't you?"

He shrugged.

"You also made sure I would be taken care of financially despite the fact that legally I would have no way of pursuing any monetary interests in the future."

"You are my wife. I wanted you provided for."

"I bet the king just loved the terms of the prenup."

"He agreed to them."

She was sure there was a story there, but right now she wasn't interested in hearing it. "You came after me with the intention of securing Volyarussian economic stability, no matter the cost."

"Yes." The word sounded torn out of him.

"You could have just asked me to sign the shares over and I would have done it. Especially after reading my grandfather's diaries."

"His diaries?"

"He spelled out his intention of leaving the shares to the people of Volyarus, but at first he was still holding out hope your great-uncle would marry my great-grandmother, then he got his hopes set on the next generation. He died before he could try to make that alliance happen."

"I am aware."

"What you didn't know was that he'd written my great-grandmother and told her that he planned to leave his interest in Yurkovich Tanner to the Volyarussian people. I never would have tried to undermine his clear wishes."

"Your stepfather would not be so sanguine. He might well have convinced your mother to bring suit on her deceased husband's behalf."

"A suit that wouldn't have gone anywhere without my cooperation, and I wouldn't have given it."

"We did not know that."

"You had to have realized, as you got to know me."

"Once I commit to a purpose, I do not change my direction on a whim or the hope of a different outcome."

"Maybe you decided you *wanted* to marry me." It was hard to say the words, to put it out there like that, but this man was about as in touch with his emotions as the puppet he was so adamant he was not.

"I did want to marry you."

"Why?"

He stared at her, his expression so open she wanted to cry. Because it showed so much that he so clearly didn't know how to express verbally. One thing was really obvious. This man did not know what to do with his emotions.

"We are very compatible."

"Are we?"

"You know we are."

"You're a prince. I'm a scientist."

"Those are our titles, not who we are at the core."

"Okay, then you're ruthless and I'm insecure. We're both emotionally repressed."

"But you are more secure about yourself with me."

"And you are less ruthless with me?" she asked, already knowing the answer.

Looking back on it, she saw that the prenuptial agreement was practically a love letter from Demyan.

The uncertainty in his expression was heartbreaking. "Yes?"

She couldn't hold back from touching him any longer. She stepped right into his personal space and he wrapped his arms around her like it was the most natural thing in the world to do.

"Yes, Demyan. *Yes.*" His ruthlessness wasn't always a bad thing, but she brought out the best in him, too.

Now, if she could just get him to realize what that meant.

"You turn me on like no other woman ever has." He spoke as if that fact confused him. "I don't like being without you. Not even for a couple of days. It makes it hard to focus."

"I'm glad to hear that. I feel the same way."

"I miss you," he stressed. "Every hour we are apart. Even when I am working."

No matter how this thing between them had started, it had caught Demyan in the whirlwind of emotion right along with her. Which was the conclusion she'd finally come to after a lot of pain-filled soul-searching and examination of every memory from the moment they'd met.

"It hurt finding out about the will and your reason for marrying me from your sperm donor."

Pain twisted Demyan's features. "I am sorry." He reached up to wipe along the tear streaks on one cheek. "You cried."

"At first, all I could think was that you'd tricked me into loving you when you felt nothing for me at all. That you probably planned on getting rid of me as soon as the ink was dry on the marriage certificate."

"No!" He kissed her, the connection between their mouths infused with a desperation stronger than anything she'd ever felt from him.

It was a magnified version of the feelings that emanated off him at night when making love since their arrival in Volyarus.

She did nothing to stop the kiss for a long time, needing this connection as badly as he so clearly did.

But eventually, she broke her mouth away. "Were you going to tell me?"

"Maybe someday. I do not know. I did not want to."

"You were afraid."

"I am never afraid."

"Not usually, but the idea of losing me scared you."

"Have I lost you?" His arms tightened around her even as he asked the question.

"No."

"No?" he asked, his voice breaking so the word sounded as if it had two syllables.

"Definitely not. Yet."

His big body went absolutely rigid. "Yet?"

"It all depends on your answer to a question."

He stared down at her.

"You never break your promises, right?" She let her body mold completely to his, trying to give him strength.

That's what people who loved each other did—they lent their strength when it was needed.

"Right."

"Tell me you love me."

The tension emanating off him increased exponentially.

"Your mom told me what she made you promise her."

Demyan's expression was haunted.

"You promised not to say you love me unless you really mean it," Chanel reminded him. "You can say it now, Demyan. I will treasure your love forever, too."

"But…"

"You love me."

"I do?"

"That stuff you were saying earlier, about missing me, being afraid to lose me, even the way you changed the prenuptial agreement, it all means one thing."

"It does?" Comprehension and acceptance dawned over his features, making him smile with heartbreaking happiness. "It does. I love you, Chanel, more than my life as a prince. More than anything."

More tears filled her eyes, but these didn't burn or hurt her heart. "I love you, too."

"I mean it."

"I know."

"No, I mean…we don't have to live with the whole royalty thing. I know it's not the life you want. I can abdicate my role."

It wasn't an empty promise and it would not come without significant cost to this amazing man. Especially after finally acknowledging his true role as son of Oxana and Fedir, but Demyan was entirely sincere in his offer.

"No. I love you, Demyan. Ruthless prince. Corporate king and shark. All of you."

"I love you for all that you are, too, Chanel, and that includes the woman who has never aspired to be a socialite."

"I'm not going to be one now, either."

"My uncle…father is not going to know what to do with you."

"He'll probably call me princess just to annoy me."

Demyan laughed, the sound freer and filled with more joy than she'd ever heard from him. "You may well be right."

"So long as you call me love."

"*Koxána moja*," he said, calling her his love in Ukrainian. "Always and forever. You are the very heart that beats inside my chest."

And then he took her back to the rooms they would share whenever staying at the palace for the years to come and made tender, night-long love to her, using those words and so many others to tell Chanel that this man truly loved her and always would.

Later she snuggled into his body and yawned as she said, "I guess it's a good thing you've got a sneaky, underhanded side."

"Is it?"

"Yep."

"Why?"

"We never would have gotten together otherwise. You snuck past all my barriers."

"It is only fair, since you destroyed mine."

Two broken people who had not even realized they were broken had been made whole by love.

Yes, Chanel thought, that was exactly right and fair.

"Love you, Demyan."

"I love you."

"Always."

"For the rest of our lives."

"And beyond." Eternity would not end a love so strong.

"And beyond."

EPILOGUE

OXANA CUDDLED HER latest grandchild. The tiny infant was only three days old, but he was so alert that the queen could not help smiling into soft gray eyes so like his mother's.

Little Damon was her fourth grandchild and she had no doubts he would bring her every bit as much joy as the other three she'd been gifted by her sons and their wives.

The oldest, Mikael, was five and the only child Gillian and Maksim had conceived. Their youngest was adopted, a beautiful little girl who had both her besotted parents wrapped around her dainty little fingers.

Demyan and Chanel's oldest had turned two, four months before the birth of her little brother. Both children were cosseted and adored by parents who showed a decided ruthlessness when it came to putting their family first.

Oxana could not be more pleased. She'd given up a lifetime of love and found little personal happiness in order to give her sons the best chance at a better life. One would be king, the other would continue to oversee their business interests, but both were blissfully happy.

And Oxana thought that a more-than-fair compensation for the sacrifices she'd made. After all, she had her grandchildren around her now. They called her Nana, not Your Majesty, and didn't hesitate to muss her designer couture with messy fingers.

How incredibly blessed she was, but her sons had received the true gift beyond measure.

A lifetime love with women who not only knew but accepted both men for who and what they were.

Fedir often didn't know what to make of his independent-minded daughters by marriage, but he loved being a grandfather and already had grand plans for the children.

Oxana didn't tell him, but she had plans, too, and she knew exactly what each grandchild needed for the future. Love.

Just as she had done her best to make sure both her sons realized their loves, she would do whatever it took to ensure each of her grandchildren knew true love, as well.

Fedir could plan all the machinations he wanted, but in the end? Love would triumph.

Just as it had for her children.

* * * * *

Look out for
Mills & Boon® TEMPTED™ 2-in-1s,
from September

*Fresh, contemporary romances
to tempt all lovers of
great stories*

A sneaky peek at next month...

MODERN™

INTERNATIONAL AFFAIRS, SEDUCTION & PASSION GUARANTEED

My wish list for next month's titles...

In stores from 16th August 2013:

❏ Challenging Dante – Lynne Graham

❏ Lost to the Desert Warrior – Sarah Morgan

❏ Never Say No to a Caffarelli – Melanie Milburne

❏ His Ring Is Not Enough – Maisey Yates

❏ A Reputation to Uphold – Victoria Parker

In stores from 6th September 2013:

❏ Captivated by Her Innocence – Kim Lawrence

❏ His Unexpected Legacy – Chantelle Shaw

❏ A Silken Seduction – Yvonne Lindsay

❏ If You Can't Stand the Heat... – Joss Wood

❏ The Rules of Engagement – Ally Blake

Available at WHSmith, Tesco, Asda, Eason, Amazon and Apple

Visit us Online

You can buy our books online a month before they hit the shops! **www.millsandboon.co.uk**

0813/01

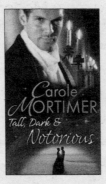

MILLS & BOON® Book Club

Join the Mills & Boon Book Club

Want to read more **Modern**™ books?
We're offering you **2 more** absolutely **FREE!**

We'll also treat you to these fabulous extras:

- 🌹 **Exclusive offers and much more!**
- 🌹 **FREE home delivery**
- 🌹 **FREE books and gifts with our special rewards scheme**

Get your free books now!

visit www.millsandboon.co.uk/bookclub
or call Customer Relations on 020 8288 2888

The World of Mills & Boon®

There's a Mills & Boon® series that's perfect for you. We publish ten series and, with new titles every month, you never have to wait long for your favourite to come along.

Blaze®

Scorching hot, sexy reads
4 new stories every month

By Request

Relive the romance with the best of the best
9 new stories every month

Cherish™

Romance to melt the heart every time
12 new stories every month

Desire™

Passionate and dramatic love stories
8 new stories every month